Taming an Impossible Rogue

SUZANNE ENOCH

D0060488

St. Martin's Paperbacks

This is a work of fiction. All of the characters, organizations, and events portrayed in this novel are either products of the author's imagination or are used fictitiously.

TAMING AN IMPOSSIBLE ROGUE

Copyright © 2012 by Suzanne Enoch.
Excerpt from *Rules to Catch a Devilish Duke* copyright © 2012 by Suzanne Enoch.

For information address St. Martin's Press, 175 Fifth Avenue, New York, NY 10010.

ISBN: 978-0-312-53452-3

Printed in the United States of America

St. Martin's Paperbacks edition / April 2012

St. Martin's Paperbacks are published by St. Martin's Press, 175 Fifth Avenue, New York, NY 10010.

10 9 8 7 6 5 4 3 2 1

*The risk is
its own reward.*

PRAISE FOR SUZANNE ENOCH
and her bestselling romances

"A joyride of a novel . . . a sensual romantic caper sure to win applause." —*Publishers Weekly* (starred review)

"Reading a book by Suzanne Enoch is like stepping into a time machine. She so adeptly transports readers."
—*New York Journal of Books*

"A highly gifted author." —*Romantic Times*

"With her carefully drawn characters and plot chock-full of political intrigue, greed, and scandal, Enoch has put a nifty Regency spin on the Beauty and the Beast story."
—*Booklist*

"Suzanne Enoch has a gift for piquing a reader's interest."
—*Sun Journal*

"Ms. Enoch provides an entertaining read . . . an often amusing and, just as often, dangerous battle of the sexes that will delight fans." —Harriet Klausner

"Dazzling, delicious, and delightful." —Karen Hawkins

"Always an eagerly anticipated pleasure." —Christina Dodd

"Indulge and be delighted!" —Stephanie Laurens

"One of my very favorite authors." —Julia Quinn

"With her fascinating characters, lyrical prose, and whip-smart dialogue, Enoch has created a novel to be cherished." —Lisa Kleypas

For Bryna Dambrowski,
a *very* patient and generous woman.

Chapter One

Keating Blackwood came awake with the sharpness of gunfire. Someone was in the room with him. Someone he hadn't invited. Keeping his eyes closed, he stirred enough that he could slip his hand under the pillow and curl his fingers around the hilt of the knife resting there.

"You do know it's the middle of the day, don't you?"

Straightening his fingers again, Keating opened his eyes and sat up. In the near total blackness of the room, he could just make out the dark figure walking to the nearest set of heavy, dark curtains. "Wait. Don't . . ."

Blinding light filled the room. The sun seemed to spear directly into his skull and lodge there, thrumming.

"Goddammit, Fenton," he growled, squeezing his eyes closed again. "What the devil are you doing here?"

"Looking for you. I need your help."

"Then close the bloody curtains and go sit in the drawing room until I join you there."

"Very well. That's a lovely black eye you're sporting, by the way."

"You should see the other fellow." With a rustling of material, the room behind his eyelids darkened again. When he opened his eyes, blinding red dots still swam across his vision, but at least for the moment he didn't feel the pressing need to cast up his accounts. "And have Barnes fetch you a very large pot of tea," he added, pressing the heel of his hand against his temple.

"I don't want tea."

"I do. Go away."

Once he was alone again in his bedchamber, Keating dug a shirt and trousers out of his wardrobe and shrugged into them. His boots were by the door, but he ignored them, just as he did the jacket and waistcoat Pidgeon had laid out for him sometime yesterday. Sending a dubious glance at his door, he did pick up the freshly pressed cravat and knot it tightly around his forehead. If he was lucky, it might hold his brain inside his skull. God, he needed to stop drinking Russian vodka—or whatever it was he'd been imbibing last night.

"Are you supposed to be a pirate?" Fenton asked, as Keating made his way into the drawing room with liberal help from the walls on either side of the hallway. "You might at least have put on slippers."

"I don't own any." Keating limped over to the far window and closed the curtains, then sat opposite his cousin. "At the risk of sounding incredulous, why do you need *my* help? And make it quick, will you? I may pass out at any moment."

"Why do I need your help?" Stephen Pollard, the Marquis of Fenton, repeated, eyeing him. "I know you've been avoiding London, but surely you've been reading the newspaper."

"I'm avoiding London. Why the devil would I wish to read about it?" The tea tray arrived, and without being asked, Barnes poured a cup, dropped in five lumps of sugar, and carried it to him. "My thanks," he said to the butler, taking a long, slow swallow.

"Why bother with the tea?" Fenton asked, sitting forward to pour himself a cup and making a show of adding a solitary sugar.

Ignoring the question, Keating sipped carefully at the too hot, too sweet brew. "I thought you didn't want any tea."

His cousin looked down at the cup in his hand, then with a grimace set it aside. "I don't. I was attempting to make a point, I suppose. About sugar."

"Yes, I noticed that. I was positively wounded by the jab."

"The morning—or midday—after being three sheets to the wind, I would think sweet tea would do you in."

"I've had a great deal of time and opportunity to experiment. Sweet tea helps. A little. Occasionally." With a breath he swirled the tea around in the full cup. "So do you actually wish to discuss tea, then?" Keating took another swallow, trying not to anticipate the dulling of the hollow chasm of pain in his skull.

"No, I don't."

"Good. Because otherwise you've traveled a great distance for a very poor reason. Let's get to your point, shall we?"

Fenton hung his hands between his knees. "Yes, of course. Do you remember Lord and Lady Montshire? The idiotic agreement they made with my parents?"

Finally Keating cracked a grin. "God, she's one-and-twenty now, isn't she? You getting the shivers over being leg-shackled to a chit you've never met? I suggest closing your eyes and thinking of England."

"She's two-and-twenty now." The marquis scowled. "The thing is, I actually enjoyed not spending the past eight years having to court chits, forgoing all that wooing nonsense. What could be more convenient than just setting a date, going to the church, and then simply getting on with fathering an heir?"

"You make domesticity sound exciting as a tombstone." More interested now despite himself, Keating kneaded a knuckle against his bruised eye. The swelling was going down a bit now. Yesterday he hadn't even been able to open the thing. "What's your trouble, then?" he prompted. "Or should I guess? You did meet her, and she has the face of a harpy. She squints. She's missing a leg. She—"

"Do shut up, Keating, will you?"

"I'm merely attempting to scribble something in the blank spots you've left."

"She's pretty enough. Just over a year ago my solicitor took the paperwork to her, she and her parents signed in all the proper places, we placed an announcement in the newspaper, and I went to the church. I even invited you to attend the ceremony."

"Fancy that." The invitation must have been buried in the middle of one of Fenton's ten-page sprawling letters. As if he had the least bit of interest in who'd invited his cousin to dine or which duke had nodded in his direction. "Last year? What happened, then?"

"The chit fled."

Despite the fact that he expected to hear that some calamity or other had occurred, Keating blinked. "She fled? Do you mean she balked at marrying you?"

"I mean she appeared in the church doorway wearing a lovely white gown, and then she turned around and ran. Knocked over a candelabra and nearly set the church ablaze."

Keating gazed at his cousin for a long moment. They'd grown up nearly as brothers, but in the past decade or so had drifted apart. The difference in destiny between the son of a marquis and the son of a marquis's younger brother, Stephen had always said. To Keating it had meant that once Stephen had realized he was to inherit a title and wealth and lands, he'd become so insufferably high in the instep that none of his lessers could stand to be in the same room with him. As for him, he'd inexorably become one of those lessers.

"Well, you're a fairly . . . pleasant-looking fellow," he returned, fighting the urge to squint his eyes even in the dim room, "and you're a marquis with a fortune you keep bragging about and then refusing to lend me, so I have to ask if you said something to frighten her."

"Frighten her? Why would I frighten her? *How* could I frighten her, when I've never spoken a word to the chit?"

"Not a single word?"

"I saw her on several occasions, from a distance, but I . . ." Fenton flung up his hands. "You know me; I'm not glib. I don't have a charming conversation like you do."

"You would, if you could be bothered to remove the broomstick from your arse and do more than look down your nose at everyone else."

"There's no need to be insulting. I am as I am. And you are as you are."

That didn't sound promising. In fact, it sent a belated alarm coursing through his already throbbing skull. "Considering that she's been signed over to you, Fenton, I would assume she won't have gone far. Perhaps you should attempt writing her a letter or—I'm merely speculating here—*speaking* with her to discover what happened."

"I would do so, except that my bride-to-be did go far. She disappeared, and when she emerged again, she'd . . . found employment."

If his cousin hadn't been sitting there, anger and

frustration and embarrassment etched into his expression, Keating would have laughed. He was tempted to do so anyway, but he'd only just gotten both eyes open. Two or three days between brawls seemed more reasonable than beginning another one immediately. "Employment as what? A lady's companion? Surely not as an actress. That would be too—"

"At The Tantalus Club."

"What the devil is The Tantalus Club?" From Stephen's tone alone it didn't sound promising, and the name was certainly evocative. Had London become even more sinful in his absence? That was unexpected. He'd thought that after he left everyone would have turned into saints simply out of fear of being compared to him.

"Good God, you *have* become a hermit."

And abruptly Keating wasn't amused any longer. Setting aside his tea, he pushed to his feet. "Considering that you know why I'm here," he ground out, "I can only wish you luck in your pursuit. If I may suggest, attempt a small measure of . . . well, if you can't manage compassion, then at least humanity. Now get out of my home."

"Damnation, Keating. It's been six years. I hadn't realized the subject was still so raw. You . . ." Fenton cleared his throat. "I apologize. It's only that everyone knows about The Tantalus Club. It's the newest rage in London. Lady Cameron—or rather, Lady Haybury now—opened a damned gentlemen's club just under a year ago, and she only hires chits."

With a breath, Keating returned to his chair. Fenton had never been concerned with anyone but Fenton, and the present fiasco certainly didn't point to the fact that the marquis had altered his behavior. Expecting Stephen to be different would simply be an error on his own part.

And if the marquis needed assistance . . . well, that could benefit his wayward cousin in several ways. "Haybury's married?"

"Yes, to the former Earl of Cameron's widow." Fenton scowled. "Don't alter the subject. This is about *my* bride, not Oliver Warren's."

Keeping his jaw clenched, Keating nodded. "Very well. The Tantalus Club. Is it a brothel, then?" he commented, deciding it wouldn't be that far-fetched for the Marquis of Haybury to be involved with such a thing. "If that's where your betrothed has gone, then you'd best look elsewhere for a bride."

The marquis's face reddened. "It's not a damned brothel. But you're not the first to think it is."

"Perception, my friend. It is what everyone thinks it is. Look elsewhere for your Lady Fenton."

Slamming his fist on the arm of his chair, Fenton scowled. "If she had become . . . soiled, I *would* look elsewhere. But the place is wildly popular, very exclusive, and members swear it's aboveboard. And I'm a laughingstock, because the daughter of the Earl of Montshire would rather work for a living, serving my peers, than marry me. She didn't even have the decency to go hide away in the country somewhere where everyone could forget her—and what she did to me."

"Then go fetch her."

"I've considered that, as well. Firstly, Lady Haybury has refused to grant me admission to The Tantalus Club even as someone else's damned guest. I've been blackballed. *Me.* Secondly, I have no idea how to approach such a . . . rebellious, self-absorbed chit, and thirdly I'm not even certain that's how I should proceed. I want her back in that church—any church—beside me, and I want her to be grateful to be allowed a second opportunity to live the kind of life she should be thankful for."

"Ah. So a bit humbled, then."

"She made a mistake. A very large one. I am willing to give her a second chance for the sake of her future and—"

"And to stop everyone from laughing at you."

"Yes, that, as well," Fenton snapped. "But you, of all people, should appreciate the rarity of second chances. She could return to her family's good graces, have a comfortable, pampered life, and see her children enjoy the same. I'm not a cruel man; yes, I suppose I'm a bit pompous, but if a ninth-generation marquis cannot be proud of that fact, then he may as well be a farmer."

Keating refrained from glancing about the morning room of his small, comfortable house. Havard's Glen might not be a farmhouse, but it was close enough. And he'd certainly sheared enough sheep to earn the title of gentleman farmer himself. "Indeed."

"All I'm saying is that she would be wise not to squander a second chance. There won't be a third."

That, he did understand. And it bothered him immensely that his cousin knew precisely how to manipulate him and seemed to have no hesitation at all about doing so. Clearly he needed to bury his scars more deeply if he didn't want anyone else picking at them. For a moment Keating gazed toward the darkened window. "I want something in return," he said.

"I thought you might. That five thousand pounds you've been asking me to give you for the past four years, perhaps?"

"That would suffice." Hm. He hadn't thought it would be that simple. Which meant that Fenton wanted Lady Camille Pryce more badly than he cared to admit. "If accompanied by an additional five thousand pounds."

Fenton blinked. "Ten thousand pounds in exchange for bringing a chit to a church? I think not."

"Keeping in mind the fact that the chit's been evading you for better than a year already, we both know it's more complicated than that. But if the price is too steep, find your assistance elsewhere."

"Damnation, Keating. You're a villain, you know."

"So I've been told. Do we have an agreement?"

"I wish you'd take that cravat from around your head. It doesn't inspire much confidence."

"I'm not here to inspire your confidence. In fact, as you're the one who came to see me, I'm perfectly content to sit here in my bare feet and glare at you until you stop insulting me and leave."

"Just say you'll do it, will you? Some subtlety is required. I don't trust anyone else to step in as my second."

"And my poor reputation eclipses your status as a laughingstock."

"There is that. I doubt many even remember we're cousins. I hope that's the case, anyway. But your presence will . . . shift that negative attention away from me."

"To gawk at me." With a sigh, Keating closed his eyes. "I don't owe you any favors, Stephen. Ten thousand pounds. And yes, you know you may trust me."

With a hard breath the marquis pushed to his feet and stuck out his hand. "Yes, damn it all. Ten thousand pounds, twenty-four hours after I am a married man."

Keating rose and shook his cousin's hand. "I want it in writing. And I expect you to do as I say in this matter. Because clearly following your own advice where this Lady Camille is concerned didn't go well."

"Yes, yes. In writing, and I will follow your recommendations. Just be in London by Friday."

"Just have the agreement ready for my signature when I arrive, or I'll be leaving again."

Once Fenton exited, Keating sank back into the near darkness to finish his tea. Returning to London. At one point he'd sworn never to do so. Lady Camille Pryce had just made a great deal of trouble for him, but at the same time perhaps she could be the means to something in which he'd ceased to believe six years ago. Redemption.

Chapter Two

"Who is that sitting at the Duke of Walling's table?"

Lady Camille Pryce frowned as she glanced up from the morning's seating plans. "I suggest you occupy yourself with memorizing the tables and stop looking for trouble, Lucille."

The petite brunette blushed. "I only asked who he is."

"He's Lord Patrick Elder," Camille returned. "He already has a wife and two mistresses. I doubt he's looking for a third."

"Cammy."

"I'm completely serious. And I see that Mr. Alving at the window table is scowling. Go smile at him and see what we might do to alter his expression."

Lucille chewed on her lip. "Which table?"

Oh, for heaven's sake. Stifling her grumbling, Camille handed the seating plans to her companion. "Lord Blansfield is arriving. He's one of our founding members, so see him to one of the reserved tables. Not near the doorway. He's very sensitive to drafts."

"But—"

"Lucille, all that is required of you at the moment is to smile and remember that you are working, not attempting to find a husband or someone to purchase you jewelry."

That was perhaps a bit harsh, but after three mornings of working with Lucille Hampton, she was beginning to think that the girl would be better suited to a position where she didn't have to give gentlemen directions. Or do anything other than flutter her eyelashes and giggle.

She stifled her sigh. A year ago, she'd been jumping at her own shadow—and everyone else's. Considering that Lady Haybury had given her both a roof over her head and a way to earn an income without having to lift her skirts, she was willing to give Lucille another few days to settle into her place at The Tantalus Club. Sometimes a small opportunity could breed a large miracle.

"Mr. Alving," she said, stopping at his table. "I heard a rumor that our chef is baking a very few peach tarts. Shall I have one set aside for you?"

The Earl of Massing's uncle narrowed his eyes as he looked up at her. "It's criminal, the way you chits know every one of our secrets."

Camille smiled. "Only the gastronomic ones." And the wagering ones, and the political ones, and most of the bed-chamber ones, and who was friends or enemies with whom—but that was not a conversation she wished to have with one of the club's membership. "I'll have the tart on your table by the time you've finished those poached eggs."

The request sent to the kitchen, she stood back for a few moments to watch Lucille seat the next groups of men at the tables. Eyelashes continued to flutter, but that was likely an ingrained part of her character. From what Lucille had said of her life before The Tantalus Club, the girl had lived alone with her mother, a woman who'd evidently craved the affection of men to the point that she viewed her own daughter as unwanted competition.

Camille sighed again, glancing about the room at the other dozen women who carried platters, poured drinks, or glided among the tables encouraging those gentlemen who lingered too long either to move into one of the even more comfortable adjoining gaming rooms, or to see to whatever appointments they might have about London this morning.

These ladies had become her friends when she thought she'd lost the opportunity to have any of the kind. Over the past year they'd become her adopted family, women who'd fled their previous lives for a hundred different reasons and found sanctuary at the oddest place imaginable. Silently she sent up thanks once more for The Tantalus Club. And to Lady Cam—no, Haybury now—for allowing her to work in the mornings when the guests were less inebriated and so less likely to speak their minds when they caught sight of her.

Even as she conjured that thought, fingers pinched her backside. Hard.

She yelped, whipping around. Her fists curling in abrupt anger, she looked up at the rotund man who was now gazing at her chest. "Stop that at once," she snapped.

The fellow lifted an eyebrow. "Don't ruin that pretty face with talking," he said. "Come sit with me, and I'll point out your charms to you."

"Farness, leave off." The man behind the ogre, Arthur Smythe, as she recalled, took his friend's elbow. "This ain't a bawdy house."

The ogre kept his gaze on her. "You promised me a grand time at this club of yours, Smythe. Stand back and let me have one." He took a step closer to her. "You're the chit who fled from marrying Fenton last year, skirts flapping. I heard you were employed here. I'll pay you two shillings to sit on my lap. Three, if you wiggle."

Camille lifted her left hand straight into the air, fingers spread. All the ladies knew the signal, though she, unfortunately, had used it more than any of the others. Even in the less crowded, less inebriated mornings at the club. The perils of a publicly ruined reputation, she supposed. Thankfully, while Lady Haybury might have preferred to have only female employees, it hadn't taken much to convince her that a handful of very large former boxers might be helpful to have about.

Out of the corner of her eye she caught sight of the largest of the Helpful Men, as she and the other girls had come to refer to them, approaching. Only an utter fool would protest Mr. Jacobs guiding him out the doors of the club.

As she faced the ogre again, a fist and a nicely jacketed arm crossed directly in front of her—and connected with Farness's chin. The round fellow fell to the blue-carpeted floor on his arse.

"When I was last in London," a low, cultured drawl came from beside her, "men did not insult women in such a manner. I can only assume, then, that either you were mistaken, or you're not a man."

The words "Bloody Blackwood" began circling all around her, in the same tone that men generally used to discuss the outcome of the most impossible and deadly of wagers. She sidestepped as the tall, dark-haired man attached to the fist bent down to haul Farness to his feet.

"Which is it, then?" he murmured. "Were you mistaken, or are you simply not a man?"

The ogre raised shaking fingers to touch his cut lip. "Good God. You're Blackwood. Bloody damned Blackwood."

"I'm aware of that. Answer my question."

"Mistaken," Farness rasped. "I was mistaken."

"Then I suggest you apologize," Blackwood pursued, in the same tone he might ask for an additional card while playing vingt-et-un.

"I—"

"To her. Not me."

Farness looked over at her. "I apologize."

"For?" her supposed rescuer prompted.

"For . . . for insulting you, my lady."

"Well done." With a light but unmistakably serious shove he deposited Farness into the grip of Mr. Jacobs. "Shall I leave, as well?" he asked, looking over at her for the first time.

Light brown eyes the color of rich tea, one of them circled by a faint, fading bruise, gazed levelly at her. Stifling the abrupt impulse to straighten her hair, she shook her head. "As long as there's no more punching, I can't fault you for defending my honor—unnecessary though it was."

A slow smile touched his mouth. "Thank you. And I've never found defending a lady's honor to be a frivolity."

Just as she realized that she seemed to be staring at the man, the circle around them stirred and parted. Diane, Lady Haybury, emerged into the small clearing. "I will not have fisticuffs in my club," she said, ignoring Mr. Farness being led away and instead focusing her attention on the punching man. "Whose guest are you, sir?"

"Mine."

The Duke of Greaves moved into the circle, his expression as cool as if he were discussing the weather. "Lady Haybury, Keating Blackwood. Keating, the proprietor of this establishment, Lady Haybury."

Oh, dear. Camille resisted the urge to back away. She'd only wished to stop a man from pinching her hindquarters. Involving Diane and dukes and disrupting the running of the club . . . Perhaps she should have simply accepted the pinch for what it was; after all, of all the ladies employed here, her fall from grace was by far the most public. With some of the things said to her back—

and even to her face—whenever she ventured out of doors, at the least she should have expected such discourtesy from time to time within her sanctuary's walls.

Diane glanced in her direction. "Is any further action warranted, Camille?"

She shook her head. "I believe there's been enough fuss, my lady." More than enough.

Diane nodded, returning her attention to the rather tall Keating Blackwood. "If His Grace is willing to vouch for you, Mr. Blackwood, then I will allow you to remain. Your motives in this instance seem gentlemanly enough. Have a good day, sir, and enjoy your time in The Tantalus Club."

Keating Blackwood inclined his head. "Thank you, my lady."

Feeling in need of a strong glass of spirits, Camille excused herself and returned to her station close to the front door of the dining room. Wasn't she supposed to have become accustomed to such assaults by now? To being ridiculed and abused because she'd done what she still considered to be the most sensible thing she'd ever managed in her life? For the most part The Tantalus Club had been her safe haven for the past year. An occasional intrusion of . . . reality, she supposed it was, was still far better than what she faced on the streets of Mayfair. Eventually everyone would forget, or some other scandal would take the place of hers. Or so she'd been hoping for the past year.

Lucille made a small sound behind her. "My goodness," she chirped. "I had no idea men would fight over us here. That's delightful."

Camille frowned. " 'Delightful' isn't the word I would choose," she returned. "I hate this. But the alternative is . . . well, there truly isn't one."

"Couldn't you have found work as a governess? Perhaps somewhere in the country?" Lucille returned in a hushed voice, pausing to bat her eyes as Lord Haybury strolled into the room.

"Yes, because everything is magical in the country, and they have no newspapers and no one knows how to read or write letters to people in London." Camille scowled. "How foolish I've been not to consider that before!"

"Oh. I merely hadn't thought much about it. There's no need to be rude."

No, there wasn't. And silly though Lucille was, none of this was her fault. With a sigh, Camille patted her companion on the shoulder. "There's no reason my problems should trouble you." She sent a glance about the room, relieved to see that everyone seemed to have returned to their seats. "Now, why don't you go to Lord William Atherton's table and mention that Mary Stanford is dealing vingt-et-un at this very moment?"

"How does that signify?"

"It signifies because Lord William Atherton believes Mary to be very pretty, and *I* need their table for the three gentlemen waiting in the foyer."

"Oh, very well. I have no idea how you keep all of this in your head." With a flounce of her skirt, Lucille pranced over to the table in the far corner.

As Camille looked up again, faint uneasiness touched her. Keating Blackwood, his gaze on her face, approached her podium without even making a show of being interested in some other possible thing or person in her vicinity. "Thank you again," she said as he stopped before her, hoping to forestall his asking for a kiss or something as a reward of his so-called heroics. "How are you finding your breakfast?"

"Exceptional," he replied, leaning an elbow on the lectern the hostesses had taken to using to keep their table charts and lists of names and menus and the preferences of individual gentlemen. "You're Lady Camille Pryce."

Hiding her flinch, Camille shuffled through her papers. "That's hardly a secret. Now, is there something you need? A bottle of wine, perhaps? We have a fine bur—"

"I'm Keating Blackwood."

"So I heard." She looked at him for a moment, catching the expectant look on his lean face. "You have a black eye."

"Nearly gone, now." He brushed a negligent finger against his left cheek. "You don't know who I am."

"You're Keating Blackwood. My memory extends past one minute, I assure you."

A quick smile curved his mouth. It was a very attractive mouth, she noted peripherally. But it wasn't the first attractive mouth to decide that as a fallen woman she must be in need of a lover or a benefactor, or worse, that she made a habit of engaging in self-destructive behavior.

"Stephen Pollard is my cousin."

The ground beneath Camille's feet seemed to turn to pudding, because she swayed alarmingly. Gripping the podium hard, she forced a breath through her lungs. Lady Haybury had thus far done a masterful job of keeping Lord Fenton out of The Tantalus Club. As long as she stayed inside its walls, insults and the occasional pinch had been the worst she'd experienced. But now trouble had breached the walls of her haven in a very alarming manner. "I—"

"I'm only telling you so that you aren't taken by surprise later if someone should mention it," he continued. "I'm making an attempt at honesty."

Camille swallowed the lump of coal in her throat. "I . . . appreciate your candor," she ventured, using every bit of her self-control to keep from backing away. "However, as you are a guest of a club member and I am merely the breakfast-time hostess, I hardly require your résumé."

"Is this your way of saying that I need not have bothered with introducing myself as we won't be meeting again?" he countered.

"Well, yes, I suppose it is."

That faint smile touched his mouth again. "My cousin is a stiff-backed buffoon, my lady. That said, I don't believe he's ever been the sort to pluck the wings off flies or . . . hurt anyone intentionally. This makes me curious. Did he harm you? Or insult you? Is that why you didn't wish to marry him?"

The question took her completely by surprise. Attempting not to gape at him, she glanced away to send a distracted smile at Lord Trask as the viscount entered the room with his two sons. When Lucille approached, Camille had her seat the Trasks . . . somewhere; it might have been in the kitchen for all the attention she paid.

"If you aren't going to answer the question, I wish you'd say so," Blackwood prompted. "I have a fine plate of ham and cheeses and an annoyed duke waiting at the table for me."

"Then you should return to them." She picked up her seating chart and went to greet the next arrival.

"Do you ever go walking?" Blackwood's voice came from directly behind her.

Oh, dear, now he was trailing her about the room. "No."

"You should. At what time do you finish your hostess duties?"

"I—at—I don't believe that's any of your concern, Mr. Blackwood. Now please cease accosting me, or I shall be forced to have you removed."

"I mean you no harm, my lady," he returned in a low

voice. "I've been away from London for six years, and as I said, you've made me curious. Few people stand against Fenton. I'd merely like to know your reasons."

Her parents hadn't even asked her that question. Camille took a stiff breath. "I will be free after one o'clock," she said in a rush, before she could change her mind. "But I almost never leave the club's premises. You may find me in the rose garden."

He sketched a shallow bow. "I shall do so."

She pretended to return her attention to the late-arriving breakfast guests, and after a moment the warmth shielding her back was gone. Of all the things she'd expected ever to occur, the cousin of the man she'd jilted a year earlier appearing and being nice to her wasn't one of them. And she'd never anticipated anyone asking what Lord Fenton might have done to cause her to flee rather than questioning why she'd lost *her* senses. Because she hadn't lost them. Not then, and not now.

If some relation of Fenton's wanted an explanation for her actions, she was certainly willing to give one. As long as he realized it changed nothing. And as long as he didn't think she might be amenable to Stephen Pollard's cousin after she'd turned her back on the man himself.

Camille gave a tight smile in response to some lordling's greeting. Yes, she was quite aware that she'd ruined her life. What no one else—men, in particular—seemed to realize was that she had no intention of making things any worse. Ever.

Chapter Three

The crunch of an apple roused Keating from his gaze out the front window of Baswich House. "I expected things to have altered at least a little in six years," he commented, watching a grand carriage emblazoned with the coat of arms of the Duke of Monmouth clatter down the street.

"You visited the one difference this morning. Where you nearly began a brawl, by the way." The Duke of Greaves leaned against the doorjamb and took another bite of apple. "I'm curious," he stated.

"Why am I not staying at Pollard House with Fenton?" Keating suggested.

"It's no fun if you guess everything I'm going to say." Greaves waved his fingers. "So answer the question you posed of yourself."

"Stephen continues to pretend that he and I are not related, which actually suits me quite well. If you want me to leave, I'll find lodgings elsewhere."

"I never said that." Greaves shifted to the other side of the doorway so he could see out the front window as well. "There are people who make a point of surrounding themselves with fellows of good character, to reflect well on their own. I, on the other hand, prefer rogues and scoundrels. Not only are they more interesting to converse with, but I look better in comparison."

Keating snorted. "I should forewarn you, then, that I mean to attempt to behave while I'm here. A new start." It sounded promising, anyway; though he could likely trust Greaves's discretion, he'd given his word to keep his true reason for returning to London to himself.

Doubt, disbelief—or something of the sort—crossed the duke's face and then was gone again. It didn't matter; Keating had his own doubts about his ability to reform his reputation and his character. A good thing, then, that he intended to make this a brief visit. And perhaps if he could manage to stay away from trouble, he could attempt it a second time.

But that was putting the cart so far in front of the horse that they were in different shires. He pulled out his old, scratched pocket watch and clicked it open. "At least you didn't say anything disparaging aloud, Adam," he commented, standing. "I have some doubts myself. But at the moment, I have an appointment."

"As do I," Greaves returned. "And Keating, if you had no qualms about your character, you wouldn't have hidden away like a hermit for the past six years. Merely keep in mind that your past poor behavior is likely still of much more interest than any propriety you exhibit now."

"Thank you for the speech. I've heard the poem they made up about me." He sighed, moving past Greaves and into the foyer. "I'll see if I can refrain from living up to it."

"In your defense," the duke returned, shifting to keep him in sight, "the poem isn't very good. And it's six years old now. I know for a fact there have been a myriad of other poems since then. Some of them at least as poorly written as the tribute to you."

Keating gave a noncommittal grunt. If the duke was suggesting that he and his exploits had been forgotten, well, that would be a relief. He had the distinct feeling, however, that there was a large difference between being set on the shelf while new game passed by, and being forgotten. And no, it wasn't a very good poem.

He had his dark gray gelding, King William Lord of Horses (as an optimistic breeder had named him), or Amble (as Keating had more realistically dubbed him), waiting on the Baswich House front drive. He swung into the saddle, and as they trotted onto Grosvenor Street for the second time that day, Keating squared his shoulders. Even with the fisticuffs, this morning at The Tantalus Club had proceeded better than he'd expected, both in regard to meeting Lady Camille Pryce and to the reaction of his fellow aristocrats on seeing him once again in London.

He wasn't certain whether it was because the club had a particular relationship with scandal that made his own past exploits less . . . noteworthy there, or if it was because he'd managed to take London by surprise. Whatever the reason for the quietude, he had the distinct feeling that the Town wouldn't be as welcoming once the residents had time to make note of his presence.

Or what if he *had* simply been forgotten? Gossiped over, raged about, and then put in the ash pan once the next scandal burst? Keating blew out his breath. That would have been perfectly acceptable to him. It was merely that he didn't much rely on good fortune these days.

He'd thought The Tantalus Club crowded during breakfast, especially on a day when Parliament wasn't in session. The amount of carriage traffic rolling onto the elongated front drive now, however, was at least double what he'd seen earlier. Keeping his jaw locked, he sent

Amble off with one of the stableboys and, rather than joining the trek up the front steps, headed around the opposite side of the house. Damned hypocrites. They all spouted the merits of living noble lives, and went to luncheon at an establishment where they were encouraged to ogle the female staff.

He wondered how many of them justified their actions by repeating the mantra he'd heard at least half a dozen times since he'd first learned of the existence of The Tantalus Club: No touching, at least not without the lady's permission. That, apparently, made the entire . . . existence of the place scandalous, but acceptable.

Camille Pryce sat on a small stone bench beneath the shade of an oak tree set in the center of a well-manicured circle of rosebushes. For a moment Keating stopped at the edge of the cobblestone path, noting that whether intentional or not, the tree blocked the bench and its occupant from the myriad windows of the club. She'd changed her attire from the sleek bronze silk of the morning; the simple blue and green sprigged muslin seemed almost absurdly modest given her place of employment.

This was the chit Stephen was supposed to have married a year ago. A demure, proper young lady, aged two-and-twenty now, sitting in a well-groomed garden and reading a book. Civilized and bloodless, the very portrait of the girl to whom the Marquis of Fenton had been engaged since his seventh birthday. Keating remembered when his cousin had learned about the agreement; the moaning and exaggerated faux vomiting had been highly amusing—to the point that he'd joined in. At six years of age, he'd agreed that females were highly overrated.

In the dappled sunlight her fair hair took on more color, though yellow seemed too strong a word to describe it. Buttermilk or whey seemed more appropriate. The color—or lack thereof—was actually quite striking, particularly in combination with her blue eyes as pale as the morning sky.

Yes, he'd been tasked with seeing her safely back into Society's—and his cousin's—arms, and yes, he'd spent several long minutes in front of his dressing mirror at Havard's Glen swearing that he would behave, earn his pieces of silver, and return home without incident. Beneath that, however, he was male. And she was stunning.

Keating shook himself. He had certainly never waxed poetical even when he'd been young enough to be considered naïve. And he was nothing close to either, any longer. Yes, she was pretty. She was also the intended of the Marquis of Fenton, *and* she was the means by which he would obtain ten thousand pounds. With that money he could finally begin to make some things right. Things he'd made wrong six years ago. *That* was the reason—the only reason—he'd returned to London.

He cleared his throat. Scaring the chit to death would cost him a great deal of blunt. "You look as though you're posing for a portrait," he commented, stepping forward.

She looked up at him. From her calm expression, she'd known he was standing there. "How should I sit while reading, then? One arm above my head and my toes turned in?"

Evidently she wasn't quite as fragile as she looked. "I meant that to be a compliment. Shall I turn around and begin again?"

Her sunrise blue eyes assessed him. "You don't look much like your cousin. I daresay if you hadn't told me of your relationship, I never would have known."

"In all honesty," he returned, moving close enough to lift the book from her lap and examine the title, "I heard that you didn't get much of a look at my cousin." Hm.

Pride and Prejudice. So she had a romantic bent. That was good to know, though he wasn't certain how it would help him in swaying her back toward Fenton, the cold fish.

Her cheeks darkened. "I agreed to speak with you here because you asked me a question that no one had ever posed to me before. If you mean to insult or bully me, Mr. Blackwood, know that you're not the first. Nor are you anyone whose opinion matters to me in the least. Clearly I was mistaken in thinking you might be someone with whom I could . . . commiserate." Snatching her book out of his hands, she stood and marched back toward the large manor.

Damnation. Seeing his ten thousand quid stomping away, Keating went after her. Clearly he needed a different approach—and quickly. He put a hand on her shoulder. "My lady, I didn't m—"

She whipped around and slammed the book into the side of his head. "Leave me alone!" she snapped, and trudged away.

If Keating had never been hit before, the thwack might have stopped him. Considering that he still bore the remains of a black eye from a gargantuan bruiser nicknamed Bully Tom, he simply strode forward to block her escape. "Nicely done," he said, tasting blood from a cut lip. "What question did I ask you?"

"I—you—get out of my way."

"Answer my question. About the question."

Camille Pryce took a deep breath. If he hadn't been behaving, he would have noted the fine form of her bosom, but he kept his gaze firmly on her face. He also kept his weight balanced on the balls of his feet, ready to dodge if she swung the book again.

"You asked me what Fenton had done to drive me

away." She narrowed her eyes, her jaw clenched. "You didn't ask what was wrong with me to leave a wealthy, titled gentleman standing in the church. I thought that was . . . refreshing. But now you've ruined it, and I'm finished speaking with you. Do not come back to The Tantalus Club."

"I scratched at old wounds, you mean." God, even as he spoke the words he realized how familiar they sounded. "I apologize. I have developed a tendency to strike first." He rubbed his fingers against his jaw. "You returned fire quite adequately," he continued, grinning. "Might we consider this a draw and begin again?"

"We've been conversing for five minutes, and that's the second time you've asked for a second chance. How many am I supposed to tolerate?" Camille folded her arms across her chest, lifting her chin to gaze up at him.

That did stop him for a moment. He had the strangest sensation, not for the first time, that he might have been conversing with himself. *Second chances.* How many was one man allowed to have? Surely he'd surpassed that number some time ago, whatever it was. Time, then, to stop backpedaling and do it correctly the first time.

"This is the last one," he said, realizing that he spoke the absolute truth. He had one thing—*one thing*—to manage. Because the assignment Fenton had given him wasn't a second chance. It was his last chance.

She gazed at him for several hard beats of his heart, while he rolled his thoughts around what he would do if she continued into the club. "I have a question for you," she finally said.

Anger and frustration curled into him, and just as swiftly he pushed them both away. No, he didn't like interrogations, but he could tolerate a damned question or two. Camille Pryce was not some random chit he'd decided to seduce. "I don't hold up well under scrutiny," he returned, attempting to sound disarming, "but ask away."

"Do you expect me to believe that you're here at this moment simply because you also dislike your cousin? I'm a kindred spirit to you for that reason, and you are not here because of some plan to further injure or embarrass me?"

"I don't know a great deal about what transpired between you and Fenton," he returned, thankful he could, for the most part at least, speak the truth. "I'm generally not well liked in London, and so yes, when Greaves told me who you were, I thought . . . I don't know what I thought."

"It's difficult to find—and trust—friends, sometimes."

The brief sadness that touched her sky blue eyes made him pause. If his intention had been to hurt or mislead her, he was fairly certain he would have changed his mind right then and there. But Fenton had offered her a second chance, as well. A chance to be embraced again by her family and friends and to not have to put up with overtures of friendship from scoundrels like himself.

"I'm not a gentleman, my lady, and you have no reason in the world to trust me. But I would like it if you called me friend."

She glanced down at the book in her hand for a moment. "I heard everyone whispering your name this morning, but because of that question you asked me, I decided not to inquire until I'd spoken to you. So who are you, Mr. Blackwood?"

She asked that as if she assumed the answer were simple. Keating looked toward the tall windows of The Tantalus Club. Actually, it *was* fairly simple. It was only that he didn't like saying it, and that his own reputation could keep him from winning this round. He took a short breath. "I'm Keating Blackwood, the grandson of the former Marquis of Fenton. They whisper about me because six years ago I seduced a woman and then killed her husband. Pleased to make your acquaintance."

Camille blinked. Given his looks—that coal-colored hair, brown eyes that looked almost amber in the sunlight, and those high cheekbones and sinfully long eyelashes—she'd thought that whatever had stirred up the club's noblemen must have been some sort of scandal involving a woman, if not pure jealousy at the Adonis suddenly in their midst. But she hadn't expected murder.

A rustle of memory touched her, from back when she'd been sixteen, still living at home and still perfect in her parents' eyes: her father returning from a night at one of his clubs and saying Blackwood had done it that time, and they would hang him for certain. And a poem popularized in one of Cruikshank's caricatures. " 'Bloody Blackwood plowed the wife, and then he took her husband's life,' " she muttered, half to herself, then blanched as the expression in his eyes cooled to winter.

"Do you make a habit of reciting people's sins to their faces?" he said quietly, taking a half step closer to her. Then visibly catching himself, he lowered his shoulders. "Apparently neither of us is particularly politic."

She swallowed. "No. I don't suppose we are." In the back of her mind, her father's upset at the actions of a man who'd been a complete stranger to her abruptly became clear; after all, his eldest daughter had long ago been promised to the rogue's cousin. And no wonder she'd never associated Fenton with this particular relation. He would have done everything in his power to keep any mention of scandal as far away from himself as possible.

"So you see," he commented, his tone very, very level,

"your flight from a church, and even your coming to The Tantalus Club for employment, pales in comparison to me. Does that put you off chatting with me? I'm a very bad man, after all."

Before her almost-marriage, the answer to that question would have been simple. So simple that she would already have been back in her bedchamber, the door bolted. She might even have been hiding behind the bed. Of course that would have been in her parents' house, when she still had her own bedchamber. Even here at the club, though, she was still hiding. And that realization abruptly bothered her.

The magnitude of difference between his scandal and hers wasn't even a near thing; she'd fled a wedding, and he'd killed a man. But there was still that question he'd asked. And now she understood why he'd been interested in *her* point of view. And the way he stood not quite facing her, his right shoulder forward as though he were ready for a blow. How many friends had he lost? Did he hope people would simply forget him, leave him be?

"The man you killed," she said aloud, her voice not quite steady. "Was it murder, or a fair fight?"

He studied her face for a moment. "He broke into my home and came after me with a pistol. But it was certainly my actions that drove him to do so."

"Do you regret it?"

"Are you my confessor?"

Camille tilted her head. "You think we have something in common. I'm testing that theory before I risk spending another minute in your company."

Finally he nodded. "I regret it. I regret all my actions where Lord and Lady Balthrow are concerned."

It might merely have been lip service, but the same thing that had compelled her to agree to meet with him out in the garden in the first place whispered to her that he was speaking the truth. And that perhaps she could learn something from him. Perhaps he could instruct her how to walk outside in London where people knew what she'd done, and not care what they said about her.

"I'm about to take my luncheon in the employees' quarters," she said slowly. "Would you care to join me?"

He inclined his head, surprise briefly crossing his handsome features before the cool cynicism dropped back into place. "I would. And I can promise that I'm generally not so macabre. I'm fairly amusing, actually."

"I'll be the judge of that."

"Then I shall save my best dialogue for you."

As he followed her into the Tantalus Club through the servants' entrance and up the back stairs to the third floor, Camille couldn't help the feeling that she was some sort of doe leading one of those sleek black Indian panthers into her den. Some of the other ladies took gentlemen from downstairs—and elsewhere—upstairs to their beds, but this was the first time she'd invited anyone from outside the club inside its walls. Into what she considered her private sanctuary.

She pushed open the door into the large common room where the half-dozen long tables had been set for luncheon. Fifteen or so of her companions were already present, including the large Mr. Jacobs and Mr. Smith. And everyone looked in her direction. Camille shivered. Oh, this was a mistake; she had enough people looking askance at her. Adding Bloody Blackwood to the mix would only make things worse.

And yet, there they were, and unless she turned around and pushed him back outside, there they would stay. *It's only luncheon,* she told herself. Surely she could manage to be brave for an hour. Camille took a seat at one of the tables, and without hesitating, Mr. Blackwood sat on the sturdy bench opposite her. "This is not what I expected to see up here," he commented, taking two of the cucumber sandwiches set in the center of the table and placing them before him.

"What did you expect?"

"Deep red wall hangings and less clothing, generally."

Her cheeks heated. "A brothel. Disappointed, then?"

His lips curved at the edges. "No. Surprised. I like being surprised. It doesn't happen often."

"You were here this morning, weren't you?" a second female voice asked.

A pretty brunette sat on the bench beside him. He could practically smell the seduction flowing from her and drawing around him. Enticing as it was, he was also struck by the difference between this forward chit and the cautious, standoffish one seated opposite him. "I was. Keating Blackwood. And you are?"

She batted lashes over her impossibly blue eyes. "Miss Hampton. Lucille." Picking up a strawberry, she made a show of sliding it into her mouth. "You were very gallant."

"I bloodied a man's nose, Miss Hampton."

"Yes, but you did it in defense of a lady's honor. That's so very gentlemanly of you."

He sent a glance across the table. Camille sat concentrating on a bowl of pea soup, her shoulders lowered. She looked very like someone who'd been broken, resigned to accept whatever happened to her. Damn Fenton for being so oblivious, ham-fisted, or whatever he'd done to make her run.

Returning his attention to the younger lady seated next to him, he leaned closer. "So I have a fat man's bloody nose to recommend me to you," he murmured. "Is that enough? Why don't we find a private room where you can demonstrate how much you admire me?"

Porcelain blue eyes widened, then blinked. Twice. "I—"

"After all, perhaps I am a hero. Perhaps I defend the reputations of young ladies twice every day and thrice on Sunday. Or perhaps I had an aching head and the idiot's yammering annoyed me. Or perhaps I simply enjoy hitting people when I know they can't or won't defend themselves." He edged still closer. "Or perhaps you should discover who it is you might be flirting with, Miss Hampton. I might even be a murderer. You never know."

Her fair skin turned pale. "You are jesting, Mr. Blackwood. Certainly."

"Actually, he isn't."

The deep, sophisticated drawl immediately put him on alert. He generally knew better than to sit with his back to a door, but for the devil's sake, he was in the attic, in the employees' quarters, of a chit-filled gentlemen's club. "Haybury," he said, centering himself again.

"Miss Hampton, Cammy, give us a moment, will you?" the marquis said, moving around the table and offering a hand to Lady Camille. "I would like a word or two with an old friend."

Camille stood. "Certainly."

Keating eyed the marquis as he sat in Camille's vacated place. "Do you often venture into the ladies' private area of the club?" he asked, resuming his meal. "Does your wife know about this?"

Haybury continued gazing at him, light gray eyes assessing and nearly as cynical as his own must be. "Aren't we supposed to begin with general greetings before the stabbings begin?"

"Ah." Keeping his brief appreciation hidden, Keating nodded. Haybury, at least, had once had a foul reputation himself. "Haybury. I hear congratulations are in order. You've gained a wife and a gentlemen's club."

The marquis nodded. "Yes. I couldn't have one without the other."

"But which were you after?" Keating pursued, already deciding how much of a stir he was willing to raise if the marquis should ask him to leave. Or to order him to do so.

"The wife," Haybury returned immediately. "And I seem to enjoy making her happy. Which leads me to a question: Would she be happier with you in the private areas of her club making all sorts of mischief, or with you outside on your arse?"

"I know where I'd be happier." Keating rolled his shoulders. He had a destination clearly in mind; all he needed to do was behave in the manner that would be most likely to gain him what he wanted. "I have no intention of making trouble, Oliver. I'm here for a luncheon and a chat with a pretty chit."

"I don't have much faith in your ability to behave."

Look who's talking, Keating nearly said, but clamped his jaw closed over the words. "People change."

"Fenton may have done everything in his power to put distance between the two of you, my friend, but *I* haven't forgotten. Nor has it escaped my attention that you're lodging with the Duke of Greaves. That doesn't recommend you to me, either. And given that my Diane seems to have developed a need to protect the ladies in her employ, I won't sit back and let you work your mischief with Camille."

"She knows who I am."

"Everybody knows you're Bloody Blackwood."

Only six years of practice kept him from reacting to the name. "She knows I'm Fenton's cousin. I told her." He sat forward a little, noting that Haybury shifted the same distance back in response. It wasn't fear, but caution; in the past he hadn't been a brawler, but that had certainly changed. And if anyone knew of his recent proclivity to provoke fights, it would be the marquis. "What put you off Adam, by the way?" he asked, settling for a verbal jab. "You and Greaves used to be fast friends."

"This is my interrogation; not yours. And since you apparently saw the need to approach Camille, I'd like to know why. Other than to announce your relationship to her former fiancé, of course."

Keating forced a short laugh. "When did you become the purveyor of propriety, Oliver? I told you; she's pretty, and she dislikes Fenton." And like him, she'd made a mistake that had ruined her life. But he meant to keep any feelings of kinship to himself. Feelings rarely led him in the right direction. "I thought it would be unfair of me to surprise her with my cousin's identity."

"So you're commiserating."

"Yes. We're commiserating. And she invited me in." He glanced down for a moment. "She also clubbed me in the head with a book, if that makes you more inclined to allow me about."

The marquis's jaw twitched. After a moment, he nodded. "Camille," he said over his shoulder, "enjoy your luncheon. If Mr. Blackwood gives you any trouble, please inform me."

The hostess curtsied. "Yes, my lord."

Once Haybury left the room, the buzz of conversation resumed. Clearly not everyone who worked at The Tantalus Club was as ignorant of his past as Lady Camille had been. He detested being referred to as "Bloody

Blackwood," though at the same time the moniker was likely fairly apt. It was still an idiotic poem.

Camille returned to sit opposite him. "Do you mean to make trouble for me?" she asked, meeting his gaze.

"I do not." Rolling his stiff shoulders, Keating took another bite of sandwich. "As you may have noticed, however," he continued, keeping his voice cool and even, "I am frequently glared at and whispered about. Does that trouble you?"

After a long moment she lowered her head. "I thought I might be able to learn a lesson or two from you about keeping my spine stiff even with all the glaring. But perhaps this is a poor idea, after all."

Damnation. "More attention on me means less attention directed at you, does it not?"

"Or it could mean twice the attention I would warrant on my own."

He leaned forward on his elbows. "Go walking with me tomorrow. It's the only way to know for certain."

Her guarded expression deepened. "I don't think that's a good idea."

"Cammy almost never leaves the property," one of the ladies at the far end of the table offered. "Are you truly Bloody Blackwood?"

Keating began to consider that he might have been better off turning down his cousin's request and remaining at home. "Yes, I am," he said, sending the loudmouthed chit a glance that had her looking elsewhere.

Returning his attention to the young lady still seated opposite him, he swiftly reassessed the conversation. He knew he could be charming; what he hadn't anticipated was that she would be skittish as a colt after her first snowfall. "We needn't go tomorrow," he revised, inwardly cursing himself. "Or if you're worried over my intentions, bring some of your friends with you. I only thought a stroll would be pleasant."

"It used to be," she said in a voice so low he almost didn't hear it. Lady Camille visibly shook herself. "I'm quite busy, but I shall inform you if I change my mind."

He forced a smile. "Please do." So his own reputation had doomed the venture before he'd even begun it. A man as cynical as he knew himself to be should have expected that. In a sense it was even amusing that a ruined chit found him too scandalous. In another sense, what he needed was a damned drink. Several of them.

Chapter Four

"He asked you to go walking with him?"

Camille nodded, finishing with the pins holding her hair in its simple bun at the top of her head. "I told him no, of course, but it was nice to be asked. Even by a notorious rogue."

"He's the one who told you he was a rogue."

"I would have discovered that fact shortly, anyway."

In the dressing mirror's reflection she saw Sophia White blink light green eyes beneath long, curved lashes. "You know, I think his reputation is worse than yours, Cammy."

"Well, thank you very much." Camille put the rest of her toiletries back in the drawer of the dressing table she shared with the Duke of Hennessy's illegitimate daughter.

Sophia had people looking askance at her as well, but at least she hadn't done anything to warrant the tongue-wagging. Except come to work at a gentlemen's club, of course. But Miss White had grown up with the sideways looks and muttering, and it had never seemed to bother her—until she came of age and discovered that no one wished to hire a governess born to an indiscreet duke and an upstairs maid.

"What I mean is, perhaps you *could* go walking with him as your companion," Sophia pressed. "Everyone will stare, of course, but they won't be staring at you. They'll be staring at Bloody Blackwood."

"Yes, that's what he said." Camille shuddered. Not at Keating Blackwood's nickname, but at the thought of people staring. Oh, she hated that. The staring, the behind-hand whispers, were worse even than being given the cut-direct. "I would prefer to forgo the experience, who-ever they might be chattering about."

Sophia flopped backward onto her bed. "I don't like being looked at askance, either, but I've learned to ignore it."

Sinking onto the edge of the bed beside her friend, Camille shook her head. "The circumstances of your birth are not your fault, Sophia. You have no reason to pay at-tention to the spitting cobras outside."

"Then your solution is to never venture beyond the walls of The Tantalus Club ever again? Ever?"

"Not until everyone forgets me, anyway." Sighing, she stood again. "If you think me going outside is such a wonderful thing, then you go with me."

"Very well."

That stopped her exit from their shared bedchamber. "What?"

"You heard me. I'll go for a walk if you go for a walk. With Keating Blackwood, that is. I'd like to meet some-one more scandalous than I am. It'll be interesting."

Oh, dear. Camille knew she was a coward; she only needed to remind herself about how long it had finally taken for her to stand up for herself to see it very clearly. And that certainly hadn't gone well. But the other ladies here didn't know about her faint heart. They'd embraced her when her own family had turned their backs. And she didn't want her new friends deciding she wasn't worth troubling themselves over.

She took a deep breath. "I'll send Mr. Blackwood a note, then. And if anyone else wishes to join us, they are certainly welcome to do so."

Sophia chuckled as she sat upright again. "Safety in numbers?"

"We're the scandalous females of The Tantalus Club. I daresay we'll have ladies of good breeding fainting left and right."

There. That sounded brave. Sophia likely knew better, but out of everyone at the club, Camille trusted Miss White. Before she could change her mind she headed for the large upstairs common room and sat down to write out a note to Keating Blackwood. He'd said he was residing at Baswich House with the Duke of Greaves, and whatever her employer Lord Haybury seemed to think of the duke, she counted that as a mark in Blackwood's favor. If he'd been staying with his cousin, the Marquis of Fenton, she wouldn't have exchanged another word with him. And she likely would have hit him a second time.

The note finished, she delivered it downstairs to Juliet, the evening butleress. Venturing anywhere with this near stranger simply because she felt . . . drawn to him was likely a very poor decision, and by two minutes after the walk began tomorrow she was certain she would regret leaving the club's grounds. At the same time, she hadn't ventured down the street more than a dozen times since she'd been hired at The Tantalus Club. As much as she had always enjoyed long walks, the self-prescribed confinement over the past months had been nearly as difficult an adjustment as being away from her family and former friends. She'd lost both of the latter, but for heaven's sake, perhaps she could manage a walk.

But simply because she'd agreed to go didn't mean that she would leave her sanctuary without knowing everything she could about her prospective companion. He'd admitted to killing a man. If her mind had been functioning correctly, that would have sent her fleeing. His admitting it, though, and the sincere regret she'd heard in his voice . . . had set her more at ease. Not about the deed, but about the man. He hadn't attempted to disguise it or lie about it or make it sound somehow acceptable.

Frowning, she went to find Pansy Bridger. At the same time she attempted to ignore the niggling warning in the back of her skull that she was once again being behindhand, waiting until it was too late to make up her mind about anything. She wanted to know precisely what lay in store for her if she was to be seen in public with Mr. Blackwood, and if anyone knew ill facts about every man in London, it was Pansy.

She found the petite brunette reading in the common room and sat in the chair opposite. "Pansy, may I ask you a question?"

Dark brown eyes glanced over the top of the book at her. "Have you ever read *Waverley*?"

"Of course I have. Most everyone says Walter Scott is the author, you know. I'm not certain why he bothered to publish anonymously."

"And do you agree with the ending?" Miss Bridger pressed.

Camille paused. Over the past few months she'd become familiar with Pansy's eccentricities, but even so, she wasn't certain what her friend's objection might be. "It's based on a historical uprising," she said carefully. "Surely my objection would be to the fact that a civil war happened at all."

"Waverley marries Rose," Pansy said flatly. "Patient, proper Rose." She snapped the book closed. "I suppose Sir Walter couldn't tolerate the idea of a man finding happiness with someone like Flora—for heaven's sake, she's interested in politics and she has a mind of her own."

Ah. "I think Rose is symbolic for peace and order," Camille ventured, "whereas Flora is unrest and idealism. It's not so much that they're two women, as that they represent two diff—"

"I know what they represent," Pansy cut in, scowling. "And I don't like it. Logically a man should prefer an intelligent woman. I don't care if it's symbolic. It's idiotic."

Taking a short breath, Camille nodded. "*Ideally* a man should prefer an intelligent woman," she countered. "Logically I think a man chooses to pursue the woman who would best . . . benefit him—either his mind, or his pocketbook, or his bed."

Pansy pointed a finger at her. "That is well said. Now what was your question?"

She'd very nearly forgotten. "I was wondering what you knew of Keating Blackwood."

Her friend's frown deepened. "I know the poem, and I know he's been in exile in Shropshire for the past six years." Her furrowed brow smoothed. " 'Too many nights philandering, / Too much whiskey, too much gaming. / Whichever lady caught his eye, / He had no trouble claiming,' " she recited.

That sounded ominous. "Any further details?"

"Oh, yes. The victim was the Viscount of Balthrow. Blackwood was arrested for it, but the court said he had only acted to defend himself." She snorted. "I should think he would have to defend himself, after Lord Balthrow caught him in flagrante delicto with Lady Balthrow." She shrugged. "As I recall reading about it, though, Blackwood returned home and Balthrow pursued him, so by law Balthrow was the aggressor."

So he had told the truth about the circumstances of the fight between himself and the viscount. It still didn't make Camille feel any easier about being seen chatting with him in public. The two of them together were likely to set wagging tongues aflame. "Thank you," she said, noticing that Pansy still looked at her.

"I heard that he spoke to you, Cammy. He's awful, you know. Worse than men who marry to gain money or position. He only cares for one part of a woman. The rest is inconsequential to him."

"We only exchanged words, Pansy. There's no need to worry."

"Good. I'm only trying to prevent you from being further wounded."

"And thank you for that."

Camille stood again, and returned to the club's foyer. As far as Pansy was concerned, no man had anything positive to offer *any* woman, but her information at least seemed legitimate. Time for her to change her mind a second time about going for a stroll with Bloody Blackwood—before it was too late. Cammy stood back as the butleress welcomed a small party of gentlemen into the club, then approached her.

"I sent your note off," Juliet said. "No need to fret; I'll inform you as soon as there's a reply."

Damnation. The note was likely already in Mr. Blackwood's hands, then. Fighting abrupt panic, she thanked Juliet and hurried up the stairs again. Well, she'd made her decision to go walking with him based on her . . . perception of him rather than the facts of his past. That seemed the more upright road to travel, whether she'd acted rashly or not. Camille stifled a sigh. Acting rashly had yet to net her anything but pain. Now she could only wonder whether she'd just made the same mistake once again.

* * *

Keating didn't bother to look up as someone pulled out the chair opposite him and sat. Instead he concentrated on pouring the dregs remaining in the whiskey bottle into his glass. Spilling any of the liquid would be a tragedy.

"I manage to secure you a guest membership to The Tantalus Club, and you decide to spend your evening at Jezebel's?" the Duke of Greaves's low drawl came after a moment.

"I like it here," Keating returned. "It's dark, and it stinks of liquor and sweat and tallow."

"And urine. Yes, it's delightful. Was that bottle full when you received it?"

Finally he looked up to see dark gray eyes assessing him. "I don't require a nanny, Adam," he said.

"I'm merely curious," the duke stated.

"Curious enough to venture into Jezebel's yourself. Not precisely your typical haunt any longer, is it? Don't trail after me. I don't like it."

"I see that." The duke, though, remained seated. "May I ask you a question?"

"No."

"Very well. I will only suggest that you keep in mind the fact that you're not in some tavern in Shropshire, and that if you dislike that poem, you should not live up to its poorly written rhymes." Greaves stood. "Oh, and this arrived for you earlier." He dropped a note onto the table. A moment later he vanished in the direction of the door.

Keating looked after him. "Yes, well, remind me sometime to tell you what Haybury said about you," he muttered. A bit too late for a timely retort, but he would attempt to remember it for next time. After all, if he couldn't manage to set one former friend against another, what good was he?

As he reached across the table and dragged the note toward him, he noticed—not for the first time—that despite the crowd at the gaming hell, a good ten feet of space remained between him and the nearest patrons. For a moment it was as if the past six years had never happened; he was that idiotic . . . boy, one-and-twenty years old and so full of piss and vinegar that he couldn't be bothered to pay any heed to anyone.

A warm hand slid down his shoulder. "I know who you are," came a sultry whisper, and then a warm tongue licked the curve of his ear. "Come prick me, my dear, and I'll let you in for free."

He glanced up at the source of the tongue. Jezebel's wasn't anything like The Tantalus Club. The young ladies who were employed here weren't known for their education or their conversation or even their pretty faces. They were known for being inexpensive and willing. "What's your name, love?" he asked, noticing for the first time that his words were slurring.

"Lizzy, unless you'd care to call me something else. Eleanor, perhaps?"

Keating's hand was around her windpipe almost before he realized it. Slamming to his feet, he held her close, the tips of her toes just barely touching the dirty floor. "What was that?" he murmured.

She clawed at his fingers. "Nothing, sir . . . I ain't . . . said nothing," Lizzy croaked.

He released his grip and pushed, shoving her onto the lap of the surprised man seated behind her. "I thought not." Remembering the note at the last minute, he picked it up and shoved it into his pocket before he strode out of the club. Behind him the jackals were already yapping.

Inebriated as he was, he still realized that he'd been fortunate. Instead of a notoriety-seeking whore, he might just as easily have been approached by a friend of the late Lord Balthrow. As Greaves had warned him—too late, of course—London wasn't Shropshire. Attempting not to stagger as he made his way into the street, he hailed a hack and gave the driver the address for Baswich House.

Once he was settled in the bouncing, rackety coach, he pulled the note from his pocket and unfolded it. He had to blink hard to clear his vision, and then found that the interior of the hack was too dim for him to be able to read the thing. Finally he pressed the note up against the window. With the flickering lamplight outside, he slowly deciphered the pretty, looping letters.

" 'Mr. Blackwood,' " he muttered to himself, " 'I have considered your offer, and my friend Sophia White and I will be pleased to go walking with you on Wednesday. Please meet us at The Tantalus Club at two o'clock, or if you are unable, send me word to that effect. Kind regards, Camille Pryce.' "

For a long moment he looked at the last block of words on the heavy vellum. "Kind regards." He touched them with his finger. They didn't rub away. How long had it been since anyone had sent him that sentiment? Seven years? Eight?

Oh, good God. Keating punched his fist into his thigh, none too gently. Next he would have tears welling in his eyes. Drinking this much was worse than foolish, especially here. Especially when he had a task to accomplish. He needed that ten thousand pounds. Not for himself. For what his idiocy had created. For what he'd done to Eleanor Balthrow and what she'd had to hide from London. From him. From everyone.

Luckily the hack lurched to a halt before he could begin weeping, and he stumbled onto the Baswich House front drive. He tossed a coin of some unknown value to the driver, and whatever it was it made the fellow tip his hat as he drove down the street.

Adam's butler, Hooper, pulled open the front door before he could pound on it. Instead he nearly fell on his face into the foyer. Grabbing onto the small bench against the wall, he righted himself again.

"Shall I send Pidgeon up to you, Mr. Blackwood?" the butler asked, his face a mask of solemn propriety.

"No. I'll see to myself." Halfway to the stairs, he paused. "Is Greaves here?"

"His Grace returned just moments ago."

"Had he been gone long?"

"His Grace spent the evening in, sir."

"When did that note arrive for me?"

"Just before dusk, sir."

So Adam had decided to wait better than six hours—until he'd demonstrated that he meant to stay out all night drinking—before delivering it to him. Apparently he *did* have a nanny, unlikely a one as Adam Baswich made. Considering that the news was good, he was willing to overlook his friend's hovering. This once. Because generally he believed he should be left to wallow in the hole he'd dug for himself. No one else needed to be muddied on his account.

He didn't recall making his way up to the private rooms Adam had given over to him, and he didn't remember shedding his clothes or falling onto the bed. In fact, his next conscious thought was that he was going to punch his valet in the nose if Pidgeon didn't stop tapping him on the shoulder. "Bugger off," he muttered, "or you're sacked."

"I don't work for you."

Keating forced open one eye. "Bugger off, anyway."

The Duke of Greaves picked up a pitcher of water and threw it on him.

Cursing, Keating shot to his feet. Shock and throbbing pain in his head both hit him at the same time. With a growl he launched himself at the duke.

Greaves sidestepped, and Keating crashed to the floor. Before he could stumble back to his feet, Adam put a booted foot on the small of his back. "Stay down," he said evenly.

"I was down, damn it all. In bed. Now I'm on the bloody floor."

"You know, I can't decide whether you prefer hitting, or being hit." The boot heel dug into his back. "You aren't precisely prime at the moment."

"I'm not the one who threw water on me." Keating uttered another epithet. "Get your foot off me, or you'll find out firsthand."

The weight came off his back. "Pidgeon tried to wake you earlier," Greaves commented, moving backward. "I'm here because it's past noon, and I believe you have an appointment at two o'clock."

The angry retort Keating had been about to make stopped in his throat. "How far past noon?"

"It's twenty minutes of one. I had a bath drawn in your sitting room. Use it. There's tea and sugar and toasted bread in there. Do I need to dress you as well?"

Sitting upright, Keating leaned back against the side of the bed. "No." He drew a tight breath. "Thank you, Adam."

"Yes, well, I don't know what you're up to, but I'm all for creating mischief." He walked to the door. "I'll send in Pidgeon at one o'clock."

Once the door closed, Keating swiped a hand through his dripping hair. At least it was water. There were times, a few years ago, when he'd awakened in worse. He couldn't even count the number of times he'd told himself that he needed to stop drinking to such excess. Previously he'd always managed to take care of his duties as a landowner regardless of—or in spite of—his fondness for drunken oblivion.

Now, however, he had a woman's trust to gain, with ten thousand pounds at risk. And his head felt ready to pound straight off his neck. Of all the things he felt ready to do, being charming wasn't one of them. "Damnation," he mumbled, pushing to his feet and belatedly realizing that he was stark naked.

He stifled a rueful chuckle. That must have given Adam a start. To his friend's credit, the duke had awakened him, anyway. Not bothering to find a robe, he walked the short distance down the hallway to his sitting room. An upstairs maid shrieked and fled down the stairs, but other than his porcupine hair and beard stubble he didn't see what was so frightening. Unless she'd been overwhelmed with desire at the sight of his cock, of course.

Though he'd half expected the cast-iron bath to be full of icy water, it was pleasantly warm and steaming. After fifteen minutes of alternating sweet tea and submersion, he began to feel slightly less murderous. That was when it occurred to him that the Duke of Greaves had read his private correspondence.

"Sir?" Pidgeon's voice came from the door as it cracked open. "His Grace said you would require attire appropriate for strolling. Do you wish the black trousers, or the buckskin breeches?"

"The buckskins. And the new Hoby's. And the black superfine coat. That looks gentlemanly, doesn't it?"

He could almost hear the valet blink. "Yes, sir. I believe it does."

"Quickly, if you please. I don't wish to be late."

The door closed again, with a thud that made him

wince. So he could dress like a gentleman; the question was whether he could behave like a gentleman. And the answer was that he could, and would, because he had to. Stuffing a slice of toasted bread into his mouth, Keating stood and stepped out of the bath. He toweled himself dry and dressed as soon as Pidgeon reappeared with his clothes.

He supposed he owed Adam additional thanks, but that would mean admitting aloud that he'd needed the duke's assistance. Instead he went out to the stable while the groom saddled Amble, and then rode off at a cautious, mostly jolt-free walk to The Tantalus Club.

Just as he was beginning to consider that he had no idea where one went to pay a social call on the employees of . . . of anything, he caught sight of Lady Camille at the side of the carriage drive, a pretty, redheaded chit standing beside her. He took a deep breath, attempting to ignore the tingle that shot up his spine all the way to his fingertips at the mere thought that she'd defied her better judgment to be seen in his company. Swiftly he dismounted and sent Amble off with one of the club's stableboys.

"Good afternoon," he said, deciding that bowing would both be inappropriate and would cause his head to explode.

"Mr. Blackwood." Camille nodded at him. "This is my good friend, Miss White. Sophia, Mr. Blackwood."

"Keating, please," he said, taking the other chit's hand. "Do you ladies have a destination in mind?"

"Green Park," Camille answered, directly on the tail of his question.

Traditionally those wanting to be seen strolled through Hyde Park, particularly in the afternoon. Interesting. "Green Park it is," he said aloud, offering an arm to each of the ladies. "I'll purchase us ices, if you wish."

"Oh, it's been ages since I've had a lemon ice," Miss White commented with a smile, wrapping her fingers around his sleeve.

On his left side, however, Camille stood looking at his elevated forearm. "Is something amiss?" he asked. "Do I have an insect crawling on me?"

"No. It's only that I agreed to a walk. Not to doing something that would make my situation even worse." She wrinkled her nose. "And you smell like liquor."

Keating looked at her. She made a damned good point. And he liked the way she scrunched up her nose. It was . . . fetching. "I bathed," he said, attempting not to sound affronted. "But I promised I wouldn't make things worse for you." He glanced at the lady on his other side. "I'm afraid you'll have to release me. If I can't escort both of you, it'll look as if I'm courting one of you."

With a brief smile he nearly missed, Camille started off down the street. He strode after her, not waiting to see if Miss White kept pace. In a moment he'd caught up to his cousin's almost-bride. She'd donned a large, pale blue bonnet, which served to deepen the color of her light azure eyes.

"What changed your mind?" he asked, slowing as he drew even with her.

"Sophia offered to join me. And . . . I've had a shortfall of friendships lately. I decided it would be absurd to turn my back on a possible friend because he is potentially of dubious character."

"I'm flattered, I think."

Another swift grin. "I do have one request, however."

"That I stay at least twenty feet distant from you?" Keating suggested, keeping his expression still. For God's sake, he'd heard the poem; a chit's censure could hardly injure him.

"Honesty," she said.

"Beg pardon?"

"Honesty. I am here because you told me precisely who you are. Don't ever lie to me, Mr. Blackwood, or I shall decide that we actually do not have anything in common."

He nodded, something dark and heavy breaking loose in his chest. What that sensation was, he would debate later. "I agree. As long as you do me the same courtesy."

"Then we have an accord."

Keating glanced at the park coming into view ahead of them. "Shall we shake hands, then?"

The redheaded lady made a sound behind them very like a snort. Let her laugh; it was thanks to Sophia White that Camille had joined him today. He felt rather kindly toward her at the moment.

Camille held out her right hand. Resisting the odd, abrupt urge to first wipe his own palm against his thigh, Keating gripped her warm fingers. As long as she never asked precisely why he'd returned to London, everything would proceed swimmingly. Of course he'd broken his word before, but at this moment, he hoped he wouldn't have occasion to do so with Camille Pryce.

Chapter Five

Even though Sophia seemed to be of the opinion—erroneous though it was—that she was serving as a chaperone to her two companions, Camille kept dragging her up to Keating's other side. They were three . . . friends, strolling through Green Park, and in her case, at least, hoping desperately that no one else noticed them.

She took a deep breath. While it had been over a year since she'd strolled Mayfair's parks with a very different set of friends, it felt even longer ago than that. The sounds of London faded to the distance, replaced by the singing of birds and the dull rush of wind through the treetops. Peace. Slowly the tight muscles across her shoulders loosened, and she lifted her gaze above their immediate surroundings.

Beside her the much more lively Sophia was chatting with Mr. Blackwood about hats, of all things. For these few moments, at least, she could feel . . . untroubled. Her fingers brushed against Keating's black coat, and she shook out the sudden warmth that tingled through them. If anyone had ever told her that one day she would be grateful to a confessed killer, she wouldn't have believed it. And yet, standing there in the middle of Green Park with leaf-mottled sunlight making bright patches on her soft blue walking dress, she *did* feel grateful.

"How long has it been since you've been for a stroll?" Keating asked quietly.

Camille blushed. She hadn't realized she was so transparent. "A year. That's not what matters, though. It's just very pretty today."

"It is, indeed."

She sent him a sharp glance, but his gaze was on a pair of squirrels bouncing from one tree to another. Oh, for heaven's sake. Had she expected a compliment? Did she expect that he might have something nefarious in mind for her? The answer to both questions was a firm *no*, of course. "Do you go walking frequently?" she queried, attempting to be social.

"I grow wheat and have a number of cattle and sheep," he returned easily. "I'm out of doors nearly every day."

"You tend them yourself?"

"I prefer to." He cleared his throat. "Not that I've become a monk or some such. I do employ servants. And several men who also work out of doors with me, in addition to fellows who hire themselves out at harvest and calving time."

"Not what I would have expected from someone who had a poem written about him."

A muscle in his jaw jumped. "I didn't write the poem."

"Cammy, steady," Sophia said abruptly from just beyond him.

At the same moment Camille heard the telltale chatter of women approaching them. Before she could head in the opposite direction, five young ladies came into view around the hedgerow. "Earlier warning would have been nice," she muttered at Sophia.

"I didn't hear them earlier," her friend whispered back. "Let's just go."

"Did I miss something?" Keating broke in, frowning.

"No. They merely . . . say things I don't like to hear. I should be getting back, anyway."

"Ah." To her surprise, Keating took her arm, and then Sophia's. "Watch this."

Short of yanking her arm bodily out of his grip, she seemed to be trapped. Camille *felt* trapped, being dragged toward her worst nightmare. Heavens, she even recognized two of them. One had been a dear friend, until—until she'd upended her own life.

"Stop," she hissed, putting as much authority into that word as she could.

They kept moving.

At less than a dozen feet distant from the five young ladies, Blackwood released her. Then, just as Amelia Danning's pretty face, framed in its usual bouncing black curls, began to sneer out the syllables of her name, her escort surged forward.

"Ladies," he exclaimed, and, grabbing Amelia's shoulders, he tugged her forward and kissed her full on the mouth. He released her so quickly she stumbled, and then he repeated the action with Olivia Harden. Screeching, the girls fled like a flock of terrorized chickens. In a moment they were alone again, except for the other strollers on the fringes who all stared at Keating and muttered to each other. She was certain she could hear a chorus of "Of age but one-and-twenty, / By three years in Town he'd burned, / All his candles, all his bridges, / His friends and family spurned."

"What the devil was that?" she demanded, glaring at him.

"I'll wager you a thousand pounds that no one here is gossiping about you, Camille Pryce," he said with a jaunty grin that didn't touch his light brown eyes.

"But . . . but what happens when the angry papas come after you?"

"I don't think they'd dare." He motioned for her to continue along the path with him. "Shall we?"

Well. He had the reputation for being a notorious rogue, and he'd certainly just looked like one. But he hadn't scandalized her former friends because of his own lack of character. He'd done it to protect her.

With all the upset her actions had caused, she felt like the largest blot on the landscape of Mayfair. It was odd to realize that she'd stumbled across the one person whose reputation and standing were more damaged than hers. And even stranger was the idea that having him about might offer her some respite from those stares and sneers. Yes, they would still be scowling, but they wouldn't be doing it at her.

Sophia made a snorting sound, and Camille realized that her friend was laughing. "What's so amusing?"

"I don't know those girls," the illegitimate daughter of the Duke of Hennessy returned, chuckling, "but I imagine none of them has ever been so surprised and scandalized in her entire life."

"I should hope not," Keating put in. "I'd hate to think all that effort went for nothing."

"What effort? You merely pursed your lips and walked forward in their direction."

"I had to steel myself for the contact. Virgins and I generally avoid each other. Something about heaven and hell and the fires of damnation."

"And what about merely strolling with a pair of young innocent misses?" Camille asked, grinning despite herself.

"With limited physical contact, we should be safe." Reaching over, he tugged on the brim of her bonnet. "Tell me that wasn't fun."

The most fun was the realization that this man who'd crossed her path just yesterday had already shown himself to be more her ally than her parents, her sisters, or any of her previous "friends" had been in over a year.

She had thought that she'd used the last bit of her luck and fortune in finding The Tantalus Club advertisement for hostesses on the same day she'd found herself down to her last shilling at a disapproving relative's house in Chatham. And then she'd found other young ladies whose unique and frequently scandalous pasts made them her compatriots and allies and friends. And now she'd found Keating Blackwood.

"I am cautiously amused," she conceded. "If I knew for certain *why* you seem willing to take the blows meant for me, I would even be tempted to remove the modifier from that sentence."

A slow smile curved his mouth, and this time his eyes twinkled. "Then we'll have something to discuss when we go driving tomorrow afternoon, won't we?"

Keating resisted the urge to wipe the lingering taste of virginal affront from his mouth as he rode back to Baswich House. Six years ago the females' papas might indeed have come after him with torches and muskets. Being Bloody Blackwood, however, offered him a kind of protection he'd never anticipated. And apparently he was expected to misbehave to a certain degree.

At least those chits wouldn't be wagging their tongues about Camille Pryce tonight. Of course Fenton might prefer if they did; any additional incentive to drive her back to the altar would undoubtedly please the marquis. Keating scowled. That likely should have occurred to him before he decided to attempt being a hero. Or his idea of one, anyway.

Hooper informed him that Greaves was attending meetings in Parliament, so he made his way up to his friend's generous library to answer the correspondence from Fredericks, his estate manager. It was the first time in six years that Fredericks had had actual duties to see to, but the old fellow had also managed Havard's Glen for thirteen years before that, when he'd had no guidance at all.

The liquor tantalus beneath the library's center window glinted in the late afternoon sun, but he turned his back on the damned thing and went to find a book. He'd nearly missed his last second chance today because of his drinking. And apparently he smelled of liquor.

Dropping into a chair, Keating lifted his arm and smelled his sleeve. All he could detect was the faint scent of lemons from where the red-haired chit, Sophia White, had grasped his arm. He opened his coat and inhaled again, but perhaps he was too saturated with whiskey to be able to detect it himself.

"What are you doing?"

The Duke of Greaves sank into a neighboring chair, then reached over to pluck the book from Keating's hands. *"Pride and Prejudice?"* He lifted an eyebrow. "When did you begin reading romantic fiction?"

"Five minutes ago." Keating retrieved the book and snapped it shut. Wherever his search for insights into Camille Pryce might bring him, he wasn't about to share any of it with Adam Baswich. "What are your plans this evening?"

"I've been asked to a dinner party by Lord and Lady Clarkson. I would suggest that you join me, but considering you assaulted their daughter this afternoon, you might do better to remain away."

"Ah. Which one was she?"

"The one with black, curling hair."

"Good to know, then."

Silence. At the same time, he could practically hear the duke's razor-sharp mind debating, assessing, plotting. "Very well," Greaves finally said. "Don't tell me what the devil you think you're about. Don't tell me why you talk about making a new start in the morning, and then become some sort of kissing bandit in the afternoon. In return, I won't tell you to stop behaving like an ass before the entire House of Lords tars and feathers you."

Pushing to his feet, Keating tucked the borrowed book beneath his arm. "Fair enough. In fact, in thanks for your fairness, *I* will refrain from mentioning your . . . rather colorful past."

"Good."

"It's amazing how much menace you're able to put in a single word, my friend," Keating returned mildly. If he hadn't been far beyond caring, he might have found it off-putting. "As for tonight, I think I'll step out for an early dinner at The Tantalus Club and then retire for the evening."

"You— Oh." Greaves cleared his throat. "Do you have any suggestions, then, about how I should answer Clarkson's demand for your head on a platter?"

"Tell him there's a queue for that, and I'm likely to be dead long before his turn comes 'round."

"That might suffice. By the way, I'm going to spend the day at Tattersall's tomorrow. Care to join me?"

"I have an engagement." Nor did he have the blunt to purchase any horses. He headed up toward his borrowed rooms to change for dinner.

"You know if something's afoot you can discuss it with me, Keating."

He slowed, but didn't turn around. "Nothing's afoot, Adam. But thank you. And I'll attempt to be gone from London before the masses begin calling at your door for my execution."

Camille's book of choice kept his interest until well after dark. That Darcy seemed a bit stiff, but he definitely had his eye on the correct Bennett sister. Finally he stretched and sent for Pidgeon to find him something to wear to dinner. In Shropshire he'd ignored invitations—such as they were—until the other area residents stopped sending them. Consequently he hadn't had much need for proper evening attire, and he was already feeling the lack. As much as it pained him and his purse, he was going to have to purchase some additional clothes.

As he finished tying his cravat, the butler knocked at the half-open bedchamber door. "Mr. Blackwood, you have a caller."

Keating lowered a brow. "Male, or female?"

"Male."

That couldn't be good. "Is he armed?"

The butler blinked. "No, sir. It's the Marquis of Fenton."

Taking a deep breath, Keating finished dressing. "I'll be down in a moment."

"Very good, sir."

As a finishing touch he tucked the slim dagger he always carried into his right Hessian boot. Then, with a swift, reluctant glance at the bottle of whiskey sitting on his dressing table, he descended the stairs. Hooper gestured him toward the morning room, then vanished into the depths of the house. Adam had some very discreet servants.

Keating pushed open the morning room door. "Hello, cousin."

Fenton was dressed for an evening out as well, though they couldn't possibly be headed for the same club. After all, the marquis had been banned from The Tantalus Club. His cousin turned from inspecting the clock on the mantel. "What the devil do you think you're doing?"

"Going to dinner."

"It's far too late for you to play at being innocent, Keating. You are here to convince Camille Pryce to return to me. Not to make matters worse."

"I know why I'm here. And I told you to leave the details to me." He frowned. "What did you hear?"

"That you're terrorizing Green Park, kissing every virtuous young lady who crosses your path!"

Well, that sounded like something he would have done—six years ago. "With whom was I strolling, anyway?"

"I don't give a damn who was with you. There are enough people who know of our kinship that I won't have you rolling in the mud and dragging me down with you."

"Interesting. For your information, I was out walking with your betrothed. We crossed paths with her former friends, and I stopped them from beginning any additional gossip." There. It sounded like that was what he'd intended, anyway. And nothing in heaven or hell would convince him to admit that all he'd been thinking of was the hurt, wary look in Camille Pryce's pretty blue eyes.

Fenton took a step toward him. "You managed to pry her out of that damned club?"

"I did."

"You should have informed me. I might have stumbled across you by accident, before you transformed into a public menace."

"I was already a public menace, and I told you to leave this to me. Now go away before someone sees that you've been here and *you* ruin *my* reputation."

Clear annoyance on his face, Stephen nodded. "Very well. But promise me you'll stop doing that. I asked you to be discreet."

"I am being very discreet about you and Camille. If you think to instruct me on how to go about the remainder of my life, save your breath."

His cousin glared at him. "If you expect your reward, I expect you to do as I've asked. Camille Pryce has caused me a great deal of embarrassment. I suppose you did well in stopping more gossip from beginning, but you're here to see she learns a lesson about the perils of defying propriety."

"I know why I'm here," Keating snapped. "What I don't know is why you're still here. Leave."

With a last scowl Fenton stomped out to the foyer, where Hooper had miraculously reappeared just in time to pull open the front door. "Don't play about with me, Keating. I've run out of patience."

Keating reached past the butler to slam the door closed. "Idiot," he muttered, then had to pace the hallway for five minutes while he waited for his cousin to be well away from Baswich House. There was nothing worse than putting a satisfying exclamation on a conversation and then having to continue on with it because of ill timing.

Finally he went out to fetch Amble and then rode to The Tantalus Club. Since he was only being admitted because he was Greaves's guest, he likely should have made certain the duke was with him, but Greaves belonged to at least half a dozen other clubs in addition to the dozens of people who for some reason liked to schedule meetings with him. Keating couldn't very well accomplish what he needed to in one morning or one evening a week.

Camille wasn't seating members. Rather, it was the lively redhead. "Good evening, Sophia," he said, smiling as he stopped at the podium they'd put beside the Demeter Room doorway.

"Keating. Are you alone tonight?"

"For the moment. You're not allowed to dine with me, are you?"

Color touched her fair cheeks. "Heavens, no." She cocked her head at him. "You do go looking for trouble, don't you?"

"Whenever possible. Your shy friend isn't about, is she?"

"Cammy's dealing vingt-et-un tonight."

She was actually sitting at a table with men who might look askance at her? That was interesting. "I thought she only worked in the Demeter Room."

"We've all trained in every position. Sally is ill, and Cammy said she supposed she could count well enough to sit in for one evening."

The part of him that had felt . . . coiled up, steeling himself for a night of being glared at and avoided, loosened just a little. Mentally he counted the blunt in his pockets. Nine pounds give or take, about half of which he could afford to lose. Considering that he hadn't played cards in six years it was a risk, but then again he could lose five pounds in exchange for ten thousand more.

"I believe I'll go play some cards," he said, nodding at Sophia.

"We do have a lovely roasted pheasant on the menu this evening," she returned, gesturing at the crowded room.

He grinned. "I'll pass on dinner, but thank you." Looking toward the three doors that exited the dining room, he frowned. "Where do I go?"

"The Persephone Room. Don't tell her that I mentioned she was working."

"My lips are sealed."

The Persephone Room seemed to be the largest of the gaming rooms, and if he'd needed more proof that The Tantalus Club was thriving, it lay all around him. Crowded tables, the scent of expensive American cigars, the murmur of cards and conversation, and pretty young women everywhere carrying drinks and dealing cards and supervising the tables. Some of the most powerful men in London, paying for the privilege of having ruined chits tell them when they were wagering too deeply and needed to leave for the evening.

It took him a moment to find Camille. Her ash-blond hair had been pulled up into a curling knot, whitish tendrils escaping to frame her angled cheekbones. The demure muslin of the afternoon was gone, replaced by a shimmering blue gown that clung to her appealing curves. Good God. No wonder that even with the scandal attached to her, four men sat at her table while half a dozen more stood about, supposedly watching the game.

And no wonder Fenton was so determined to get her back in hand. Camille and the marquis's name were inexorably linked, and the men surrounding her spent their days at the House of Lords with Fenton, at other clubs with Fenton, at soirees with Fenton. He would never be able to move past the fact that he was technically still engaged to a woman who'd fled their wedding to work at a gentlemen's club.

That had taken courage. The young lady with whom he'd walked this afternoon had been cautious and hurt, but the one he looked at now was confident and even . . . sultry. Earlier today he'd thought swaying her back into Fenton's—and by extension, Society's—arms would be a simple matter. Camille Pryce, however, had more facets than he'd expected. He needed to discover what motivated her, what it was she truly wanted, and what it would take to send her back to her betrothed. And he needed to be someone she trusted if he meant to accomplish any of that. Which meant that he needed to stop staring at her like a cat sizing up a mouse. However much he might wish to pounce.

She glanced up, and the corners of her mouth turned up as their eyes met. He smiled back at her, nodding, shoving back at his predatory instincts until they subsided and returned to the cave. Apparently she'd decided that his kissing spree of earlier wasn't so awful, after all. Considering that he had at least two additional families cursing him now, he was glad it had been worth it.

"I think I'd like to play," he said.

"Only four players at this table, Blackwood," the Viscount of Swanslee commented, glancing up from his cards. "Go find another table."

"I'd like to play *here*."

Next to the viscount, Jonas Atherling stood. "Take my seat," he offered, gathering his coins. "I'd prefer to be in a different room from you, anyway."

"Likewise." The stodgy fellow was practically swimming in cheap French cologne, and it followed him like a cloud as he departed. Wondering how Camille had managed to breathe, Keating took the abandoned chair. "And how do your fare this evening, my lady?" he asked, putting his own blunt on the table.

"Very well, Mr. Blackwood." Camille gazed at the players. "Ready, gentlemen?"

"Deal the damned cards," the stocky gentleman on Keating's left grumbled. "Here's hoping Blackwood's ill luck alters my own."

"I don't have ill luck," Keating protested. "I make ill choices. There's a very large difference."

"Isn't that rather like debating degrees of death?" the fourth fellow, seated just to his right, commented in a low voice.

Swiftly Keating reassessed his general opinion of the club's membership. At least one of them seemed to have both intelligence and some spleen. "And who might you be?"

"That's right, you've been away for a time, haven't you?" The man gestured for a third card. With his left profile partly obscured by too-long dark brown hair, the best impression Keating could get was that he was in his mid-twenties and lean.

"What are you, my replacement in debauchery? You should be at a less reputable club." He glanced at the glass sitting at the fellow's elbow. "And you shouldn't be drinking brandy. You'll want something that sinks into your gullet quickly. Whiskey. Or Russian vodka."

Finally the man faced him. The thin white scar that ran from halfway down his right cheek and glanced off his chin was only made more striking by his milky white right eye, an unsettling balance to the dark blue left one. "I don't think I require your advice, but you make a valid point." He pushed to his feet, sliding a quid to Camille. "Good evening."

No one else took the one-eyed gentleman's seat, so Camille dealt two face-up cards to the trio of men before her. To herself she dealt the seven of clubs and the king of spades, both face up. "Gentlemen?"

"Who was that?" Keating asked, disliking that his curiosity made him ask.

"He didn't give his name, Mr. Blackwood." She glanced up. "Do you wish a card?"

So now she pretended they weren't acquainted. He glanced down at the nine and queen in front of him. "I'm staying."

Only a flicker in her eyes betrayed that she might be reading more into that statement than he'd actually said. At least he hoped that was the case; considering he'd just realized that while his reputation might help her, it wasn't doing *him* any favors, he was a bit distracted. If she pretended not to know him, he couldn't expect her to trust him. Evidently he was going to have to attempt to behave. Good damned thing, then, that he'd stopped drinking.

Chapter Six

Camille dealt cards for an hour, then signaled to the room captain that she wanted to go stretch her legs. And she wasn't the least bit surprised when Keating Blackwood left the table immediately after she did.

"Please don't do that," she muttered, feeling him walking behind her as she headed for the doorway leading into the back of the club and some privacy.

"Don't do what?" his quiet voice returned.

"Follow me about. People will think you're pursuing me."

"I'm not."

The odd responding . . . thump in her chest didn't feel at all pleasant. "Good. But it looks as though you are, and that will only have more people talking. I don't want that."

From the envious looks some of the other ladies were sending her as she left the room, she was being an idiot. Keating was devilishly handsome, witty, and fearless. And he played a fine game of cards. If not for his reputation, she wasn't certain she would be able to conjure any objection to his presence.

Then it struck her. She was doing the same thing to him that others did to her. Camille nearly stumbled in the doorway to the back rooms, and a strong hand gripped her right arm. "Steady, there."

"Thank you." For heaven's sake, if not for *her* reputation, she imagined she would have quite a few friends. Perhaps even parents and her own home again. "I apologize."

He'd stopped in the doorway, and stood looking at her. "For what?"

"For being put off by your reputation. It's hypocritical of me."

A grin tugged at his sensuous mouth. "No it isn't. It's very wise of you. We don't compare."

Glancing past him at the busy, curious room, she gestured for him to come through the door. "You might as well come in here."

With a slight hesitation she almost didn't notice, he walked into the narrow corridor and shut the door behind him. "This is nice. You can travel up and down the length of the club without men drooling on you."

"It was Lady Haybury's idea," she returned, "but men don't drool on me."

"I don't know why not. You're lovely."

Her cheeks warmed. She couldn't even remember the last time she'd been complimented when the speaker didn't attempt to pinch her or to lure her into his bed. "They speak to me in the club," she said aloud, "but at the same time they seem to think either that I've been irretrievably soiled and can be purchased for a penny, or that my being near them will give them the plague."

"If I may," he drawled, reaching out to pluck at her sleeve, "taken as a whole, men are idiots and fools. They want what they cannot have, and fear that what they do have has been gotten too cheaply to be valuable."

She was beginning to realize that Keating Blackwood

was a very unusual man. And that intrigued her, far more
than she should have allowed. "And where do you fall in
this categorization?"

"I'm the man who's learned his lesson and very clearly
sees the follies of others."

"Is that so?"

"Absolutely." He tilted his head a little, his eyes lowering to her mouth. "You have a very nice smile. You should
employ it more often. Smiles can be deadlier than pistols,
if used correctly."

Camille hadn't even realized she was smiling. Her
first instinct was to wipe it away, duck her head, and flee.
But they were alone in the hallway; only Keating had
seen her acting as though she could actually enjoy a moment of happiness. It didn't escape her that that was the
second time she'd smiled in his presence today.

And here she was, ruined, a coward, and for the moment with no one to look at her askance. With a very
handsome man standing in front of her. One who seemed,
for some unexplainable reason, to have taken her side in
all this nonsense.

Her heart stammering, Camille put a hand on his chest,
leaned up, and kissed him. Their lips touching, she felt
his surprise, and then the breathless moment as he
shifted forward and molded his mouth against hers. His
hands curled onto her hips, tugging her closer. Pure white
heat swept down her spine, and she closed her eyes at the
sensation.

Those fingers close against her skin flexed, and then
lifted her away from him. Camille opened her eyes again,
to find herself gazing into twin orbs the color of polished
bronze. Keating cleared his throat. "That . . ."

"I apologize for putting you at risk from the fires of
damnation," she managed, trying to gather her fleeing

thoughts and her breath all at the same time. "Though I don't know how pure anyone would consider me at the moment."

"Oh, it definitely singed me a bit." He continued to gaze at her, though she hadn't a clue what he might be thinking. At least he wasn't laughing at her.

"So. Do you still wish to take me driving tomorrow, or should I return to my reading?"

"Be on the front drive at half one."

Camille let out the breath she'd been holding. Whatever had just happened, at least she hadn't ruined the most interesting friendship she'd ever managed. With the one man who viewed her scandalous actions as a barely noticeable tweak to Society's collective nose. With the one man she'd ever kissed—whether he would have kissed her or not.

"Very well. I—thank you."

"What the devil are you thanking me for?" he asked, one brow lowering.

She sighed. "For not laughing, I suppose. For not just standing there looking affronted. For n—"

Keating swept forward and kissed her again. Her back bumped against the opposite wall as he pressed his mouth to hers, plying and nipping until both her mind and her body seemed to melt into a heated puddle. This time she couldn't say that he'd been surprised into kissing her back, and that he otherwise wouldn't have been the least bit interested.

"Don't thank me for being idiotic and doing something that will only make matters worse for you, Camille," he murmured against her mouth. "And don't kiss me again. You're too damned tempting. I'm endeavoring to behave, and I'm not very good at it."

With that he vanished back into the club, shutting her

alone in the hallway. For a long moment she stood there, touching her forefinger to her lips. So that was a kiss. She'd never experienced one before. Now she knew what the other girls meant when they talked of wanting to swoon because of a mere touch of mouth against mouth. Because her knees still felt wobbly.

As she put her hand on the door to reenter the Persephone Room, it occurred to her that every man in there likely thought she and Keating had been doing exactly what they'd been doing. Cold trailed down to her fingertips, and she shut her eyes.

Of course they all thought she'd been doing the same thing for the past year, and they still sat at her table and smiled when she seated them at breakfast and offered her trinkets to stray with them. Camille opened her eyes again. The chasm of mortification that had opened at her feet slowly knitted itself together again. As far as Mayfair was concerned, she'd been kissing men—and worse—hither and thither for months and months.

She touched her lips again. What did it matter, then, if she actually did kiss a man? There weren't any additional people that could look askance at her, surely. Perhaps Keating wasn't the wisest choice for folly, but she'd already been seen with him at least twice, and nothing had changed that she could detect. He might be attempting to behave, but she'd suddenly realized—thanks mainly to him—that she no longer had to do so.

"Goodness," she whispered, then had to chuckle. Goodness had nothing to do with it.

Halfway back to Baswich House it began to rain. Keating slowed Amble to a walk and turned his face up, catching the cold drops on his skin. It didn't much help.

The chit had kissed him. The damned chit had put her

dainty hands on his chest, closed her eyes, and attacked him with her mouth. And it had shivered through him down to his toes.

It was his own fault; he'd intentionally stood as her friend when no one else outside of The Tantalus Club would do so. And he'd done his best to be charming. In the past when he'd been charming he'd almost always ended up naked in some lady or other's bed. Lately he hadn't been as discerning, other than making certain the chit was unmarried. The pickings in Shropshire had been slimmer, particularly once all the women knew what a poor idea being linked with him could be, but he wasn't a damned monk.

He blew out his breath. Camille Pryce had been spoken for since her birth, and by his own cousin. He'd learned his lesson; he did not step between married couples. And while Camille and Stephen weren't married, that was precisely the mission with which he'd been tasked.

Why was he even having this conversation with himself? For Christ's sake, she was a virginal female doing her damnedest to pretend she hadn't been ruined, and he was present for the sole reason of swaying her back into Society's arms. Not *his* arms. He wasn't even interested. Whatever she was, it was definitely not his usual flavor.

This was precisely why he avoided purity. To a woman with no experience, every kiss meant something special, every murmured word was a promise of some sort. Even before the chaos with Eleanor and her husband, he'd disdained the white-wearing chits of Almack's in favor of more experienced ladies. Of course that hadn't precisely ended well for him. But he knew better than to think eschewing the jaded in favor of the virginal would make things any better.

Whatever the devil had happened, he was already

making mental note of where Adam kept his bottles of liquor back at Baswich House. Evidently he couldn't remain sober for even one day. Yes, he had something of a reason for drinking at the moment, but being three sheets to the wind wouldn't alter anything. Nor would it make anything easier.

Nudging Amble in the ribs, he sent them at a canter toward Hyde Park and Rotten Row. He refused to drink tonight, but he could certainly ride. Even though the hour was fairly early, especially by Mayfair standards, the park was generally deserted at night. With the rain pelting the grass and the packed earth of the Rotten Row riding trail, he could believe himself the only man in London.

That would have suited him quite well, in fact. For an hour or so he galloped through the water and mud, until both he and Amble were breathing hard and sweating. By the time he returned to Baswich House and handed the gray gelding over to a disapproving groom, he was soaked past his skin.

"Hm," Adam's deep voice came from the balcony overlooking the foyer. "Not what I expected."

Keating shook out his hair and started up the stairs. "It's raining. Or did you think any God-fearing raindrops would avoid landing on me?"

"You have mud up past your knees and halfway up the greatcoat I loaned you. And you're tracking it on my rug."

"I'm tired, Adam. I'll joust with you tomorrow, if you'd like."

The Duke of Greaves continued to eye him, though Keating didn't know what he might be looking for. "Do you wish me to pretend I don't know that Fenton called on you earlier?" he finally asked.

Keating slowed at the top of the stairs. "He doesn't like

me making a stir that might tarnish his good name," he
returned with a shrug. "You can't be surprised by that."

"Did he have anything to say about the fact that you're
going for strolls with his former fiancée?"

"Are you going to keep prying until you've worn me
down to dust?" Keating walked past his friend and continued toward his borrowed quarters.

"Very likely."

"It's not my secret I'm keeping."

The duke followed him. "Just tell me, for God's sake.
I detest not knowing things."

That made Keating grin. "No. I'm being honorable.
And go have your apoplexy elsewhere."

Once he'd shed his clothes and dried himself thoroughly, he dropped into bed and shut his eyes. When
he considered it, his path was actually very clear. Guide
Camille back to Fenton's side. And no more kissing. And
no more absurd imaginings that the touch of her lips to
his had meant something. That he'd felt something. Because he hadn't. He couldn't afford to.

When Keating turned the Duke of Greaves's high-perch
phaeton up the curved drive of The Tantalus Club, he
half expected that Camille would be nowhere in sight.
Instead, however, she stood to one side of the front portico chatting with the lady butler.

He attempted not to notice that she wore a pretty
green and yellow muslin or that she carried a delicate-
looking white parasol in one hand. And he pretended he
wasn't gazing at her face to see whether she would smile
when she caught sight of him. If she did smile, it only
meant that he'd gained her trust and that he could begin
the second part of his task. He took a low breath, the
predator in him stirring again.

She looked up, and that shy, fleeting smile touched her mouth. Bloody hell—she was smiling for him. *Him.* Belatedly Keating fixed a jaunty grin on his own face as he pulled the black pair of horses to a halt. "You look very fetching," he said, leaning over to offer his hand to help her onto the high seat.

"Thank you." Warm, slender fingers gripped his. Swallowing, he pulled her up beside him.

"Where would you like to go?" Considering her reaction to seeing her former friends in Green Park yesterday, he imagined they would spend the next hour simply driving the streets around The Tantalus Club. It didn't matter, as long as he had a few moments to chat with her. In fact, no privacy would be better. Much, much better.

"I doubt Amelia Danning will venture back into Green Park today," she returned. "I would like to drive through there."

Keating lifted an eyebrow. "You're certain of that?"

"No, but I think we should do so, anyway."

With a cluck to the team, Keating set off in the direction of the park. Evidently the chit had found some courage over the last day. At the moment he wasn't certain whether that boded ill or well for him, but clearly he couldn't afford to delay any longer—literally or figuratively.

"I've a question for you," he said after a moment of silence.

"And I have one for you," she returned, "but I suppose you should go first."

He resisted the urge to close his eyes. In a sense, this . . . uneasiness was so odd, especially considering that in the past, he'd enjoyed creating mayhem. "Fenton," he said aloud.

"I don't want to talk about him," she returned, facing

the row of shops and then changing her mind when some of the shoppers looked back at her.

Not quite so brave out among her peers—former peers—then. "You never told me what he so stupidly did to drive you away."

"Does it matter? I ran away, and there were—are—consequences."

"No, I don't suppose it does matter," he conceded, reflecting that if she'd been more malleable she would be married to Fenton and he would still be in Shropshire. "But tell me anyway."

"Why?"

"Because . . . because you've likely never told anyone else, and if you can't trust a charming, liquor-scented rogue, who can you trust?"

She chuckled. It was a very pleasant sound, like water skipping over pebbles. "You don't smell of liquor today."

"Good. I haven't been drinking any."

"Good. Was that because I insulted you?"

"Partly. It was also because I'm beginning to believe that the next time I overimbibe, my skull may shatter. Now don't alter the subject. You. Fenton. Flight from the church. Explain."

Light blue eyes met his and then turned away again. Finally she sighed. "He didn't do anything."

Keating guided the phaeton into Green Park and slowed to a walk to avoid crashing into the dozen other carriages on the path in front of them. Despite Camille's stated belief that any chits were likely to have fled the area, they seemed to be everywhere. After a passing thought that he could likely roll a lawn bowl across the clearing and knock over a dozen of them, he put that aside. The young lady seated beside him would have been the most interesting female in the park even if he hadn't been assigned to speak with her. "I don't believe you. If he'd done nothing, you'd be married to him."

Camille tilted her parasol between her and the trio of horseback riders passing by them. Whether she'd decided not to care what anyone else might think of her, she didn't need to encourage their scrutiny. She didn't actually want Keating's scrutiny, either, but she'd been silent for a year. And he made a good point, in jest or not. If there was anyone who could commiserate with her situation, it was him.

Good heavens, there were young ladies everywhere in the park today. With a frown she settled herself to face Keating, putting her back to half of them at least. Green Park was never this occupied. Hm. She wondered if that had anything to do with a certain extremely handsome kissing bandit with a dark and deadly reputation.

"Camille, you're not talking."

No, she actually seemed to be gazing at his rather fine profile. She shook herself. "Fine. I mean I refused to marry him because he didn't do anything," she clarified.

From Keating's expression, he was wishing that he hadn't avoiding drinking, after all. "Would you . . . elaborate?"

"Stephen Pollard and I became engaged when I was three days old, and he was seven years of age. When I was younger, I thought it romantic. I imagined he would be so very handsome, and he would bring me roses and write me poetry and letters. I received nothing." She took a breath, remembering how naïvely eager she'd been, pestering her father about the mail for the week before and after her birthday, the anniversary of the signing of their marriage agreement—any occasion for Fenton to acknowledge the connection between them.

"Did he contact you at all?"

"No. Never. I saw him once or twice at soirees after my debut, but it seemed as though the moment he heard a whisper that I might be present, he would flee. Or at the least, make every attempt to avoid me."

"Halfwit," he muttered, and she saw his fingers tighten on the reins. "If I said that was typical of him, would it make a difference?"

It was far too late for it to make any sort of difference, but she couldn't help being curious, anyway. After all, she'd had questions about her betrothed since she'd been old enough to know she had one. "Typical how?"

"He's . . . not charming. At all." Keating's sensuous mouth turned down into a scowl. "I mean he's annoyingly bland and has no idea how to chat with people." He looked down for a moment, another expression, one she couldn't read, crossing his face for a heartbeat. "As much as I hate to say it, though, he isn't evil."

"Evil?" She forced a laugh. "I never thought he was evil. I just decided at that moment, when I was standing there looking up the church aisle at him, that I didn't want to spend the remainder of my life married to a man who couldn't be bothered in twenty-one years to introduce himself to his bride."

In the ensuing silence she could almost hear what he must be thinking. That she was a childish fool, that she'd taken the most extreme action when she might have simply sat down with her husband after the wedding and informed him of her displeasure, that many marriages began without love or even acquaintance and none of the other brides had fled.

"You should have punched him square on the nose before you left," he said with a grim smile. "That would have been something to see."

Camille opened her mouth to reply, then closed it

again. She had no idea what to say. Every part of her had expected that she would be hurt and humiliated again, not . . . applauded. A tear ran down her cheek, and she impatiently wiped it away. "I told my mother several times," she continued, wishing her voice would stop quavering, "a hundred times, that I thought we needed to wait a bit longer. I wanted to give him time to prove that he was who I wanted him to be, I suppose. Or to do *something*. She said that I was being stupid to suggest that keeping a marquis waiting could be a good idea. Especially when he'd already been waiting for better than twenty years."

"He didn't want to marry you when he was seven, believe me," Keating returned with a snort. "I joined him in the game of pretend vomiting."

"Oh, that's very nice." She grinned despite herself.

"Perhaps I'm inclined to take your side over his," he continued, grinning back at her, "but I agree that he should have made an effort to become acquainted with you. And I also agree that you aren't foolish for wanting an assurance of happiness before devoting the remainder of your life to a man who deliberately remained an aloof stranger."

Another tear joined the first. "Thank you."

"Don't cry, Cammy. It upsets my masculine feelings and I don't know what to do."

She put a hand over her mouth to cover her damp laugh. "It's not funny," she protested, sobering again. "When I arrived back at home that evening, my parents were waiting by the front door. My father said I was an ungrateful wretch and turned his back on me. My mother told me I was selfish and had ruined my sisters' chances of making good marriages, and then she slapped me. They closed the door in my face."

He muttered something that sounded like a curse. "Did you go directly to The Tantalus Club?"

"It didn't exist yet. When I stopped crying enough to see, I walked to Amelia Danning's house. They wouldn't even open the front door."

"That's the chit I kissed yesterday, yes?"

"Yes."

His smile this time looked a great deal less friendly. "Good." His fingers tugged at her skirt as they moved sedately along the main driving path in Green Park. "Where did you go, then?"

Just remembering that night made her shudder; she'd walked for what felt like hours, still wearing her wedding gown and with three shillings and twopence in her silly little lace reticule. Everyone had stared at her, and the only offer of help had come from a dirty-looking man who'd offered her a roof in exchange for what he'd termed "kissing his pig." She shivered again.

"I walked. All night. I was afraid to stop anywhere, and falling asleep out in the open seemed a very poor idea. Finally a farmer offered me a ride in the back of his wagon, and I went to my aunt's home in Chatham. She permitted me to sleep in the maid's quarters and had me polishing things. I don't think she ever told my mother I was there. One morning I was cleaning the dining room and I saw the newspaper, and an advertisement seeking well-educated young women for employment at The Tantalus Club. I left for London before noon."

"And that was what, a year ago?"

"Just under." She nodded. "I owe Lady Haybury everything. Without the club, I have no idea where I'd be now." Or rather, she *did* have an idea, and it terrified her every evening in her dreams.

"So you've only known Sophia White for a year? You two seem very close."

"We are. Sophia may not have done anything scandalous on her own, but she has a unique . . . understanding of what happened to me."

"She didn't flee a fiancé, then?"

Camille sent him a sideways look. "You don't know who she is?"

"I've been in Shropshire for six years. I missed out on a great deal of juicy gossip."

For a moment she debated whether to say anything more. Telling other peoples' secrets simply didn't sit well with her, but then everyone else in London already knew about Sophia. And she'd never made any pretense about secrecy. "Sophia White is the Duke of Hennessy's daughter. By his wife's favorite personal maid."

He didn't flinch or even hesitate. "Her mother must be a goddess, to compensate for Hennessy's rhinoceros face."

Coughing, Camille nudged him in the shoulder with the handle of her parasol. "You aren't supposed to make me laugh when I'm discussing scandal and ruination."

"I like a challenge."

"Nothing shocks you, does it?"

Keating shook his head. "Very little. Remember, I'm the worst blackguard I know. But I am relieved, actually, to discover that Stephen's fault was one of omission. In a sense I suppose that's better than if he'd actually done something unsavory to drive you away."

Some of the things the Marquis of Fenton had said after her flight had been less than polite, but she supposed she deserved them. And Keating was Fenton's cousin; he didn't need to know all the details. Particularly not when she couldn't help the nagging thought that she'd been relieved to have an excuse to run away.

And particularly not when she'd met Fenton's much more interesting cousin. Heat and sin seemed to radiate from his skin, tantalizing and very, very naughty. She sent a quick glance around them, not surprised to see most of the women present looking in their direction. The odd thing, though, was that the ones who gazed at her didn't have that expression she'd been accustomed to seeing on even strangers' faces. For a bare moment, she imagined they were . . . jealous. Of her. Because she sat beside Keating Blackwood.

For a heartbeat, she allowed herself to smile. Perhaps her luck was finally beginning to change—and not at all in the way she would ever have expected.

Chapter Seven

Keating could measure how close he was to Pollard House by the growing tightness in the muscles across his shoulders. It was one of life's peculiarities, he supposed, that while he'd been quite close to Stephen Pollard as a boy, he didn't particularly like his cousin now that they were both adults.

As he'd expected, the butler kept him waiting in the morning room. Even though it had been seven or eight years since he'd last been inside the house, not one thing seemed to have been changed. Candlesticks sat in their same place on the mantel, the same volumes of leather-bound plays by Shakespeare still kept their same place on the bookcase.

"Do you actually live in this house?" he asked as the Marquis of Fenton walked into the room.

"I like things a particular way. You have some news, I take it?"

So much for familial banter. "I do. I need a piece of paper, a pen, and for you to sit down and pay attention to what I'm going to tell you."

"I'm not an infant, Keating. Say what you've come to say, and leave. I have friends coming to take me to breakfast, and I don't wish them to see you here."

Keating sat at the small table in the corner. "You have the oddest way of asking for help. Paper."

Fenton glared at him for a moment, then rang for the butler. "I need paper and a pen," he said, and with clear reluctance sat down opposite his cousin. "I saw Greaves in Parliament yesterday," he continued. "He gave me a look. If you've told anyone that you're here at my behest, our agreement is going to change."

"Are you attempting to tell me that Greaves has never looked at you before?"

"Well, n—"

"He knows we're cousins, and he doesn't like you," Keating interrupted. "I'm prepared to wager that he glares at you quite frequently. I haven't said a word to him. Or to anyone." He leaned closer. "And our agreement is *not* going to change. You marry Camille Pryce, and I receive ten thousand pounds."

"Yes, yes."

The butler returned with the writing implements and set them down, then left the room again. As soon as the door was closed, Keating pulled the paper over in front of him and dipped the pen in the accompanying inkwell.

" 'Number the first,' " he said, writing out the number as he spoke, " 'Send Camille flowers. Tomorrow.' "

"What? The chit abandoned and embarrassed me. I am not sending her posies. *She* needs to apologize to *me*."

" 'Number the second,' " he continued writing, ignoring the protest, " 'In two days, send a second bouquet of flowers, and a note. The note will read, "A much-delayed gift for your tenth birthday." Nothing else. Not your name, or anything.' "

Fenton slammed his fist on the table. "No. I refuse. This is not what I agreed to."

" 'Number the third, each subsequent day you will

send Camille flowers, each with a note for the next-numbered birthday, until you reach the twenty-first birthday.' " Keating looked up. "You can count that high, yes?"

"Why are you putting this on me?" his cousin snapped, the red of his face deepening. "Stop insulting my intelligence and explain yourself."

Taking a breath, Keating put the pen aside. As he'd noted on more than one occasion, Stephen had never been impulsive, warm, or . . . sensitive to the needs or emotions of anyone other than himself. Getting angry with him now for nonsense he'd begun—or rather, not begun—twelve or fifteen years earlier was pointless. In addition to that, it annoyed him that Camille's story of yesterday *had* angered and troubled him.

"Very well," he muttered after a moment. "In Camille Pryce's eyes, this debacle is your fault."

Fenton slammed to his feet. "W*hat*? *My* fault? I offered her a home, a husband, stability, a family, th—"

"That's the point," Keating interrupted. "You didn't offer her any of those things. You relied on a piece of paper she's likely never set eyes on to offer things to her. She's a young female, Stephen. She had expectations that you would at least send her a note introducing yourself. At the best, she wanted to be courted."

"You mean she fled—she left our wedding because I didn't *woo* her?"

That was likely as much as Fenton would ever understand about it. "Precisely," Keating said aloud. "And in order for her to consider returning to marry you, you need to alter her perception of you."

Fenton strode to the window and back. "No. I refuse. This arrangement was made by our parents. She benefits from a union even more than I do. I'm a marquis, after all. She would be a marchioness. No one wooed me, but I didn't flee."

"You aren't a chit."

Returning to rest both fists on the table, the marquis drew in a hard breath through his nose. "Let me make something clear, Keating. She embarrassed me. Her presence at The Tantalus Club continues to embarrass me. At least once a day one of my peers comments that they saw my almost-bride the evening before, putting bread on a table or dealing cards or seating them at breakfast. And then they laugh behind their hands, muttering to each other."

For someone with Fenton's strong sense of self-importance, that would indeed have been intolerable. Keating was somewhat surprised the marquis hadn't fled London. And yet he remained, and persisted in the idea that he would make this right. For himself, of course.

"I could choose some other female and marry, but I am still willing to honor the agreement," Fenton continued. *"That* is the best way to improve Society's view of me, and of her. Tell her that. I am not going to send her flowers after what she's done."

"Stephen, this isn't a business arrangement. It's a man and a wo—"

"I am willing to give her a second chance. See that she understands that she won't receive another. If she still expects posies and poetry after what she did, she is sadly mistaken." He bent his arms, moving his face closer to Keating's. "And I'm paying you a very handsome sum to see to this unpleasantness. Don't expect me to do your work unless you wish to forfeit your reward."

The old Keating would have flung the contents of the inkwell directly into his cousin's face, closely followed by a fist. The reformed Keating, however, merely took the piece of paper and tore it in half. "Very well," he said, rising. "I hope, however, that you are keeping in mind that once you're wed it would be easier on both of you if you weren't enemies."

"You are the very last person I would ever ask for advice on the sanctity of marriage."

Keating's right fist coiled. At the same moment that Fenton saw the motion and backed away, Keating reminded himself about the very large stack of blunt that would vanish if he struck the blow. Using every ounce of his willpower, he straightened his fingers again. "Interesting, then," he said instead, "that you are doing precisely that. If I may remind you, you are relying on me to put your little ceremony back together."

Before Fenton said something that truly would get him flattened, Keating left Pollard House for luncheon with the Duke of Greaves. Clearly his cousin didn't understand the workings of the female mind. Camille might blame herself for overreacting, but she blamed Fenton for causing the dilemma in the first place. And considering how well he knew his cousin, he couldn't blame Camille for hesitating.

If Fenton refused to make any overtures, the equation wouldn't change. After all, while she might have acted rashly and underestimated the ramifications of her flight from the altar, Camille had decided she valued love—or at least friendship—over marriage to a previously well-respected marquis. Asking her to make a different decision while changing none of the circumstances wasn't precisely reasonable.

Of course she found herself in different circumstances now. He couldn't even imagine the difference between being the pampered eldest daughter of a wealthy viscount and being an employee in a gentlemen's club. Perhaps if given the chance again she *would* decide that security was more important than something intangible like affection. The truth of the matter, however, was that he didn't want her to have to do so.

Greaves waited for him on the steps of the Society Club. "You weren't banished from here, were you?" the duke asked, straightening from leaning his hip against the railing. "I forgot to ask you, so I thought I'd best remain outside. Just in case."

"I don't remember," Keating supplied. "Shall I attempt it?"

The footman at the front door only blinked at him once or twice, so Keating surmised that he hadn't been banned from entry. Thanks to Greaves's presence they were seated at a table in the front window—though it might also have been the maître d's attempt to bring more attention to the club. How many of them could boast a murderer enjoying a roast pheasant in their establishment, after all?

"Lady Ogilvy asked after you last evening," Adam commented twenty minutes later, over a baked game hen.

"Did she? She's the one with the very ample bosom, yes?"

"You don't truly expect me to believe you've forgotten the name of anyone whose path you've crossed, do you?"

Keating took a swallow of tepid lemonade. He'd wanted a whiskey, but considering that he seemed to be having difficulty lately staying sober, he'd decided that lemonade was a wiser choice. "Very well. What did you tell darling Marianne?"

"I told her you were well, but only meant to remain in London a short time. She said that was a shame, and then wanted to know if it was true that you'd run about Green Park kissing chits. Because she thought she might take a stroll there tomorrow."

Lemonade caught in his throat, and he coughed. "That actually explains why chits seemed to be practically blanketing the park yesterday," he managed. "Good God. They *want* me to kiss them?"

"You're a rather handsome scoundrel, a famed lover, and you've been absent for six years. The debutantes only know the stories, my friend. To them you're a legend, not a—"

"A fiend?" Keating finished.

"I was going to say a bounder, but I suppose it's the same thing." Greaves indicated the glass in Keating's hand. "Have you given up the demon rum, then?"

"For the moment. I find that I seem to cause less trouble when I'm sober. Relatively speaking, of course."

"*Why* are you attempting to cause less trouble, Keating? I mean, you say that you are, but then you become Green Park's kissing rogue. And you had to know that in coming back to London, you would be stirring those old rumors and stories to life once again. Not to mention the bushels of lovers you left behind."

Keating took a breath. "You're a persistent bastard, aren't you?" he finally grumbled.

With a swift grin the duke resumed his meal. "I've barely begun digging at you."

Greaves had his own secrets and his own agendas, and Keating didn't have to be particularly keen-sighted to know that something had happened to cause a substantial rift between the duke and the Marquis of Haybury. But as far as he was concerned, Adam Baswich had never been anything but a true and steadfast friend even when it would have been much easier to turn away.

"I'm doing a good deed," he said slowly, quite aware of how his cousin would react if Fenton discovered that anyone else knew the particulars of his request. "In exchange for a substantial reward. I can't tell you anything else."

The duke chewed and swallowed. "You're hardly the person I would have chosen to maneuver a chit back to the altar," he finally commented, "given how far you generally sway them away from it. But you've certainly got a better chance at convincing her than Fenton does."

"I never said any of that. And I have no idea what you might be gabbing about." He wasn't even surprised that Greaves had put the puzzle pieces together. The duke was masterful at games.

"I'm just astonished to see you at Fenton's beck and call for any reason. I thought he'd disowned you years ago."

"Not so much disowned me as simply pretended I didn't exist. Which suited me quite well, believe me."

"That must be quite a substantial reward, then."

"It is. So don't go about glaring at my cousin. Not all of us are descendants of Croesus or Midas or whoever it is who left you his fortune."

"We both know I inherited from Lucifer himself, but I take your point." Greaves frowned. "I could lend you a sum, if that would aid you."

"A loan won't do, Adam. But thank you for offering." He'd actually considered asking the duke for blunt from time to time, when the crops produced poorly or the price of wool and mutton dropped, but this was his penance. He needed to suffer for it. More importantly, he needed to be the one earning the money to pay for his mistakes. Even if he had to resort to unconventional means to do so.

The duke cleared his throat. "Very well, then. Suit yourself. In fact, I'll help you. What would you say if I were to offer a private tour of the Tower menagerie as an excursion? Your project could bring along her scarlet-haired friend for safety again. And I'll lend you some of my so-called propriety."

"You mean you're offering to escort us on an outing?" Keating asked, surprised.

"It just seems that with the combination of your reputation and her standing in Society, without my assistance you're limited to walking in an abandoned corner of some park or playing cards at her table."

He'd been thinking the same thing himself. As charming as he intended to be, there were only so many times they could walk in the park before she realized that he couldn't actually do anything to improve her reputation. Particularly when she disliked being looked at askance as much as she seemed to. "I accept."

"I'll make the arrangements. Thursday afternoon?"

"Could you make it Thursday morning?"

"I thought she had duties then."

Keating nodded. "She does. I think a demonstration of what she could be doing if not working at a gentlemen's club is in order."

"Ah. Very devious of you."

If Keating were the suspicious sort, he would think that Adam might be plotting at something. Well, he *was* the suspicious sort, but considering he could count his good and loyal friends on one finger, he decided that perhaps the duke was indeed feeling charitable and was attempting in his own way to assist matters. "It's all a means to an end, my friend," he said aloud.

"Just keep in mind that you can't save her if you ruin her in the process."

Attempting to hide his flinch, Keating muttered something that not even he could decipher and resumed eating his pheasant. Publicly ruining Eleanor, Lady Balthrow, had been only a consequence of a night's other events, but in one evening he'd managed to accomplish both that and kill her husband. Of course, by the time he realized precisely everything that had happened, it had been far beyond his power to save her reputation, but at the least he could keep her comfortable in the shadows where she was now forced to live.

"Yes, thank you for reminding me," he finally grumbled.

Greaves was eyeing him again. "As I said before, my friend, I shall be the soul of discretion if you ever want to talk."

"Tell me why Haybury detests you these days, and I'll tell you my sad tale," Keating suggested.

"Bugger off."

"I thought so."

Curiosity satisfied or not, that bit of conversation had served its purpose; Greaves stopped asking him those sticky questions he couldn't—wouldn't—answer. Ever.

"How is it that you have all this if you've only been in London for just over a year?" Camille asked, looking up from the newspaper spread on the floor in front of her.

Genevieve Martine set another neatly bundled stack of newspapers out and sank down onto the floor beside her. "I have found it wise to always be informed of London's goings-on, wherever I happen to be," Jenny returned in her unusual French accent.

Lady Haybury's oldest and dearest friend, Jenny had no official title at The Tantalus Club. At the same time, she frequently knew more of what transpired than anyone else, and she had the uncanny ability to be precisely where she was needed. The rumor was that she had once been a spy for Wellington, but for heaven's sake, despite the severe blond bun and the demeanor of a governess, Genevieve was only three-and-twenty.

And yet, Camille didn't know anyone else who kept ten years of past issues of the *Times* to hand, neatly organized and bundled by month. "Do you know anything about Keating Blackwood?" she asked.

"I know the poem," Jenny returned, untying the string holding the bundle together and unfolding the top issue. "I know that Lady Balthrow has spent much of the past six years living abroad on the Continent. And I know that . . ." She turned a page, then nodded and handed the paper over to Camille. "And I know that most of Lord Balthrow's property was entailed and went to his nephew."

An odd hitch stuttered through Camille's heart. "You think Keating is supporting her. Lady Balthrow."

"I didn't say that. You asked what I *knew,* and that is what I'm telling you." She slid over another newspaper. "Here's another."

Keating Blackwood's name seemed to appear in the pages of the *Times* more often even than Prinny's six years ago. Outrageous wagers, deep gaming, and women. The gossip sheets mostly used initials for the ladies he was apparently escorting. On four different evenings he was seen with five different women; after six years she wasn't certain who Lady M, RS, WA, or VV might be, but she had a good idea who Lady B must be. And that was all in only one week's worth of papers.

"Goodness," she muttered, picking up another newspaper. "I'm somewhat surprised he's alive."

Jenny chuckled. "A man raised by relatives who already had a young marquis to see to apparently looks for other ways of being noticed. Or perhaps he's merely a bit mad."

Camille paused in her page-turning. Jenny's first supposition sounded logical enough; given Keating's own stated dislike of his cousin, she could well imagine that he'd been the neglected one of the two of them. On the other hand, his wildness, his apparent penchant for causing havoc simply because he could—perhaps he *was* a bit mad. And that made him so much more interesting. Even more interesting than she already found him.

"Do you have the newspapers that reported the death of Lord Balthrow?"

"I believe so."

They found them three stacks later. Other than the scandalous, lurid details of his affair with Lady Balthrow, from the writers' word choices alone it was clear that Mr. Blackwood's antics were no longer amusing to London at large, or Mayfair in particular. For two days in a row the headlines reported that he was to be hanged at Newgate.

Camille put a hand to her throat. He'd told her that he regretted everything that had happened with Lord and Lady Balthrow, and she could guess that was partly because the scandal had brought an end to his fun. "He wasn't ordered to leave London," she mused, half to herself.

"It couldn't have been pleasant to stay. Balthrow wasn't terribly popular, but he was a member of the nobility. Killing one of them is rather frowned upon, particularly by their fellows."

Lower on the page, announcing that the Blackwood deed had been deemed self-defense by the courts, she caught sight of a much smaller headline. "Lady Balthrow left London even before Keating's trial ended."

"She did have an affair that ended in the death of her husband."

"I mean, if she'd truly cared for Keating, wouldn't she have stayed to speak for him at his trial?"

Jenny smiled a little. "That is a nice thought, Cammy."

Ah, she knew that look. She was being naïve. Of course Lady Balthrow would have been more concerned with her own freedom than with assisting Keating in gaining his. But if what Jenny . . . insinuated was true, Keating was still aiding Eleanor Howard six years after his acquittal. Not that that was any of her concern, except now that it had occurred to her, she couldn't seem to get it out of her mind.

"Might I borrow these?" she asked, motioning at the newspapers they'd pulled from the stacks.

"Of course." Jenny stood. "If you find that having Mr. Blackwood about is too unpleasant, I can see that his guest membership here is revoked."

"If you and Lady Haybury denied entry to all the men that one of your employees here dislikes for some reason or another, you wouldn't have much of a gentlemen's club."

"Fenton's absence hasn't destroyed us, by any means. And when Diane hired you, she promised you would be safe here, Cammy. That doesn't change."

"Thank you." Gathering up her armload of newspapers, she rose from the floor as well. "If not for you and Lady Haybury, I don't know what I would have done."

"We have succeeded together, where I do not think we could have done so separately." Genevieve followed her to the door. "If I may, be cautious, Camille. In the past Blackwood tore through London rather like an exploding cannon. I cannot help but think that an aimed cannon could be even more troublesome."

"I think I am already too cautious these days, but thank you, Jenny."

"Do as you will."

Back in the bedchamber she shared with Sophia, her friend sat practically bouncing on the edge of the bed. "You have a note," she said with a grin, waving the paper in the direction of the windowsill. "And flowers. And another note."

Camille looked where she indicated. A lovely bouquet of yellow roses bound in red ribbons sat in a vase that had clearly been borrowed from elsewhere in the club. Flowers. She'd never received flowers in her life. Her fingers shaking a little, she walked over and pulled the folded note from the middle of the blooms. " 'A very belated happy tenth birthday,' " she read aloud.

"*Very* belated," Sophia agreed. "Who is it from?"

She looked again, and turned over the note. "It doesn't say." Leaning down, she breathed in the soft spice of the roses.

"Blackwood," her friend supplied. "Don't you think?"

"I did mention to him that Fenton never sent me so much as a letter," Camille said slowly, "but my tenth birthday has no special significance. How did Grace know the flowers were for me?"

"I don't know. She had them sent up, and Mary said they'd arrived for you." Sophia waved the note again. "Perhaps this explains it."

As Camille took the folded paper, she had to acknowledge that she hoped the flowers were from Keating. Otherwise she could only think of one person who might have sent them, and she didn't wish to contemplate that. She unfolded the note and read through it. Then she read it a second time.

"What does it say? Is it from Blackwood?"

"Just a moment, for heaven's sake." She took a breath. " 'Dear Camille,' " she read aloud for Sophia's benefit. " 'If you and Sophia can arrange to have Thursday morning free, the Duke of Greaves has offered to escort us on a private tour of the menagerie at the Tower of London. As I'm terrified of being eaten by a lion, I hope you will be able to attend. Please inform me of your decision. KB.'"

"Oh, the Tower!" Sophia exclaimed, bouncing on the bed again. "Say yes, say yes!"

"We have duties on Thursday morning, Sophia." Inside she felt like jumping up and down herself, but she sternly resisted the temptation. "We need to speak with Jenny or Pansy first."

Sophia shot to her feet, grabbed Camille's hand, and pulled her out the door and down the hallway. "Then let's speak with them. Oh, he didn't say anything about the flowers, did he? Do you think that means he didn't send them? Who else could it have been, then? Oh, the Tower. I've always wanted to go, but who in the world could I have convinced to accompany me?"

Camille wished Sophia would be quiet for a blasted minute. Because while she did hope they would be able to join Keating for an outing, at the moment she was more concerned over who must have sent the flowers if it hadn't been him. Because she could only think of one person who'd failed to acknowledge her tenth birthday and might wish to do so now. And the idea that the Marquis of Fenton might suddenly have decided to make amends to her made her distinctly uncomfortable. Especially now, when she'd just met his very compelling cousin.

Chapter Eight

Joseph Bullock, the keeper of the Menagerie himself, guided them through the collection of beasts. Keating stayed back a little, watching, as the fellow proudly paraded them past a bored-looking wolf, a jackal, and a white fox who refused to emerge from his box despite offers of some sickly looking chicken's wings and a pig's snout.

"He's nocturnal, you know," the keeper announced, pelting the box at the back of the cage with one of the wings. "From Greenland. It's dark there much of the winter."

"Perhaps he's worried he'll be made into a fur muff," Greaves commented dryly.

Camille was leaning down, attempting to gaze into the recesses of the box set in the cage's far corner. "Poor fellow. He merely dislikes being gawked at, I'm certain."

"I'll fetch one of the underkeepers with a hot poker, and we'll have him out for you to see, Your Grace."

"That's not necessary, Bullock," the duke replied, after Sophia gave an dismayed squeak. "Let's move on, shall we?"

"Of course."

They turned the corner to another set of cages, several of them emitting low rumbling growls. Camille edged a shade closer to Keating, and he offered his arm. "You're to protect me, I thought," he drawled.

She wrapped her fingers around his sleeve. "Well, I need to be close by to do that, don't I?"

He chuckled. "A brilliant strategy, my dear."

"Ah, you'll enjoy this. We haven't fed the hyena, so you may see how powerful his jaws are." An underkeeper approached with what looked like the leg bone of an ox, and Bullock banged it against the metal bars of the cage before he stuck it partway in.

With a gurgling growl the beast leaped forward, snatching the bone out of the keeper's hand. Only a second or two later the bone cracked into two pieces. "Good heavens," Camille said. "He can't chew through the bars, can he?"

"Oh, no, my lady. They are specially constructed iron."

"I don't know about you, but I'm completely reassured," Keating said in a low voice.

The whisper of her stifled laughter sank into him. In his past he'd heard the wild, intoxicated laugh of women, their cries in the throes of passion, and their snickers at some cutting jest or other he'd perpetrated on someone. But genuine, amused laughter—the rarity of it struck him squarely in the chest.

He shook himself. Yes, he could appreciate laughter. But that was not why he'd come to London. Taking a breath, he glanced over at Adam and Sophia on the opposite side of the cage. "I'm pleased you managed to escape your work at the club today," he murmured. "Greaves has Parliament this afternoon, so this was our only opportunity."

"Sophia and I traded with Emily and Jane, so I'll be in the Demeter Room this evening."

"That's a shame. I'd hoped you might join me at the theater tonight." It sounded good, at any rate.

She looked up at his face. "Keating, are you . . . pursuing me?" she asked.

Light blue eyes as deep as the sky looked straight inside him. Keating opened his mouth, then closed it again. Whatever he said next would be a lie. There was no way around it—unless he told her that he was in London as Fenton's lackey and that yes, he was pursuing her. Just not for himself. And then she would kick him in the balls and he would have neither his manhood nor his ten thousand pounds.

"Do I have to have an answer for that?" he asked slowly, wondering if there was a lower pit in Hades than the one already holding a place for him, name card and all. "I like being around you. I know that much. Generally I have very little in the way of plans. And forward-thinking makes my skull ache."

Her quick smile flashed again. "Planning has never served me very well, either."

"Good. Then the two of us can just bumble about until we either decide where we're headed or we fall into the Thames."

When she nodded and then released him to go view the tigers with Sophia, he let out the breath he'd been holding. Damn Fenton for leaving all the maneuvering to him, and damn his cousin for being such a cold fish that all he could see was honor and money and pride. From what he'd been able to determine, Camille had never wanted to rebel. It had taken Fenton's stupidity to send her running. And of course Fenton didn't think he'd done anything wrong.

"She's going to figure you out, you know," Greaves's low voice came from just past his shoulder.

"I haven't even figured me out, so I can only wish her good luck." He straightened. "She's ten thousand pounds. That's all."

"Yes, I can see that you care nothing for her."

"Shut up." He wanted to hit something, and Greaves was making himself the most likely target. Frustration seemed twined into every nerve—frustration with his cousin, with the entire mess he'd gotten himself into, and with Camille. Mostly with her, though at least he knew why that was. Just being in her presence practically set him to vibrating.

He'd lusted after women before, far more often and for less reason than he should have, but he couldn't recall that he'd ever actually *liked* any of them. Liked, appreciated, enjoyed. This realization seemed very significant, but his mind insisted that it didn't matter. He had obligations that superseded his affection for a woman he'd barely met. In addition, if he'd learned one lesson in the past six years, it was to never step between a woman and another man.

Even if it was becoming rather clear that the other man didn't deserve her, and particularly when that other man was his own cousin.

"Would you like to see the cubs?" Bullock asked, returning Keating from his useless musings.

"Could we?" Sophia asked, eyeing the massive lioness sleeping in the cage before her. "Are they very fierce?"

"They were only whelped a month ago. They've barely opened their eyes." Gesturing at another keeper, Bullock walked them over to a heavy-looking, closed door.

A moment later two keepers appeared, each of them bearing a pair of small lion cubs in his arms. "Oh, they're darling!" Camille exclaimed the moment the babies were set onto the brick floor. She plunked herself down beside them and pulled one onto her lap. "Keating, come over here. Her fur is so soft."

While ordinarily he would have given several hard-earned quid to avoid sitting on the floor with a virginal chit to ruffle a very large kitten's fur, this time he didn't even bother with attempting to resist. He sank down beside her and immediately had his cravat pounced upon by another of the cubs.

"Clearly you have no sense of fashion," he told the thing, noting that even the notoriously standoffish Greaves was assisting a giggling Sophia with removing tiny lion claws from the hem of her gown.

"But if anyone asks about the state of your cravat, you can tell them you were attacked by a lion."

"Yes, I suppose it sounds more impressive than it looks." He started to say something more, but then Camille bent her head to rub her cheek against her cub's, and he completely lost the track of his thoughts.

Her hair was lighter in color than the lion's tawny fur, but the thing that struck him was the expression of absolute delight on her pretty face. He wondered how long it had been since she'd felt such unfettered joy, and a moment later a keening knife of need to allow her to feel that way again plunged into his heart.

To cover his discomfiture he tussled with the cravat-eating cub until it began its miniature growling and attempted to do away with his left sleeve. "Good God, I'm being devoured," he said mildly, while Camille choked with laughter.

"Clearly the animal recognizes you as a fellow predator," Greaves noted, motioning for Bullock and his fellows to gather up the scattering cubs.

"I don't know about that," Keating returned, stifling a frown. "I felt distinctly antelopelike just there." He stood, then reached down to help Camille to her feet. All he needed was for Adam to begin reminding the chit that he couldn't be trusted.

Her dainty gloved hand gripped his, and he pulled. "That was remarkable," she commented, still smiling, "though I wouldn't want to repeat the experience with them in another year or so."

"Oh, they'll be lethal in six months, my lady," Bullock put in. "Good solid-bred English lions, you know."

Belatedly Keating realized he still held her hand. Shaking himself, he released her. "Don't you have a large bear or some such?"

"Yes, Old Martin. He was a gift from America—the Hudson's Bay Company. Prepare yourselves, my friends, as he's quite large—nothing like his European brethren." While the ladies followed directly behind the keeper to the cage of the massive, grizzled old bear who evidently had a fondness for biscuits, Keating grabbed Greaves's shoulder. "You're not here to make me look poorly," he hissed.

"I thought I was helping," the duke returned in an equally low voice. "Pointing out how ill-suited you are to be a . . . well, a suitor."

Damnation, Adam made a good point. "I need her to trust me."

"Why, so you can lie to her about the reasons for your presence?"

Keating pushed the flattened palm of his hand into the duke's chest. "Leave be."

Greaves looked down at his hand. "And here I thought you only brawled when you were drunk. Very well. Suit yourself. I shall cease offering my assistance."

"Good." As Keating removed his hand, he frowned.

"Though I may need to ask you for use of your box at the theater."

"You are not easy to have as a friend, my friend."

"Yes, I know. All the more credit to you for tolerating me."

As they finished their tour of the grotto with a walk past the small selection of eagles and other falcons on display, Greaves offered his arm to Sophia. That rendered it acceptable for Keating to do the same for Camille, and she wrapped her fingers around his sleeve.

"Was this worth altering your working schedule for?" he asked, following the other pair to the duke's barouche.

"Oh, definitely." She grinned up at him. "I held a lion cub."

Bathed in that smile, for a heartbeat, six years of shame and pain washed away. "And you're certain you don't wish to join me at Drury Lane tonight, for a performance of . . ." He shot a glance at Greaves.

The duke sighed. "I believe it's *A Midsummer Night's D—*"

"For *A Midsummer Night's Dream*?" he interrupted.

"I cannot. I've already upended the working schedule, and—"

"You know Emily would stand for you tonight, Cammy," Sophia broke in. "For heaven's sake, go to the theater. You've been complaining about missing all the performances for the past year, as it is."

Camille blushed. "It's not proper." She lowered her head. "I know that sounds so foolish, especially coming from me, but I don't want to make things any worse."

"I'll have someone chaperone us," Keating said, working hard to keep his tone light. "Someone female, because otherwise, well, that wouldn't . . ." He frowned. "It will be proper. And anyone who glares at you will have to face me. You're one of the few people who tolerates my presence, and Greaves would inevitably be snoring by the second act. Just as friends."

"Dukes don't snore," Greaves commented succinctly.

Oh, Camille wanted to go, and clearly from Keating's ramble of words he wanted her to go, as well. She hadn't been to the theater in ages, even before she'd refused to marry. She looked from his almost impassive face to Sophia's clearly expectant one to the Duke of Greaves's faintly amused expression. "I cannot," she said, unable to keep the slight shake from her voice.

Why did it feel as if she were saying no to more than a night at the theater? She wanted to say yes for more reasons than just seeing a play. Yes, legally she supposed she was still betrothed to Lord Fenton, but her hesitation wasn't because of any twenty-two-year-old agreement. Whenever she looked at Keating Blackwood, heated thoughts danced through her mind, her spine shivered, and her toes curled. It was so tempting—*he* was so tempting—but going to the theater in his company wasn't nearly the same as walking through the park.

Too many people—and especially too many that she knew, and who knew her—would be present. Perhaps she was brave enough to hold a lion cub, but the animal had been a precious, wee thing and had no idea she was a societal pariah. Keating knew, of course, but he was worse than she was.

His expression didn't alter. "Very well. Inform me if you change your mind."

She'd already changed it seventeen times since he'd asked her. "I shall," she said aloud.

Thankfully Sophia led the conversation for the next

twenty minutes it took to return to The Tantalus Club. Camille had no idea how her friend managed to accept her own scandalous parentage and simply . . . not care what others thought about it. The only reason she'd sought employment at the club was because no one would hire her as a governess, and none of her relations on either the duke's or her mother's side would take her in.

Both men exited the barouche to walk them to the front door of The Tantalus Club. And other men saw. Camille straightened her spine a little, wondering what they must think to see two of the Tantalus Girls, as some had taken to calling them, being escorted by a duke and an impossible rogue. Of course, part of the attraction at the moment was that no one would dare speak a cross word in that particular company. On her own . . . well, she wouldn't have been caught out of doors on her own.

"I had a wonderful time," Sophia said, sketching a curtsy. "Thank you so much for asking me along."

"You weren't asked along," the Duke of Greaves returned with a smile. "You were asked. And it was my pleasure."

"Yes, thank you so much," Camille seconded. "I shall never forget that I held a lion in my lap."

From the quirk of Keating's cheek he wanted to say something amusing, but instead he only nodded. "It was also my pleasure. Might I call on you tomorrow?"

For someone who wasn't courting her, he certainly paid her a great deal of attention. And while stopping this before it could become messy and painful was likely the wisest course of action, she'd gone through life with men knowing she was already spoken for. A bit of mild flirting couldn't hurt anything. Not when she knew it was only the rather scandalous way Keating had of speaking. And today had been very, very nice. "Certainly," she said, relieved that he didn't seem to be angry that she'd declined to join him at the theater. "As a friend, of course."

He inclined his head. "Of course."

Just inside the foyer, Grace caught her arm. "Those are for you," the daytime butleress said, indicating a very large bouquet of white roses on the foyer side table.

Camille pulled out the note. " 'Happy twelfth birthday,' " she read to herself. " 'You're becoming a lovely young woman.' "

She smiled, leaning in to smell the posies. At the sound of the duke's barouche outside clattering down the drive, though, she straightened. Her heart stammering, she hurried outside, dodging past a trio of surprised club members as she did so. "Keating!" she called.

The barouche practically skidded to a stop. A moment later Keating was on the drive, striding back up to her. "Is something amiss?" he asked, his voice devoid of its usual cynical humor.

That stopped her. He was concerned about her. Genuinely. And it made her abrupt, stubborn impulsiveness much easier to tolerate. "The invitation to the theater tonight. I accept."

He grinned, taking another step toward her and lifting his hand as though to caress her cheek. At the last second, just before she could lean into him, he stopped, lowering his arm again. "I'll be by at seven o'clock."

"I'll be ready."

"Very good. I . . ." He looked over his shoulder toward the waiting barouche. "I should go now."

Camille had the strongest urge to giggle. "I'll see you this evening."

"Yes. Good. Good-bye."

His genuine pleasure at her response warmed her insides in a way she'd never felt before. And it decisively answered the question that had been nagging at her for the past three days, since her first birthday bouquet had arrived. Keating might wish her to think that Fenton was finally and belatedly attempting to woo her, and she didn't know why he might be attempting to do so. But the Marquis of Fenton didn't have the imagination or the . . . warmth to make amends or to apologize or to even approach her in such a roundabout way. Whatever he might be up to, the flowers—and the very kind sentiments with them—were from Keating Blackwood.

And that pleased her very, very much.

Keating sat at the library worktable and rested his chin on his folded arms. Just beyond the tip of his nose, near enough that he could smell it, sat a glass full of whiskey. Lamplight turned its amber hue golden, a cool honey that would sharpen and heat as it went down his throat.

He wanted it. He wanted the softening of the edges of his frustration and anger that it would bring. He wanted the way it would make him not care quite so much that he was becoming friends with someone he was priming to give away to a man who, he was beginning to realize, didn't deserve her.

"Mr. Blackwood, you have a caller."

Not moving, Keating closed his eyes. The image of the full glass stayed clear in his mind, anyway. "I'm not here."

The butler shifted in the doorway. "I'm to tell you she's quite determined to see you."

Keating lifted his head, something jolting in his chest even as he realized he knew far too many females to think it might be . . . well, the one who'd first entered his thoughts. "She, who?"

"The lady wouldn't give me her name, but I believe her to be Lady Vandress."

The whatever it was that had sped his heartbeat fled again. "I'll see to her," he said, rising.

"Thank you, sir."

"And leave that there," he said, indicating the full glass on the table.

Given that Greaves's butler was practically made of stone, Keating couldn't tell whether the fellow was annoyed or amused at all of this. With a last, reluctant look at the glass of whiskey, Keating stood and went down the hallway to the morning room. "Charity Vandress," he drawled, stepping into the cozy room and shutting the door behind him.

The tall, willowy brunette turned from her gaze out the window. Despite the warm day she was well bundled in a long cloak, the hood pulled up to mostly conceal her face. "Shame on you, Keating," she said in a voice that would melt butter. "You come all the way back to London and don't bother to call on me."

He remembered that voice. And other things. "I apologize. I had some obligations to see to."

"Yes, I've heard what you've been up to. Kissing virgins in the park. And there's that other thing. What was it? Oh, yes. Trailing after ruined little Lady Camille Pryce. Very scandalous of you."

Keating snorted. "Don't even attempt to pretend jealousy, Charity. You do it very badly."

She pushed the hood back from her face, exposing brilliant green eyes and lip rouge that seemed a little too bright. "I'm not jealous. I'm merely pointing out that after six years you might have come to revisit your old sins rather than creating new ones."

With that she unbuttoned her brown cloak and dropped

it to her feet. Beneath it she wore . . . nothing. Absolutely nothing. And her stunning body was nearly as breathtaking as it had been six years earlier. Of course he was seeing her bare skin sober for the first time, which might account for his noticing the differences time and hard living had wrought.

"Put your clothes on, Charity. I'm not going down that path again."

"But you are," she countered, sidling up closer to him. "You're merely doing it with someone else. You never used to limit yourself to one woman. Why begin now?"

"I'm at least as surprised as you are, my dear, but I'm not going to play with you." And he *was* surprised. The male part of him did find her attractive and desirable, but his . . . heart, he supposed it was, or perhaps his battered soul, demanded that he send her packing at once. Before Camille could hear any rumors and decide that he hadn't changed from the rampaging, inebriated madman he'd been six years ago. And not solely because her loss of trust could cost him ten thousand pounds.

"I hear your voice, but I don't think you mean what you're saying." She slid her hands down her front, cupping her breasts invitingly.

"I'm attempting to be kind," he retorted, beginning to lose patience. "I've never thought ill of you, and I hope we might remain cordial. But you need to leave."

A blush began at her cheeks and spread down her neck to her chest. "You used to be fun, Keating," she murmured, bending down to pick up her cloak. "This isn't because of my husband, is it? That never stopped you before."

Yes, but that was before he'd killed someone else's husband. "Suffice it to say that I'm a leopard attempting to alter his spots."

"Hm." She shrugged into the heavy wrap and buttoned it closed again. "More like a fox pretending he dislikes chickens. I know the truth. We all know the truth."

"Then I suppose I'm the last to know. Feel free to laugh at me later."

"Oh, I shall. Believe me."

After Charity left, Keating sank down in one of the morning room chairs. For a fleeting moment he wished Greaves had been home, because as little as he liked discussing his private matters, being prodded at by Adam occasionally helped him find his path.

Closing his eyes again, he frowned. Having a path was a damned nuisance. Particularly when the path he was beginning to find very interesting wasn't the path he was going to take. Of course the problem could be as simple as the fact that he'd never attempted to have an actual conversation with a female before, and he was finding it more compelling than he'd expected. Camille said thoughtful things, and didn't attempt to strip naked on every occasion. Thus far, he'd kept his own clothes on, which he had to count as something in his favor.

Confusing as all this was, the only consolation was that helping return Camille to the arms of Society would provide him with the means to see to his other obligation. After that, he could do whatever he damn well pleased.

At least he'd weathered an initial storm or two. If he could manage tonight without driving Camille away, he would call it a success. If he could do it without losing her friendship, that would be a miracle. And if he could do it sober and without putting his hands on her, he could face anything.

Chapter Nine

"I should send over a note telling him I've changed my mind."

Sophia frowned at Camille's reflection in the dressing mirror and continued with pinning up her friend's hair. "No you shouldn't."

"Yes she should." Emily Portsman leaned in the doorway and eyed the two of them with her typical skepticism. "In the theater she won't have anyone else to rely on, and nowhere to run if something should go wrong."

"Simply because you don't trust anyone, Emily, doesn't mean you have the right of it."

"Simply because you're naïve, Sophia, doesn't mean you should go about trusting everyone."

Camille wanted to clap her hands over her ears. She would have, if it would have stopped her own mind from arguing so loudly with itself. "Please stop it," she said aloud. "You aren't helping."

With a sniff Emily vanished from the doorway. "Don't listen to her," Sophia said, grimacing as she pinned a last strand of straying blond hair into a surprisingly attractive tangle. "I think Keating Blackwood is very nearly in love with you."

"But we've only met on three occasions, you daft thing.

I'm certain he's far too jaded to fall in love so easily, if at all. And aside from that, he's Fenton's cousin. It's not as though he would marry me or anything."

"My dear, you're one of the Tantalus Girls. You don't need to marry anyone. In fact, I imagine Lady Haybury would thank you for creating a bit of scandal. The club attendance always grows when there's wickedness in the air."

"So you're suggesting we become illicit lovers?" Goodness, she couldn't remember ever saying such a thing—or even thinking such a thing—before she'd come to The Tantalus Club.

"Why not? It's not as though you have a reputation to protect."

Camille stared at her friend for a long moment. Of all the things she'd ever felt about ruining herself, a sense of freedom had never been one of them. But Sophia made a very good point. All it would take was some courage. She certainly already had the desire; she could barely look at him without her fingers twitching. She glanced down at her hands, still twining into the handkerchief she'd demolished with her worrying.

Sophia kissed her on the cheek. "It might not make anything easier for you, but you'd have much more fun being an outcast."

Chuckling and trying to shove her nerves back down someplace where they wouldn't trouble her, Camille stood and left the bedchamber. "You could follow the same advice yourself, you know."

Taking her arm, Sophia grinned. "I'm waiting for just the perfect wealthy, handsome outcast to sweep me off my feet and into bed."

"Ah. I see."

Before she could sort out what she wanted from what

she required and everything in between, they reached the foyer. And then she couldn't think at all, because Keating was there already, chatting with Juliet at the butler's station. He straightened as she approached.

"You look very nice," she said, sweeping her eyes up and down his sleek black jacket and waistcoat and trousers and his tassled Hessian boots. The stark white of his cravat, broken by a black onyx pin, completed the striking effect. He reminded her all over again of a panther, relaxed and still deadly, just waiting for the opportune moment to strike. Sophia's advice abruptly didn't seem so outlandish any longer.

"I'm supposed to say that to you," he countered. "Now I have to think up something better. Let's see. You look like the morning." He frowned. "No, that won't do. It's entirely too pedestrian." Slowly he tilted his head, the keenness of his gaze discomfiting and warming all at the same time. "'She walks in beauty, like the night / Of cloudless climes and starry skies; / And all that's best of dark and bright / Meet in her aspect and her eyes.'"

"Goodness," she said with a chuckle, genuinely impressed. "Lord Byron. I'm honored."

"I was hoping you'd be dazzled, but honored will do." He offered his arm. "Shall we go?"

Camille intentionally avoided the gaze of Juliet and of everyone else entering the foyer. It was easier to be bold if she didn't notice anyone else noticing her. Out on the drive, though, faced with the Duke of Greaves's enormous coach and four fierce black horses, she stopped. "What about a chaperone?"

"Inside the coach."

"But how could you ride here with her and still expect—"

"Oh, for God's sake," he muttered, pulling open the

door. "I rode up with Samuel. The driver. Ask him if you don't believe me."

She peeked inside the vehicle to see a very demure, almost mouselike older woman seated there. "Hello," Camille said.

The woman nodded, scooting sideways to make room on the deep brown, well-cushioned seat. "Very nice," she said in a warm, musical tone.

Before she could change her mind yet again, Camille stepped up into the coach and sat beside her chaperone. A moment later Keating joined them on the seat opposite, and the coach rolled back out to the street. "You see? All very proper."

Camille smiled at her seatmate. Somehow, he'd accomplished it. He'd found her a chaperone, then taken steps to see that even said escort had a protected reputation. "What is your name?" she asked.

The woman smiled back at her. "Very nice," she repeated.

Hm. "Where are you employed?"

"Very nice. Good."

Turning to face the amused fellow opposite her, Camille lifted an eyebrow. "She doesn't speak any English."

"No? That would explain a few things."

"Keating, where did she come from? You didn't abduct her, did you?"

A wicked glint entered his gaze. "Thank you for thinking so well of me. She's a Gypsy. I rode by the camp, offered her five shillings, threw that dress in her direction, and opened the carriage door. She climbed in and she's now wearing the gown, so you have a chaperone."

"Good heavens. What if she thinks you've taken her away to marry her? Or that you want to . . . sin with her?"

"She's old enough to be my grandmother." He shifted, then tapped himself on the chest. "Keating," he said, looking at their escort. He pointed at Camille. "Camille," he said, then gestured at the old woman.

"Ah. Rosa."

"See? This is Rosa. Stop complaining."

Camille sat back in the comfortable coach. "So you acquired seats at the theater for us with what, five hours' advance notice? Th—"

"A box," he corrected. "Greaves's box."

"You acquired a private box on the day of the performance," she amended, ticking the points off on her fingers, "borrowed a very fine coach, found a companion's dress, sent me flowers, stole a chaperone, and convinced me to accompany you. If you didn't keep denying it, I would begin to believe that you *are* pursuing me."

She was watching for his reaction, and so she noticed the swiftly downcast eyes and the tight expression that crossed his face. "Flowers?" he said after a moment. "I sent you flowers?"

And she'd thought that by concealing it in the middle of her list she might pass it by him, leaving him to confess merely by omission. "I know they're from you. Fenton has no imagination. And no inclination to apologize to me for anything."

Keating tilted his head. "I'll grant that Stephen can be a self-important fool, but are you so certain he's irredeemable?"

For a moment she felt as if someone had pulled the carpet from beneath her feet. "What?"

For a long, hard beat of her heart he gazed at her. Then before she could move he sat forward, wrapped his fingers into the front of her cloak, and kissed her. Heat soared through her, heady and intoxicating. Camille swept her arms around his neck, sinking into his embrace. This was what she'd wanted—for him to stop teasing and prove that he did want her.

With the same abruptness he pushed her back into her seat again. "I wanted one more of those," he murmured, his eyes dark and snapping, "before you decide you hate me."

"I don't hate you, Keating," she returned unsteadily, unable to remove her gaze from his very capable mouth and noting in the periphery of her thoughts that Rosa the chaperone was gazing out the window. "Why would you say that?"

"Because Stephen asked me for a favor."

Close your ears. Don't listen. "Stop jesting. It's not at all amusing." She swallowed. "Tell me how you became friends with the Duke of Greaves. After all, I keep telling you my secrets, and you've divulged almost none of yours."

"That's what I'm attempting to do."

She dug her fist into her thigh. "But I don't want to hear that. So stop it." Didn't he realize that he was the closest she'd come to making a friend still attached to the aristocracy? As impossible and scandalous as he was, he could still attend soirees and sit in boxes at the theater, and he liked her. And she liked him. Very much, and in ways she was certain weren't at all proper. Oh, she couldn't even stand the thought of discovering another friend was not who she *knew* they were.

"Just consider," he pressed, leaning forward, hand outstretched toward her knee. "What if you could return to your parents' home?" He curled his fingers and sat back again without touching her. "What if you could be invited to grand balls and be mistress of a lovely home and have lordling babies gathered at your feet?"

A tear ran down her cheek. "You lied to me. You said we would be honest with each other, and you lied to me. Bastard. Stop this coach and let me out."

"No."

"So now you're kidnapping me, as well? You'll have to flee back to Shropshire after this—even if Rosa and I are little nobodies. Heavens, if we were actual people, you might be transported. Lucky you."

"Ask me why," he snapped, cutting off her protests.

"What?"

"Ask me why I would let my cousin talk me into coming back to London where I'm not nearly as popular as you seem to think I am. Ask me why I would agree, knowing you would look at me like you are right now," he growled, his voice rising. *"Ask me."*

Even Rosa began to appear alarmed, and the woman squeezed against the far wall, looking from one of them to the other. Camille knew he had a temper; she'd seen evidence of it the first time they'd met. But he'd never directed it at her, even verbally. Until now. "Fine," she retorted, keeping her shoulders straight and reminding herself that she was the injured party in this little play. "Why?"

"Because I have no money," he returned, finally looking away from her. "I have a small house and some land, and it would have been enough, except for what I did six years ago."

"Lord Balthrow?" she asked, curious despite herself. "How is—"

"Lady Balthrow," he corrected. "She's been ruined, too, and widowed, left without a penny by her cousin-in-law the new viscount. And . . ." He took a deep breath, looking as though he would rather be standing naked in a pen of lions than speaking with her now. "And she had to go abroad."

"What does that . . ." Camille paused. She'd had a friend once who'd had to go abroad. Elizabeth had been whisked away, and then had returned ten months later and married someone they previously all would have thought well beneath her. They'd never really spoken again. "A child?" she whispered. "She has a child?"

He nodded stiffly, glancing at her and then away again. "To spare us both the niggling questions, her husband was impotent. It's mine. The boy. And she won't let me see him, because she still blames me for all this. But I'll be damned if I won't pay for his upbringing and his education, and for Eleanor to be able to have a decent life somewhere. So when Stephen asked me for a favor, I agreed."

"You mean he's paying you to trick me into . . . into what?"

"Returning to the church. The altar, rather. And I'm not tricking you into anything. I just told you my entire plan."

Camille stood up, then banged her head on the low roof and sat down hard, seeing stars. "Ouch! Damnation."

Keating pulled her across the coach to sit beside him and placed a warm palm on her head before she could even protest that she was fine. "Stephen doesn't know the particulars about my circumstances," he resumed, tucking her against his shoulder, "but he does know I'm rather particular about second chances. He's willing to offer you a chance to return to Society's good graces. And he asked if I, with my personal experience in scandal, would deliver the message."

He hadn't meant to do it this way. Cursing himself silently, Keating watched her every expression, the tears slowly sliding down her smooth cheeks, the way her hands shook because she'd clenched her muscles so tightly. He was somewhat surprised she hadn't punched him; if he had been her, he was fairly certain he would have done so.

When she'd agreed to go to the theater with him, he'd decided she needed to know the truth. If not, he would have to begin lying. And he'd given his word to her about that. He'd meant to tell her about his agreement—or part of it, anyway—once they were safely in Greaves's private box, in the view of every other theatergoer. Then he would have been assured that she couldn't flee, and likely wouldn't make a scene. Perhaps that had been cowardly of him, but it was all moot now, anyway.

"What . . ." She wiped at her eyes, which relieved him. It hadn't used to bother him to see or to cause women to cry, but apparently that had altered. At least where she was concerned. Camille cleared her throat. "What is your son's name?"

"Michael. I don't expect your sympathy, Cammy. That is not why I told you. I only want you to understand why I'm here. Because I promised to be honest with you."

For a moment that tore at him more than he would ever let her know, she gazed at him. "So there is no . . . friendship?" she finally asked, the twist in her voice going straight to a heart he no longer thought he had. "Between us, I mean."

He heard her hesitation, and did his damnedest to ignore it. If he discovered that she wanted him with the same intensity that he wanted her, he would be undone. "There is absolutely friendship. Otherwise I wouldn't have told you anything about this." And what he wanted from her in addition to friendship didn't signify, anyway. Men like him didn't win the hearts of virginal chits. He might warrant an infatuation from her, but anything else would only leave her bloody, battered, and bruised. And of course in this instance there was also the fact that technically she was still engaged to another man.

"I don't understand how you can say we're friends, when the entire time you've been scheming to—"

"The only thing I've been scheming about was how to tell you what I just told you without you clubbing me with a shovel." Deciding to risk a pummeling, he reached down and took her hand. "If you want your walks in the park, your dances, your afternoon teas and the latest fashions from Paris, you have another chance at them."

"Just like that?"

"Just like that. I think you'll find that being a wealthy marchioness causes other people to completely forget the past." Belatedly he released her hand again. "I'm not saying you should marry Stephen tomorrow; at this moment I'm only suggesting that you consider your options."

She flexed her fingers, then to his surprise she took his chin, leveling his gaze even with hers, holding him there. "Did you send me those flowers?" she asked levelly, not blinking.

Keating took a low breath. "I suggested that Fenton might be better served if he stopped being so stuffy. And I did suggest flowers." She had such pretty eyes. Like the sky at sunrise. He wanted to devour her. "Does that answer your question?"

Camille released him. "I suppose it does. Are you taking me back to the club now?"

"I'm taking you to the theater." He forced a smile. "I promised Rosa a special night out. I can't go back on my word."

"You are impossible."

"Yes, I believe I am."

When a brief smile quirked her luscious mouth, he began breathing again. Thank God. He hadn't ruined it.

A moment later it occurred to him that the "it" he'd been thinking of hadn't been his chance at ten thousand pounds. It had been his friendship, for lack of a permissible word, with Camille Pryce. By the time they arrived at Drury Lane Theater he'd managed to regain most of his sensibilities, and Cammy hadn't decided to begin thrashing him and run for The Tantalus Club. He had to consider that a victory, minor or not. They walked into the large lobby, a bewildered Rosa clumping along behind them and chattering something in her Gypsy tongue that might have been a recipe for rice pudding or a curse on everyone's soul. Even if both of them hadn't been notorious they likely would have attracted attention; no one else seemed to have brought along a Gypsy grandmother as a chaperone.

Camille shifted a breath closer to him, and he put a hand over the one that rested on his left arm. "One of the good things about being a known killer," he murmured, looking a young lady in the eye and noting the speed with which she gasped and turned around, "is that while people may stare or look askance, they rarely say anything insulting within my hearing." He glanced sideways to see her biting her lip. "Or they may simply be terrified of Rosa. I can't be certain."

Her jaw relaxed a little, her cheek rounding with her quick smile. "Let's just get up to the box, shall we?" she muttered back.

Well, he had to count that as an improvement. A week ago she would have been on her way out the door already. As for him, it felt like nearly every woman he'd ever known, and a great many he'd never seen before, were all sizing him up as they would a succulent pheasant. What the devil was the attraction? He'd ruined a wife and killed her husband, for the devil's sake. Did they think to fare any better?

If he'd been alone he might have stopped and asked several of them that very question, but Camille was clearly uncomfortable, and he'd dealt her enough blows this evening. Keeping his mouth firmly closed, he ascended the left-hand staircase with her at his side and the Gypsy behind them. "Here we are," he said, stopping to pull the heavy red curtain aside.

Camille stopped beside him and looked into the large box. "I can't do this."

"You can't walk forward ten feet and sit in a comfortable chair?"

"I can't sit there for three hours while everyone else whispers about me."

To punctuate her protest, a group of theatergoers walked past them, whispering and giggling and sending them glances. That was damned well enough of that. Keating released the curtain and strode after them. "Good evening," he said, moving in front of them.

The man in the middle of the three chits paled. "Blackwood. Wh—"

"Unless I'm mistaken," Keating interrupted, "there are no more boxes in this direction. I know this because I'm utilizing the Duke of Greaves's accommodations, and his box is located directly to the right of the stage. There are no closer seats."

"Oh." The pale man fumbled, digging for his pocket watch and opening it. "I—we—"

"Unless that watch of yours is a compass, I am going to assume that you are here so you can gawk at my friend and me." He took another step closer. "I don't like being gawked at."

"I—we—very sorry, Mr. Blackwood. We apologize."

Keating sent a glance at the chits. Little kittens all of them, thinking they had claws until it was time to use them. "Don't apologize. Go away."

The tallest of the young ladies sniffed. "I don't know what you're talking about. There is nothing here we would wish to see. And certainly no *one*."

He narrowed his eyes. "Then perhaps there's something you wish to do. Receive a kiss? Or did you have something more intimate in mind?"

She backed away a step. "Albert," she snapped, a squeak in her voice, "please remove us from this . . . man."

"Of course, Edwina."

Keating let them pass. "Good night, Edwina. Sweet, sweet Edwina. I shall dream of you naked in my arms."

When he turned around, the entrance to Greaves's box was empty. Something in his chest bumped. Had he frightened her away? Cursing himself, he strode down the few steps to yank the curtains back—and froze.

Camille stood two inches in front of him, a grin of pure delight on her face. As he nearly ran her down she stumbled backward, and Keating reached out to grab her shoulder and keep her from falling onto her backside. "You heard that, I presume?" he drawled, the relief that coursed through him making him feel almost light-headed.

"Oh, yes. You're a very bad man." She chuckled.

"Don't you forget it, my dear."

He should have moved past her, should have gestured for her to move to the front of the box, should have made some query about how they would manage to remove

Rosa from the front seats where she'd plunked herself down to gaze at the audience below them.

Instead he continued gazing into her light blue eyes, noting both the slow fade of her smile and the way he couldn't seem to stop himself from leaning toward her. Just a kiss. One more kiss. No one would see them from the back of the box, surely. And it didn't mean anything. It was only that he liked kissing her, and he hadn't been able to indulge himself nearly enough. Except that he imagined more than kissing her. He imagined sliding his hands along her bare skin, burying himself deep inside of her while she held him close against h—

"May I bring you some wine, sir?" a footman said from directly behind him, making him jump.

Keating blinked, straightening again. "Nothing for me. Camille?"

She looked slightly dazed as well. "I . . . think wine would be lovely. What about Rosa?"

"She looks like a woman who drinks whiskey," Keating decided. "Wine and whiskey."

"Very good, sir." The footman descended the stairs again.

When he looked at Camille again she was taking a seat beside the Gypsy, which only left the seat on Rosa's other side. The damned woman was a more efficient chaperone than he'd expected. "Do you think we should attempt to get her to move?" he asked, lingering in the dark at the back of the box until he could convince his stubborn cock that saluting now would only get them into trouble.

"I don't know. She seems quite happy here."

"But I want to chat with you." Even as he spoke the words he knew he sounded like a raw schoolboy being turned down by a pretty chit at his first soiree.

"Then you'll have to call on me tomorrow, I suppose."

She was half turned away, facing the parting curtains on the stage, but he'd studied her contours well enough to know she was smiling. He'd thought that convincing her to listen to his plea on Fenton's behalf would be the largest stone in his path. He hadn't realized that convincing himself to step aside in favor of his cousin would be even more difficult.

Chapter Ten

"And that, ladies," Lady Haybury said, clapping her hands together, "is why I have decided that our experiment over the past winter and spring was a complete success. I intend to keep The Tantalus Club open year-round permanently."

"Oh, thank goodness," Sophia whispered, gripping Camille's arm as they sat at one of the empty breakfast room tables. "I had no idea where I would even stay this year if we closed after Derby time."

"But didn't you think it dull?" Sylvie put in from across the table. "I mean, I appreciate that we'll have a roof and an income, reduced or not, but London is not to be tolerated between August and March—except for the Little Seasons, of course."

"Lady H said we could go away on holiday if we wanted to," Sophia returned. "So you don't have to stay."

"I'm staying," Emily put in from beside Sophia. "If Mr. Jacobs and Mr. Smith will be staying on as well, that is."

Camille looked at her friend. If there was anyone who left the club even less frequently than she did, it was Emily Portsman. But Emily had never spoken of her past or even of anything that occurred before she walked through the club's front doors.

"Emily?" Lady Haybury called from the front of the room. "Do you have any schedule changes?"

"Yes, I do." Picking up her notepad, Emily rose and walked over to make her announcements.

"Forget keeping the club open," Sophia whispered, nudging her elbow. "How was your outing last night? You didn't even wake me up to tell me."

"It wasn't at all what I expected." Camille didn't think she'd ever made such a large understatement in her life. Weariness dragged at her; in fact she wasn't certain she would do any sleeping at all in the foreseeable future.

"How so?" her friend pressed.

"I don't wish to discuss it yet, Sophia. I have to decipher my own thoughts first."

"Did someone insult you? Why didn't Keating thrash them? He seems very proficient at thrashing. Being so very muscular, I mean."

"Sophia, please."

"No. I waited twenty years to have a dear friend, and no one is allowed to harm you. I'll go thrash them myself, if necessary."

Camille snorted. "Oh, dear. It's not . . ." She took a breath. Her friends—these friends, who'd embraced her when the rest of London had turned its collective back—would support her regardless, but the last thing she'd expected had been the offer of a second chance. Especially when she'd begun looking forward for the first time in months. "Keating told me that Fenton is still interested in marriage."

Sophia's eyes widened. "After some of the things he's said about you? To you?"

"Apparently so."

"What did Keating think about that? He must have been angry, since he's been pursuing you himself."

That was the difficult part. Nearly since his arrival in London she'd viewed Keating Blackwood in a certain . . . carnal manner. It set her back on her heels to think that he hadn't been looking at her in the same way—except that he'd kissed her. More than once. And that look in his eyes at the theater had made her feel completely naked.

"Keating came to London on Fenton's behalf," she said slowly.

Sophia lurched to her feet. "What? That traitor! I'm going to kick him very hard in the man area the next time I set eyes on him."

"Ladies," Lady Haybury said, stopping her announcements and walking over to them. "What's amiss?"

"Keating Blackwood lied to Cammy."

Camille frowned. "No, he didn't lie. Not precisely. He merely didn't tell me all the facts."

"What did he lie about?" Juliet Langtree demanded, leaving her own table and joining the growing group at Camille's.

"I knew he couldn't be trusted." Pansy Bridger put a hand on Camille's shoulder. "I tried to warn you."

"No, no, no." Camille pressed her hands against the tabletop. "There's no need for torches or pitchforks, for heaven's sake. I don't even know all the details yet. All I do know, in fact, is what Keating told me—that Lord Fenton knows he erred in the way he approached this marriage, and that he's willing to begin again."

Among the general shouting and opinions and chaos, a hand took her shoulder and pulled her to her feet. Lady Haybury parted the sea of females with her free hand and led the way toward the private hallway to one side of the room. Once they were alone, the marchioness released her.

"The flowers you've been getting. They're from Fenton?"

Camille wasn't surprised that Lady Haybury knew about the flowers. She and her husband the marquis seemed to know everything that was afoot. They always had. "I thought they were from Keating, but he said he'd never sent me any. So yes, they must be from Fenton." Part of her still wasn't quite ready to believe that, but it made more sense now if Keating was somehow directing the course of his cousin's courtship. Mr. Blackwood, at least, knew how to properly—or improperly—woo a lady.

"I only wish to tell you to be cautious, Cammy," the black-haired marchioness said in her low, honeyed voice. "Men for the most part want things that benefit *them*. I may be wrong, but I can't help thinking that your well-being and happiness are not the first items on Lord Fenton's list. Particularly given the way he's behaved over the past year."

"But you had no objections when you thought Keating might be courting me?" Camille asked, more curious than annoyed.

"Keating Blackwood is a rogue." She smiled a little. "And so are we all, here."

"Thank you, my lady. I appreciate your concern."

"I do wish the lot of you would call me Diane. We're family now, whether that was what we expected or not."

One of the hallway doors swung open, and Lord Haybury emerged into the narrow corridor. "Do I need to shoot Blackwood?" he asked, his brow lowered. "Or Fenton?" he asked, gray eyes snapping despite the lightness in his words.

Diane took his hand and kissed his palm. "I'm still determining that, Oliver. Do be patient."

"No shooting, if you please," Camille put in, scowling. "Whatever happens, I've done it to myself. At least my eyes are open this time."

"You don't stand alone, whatever happens," Diane said forcefully.

"Yes. Evidently we defend our employees to the death," Haybury seconded. "What's occurred?"

"I'm not certain. Something about Blackwood lying, and Fenton still wanting to marry Cammy. And sending her flowers. Wh—"

"Keating didn't lie. For heaven's sake, I left that church because I wanted to dictate the direction of my own life. Pray don't begin throwing rocks and shooting people. I don't know what I'm going to do. I only just heard about it last night, you know."

She should have kept her mouth firmly closed, at least until she'd sorted out a few points in her own mind. And until she'd decided for certain whether Keating was merely a contrary messenger, or an ally, or something else entirely.

"Very well," Lady Haybury said, putting a hand over her husband's mouth when he looked ready to protest again. "Just know that you will have employment and a roof over your head for as long as you want it. I won't see you forced into reconciliation because you have no other choice. My first marriage was arranged, you know. It was not . . . pleasant."

"Thank you, Lady Hay—" Camille stopped herself. "Thank you, Diane," she corrected. "I'm hoping I'm done with acting before I've weighed all the consequences. *All* of them." With a nod, the marchioness patted her on the shoulder and left the hallway. Lord Haybury, however, remained. "I'm not one for giving advice," he said after a moment. "I don't know what Blackwood might be up to, but I've never trusted him. Of course back when I knew him, neither of us was particularly trustworthy, so I don't know how much merit that comment has. Anyway, all I mean to say is that sometimes a particular action is worth facing the consequences over. The trick is knowing which action, and when to take it."

Well, that hadn't been at all helpful. Before Camille could find a more diplomatic way to tell him precisely that, however, the club's employees flooded into the corridor as the weekly meeting ended. Sophia appeared to grab her arm and begin jabbering at her again, which didn't help the way her head was beginning to throb.

Camille pulled her arm free. "Give me a moment, will you?" she asked, and walked over to find Lucille Hampton flirting with Mr. Jacobs, the captain of the club's Helpful Men. "Lucille, I'll be a few minutes late. Will you be able to manage the crowd yourself?"

"Oh, yes," Lucille returned with an excited smile. "No one ever comes by on Wednesday mornings, anyway."

That was why they'd chosen the day that Parliament had its earliest session for their weekly meeting. "Very well. I'll be in shortly."

"Cammy?" Sophia asked, following her.

"I need a breath of air. I'll be out in the garden."

"Do you wish company?"

"I wish the opposite of company."

She made her way through the large kitchen at the rear of the combined manor house and gentlemen's club and escaped out to the garden. With a deep sigh she headed for the bench beneath the oak tree and plunked herself down on the chilly stone.

Last night she could still pretend that perhaps she'd misheard, or that what Keating had told her was a large, nebulous cloud without form or substance. Now, with everyone chattering in her ears and throwing brick-shaped pieces of advice and opinion at her, it seemed so much more real. And very frightening.

Another chance. What did that mean, precisely? And how would they go about it? Would everyone who'd been friendly and admiring before be so again? Would they—and could she—forget all the horrid things they'd said and done over the past months?

And what about Stephen Pollard? Had her would-be husband changed from that cold, stuffy man who'd stood at the altar looking as though he would rather have been at one of his clubs than marrying her? And then there was Keating Blackwood. What part did he play in all this? Had he been kind simply so she would listen to him when the time came for him to present Fenton's terms? What about—

"I thought I might find you here."

She looked up to see Keating leaning against the tree trunk. "You've done your duty," she said, not having to feign annoyance. After all, she'd found friends and an odd sort of life again. And now Keating had upended everything once more. With an entire sleepless night to consider it, yes, she was annoyed. More than annoyed. "Now go away and let me think."

"Thinking never did anyone any good," he returned, coming forward to sit on the bench beside her. "Come driving with me."

"No. And you needn't continue being charming. Or is it that you don't receive your reward until I have Fenton's ring on my finger?"

"I'm not your enemy, Camille." He touched his fingers against the edge of her gown, then looked away. "I'm one of those fellows who runs about on the battlefield waving a white flag and offering terms to keep the opposing sides from slaughtering each other."

"I've already been slaughtered. And I was just beginning to mend."

"Yes, I know. And I apologize for that."

"Do you?"

Keating blew out his breath. "I know what it's like to damn the consequences and throw yourself out beyond the ragged edges of propriety. And I've spent the past six years attempting to live with what I did. There are days now, more often than not, when I enjoy being a gentleman farmer. But the consequences still remain out there, as I'm reminded every time I step out of doors here. And I'm still paying for them."

He meant his son. She couldn't even imagine having a child and not being able to see him—ever. The fact that he continued to send money to Lady Balthrow spoke well for his character, though he would likely argue with that. "Did you love her?" she asked after a moment.

"We're not discussing my errors. We're discussing how to make yours vanish."

Camille lifted her chin. "You're the one who needs to convince me that this entire 'friendship' business wasn't a fraud, a ruse, and a lie."

Eyes the color of autumn leaves met hers. "Do I, now?"

She heard the harder edge come into his voice, and while she didn't relish the idea of facing him down, this was certainly more important to her than his smiles. "If you expect me to listen to any advice, you do."

"Then no. I didn't love her. She was pretty, and energetic in bed. As I recall, she was also extremely overdramatic. In all honesty, even if Balthrow hadn't broken into my apartments and attempted to shoot my head off my shoulders, I'm not certain I would have . . . visited her again."

"So it was the challenge you were after?" Fleetingly she wondered how much of a challenge she presented. Not much, considering she'd kissed him after only chatting with him two or three times.

"Did I mention that I was two-and-twenty and had decided that no one would ever order me about or even advise me on anything ever again? It's quite invigorating to realize that you know everything." He shrugged. "Until you realize that you don't, of course. After it's too late."

For a long moment she studied his lean profile. "You do a very convincing job of not seeming to care what anyone thinks of you, these days."

"That's because I don't care what they think of me. I did something wrong, and these are the consequences. Do you think that anyone could ever say anything to me that would make me feel more wrong or more guilty than I already do?"

"I hate it when people look sideways at me."

"That's because if everyone had been sane and rational, they would have considered that what you did made perfect sense. They can't very well condone it, however, or there would be mass hysteria. Women only marrying men they love? Expecting kindness and friendship in a mate? Good God, can you imagine the chaos?"

She chuckled. "So my former friends are all jealous of me."

"They're frightened of you. If independent thought is a disease, and they were to catch it from you, well, you can envision the results. They would have to think for themselves." He gave an exaggerated shudder.

"Mm-hm. And if I were to marry Fenton after all, I would be forgiven?"

"All transgressions forgotten, because they would prefer to forget all about it. Especially considering the bags of money in my cousin's possession."

He made it sound so simple, and so appealing. "You can't know that they'll forget anything."

"Mm. Lady Taviston."

Camille blinked. "I'd forgotten about her."

"And that is my point. If she can run off with a damned American, live in Scotland for a year, and then return to her grateful husband and her gaggle of babies who don't look a bit like Lord Taviston, then, well, I sincerely doubt your notoriety will last beyond the church doors."

Goodness. Her actions did certainly pale in comparison with Lady Taviston's—though that incident had been finished with a good dozen years ago. In a way, it helped her find a bit of perspective. Unexpectedly, though, it didn't leave her feeling any easier about the choice with which she'd now been presented.

"I've asked myself several times," she said aloud, "if I would have fled the church if I'd realized the consequences. If I'd known my parents would disown me and all my friends would . . . behave as they have."

He slid an inch or so closer to her. "That's the rub, isn't it?" he commented, as though he could hear her thoughts. "Has Fenton become more tolerable in the intervening year? Or would you be walking back to the exact same circumstances that caused you to leave before?"

Camille liked the way Keating had never called her a fool for simply wanting to be happy. Perhaps she had been one; from the results, she would agree that she should have reweighed the value of happiness against comfort, as she'd found herself with neither. Whatever happened next, however, she would never forget the look in Fenton's eyes. The marriage, her, had meant almost nothing to him. He'd had more affection for the pocket watch he kept flipping open than he had for her.

Taking a breath, she looked over at Keating again. "He's sent me flowers for the past four days," she conceded, still searching for any sign that the bouquets had actually been a gift from the unusual man beside her.

"Apparently we've made amends up to my fourteenth birthday."

"I would imagine he doesn't quite know how to approach this, either," he said slowly. "Are you pleased he's making the effort?"

"I'm supposed to say yes to that, am I not?"

His brow lowered. "Now you've gone and baffled me. You don't want him to be kind to you now?"

She stood. "I'm still attempting to decipher all of this," she stated, before she could begin blurting out any half-formed thoughts or hopes or dreams that had been killed before she could even enjoy imagining those very naughty nights she'd decided to spend in Keating's arms.

"Then walk with me," he repeated, standing as well. "I swear to keep silent unless you have a question for me or wish me to commiserate with your annoyance at my cousin."

Camille knew she couldn't have told Sophia to please be quiet for a blasted minute without hurting her friend's feelings. Keating, however, was much more thick-skinned. "Very well. Silence."

Gazing at her, he lifted both eyebrows and then gestured for her to lead the way. With a snort, Camille circled the back of the house to avoid the crowded carriage drive. Keating fell into step beside her.

"I'm certain more marriages than not have begun without love," she mused after a moment. "After all, there seems to be no surer way to secure a political or an economic alliance."

Silence. Just his tall, warm, compelling presence strolling beside her.

"I even know there have been marriages where the husband and bride had never met, had never even set eyes on each other, before the wedding."

A hand cupped her elbow, guiding her around a small scattering of horse manure.

"Those couples, of course, came from different villages or countries or Highland clans, where they *couldn't* become acquainted with each other beforehand."

He made a small sound that might have been amusement or agreement, but she couldn't be certain which—or even if he'd merely cleared his throat.

"Yes, I know my facts are partly based on those dreadful gothic romances, but the odds say that each circumstance must have happened at least once." Camille paused. "You may commiserate with me now."

"Of course you're correct," he said promptly. "The world is a vast and strange place."

"Oh, you're quite good at that."

"Thank you."

"But my point is, circumstance kept these couples apart. War, oceans, vast uncontrollable things. Fenton lived only a day or two distant from my father's estate for eight months out of each year. During the Season, I resided twenty minutes away from his residence. I *saw* him from time to time, for heaven's sake. What was I supposed to conclude, then, when year after year, especially when my friends began to talk of beaux and courting and receiving flowers, I heard nothing?"

"What *did* you conclude?" he queried after a moment.

He'd broken his vow of silence, but it was a pertinent question.

"I thought he was being forced to marry me. I thought perhaps he had another love, or that he'd seen me when I saw him and he found me utterly . . . lacking."

"Cam—"

"Hush."

"Oh. I apologize. Go on."

"And then because I was young and much more naïve, I began to make excuses for him. I decided he was shy and awkward. I thought he must have had no experience with women or courting and didn't realize he was to send flowers and write letters. Then I had the thought that he was overwhelmed by my . . . splendor and simply didn't feel as though he was worthy of my hand."

She glanced at Keating, but if he was amused, he didn't show it. No one had ever heard any of this before, because she'd never said it aloud. Not even to Sophia. It still surprised her that she'd been so stupid such a short time ago. Over the past year she'd heard, seen, and learned lessons she'd hadn't even known existed.

"Finally, I thought he must have been planning something at the church. A hundred hundred roses, or a gift for me to wear during the ceremony. And so I walked through the church doors with my father beside me, and there was nothing. No flowers, the smallest number of witnesses possible, no ribbons on the coach waiting outside. And when I caught sight of him . . . he was looking at his pocket watch. As though he had somewhere he'd rather be."

Keating bent his arm, offering it to her. Almost without thinking she wrapped her fingers around his sleeve.

"Do you know what it's like, to have your every dream and imagining simply . . . die all at the same time? To realize that whatever romantic idea you had of the person with whom you're meant to spend the remainder of your life was wrong? I had this odd sensation that if I took one more step into that church, I would expire. There, on the floor."

Without warning he pushed her sideways, behind the high wall bordering Clemency House. As she stumbled, he took her arm and caught her up against the bricks. And then he kissed her.

Heat speared through her at the soft, firm touch of his mouth against hers. Closing her eyes, she tangled her fingers into his deep chocolate hair. This was what it was like to be wanted. This was what she'd craved—continued to crave, actually—from a man who'd had more cause to ingratiate himself with her than any other. Fenton had failed utterly. His cousin, however . . .

Straightening, Keating cupped both sides of her face. An intense, almost fierce expression on his face, he leaned in again. Hunger, yearning, need—it was as if her body had suddenly discovered a new recipe it now required in order to survive, and Keating Blackwood was the only one who knew the ingredients. And he tasted delicious.

A carriage rattled down the street just out of sight, and Camille jumped. Shattered reputation or not, her circumstances could always be worse. And so, even though she wanted to tangle herself into Keating and never let go, she pushed against his chest. His grip on her loosened a breath, and she looked intently into his eyes.

"What was that for?" she asked, panting.

He lifted an eyebrow, reaching out to straighten her sleeve—or to run his fingers along the skin of her arm. She couldn't be certain which it was, but it made her shiver.

"Speak," she ordered.

"I'm commiserating."

"Ah. I see. You're a *very* good commiserator, then." So good that if not for that carriage she would likely be naked by now.

Keating inclined his head. "Thank you. And I apologize. You have enough apples in your cart without adding my rotten fruit."

She didn't want him to apologize for delivering the finest kiss in her entire life. "I have a question."

"Ask away, my dear."

For someone who considered herself a coward, Camille felt surprisingly calm as she held his gaze. At the same time, she doubted there was anyone else in the world with whom she could be having this conversation. With whom she would want to have this conversation. "Would *you* marry Stephen Pollard if you were me?"

He cleared his throat. "That isn't what I thought you would ask. And I can't give you an honest answer, because I have ten thousand pounds at stake."

"And yet, I think you just did give me an honest answer." And he'd given her a great many things to think about. "You are a very unusual man, Keating Blackwood."

A slow smile curved his mouth. "Considering what I would want of you if I could have my way, Cammy, that is a very nice thing to say."

She could imagine to what he must be referring. Keating wanted her. Even with ten thousand pounds at stake. And this little play had just become a completely new degree of interesting. Sooner rather than later, she would have to decide whether she meant to remain a coward. And whether she could tolerate being a pariah for the rest of her life. And whether she wanted back into Society more than she wanted . . . more than she wanted Keating Blackwood.

Chapter Eleven

What the devil was he doing? If he didn't pull himself back every other minute, Keating couldn't seem to stop flirting with, touching, or kissing Camille.

At first glance he'd put it to novelty and curiosity; after all, he had never been well acquainted with shy, virginal, overly cautious females. But the better he came to know her, the more he liked her contemplative manner, and her surprise and pride when she stepped beyond the protective shell she'd built around herself.

All this, even when they both knew precisely why he was there. Well, she didn't know precisely, because he hadn't mentioned the part about Fenton wanting her humbled and grateful. He hadn't heretofore been attempting to tear down her remaining resolve. Nor would he do so. He cleared his throat. "Perhaps we should exit the shrubbery."

"You're the one who dragged us into it," she commented with a half grin, taking his hand for balance as she stepped over some low irises.

At least she wasn't sad and miserable, as she had been when he'd spied her in The Tantalus Club garden. If he said so himself, she seemed to smile much more often now than she had when he'd first set eyes on her. If any part of that was due to him, well, it was likely the best deed he'd ever done.

What he needed to keep in mind, though, was that Fenton had given him the opportunity to do another good deed. "What would you think," he began slowly, "of my arranging for you and me and Fenton to have luncheon together somewhere?"

Her fingers in his clenched. "I won't make an appearance so he can take another opportunity to insult and ridicule me."

Keating stopped, his attention arrested and an abrupt anger shooting down his spine. "What do you mean, 'another' opportunity?"

"Nothing. I . . . I could hardly blame him for it. I was thinking the same thing myself."

"No. You've mentioned it, so you must tell me. Those are the rules."

"Is that so?"

"Camille."

She sighed audibly. "Don't think I haven't noticed that you make up a new rule every time you please, and that they never apply to you." With a sideways glare she shifted her fingers from his hand to his arm. "Two days after my parents closed their door on me, I hadn't yet run across the farmer who drove me to my aunt's. I was hungry and had a penny, so I went into a bakery for some bread. When I emerged, Fenton was in his phaeton passing down the street. He said an unpleasant thing or two. That's all."

"What unpleasant thing?" Keating insisted. Fenton had never mentioned this, of course—likely because he didn't show well. The marquis, as he frequently used to insist, was perfect.

"He called me a whore and an ingrate who deserved to remain on the streets until I died." She took another breath. "That's all I recall of the encounter. I began running, so if there was anything at the end, I might not have heard it."

Clenching his jaw, Keating nodded. "You know, I think he said very nearly the same thing to me after Balthrow. He dislikes being embarrassed; I believe his sense of pride outweighs his spleen."

"I did embarrass him. But I won't be embarrassed *by* him ever again."

"If I could guarantee that wouldn't happen, would you consider luncheon?" Keating repeated, vowing to himself that he would damned well see to it that Fenton never said anything like that to her again. If his cousin wouldn't give his word, well, the marquis would have to manage without teeth for the remainder of his life. "Just consider; I haven't reserved a table yet or anything."

"If you were there, I would consider it," she said in a tight voice. "And if I could leave whenever I chose, and if it wasn't terribly public, but public enough that everyone would have to behave themselves."

For a theoretical meeting, that seemed fairly well thought out. Keating nodded. "I'll see what I can do. If he won't agree to all of those conditions, then it won't happen."

"And you'll be out ten thousand pounds. That hardly seems fair."

He grinned at that. "Thank you for thinking of my plight, but you're my friend. I'll see that he behaves himself."

"If you continue saying nice things like that, I'll wish to kiss you again." Camille released his arm as they reached the safety of the large garden he'd begun to consider her private sanctuary.

"Well, you can't. That was a mistake." And if he kissed

her again, he wouldn't wish to stop there. There was only so much temptation someone with no self-discipline could manage.

"A several-times-repeated mistake, Mr. Blackwood."

"I'm a slow learner."

She snorted. "You are not. And I'm beginning to wonder something."

"What might that be?"

Her cheeks darkened, then paled. "I need to consider it a bit more before I say anything aloud. I apologize for no longer being impulsive."

"For the last damned time, Cammy, running from that church might have been impulsive, but your conclusion to do so was certainly justified. Even well considered. I'd have run, too."

"But you want me to have luncheon with him."

Actually, it hadn't seemed a good idea to begin with, and with every moment that passed he liked it less. "If this is about a second chance for a more comfortable life, I suppose he deserves another opportunity as well."

Sky blue eyes searched his. "I cannot figure you out."

"It's not so difficult. I'm a former hedonist whose recklessness caught up to him. I'm a sad sack full of regrets and too much whiskey." He held her gaze. "And you would seem to be my last hope."

Those lovely eyes narrowed. "And you were doing so well. I'm late; Lucille is entirely unqualified to seat gentlemen, as she tends to fall all over them."

Damnation. Keating caught her arm as she turned away. "I was attempting to be facetious."

"No you weren't."

"Very well, I meant it. But I also meant it when I said we were friends. I won't allow you to step into something that is not to your benefit. I swear that."

She faced him again. *"That,* I believe. Lead on, then. It seems I trust you." When she disappeared through the club's kitchen door, Keating sat on her abandoned stone bench and took a deep breath. Evidently and despite repeated reminders, he'd learned nothing over the past six years. Otherwise he wouldn't be kissing—or lusting after—the bride-to-be of his cousin. He lowered his head into his hands.

If she'd been a shrew or a self-absorbed ninny, this would have been so much easier. He'd never expected a charming, clever young woman whose largest fault was that she'd expected a romance and had decided—albeit foolishly—that she would be better served by fleeing anything less than perfection.

Keating straightened again. Perhaps his test was not whether he found her interesting and desirable and eminently bedable, but whether he acted on those sharp-edged desires. Which he wouldn't, because he had a child who needed a roof, a decent education, and a chance at a comfortable life. That had to be more important than whatever he wanted for himself.

It seems I trust you. The best and worst thing she could possibly have said to him, bloody chit. Shaking his head as much out of annoyance as to clear it of the rose-scented memory of kissing her, he stood and returned to collect Amble from the front drive. Now all he needed to do was convince Stephen to have luncheon with her, and the paving stones of this path would be all set out. As for him, if he could manage to keep his mouth and other, currently uncomfortable body parts to himself, he could very nearly touch success. And he refused to think of anything else. Of other opportunities he might very well be watching pass by.

* * *

Eleanor Howard, Lady Balthrow, sat down with her cup of tea and pulled the three-day-old London newspaper over in front of her. Reading it had been much more amusing six years ago when she'd been personally acquainted with most of the persons mentioned in the Society pages, but from time to time the exploits of some debauched lordling or other still made her giggle.

As she opened the newspaper her gaze immediately dropped to the second article on the page. "Several wagers set at White's were lost today when Mr. Keating Blackwood proved to be alive and emerged from the wilds to step back into the London Season's maelstrom. The infamous Bloody Blackwood is said to be lodging with the Duke of Greaves, and has already been seen several times with a particular lady sporting her own scandalous reputation."

Finishing the paragraph, Eleanor sat back. Then she lurched to her feet and sped out of the small breakfast room. "Moleaux!" she called. "Sally! Pack my things at once!"

The butler appeared from down the hallway. "My lady?"

"Have my travel chest brought down, and hire me a coach. I need to travel to London without delay!"

"Is something amiss, my lady?" the butler asked in his heavy French accent, even as he summoned the pair of footmen.

"Very much so. I am in danger of being forgotten!"

Keating Blackwood in Shropshire was one thing. Putting him back in London with so many distractions and so many other ladies no doubt eager to share his bed—that would never do. Not for her continued income, and not for what remained of her reputation. And certainly not for her future.

He needed to keep in mind what he'd done, not go about spending his blunt on wagering and drink and women. And he couldn't be allowed to find something as ill-fitting as peace—not when she had none. Above all, he needed to be reminded of his obligations. The sooner, the better.

"You wanted to meet at the Society Club so I would be forced to keep my voice down, didn't you?" Fenton asked, walking over to the nearest bookshelf in Greaves's library and running a finger along the tomes.

Keating didn't know whether he was reading the titles or checking for dust. "Perhaps I wanted you to purchase me a meal. I'm completely to let, if you'll recall."

"I recall. And I came here instead because I don't wish to be seen in public with you. The fewer people who know we're related, the better."

"That might be a bit of a problem."

Stephen faced him. "Why is that?"

"Because I'd like you to join me for luncheon tomorrow. I've invited Lady Camille and one of her friends to dine with us."

For a moment he wasn't certain whether the marquis would hit him, or simply stomp out the door. The former would be exceedingly unwise, but the second would cause him even more trouble. Finally Fenton turned away again. "I'll presume that's your idea of a jest. It isn't amusing."

"I'm not jesting. How do you expect the chit to change her mind about marrying you if you can't demonstrate that you're no longer an ice-hearted ass?"

"I am not the one who needs to alter my character."

Movement in the room's doorway caught his eye, but when he looked directly, no one was there. Still, he would guess that Greaves was close by. If so, then anything the duke heard would be Fenton's fault, and that suited him just fine. He'd been wanting to talk to Adam about his . . . circumstances for a fortnight, and the only thing stopping him had been the idea that if he broke his word to his cousin it would be the last straw and the devil would rise to claim him without any further delay.

"I repeat, if she doesn't think anything's changed, then she has no reason to change her mind. Be logical at least, Stephen."

The marquis blew out his breath. "Somewhere outside of Mayfair, then. The rumor should be that she returned to me, not that I reconciled with her."

"I can't control the tongue-wagging, but I'll hire a private room at an inn on the outskirts of Town. And you will be as polite and charming as you can possibly manage."

"And I suppose you've suggested that she be humble and agreeable in return?"

Anger pushed at Keating, and he shifted his seat in the library's most comfortable chair. "Are you the least bit interested in her actual character, or merely the one you'd like her to have?"

"Don't be a hypocrite. You're instructing me to be other than who I generally am—according to you, at least." Fenton took a book from a shelf, paged through it, and set it back again. Not enough drawings, most likely. "This had best be worth my time."

"If you bother to pay attention and learn how to deal with her, it will be."

Finally the marquis faced him again. "Your task is only to get her into the church. And watch your tongue. I've been tolerant of your . . . methods to this point, but I am not one of your drunk, fist-wielding, sycophantic cronies."

"I don't have any cronies, boot-licking or otherwise.

Now go away, and I'll send you a note with the address of the inn. Pray don't be tardy."

"I won't be." Fenton, looking relieved that the conversation was finished, headed for the door.

"One more thing," Keating said, inwardly wincing.

His cousin paused in the doorway. "What might that be, Keating?"

"If she mentions flowers or bouquets or birthday sentiments, simply tell her that it was your pleasure, and sorely overdue."

"What?" The marquis strode back into the room again. "I told you that I would not send her posies or any other gift to excuse or forgive her abysmal behavior."

"Too late. You've sent her several bouquets. Not overly sentimental, but thoughtful. As if you truly wish to have an amiable friendship with your would-be bride. *If* you wish her to be your bride."

"Do not go behind my back again, Keating." Fenton jabbed a finger in his direction. "If you do, then our deal is finished with."

"Yes, my lord."

"Bah." The marquis stomped down the Baswich House hallway and out the front door.

"Well, that sounded pleasant."

Keating didn't look up. "I thought that was you skulking by the door."

"I'm a duke. I don't skulk; I strategically overhear." Greaves walked past the chair and over to the liquor tantalus. "I'd offer you a whiskey, but you look too much as though you'd take me up on it."

"I likely would."

"So if I heard this correctly, I now have official confirmation that you've made an agreement with Fenton to sway Lady Camille back into a wedding on his behalf."

"Did I? You didn't hear it from me."

"Mm-hm. He seems serious about it, the way he kept threatening you if you didn't succeed."

"I believe he's tired of being laughed at. He never could tolerate that sort of thing. And he knows I need the blunt." Fenton didn't know why, of course, and he never would.

"But he doesn't know that you have a certain fondness for the lady."

"What does that have to do with anything?"

For a moment he hoped Greaves would have the answer to that question, because he'd been asking it of himself almost since the moment he set eyes on the fair-haired conundrum. Might-have-beens and should-have-beens weren't for men who'd dealt with life as he had, but it didn't stop him from dreaming about them, damn it all.

"I'm glad I'm not you, my friend."

"Now I'm jealous. I wish I wasn't me myself. It hasn't helped." He stood and went to go search out a promising inn where they would have enough privacy to be seen together, and enough of an audience that everyone would have to behave him and herself.

After Keating left the house, Adam Baswich finished off the whiskey he'd poured and then called for his own horse. He had more pieces to the puzzle, but a few of the bits didn't quite seem to fit together. And he disliked things that didn't make sense. Especially when they concerned friends of his.

"Thank you so much for doing this, Sophia."

Camille's friend shrugged. "You couldn't very well take Lucille with you. She'd either flirt with Fenton until he fled, or faint at being in the company of lords and rogues." With the flash of a grin she nudged Camille in the shoulder. "I know you won't flirt with him."

"No, I won't. I may faint, however." She felt sick to her stomach as it was. Even her hands felt sweaty, and that certainly wasn't due to the idea that she would be seeing Keating in a very few minutes. Not this time, anyway.

"You don't have to go."

"Yes I do. I gave my word. And I prefer knowing the facts to hearing the rumors, even from Keating. If Fenton has become more . . . warm, then I want to know it."

"So you truly would consider marrying him, even after all this?"

"That, I don't know about." She didn't even want to think about it. This was about having luncheon. Nothing more. It had to be that way, because if she even thought too closely about what was to come this afternoon, she would drop dead from an apoplexy.

The club's foyer cleared a bit, and she and Sophia made their way out the front door and onto the drive. "Answer me this, then," Sophia commented, adjusting her wrap and for the first time looking a little ill at ease. "What do you mean to do with Keating?"

"Do with him?" Camille repeated, scowling. "Nothing. What do you mean by that?"

"I mean I've seen you look at him. You like him."

"Of course I like him. He's proven to be much more tolerable than I first expected."

"Fine. Keep your own counsel. May I flirt with him, though, if you're to marry the man who called you a whore?"

Thankfully Keating and his borrowed barouche arrived before she could answer that. Because she didn't want Sophia to flirt with Keating. She didn't even like when any other female *looked* at him—and that happened at every other moment when she ventured off the club's grounds with him. At least she wasn't the only one

who knew of his reputation and still found him attractive,
though she didn't know how many other women might be
kissing him on a nearly daily basis.

An uncomfortable peach pit lurched around in her
stomach at the thought. Oh, for heaven's sake. If there
was a worse man to feel jealous over than Keating Blackwood, she'd never heard of him. And if she felt like this
because he was simply the one man—aside from the very
married Lord Haybury—who'd been kind to her in the
past year, then she was a fool.

"Good afternoon, my dears," he said, standing to hand
them into the open vehicle. "Did you notice that you've
made me the envy of everyone at The Tantalus Club?"

She glanced over her shoulder to see the dozen or so
men in the process of entering or leaving the club all looking in their direction. In the past she would have been
mortified, but it abruptly occurred to her that Keating was
correct. Whether these men dared to be seen in public
with her or not, they envied Keating for doing so. They
wanted her company—for something nefarious, no doubt,
but it was an eye-opening realization, nonetheless.

"Perhaps I should have mentioned," Keating murmured
as he helped her sit beside Sophia, "there is a certain . . .
allure to being notorious. Not always, but there are moments when one realizes that there is a freedom to having
no boundaries. Or in being seen that way, at least."

"I believe the 'freedom,' as you call it," she countered,
"only occurs when one isn't attempting to do anything
within Society."

"True enough." He tightened his grip on her fingers,
then released her hand as the barouche rolled into the
street. "Thank you for trusting me today."

"I'm attempting not to think about where I'm going,
thank you very much." She shivered, then resolutely set

her gaze on the scenery and attempted to concentrate on the latest fashion in hats.

"Am I to be silent and polite?" Sophia asked, patting Camille's knee. "Because I shall volunteer to punch Lord Fenton in the nose if the opportunity arises."

"You'll be behind me in the queue, Sophia," Keating returned, a smile in his voice.

Camille looked back at him. "Are you going to tell me whether this was his idea or yours?"

"He wants an opportunity to chat with you. I've been put in command of arranging the details. The matchmaking liaison, I suppose."

"You're very masculine for a matchmaker." Sophia giggled.

"Thank you for noticing. And Cammy, he will behave himself. If he doesn't, he'll answer to me."

Yes, to the man who stood to make ten thousand pounds if the match—or rematch, rather—was successful. If anyone had divided loyalties, it would be Keating. Even so, to this point he'd been honest and forthright with her. And blasted charming and intriguing and eminently kissable. She sighed, irritated that she couldn't put the heat and allure of him out of her mind.

"A penny for your thoughts," he said, treading on the tail end of them.

She narrowed her eyes. "I was just thinking that your methods of matchmaking would leave most mamas horribly scandalized."

His expression darkened. "Put that to my weakness and general lack of good character. If my poor behavior offends you, I shall attempt to restrain myself."

Oh, she didn't want that, either. In front of Sophia, however, she wasn't about to tell him that she very much wanted his kisses and caresses to continue. Of course if—*if*—she and Fenton reconciled, the kisses would have to stop. That shouldn't even be figuring into her equations for her future. But it was. She decided not to reply; there didn't seem to be a good response. He could make of that whatever he wished.

It only took a few minutes before she realized they weren't going anywhere in Mayfair. "So it's to be Cheapside, is it?" she muttered, curling her fingers into a fist. "Or perhaps Charing Cross?"

"No. The Mug and Pipe just to the north of Town. No one who knows either of you to gawp and gossip, hopefully." Keating sat forward, taking her hand and uncurling her fingers one by one. "This is a second chance, Camille. Nothing more, nothing less. If it pleases you, take it. If not, pass it by."

"And you'll stop your matchmaking, just like that?" She snapped the fingers of her free hand.

A muscle in his jaw jumped. "I don't know."

"I see. Then I still thank you for making this attempt on my behalf, but stop pretending that you're merely the Samaritan of happy matches."

He released her and sat back again. "Very well."

Sophia looked from one of them to the other. "Did I miss something?"

She'd missed ten thousand somethings, but Camille didn't feel inclined to tell her. That would mean admitting that she'd been duped from the beginning, and that she was now an idiot for trusting him when she knew he had ulterior motives. "Suffice it to say," she commented after a moment, "that Keating isn't quite the neutral party."

"Well, neither am I." Sophia scooted closer to Camille. "I side with you, my friend."

"You—" Keating snapped his mouth closed. "I am not accustomed to being the voice of reason. Clearly I'm not very proficient at it, but just . . . don't make up your mind until after luncheon. Please."

For a moment she heard the desperation in his voice, and it made her stop the retort she'd conjured. Clearly he didn't care overly much for his cousin, and in a sense he was as trapped in this mire as she was. Ten thousand pounds was a fortune, and she had no idea how truly badly he might need the money. "I gave you my word that I would come with you today," she said stiffly. "I didn't do so lightly."

He nodded. "That will suffice."

They sat in silence for the next twenty minutes. That gave Camille enough time to decide that she likely should have waited until after she returned to The Tantalus Club to begin a fight with Keating, because when she wasn't bantering with him she had far too much time to think about what would happen when she walked into the inn.

Would Lord Fenton be pleased to see that she'd kept her word about sitting down with him? Would he take the opportunity to lash out at her again? Would he be as cold and distant as she'd known him to be even from the far side of the church aisle? Would he look at his pocket watch?

She sent a sideways glance at Keating, who sat with his arms crossed, his gaze fixed on the opposite view from her own. The question that pressed at her most, even angry with him as she attempted to be, was what would happen if Fenton was perfectly pleasant. Camille took a breath. One blasted disaster at a time.

Chapter Twelve

Despite her stated resolve to go forward with this meeting, Keating kept an eye on Camille as they left the barouche and walked into the small inn. It had taken years of disinterest on Fenton's part to cause her finally to flee once, but it would only take a misspoken word or—God forbid—a single check of a gold-inlaid pocket watch to send her out the door a second time. Hopefully Fenton was aware of how thin the ice was, and hopefully he would at least make a minimum effort to be polite and politic.

Sophia edged closer to him as the proprietor showed them past the crowded common room and into a private sitting room at the back of the wood and stone building. "Are you two fighting?"

"Evidently," he muttered back, watching Camille's spine stiffen as they all caught sight of the lone figure seated before the fireplace. "If being angry with me lends her courage, well, my hide is thick enough to withstand it."

"Just remember that you promised to keep her safe. And that a large part of Cammy is her heart."

He glanced sideways, attempting to reconcile Sophia White's sudden thoughtfulness and insight with her general effervescent humor. "Don't bother pretending to be silly and frivolous with me any longer," he whispered, "because I shan't believe you."

"We all do what is necessary to survive, Mr. Blackwood."

While he digested that further bit of wisdom, Camille stopped a few feet into the room. *Get up*, he silently urged Fenton, doing his damnedest to shout at his cousin without making a sound. Finally the marquis stood. "Lady Camille," he drawled.

Camille inclined her head. "Lord Fenton."

That looked to be the end of their conversation. Before the silence could deafen the lot of them, Keating ordered a whole pheasant from the curious innkeeper and closed the door on the man's face. "Stephen, this is Miss White. Sophia, Lord Fenton." He pushed past Camille and took a seat at the long table. "I hope you requested a good wine, Fenton."

His cousin stirred, then slowly approached the table. "French and red."

"Excellent. Now for God's sake, everyone sit down. Fenton, was that a new pair I saw pulling your coach outside?"

"Yes. I'm partial to bays. They're called Achilles and Ajax, and according to the breeder, they're half brothers."

"They're well matched," Keating returned, shifting a little so Camille could sit beside him. Sophia took a seat on his left. Fenton likely wouldn't appreciate being glared at by a trio of unacceptable persons, but with no witnesses, hopefully the stiff-spined marquis would tolerate it.

"I wouldn't have purchased them, otherwise."

Keating mostly refrained from rolling his eyes. Just when he'd become the levelheaded arbiter of cordiality for the outing he had no idea, but he felt supremely unsuited for the position. "Stephen, tell us about Fenton Hall. I know it used to have good fishing in the pond there, but I haven't visited the grounds in some time."

"I would rather hear Lady Camille explain her actions over the past year, beginning with her embarrassing performance at the church."

Even though they weren't touching, Keating could feel Camille stiffen beside him. From someone as socially obtuse as Fenton was, it was likely a reasonable, honest question, but Fenton was supposed to have been pretending to have a heart. "I thought we might begin a bit more slowly than that," he said aloud.

Thankfully the innkeeper and two serving maids reappeared before anyone could say anything too damaging. He poured the wine himself, reluctantly dismissing the trio of witnesses. For a long moment he eyed the slowly swirling ruby liquid in his glass, then he downed the lot of it. Anything to dull the sharp edges of his temper for today.

"First I suppose I should thank you for the flowers," Camille said unexpectedly. "I'm very fond of lilies."

Keating flinched. *Roses*. They'd been roses.

"Yes, well, I suppose I might have paid you a bit more attention over the years," Fenton grumbled with clear reluctance.

If she'd discovered the ruse, Camille gave no sign of it. "And I might have sent you a letter or two myself, instead of waiting for you to begin a correspondence."

Fenton set down his glass of wine. "Excuse me, but are you saying that you refused to marry me because I failed to correspond with a female I had no need to woo or flatter or otherwise coerce into marriage?"

"Stephen, we're commiserating here. Don't lose the trail," Keating put in, swearing inwardly.

"I know if I had a husband-in-waiting," Sophia said, as she finished a bite of pheasant, "I would hope he considered me to be more than a piece of furniture. A kind word or a smile or a *rose* over fifteen or twenty years isn't too much to expect, I don't think. A measure of human kindness, I mean."

"And who the devil are you? Sophia what?" Fenton demanded, his face darkening.

"Sophia White," Sophia said very distinctly. "I'm employed with Cammy at The Tantalus Club."

"White." Blinking, Fenton lurched to his feet. "You're Hennessy's by-blow. For God's sake, Keating, what the devil are you attempting to do? I've told you countless times that I won't be subjected to your penchant to associate with degenerates and dishonorables."

"Sit down, Stephen." No longer amused, Keating slammed his hand onto the wooden tabletop. "None of us are saints or angels, or we wouldn't be here. You're at fault in this as well, and the sooner you loosen your spine, the sooner you'll find yourself where you wish to be."

The marquis sat again. "If anyone outside that door recognized me, I'll never live this down. You'd best pray you managed to find the most discreet establishment in England."

"I pray for other things, but I take your point." Keating refilled his glass and emptied it again. "You're angry and embarrassed that you were left standing with a priest and no bride. Camille is worried that she'd been doomed to a life with a cold, uncaring boor. Sophia, well, Sophia is here because I asked her to join us. Don't insult her again." He banged his fist on the table a second time. "Now. Stephen, do you enjoy riding or walking out of doors?"

Silence. Then his cousin slowly lifted his fork again.

"Yes. I enjoy a bit of exercise. And I like fox hunting, especially."

"Camille," Keating pursued, wondering if he would next be forced to wear a judge's white wig, "do you enjoy a walk or a ride out of doors?"

"I quite enjoy either. I miss being able to do so."

"Fenton. Your favorite poet."

"William Browne." The marquis took a breath. " 'Now as an angler melancholy standing / Upon a green bank yielding room for landing, / A wriggling yellow worm thrust on his hook, / Now in the midst he throws, then in a nook.' "

Oh, grand, a fishing poem. "Very nice," Keating said aloud. "Camille, same question. Favorite poet."

"Lord Byron," she answered without hesitation, a touch of defiance in her voice. " 'In secret we met / In silence I grieve, / That thy heart could forget, / Thy spirit deceive.' "

"So we're engaged in dueling quatrains now? At least this is more entertaining." Despite the unhealthy urge to grin at the way Camille had just demonstrated the very great difference between the potential bride and groom, Keating ventured a bite of pheasant. "Very well. Shakespeare. Favorite play, Stephen."

"King Lear."

"A Midsummer Night's Dream," Camille put in.

This likely wasn't going to help them to get along, but they were becoming better acquainted—whether they realized it or not. At the same time it struck him that she'd named the very play he'd attended with her. He just barely refrained from looking over at her. "Gemstone," he continued aloud, attempting to keep the luncheon from running into the hedgerow.

"Diamond." Fenton actually offered a competitive nose flare as he sent a glare across the table at Camille.

"Sapphire."

"Favorite vehicle."

"Coach and four."

"High-perch phaeton," Camille contributed, and he began to wonder now if she was being intentionally difficult. Of course he could hardly blame her for that. Fenton was as warm as a fish.

"Dance."

"The waltz." Camille slipped in, before Stephen could comment. She lifted an eyebrow. "I don't like always being second."

Stephen looked directly at her. "I don't dance. And as I will be the head of household, you *will* be second." The marquis sent Keating a glance. "Which is still an improvement over being an employee at a gentlemen's club."

"And *I* would like to point out that *I* never signed any agreement to marry anyone, and to this point your efforts to convince me to wed you have been, well, nonexistent. Perhaps legally I am property, but I doubt you'll find any chairs that object to being pushed about and sat upon. And I am not a chair."

Keating pushed to his feet. "Camille, I had a question for you," he said over the rumbling beginning to emanate from his cousin's direction. "Excuse us for a moment." He pulled her to her feet by the arm and half lifted her over the bench.

Once he had her in the small cloakroom dividing the private room from the rest of the inn, he let her go. "Where the devil did that come from?"

She lifted her chin. "I don't know. But I rather liked it."

So did Keating. In her presence now, he practically vibrated like a mandolin string. "He would prefer you cowed, you know," he pushed, attempting to stay on the road, "and while thoughtful sangfroid would do fine for me, I don't think insults and defiance will serve anything."

Her face folded into a scowl. "Yes, you're correct. Of course. But he's making me angry. Could he possibly be more stodgy and arrogant?"

"Not even if he tried," Keating conceded. "Think about what he offers your life, rather than how dull he is."

Camille looked toward the closed door. "I will attempt that," she said after a moment. "But first I think you should kiss me."

"Wh . . . what?"

Taking a step closer to him in the small room, she slid both hands up his shoulders. "Sophia reminded me of something. I am a ruined woman. Short of running naked through Mayfair, my reputation couldn't be much worse than it is. And yet here I stand, in your odd version of negotiations for a proper marriage. What do I have to lose?"

He could think of several things, but the twitch of his cock rendered them insensible. "I'm no good for you," he said, his mouth dry.

"I don't want you to be good for me. I would like to kiss you." Her long eyelashes lowered briefly. "If you would like to kiss me, that is."

If. Keating swept his arms around her waist, lifting her against him. At the same moment he captured her mouth with his. The softness of her lips, the eagerness of her embrace, intoxicated him the way no amount of whiskey had ever managed. She wrapped an ankle around the back of his calf, and he just barely managed to stifle his groan.

Good God. This was the man he used to be. The one who seduced other men's women in closets. Taking an unsteady breath, he set her back on her feet. "Stop it," he rasped, retreating as far as he could in the tiny room. "My cousin is fifteen feet away. I won't do this again."

"Again? What . . . Oh." Her flushed cheeks paled. "You mean because of Lord Balthrow." She closed on him again.

Keating put a hand out, holding her at arm's length. It wasn't nearly enough, but he couldn't exactly flee the premises. "Give me a damned minute, will you?"

Thankfully she halted, and in fact took a step back to lean against the far wall. Despite the solemn expression on her face, he could swear that her eyes were smiling. "You like me," she finally said.

"Of course I like you. Not at this moment, but yes. If I didn't, I would have bullied or frightened you into being here today."

"But I would still be here." Her eyes weren't smiling any longer.

"Yes, you would."

"Because you need ten thousand pounds."

"Because I need ten thousand pounds, and because you would be happier being able to go for walks without people looking askance at you, and because you like to waltz. With Fenton, annoying as he is, you would have that again. *That* is what this should be about for you. You'll find happiness in being comfortable."

"But not love."

He shrugged; the blood seemed to be slowly returning to his brain. "Love is more dramatic, I'm certain, but being comfortable will last you longer."

"I don't know about that." Camille tilted her head. "Have you recovered your . . . comfort?"

Now *that* was a complicated question. "At times." He felt comfortable in his own skin more often since he'd returned to London, and he thought he knew why, but he didn't intend to dwell on that fact. Not at the moment, and not in this company. "Now, give me your word that you'll be polite."

"For you, I'll be polite. Not for him."

That shook him even more than the kiss, but he nodded. "I'll accept that. And when I ask what your favorite treat might be, say sugared orange peels. Then at least you'll have something in common."

Her nose wrinkled attractively. "At least I've discovered one thing about Lord Fenton."

"And what might that be?"

"He's not as intimidating as I thought he was. I don't seem to be afraid of him."

Before she could pull open the door, he caught her shoulder. "You were afraid of him?" That would change the situation considerably; ten thousand pounds or not, Fenton was not permitted to harm her in any way.

"I'm afraid of everything. But I think I was afraid of the idea of him. After all, this is the first semicordial conversation with him I've ever had. Actually, it's the first conversation at all."

The matter-of-fact way she announced her uneasiness made him gaze at her as they returned to the stiff silence of the private room. Yes, she could be timid, but for God's sake, she kissed with a passion that stunned him. She saw herself, though, as a coward. Considering that the second day they'd met she'd clubbed him with a book, this fear didn't seem to extend to him. And he was glad about that—even though her fear or antipathy or even caution where he was concerned would both have been much safer for her, and would have made things much easier for him.

Once they sat again, he poured himself another glass of wine. As accustomed as his body was to liquor he might as well have been drinking water, but he was quite aware that he was breaking his promise to himself. At the same time, without dulling his edges a bit he wasn't certain he would survive through the end of luncheon without pounding his fist against Stephen Pollard's face or stripping Camille naked and laying her on the long table.

Considering that Fenton was actually being more co-operative than he'd expected, he wasn't entirely certain where the rising anger in his chest came from. The longer the luncheon proceeded, however, the deeper it flowed through him. "Well," he said aloud, forcing his voice to remain cool and level, "we've established that you both enjoy the out-of-doors, Shakespeare, and reading. Not a bad beginning, I think. Perhaps we should conclude with a discussion of desserts or sweets. Stephen?"

"I enjoy sugared orange peels," the marquis said, finishing off his own glass of wine—his first, if Keating's count was correct.

"I recall. Camille?"

"Lemon syllabubs," she answered, swirling her own glass before she sent a furtive glance in Keating's direction. "Though sugared orange peels are quite good."

Difficult chit.

At the last moment he noticed Fenton stirring, reaching down to his waistcoat pocket. *Damnation.* Swiftly he pulled his own battered pocket watch free and clicked it open. "Well, my friends, I believe Lord Fenton has an afternoon session in Parliament. Perhaps we should set him free for today."

"Yes." Standing, Fenton actually inclined his head in

Camille's general direction. "Perhaps, given your enjoyment of the out-of-doors, we might arrange for a stroll. The four of us, of course."

Camille nodded. "I'll leave it to your discretion. Somewhere off the main path would be more welcome, I think."

"Indeed."

With that Keating offered Sophia his arm and ushered the two young ladies out through the main part of the inn and into their waiting barouche. "Lemon syllabub?" he said, once they were moving. "You did that on purpose."

"I agreed with his awful orange peels. I was merely indicating that I have other interests, as well."

As did he. "Fair enough. What did you think of him, then?"

"I think he's an overstuffed peacock, but don't mind me." Sophia laid her chin on her arm to look out over the lip of the carriage.

"I will concede that it must have been difficult for a man as proud as he is to agree to a meeting," Camille said quietly. "I'm somewhat surprised he hasn't simply publicly denounced me and found someone else to marry."

"He did denounce you publicly," Sophia countered. "You told me so."

"No, he called me names in public. In the heat of the moment, I presumed. That's hardly the same as making repeated accusations or going to court and having our parents' agreement dissolved." She frowned. "He must have been embarrassed when I left the church. I never actually thought of that before now. So I have to say that it speaks well of him that he's willing to make another attempt at all."

"I'm glad you're feeling more diplomatic," Keating commented, pleased that he'd asked Greaves for the loan of the open vehicle and much less happy at the pronouncement than he would have expected. A coach would have been too clandestine. And he felt grateful for the breeze cooling his heated skin.

"Don't tell me you're actually considering becoming proper again, Cammy." Sophia kept her gaze on the passing scenery. "We won't be able to be friends any longer."

"First of all, you will always be my friend, Sophia," Camille said forcefully. "And second of all, I'm not certain what I'm considering. I'm merely thinking aloud." She slid a glance at Keating. "You shouldn't have lied to me about the flowers."

"You shouldn't have been clever enough to quiz him about them," he retorted. "And I didn't lie about them. All I said was that I suggested he should send you bouquets. Which I did. You received them, and half the members of The Tantalus Club saw you receive them. If they all happen to believe the sender was the Marquis of Fenton, then it can only help your standing."

"That's a very thin truth, then. And I still would have liked to know they came from you, Keating. Even if you sent them on someone else's behalf." She folded her hands together on her lap. "Shall I guess why he refused to send them himself? He thought it would look too much like he was apologizing to me rather than the other way around. And you went ahead and sent them, anyway, without informing your cousin."

Evidently he had lost the ability to deceive anyone about anything. "You should have had flowers," he commented, and crossed his arms over his chest before he sent his own gaze outside the barouche. Let her say something slighting about that.

"Thank you for them. They were lovely."

Her voice was so quiet that for a moment he almost

thought he might have imagined it. Clenching his jaw, he inclined his head. "My pleasure."

"Sophia has expressed an interest in driving through Hampstead Heath. I wonder if you might escort us."

"Hampstead Heath? You know there are highwaymen there."

"It's supposed to be lovely. I was never allowed to drive through there before."

This didn't bode well. The idea behind convincing her to wed Fenton after all was that she longed to return to the arms of proper Society. Apparently, however, she abruptly seemed interested in stretching her wings and exploring the . . . scandalous side of life in Mayfair. Was that Sophia's influence? Or worse, was it his?

"I'll see if I can arrange something," he said aloud. Damnation, but he was becoming pitiful. Any excuse to spend more time with her—even if it meant fending off outlaws and cutthroats.

"I believe we can arrange to be free on Thursday."

Nodding, he sank back onto the plush leather seat again. He hadn't survived being a blackguard for as long as he had by being obtuse, and every sense he possessed bellowed that something was afoot. What it might be, though, he didn't know. Not yet, anyway. "I'll ask Fenton about his schedule, as well. I wouldn't recommend the Heath for a stroll, but perhaps one of the smaller parks. Or Primose Hill in Regent's Park."

"I'll leave it to you," Camille said.

He wanted to ask her what had happened, why she abruptly seemed so calm and confident when she'd been ready earlier to cast up her accounts at the mere idea of meeting face-to-face with the Marquis of Fenton. This . . . agreeable side of her should have been welcome, and he supposed it was, but it was also very odd. And suspicious.

If they'd been alone he would have pursued his questions. They weren't alone, however, and given the way he'd mauled her at the inn, that was more than likely for the best.

In fact, he should make certain he wasn't ever alone with her again. Fenton had become a visible part of the play now, and he wouldn't risk placing himself between two people who were all but married. Not even if he found Camille bloody attractive. Not even if he couldn't seem to sleep without dreaming of her light-colored hair and fair skin sprawled across his bedsheets. Especially not because of the unbearable, taunting . . . itch she'd begun beneath his skin.

"I'll send you a note when I have an answer," he said, standing as the barouche stopped directly in front of The Tantalus Club's front doors. Stepping down, he turned to offer his hand to the two ladies.

"Blackwood!"

Instinct made him drop his hand toward the knife in his boot even as he faced the low, booming voice. "Rendale."

The large, bear-shaped, bear-colored earl charged down the club's shallow steps in his direction. "You should not have come back!" the ursine snarled, cocking his fist.

"Get back in the barouche," Keating said over his shoulder and ducked the swing. At the same moment he twisted forward and lifted, hurling the behemoth over his shoulder and headfirst into the cobblestones.

A glance told him that both Camille and Sophia had complied, and they were standing with the sides of the carriage keeping them safe from any flinging fists. When Rendale rolled onto his knees and clambered to his feet again, Keating backed away a bit, putting a touch more distance between the fight and the women.

"You slept with my wife!"

"Did I? I don't recall. There were so many, though." Keating ducked another blow, and landed a lightning-fast punch on the earl's chin.

"I found the letters! Don't deny it!"

"I'm not denying anything. Perhaps you could describe her to me." Another punch, and then he flung all his weight, shoulder first, into Rendale's gut. The surge lifted the earl off his feet and put him down onto the ground again. A third punch bloodied and likely broke the man's nose.

"Keating, stop it," Camille hissed.

He straightened, stopping the next blow he'd been about to deliver. She had both hands to her mouth, her expression both mortified and horrified. "Whatever I did, Rendale," he panted, "it was seven years ago. And I apologize for it."

Lord Haybury and two of the club's large footmen charged out of the building and stepped between the two combatants. "As much as I enjoy a good fight," the marquis said in his usual deep, dry voice, "this is not the place for it. Rendale, you were on your way out. Pray continue. And Blackwood, deliver your companions and leave."

Generally being ordered to do something would only spark another brawl, but very aware of the chits behind him, Keating pulled his anger back in and nodded. "Of course."

"He didn't begin it, my lord," Camille said, leaving the barouche for the second time.

"Yes I did. It merely took him seven years to respond." Inclining his head, he stepped back into the carriage. "Good day, Lady Camille, Miss White. I'll send you word."

"I'll be waiting, Keating." Camille took a step back in

his direction. Back toward the chaos and infamy that he represented. That small movement nearly did him in, and he snapped at the driver to leave before he could do something even more foolish and kiss her. Because apparently even with the evidence of his past sins splattered on the ground around her feet, she still liked him. And that wasn't supposed to happen.

Chapter Thirteen

Camille didn't need to see Sophia attempting to catch her eye every three minutes to know that her friend wanted to speak with her. Since their return from luncheon Sophia had been attempting to arrange a moment in private, and Camille had spent the same amount of effort to avoid being anywhere alone with her dearest friend.

She wanted to think. And conversely for her, standing at her podium and seating gentlemen in the Demeter Room was the best time for her to take a minute for herself. After all, she need only smile and say something mildly flattering, and no one required anything more. And after Lord Haybury had ordered the two brawlers of earlier off the club's grounds, no one was likely to overtly insult her—or any of her friends—this evening.

"That's two fights you've witnessed since I've been here," Lucille whispered during a momentary lull. "Both involving your new friend. Does he scrap often?"

"Evidently," Camille replied, wishing Lucille hadn't made the same arrangement to trade with the evening greeter's assistant that Camille had with Patricia Cooper. The other girls might engage in chitchat, but Lucy's naïveté continued to rankle.

"I heard that during the last Ladies' Night here, they

opened a new page in the wagering book over who would bed him first. They have to supply proof of some sort. A ring of his, I think. Some of the ladies were writing down their own names. And then they started a second wager about who would be the one to shoot him. Now they'll have to change the odds on Lord Rendale, because he was only at eight-to-one before. I don't know if Bloody Blackwood would have to be killed or merely be wounded for anyone to win the wager."

"Lucille, do shut up," Camille snapped. Waving a hand at Jenny Martine standing toward the rear of the large dining room, she started in the coproprietress's direction.

"Is something amiss?" Genevieve asked in a quiet voice, her French accent somehow making her sound older than Camille knew her to be.

"I need a breath of air."

Jenny frowned, her light-colored brows dipping. "No."

"No?"

"We are a scandalous place, you have a scandalous reputation, and you have befriended a very scandalous man. Either change one—or all—of those things, or . . . make yourself a thicker skin, Cammy."

Camille blinked. In the past both Jenny and Diane had been so patient and understanding with her. What had happened? Or was it rather a question of *who* had happened? She'd become friends with Keating Blackwood, and now they'd decided she was simply asking for trouble. She gave a tight nod. "I understand."

Evidently even her new, more tolerant friends had limits to their patience and understanding. The realization was like another blow to her heart. And abruptly the idea of leaving The Tantalus Club and returning to Society didn't seem such a far-fetched or unreasonable one.

Before Camille reached her podium again, Sophia

swooped in to grab her arm and drag her through one of the private doorways. "I want to talk to you."

"I don't want to hear it." Camille rubbed her face, attempting to convince herself that the wetness on her palms was sweat rather than tears.

"Well, then, don't listen. I'm still going to talk."

"I need to return to my station, Sophia."

"While you were in the coatroom at the inn arguing with Keating, I kept an eye on Fenton, you know. He got up once to leave, then changed his mind and sat down again. Then he looked right at me and said, 'How many men has she taken to her bed? Not that I expect an honest answer from a duke's by-blow, but give me some idea.'"

Listening in spite of herself, Camille lowered her hands again. "And what did you say to that?"

"I said, 'If you think the answer is a number other than none, why are you sitting here speaking with her?' And he said, 'None of your damned business, except that I'm tired of the lot of you having a laugh at my expense. I didn't run from the church, and I've never received a note or a posy from her. And yet I'm the one who's been punished for it. She owes me a marriage.'"

"How has *he* been punished for it?" Camille asked, scowling. "While I concede that perhaps people laugh behind their hands at him—which *isn't* his fault—he's still invited to soirees and his friends still talk to him, and he hasn't been ordered to leave his home and been put out on the streets. I expected some sputtering, but it sounds as if he genuinely expects me to apologize to him."

"I don't think he considers his lack of . . . tenderheartedness to be a fault." Sophia leaned closer. "Nor does he expect that you'll return a virginal young miss."

"But I *am* a virginal young miss."

"A fact he will never believe, whatever you do."

Camille gazed at her friend. "And what is it you're suggesting I do? Sneak out of The Tantalus Club and go waylay Keating somewhere? That's what you're intimating, isn't it?" She attempted to sound offended and cynical all at the same time, but her heart had begun pounding so loudly she couldn't tell how well she'd managed that particular feat. Heat spun down her spine at the mere thought of putting her hands on his warm, bare skin.

"I meant to speak a bit more subtly than that. But you've caught onto my meaning, so I'll return to my duties." Mindful of Jenny's comments, Camille immediately returned to the Demeter Room, as well. She supposed that Sophia's suggestion should have shocked her, and would have shocked the young lady she'd been a year ago, but she'd been thinking endlessly about a naked Keating for better than a fortnight. Everyone—including Fenton— thought her ruined both socially and morally. Apparently in her would-be betrothed's mind he preferred that things look proper rather than actually be proper.

Whispering, muttering, giggling—it had all been flung in her direction for months, and she'd cringed every time. Every blasted time. At least people didn't come running out of the shrubbery to attack her like they did Keating, because she likely would have sunk into the earth rather than face the looks that would come after something like that.

He'd fought. He'd punched and torn a sleeve of his coat, and then he'd apologized to the man who'd attacked him. Impossible rogue or not, he seemed to genuinely regret what he'd done in the past, and she'd seen every indication that he meant not to repeat his mistakes. No one else seemed to believe that, if the wagers in the Ladies' Book here were any indication. At the least, the wager of who he would bed still remained open.

A small smile tugged at her mouth, and she flattened it again before anyone could notice. All the proper ladies who gathered at the club every other Tuesday night wagered over who Keating Blackwood would take to his bed. And these same ladies looked askance at her. Well, wouldn't it be amusing if *she* was the one he took to his bed, and none of them knew it? They could all pant after him, and she would know the truth of it.

His second chance and her second chance seemed very much at odds with each other. Damnation. Shaking herself, she attempted to attend to her duties and not end up stacking gentlemen ten deep at the same dining table. For the entire evening, however, all through the lull of the theater and then the renewed crowds directly afterward, she couldn't help thinking about where she wanted to go. With whom she wanted to be.

Finally Jenny nodded at her, and with a rehearsed smile she vanished through the private doors at the side of the club. Weariness and frustration pulled at her with equal strength. Considering that she had an early morning and her regular schedule ahead of her in a very few hours, logically she should retreat to her bedchamber and find some sleep. Not that that would be an easy task in itself.

"Did you see Lord Burkis tonight?" Sophia asked as Camille stepped into their darkened room and shut the door behind her. "He keeps offering to purchase me a small house in the country where he might come and call on me."

Camille made a face in the dark. "Oh, now I shall have nightmares."

Sophia chuckled, her bedsheets rustling as she turned onto her side. "It's especially amusing given how he pretended not to know me when I crossed paths with him on

Bond Street the other day. He nearly fell over a dog, he was trying so hard to avoid looking directly at me."

"And that doesn't bother you?"

"As I keep telling you, I've been notorious for my entire life. Everyone knows who my father is, even if Hennessy would never acknowledge me. And they all know who my mother is, because the duchess made such a show of sending her off to the country and then sacking her. None of it, however, is my fault. So yes, from time to time I very much wish to spit on people and demand that they look me in the eye for once, but my life isn't so terrible. Not any longer. I like it here."

"As do I, most of the time."

"No, you don't. You like having a roof and an income. That's different from looking forward to being in the room with all those handsome, wealthy men or happily chatting away with them even knowing they would cut you in public."

Camille sank down on the edge of her bed. "Yes, I suppose so."

"Lucky, then, that you have a way to reclaim your life. Do you mean to make use of it?"

"Of Fenton, you mean?" Gazing toward the curtained window, Camille slipped her toes in and out of her shoes. "He's . . . stuffy, and I certainly don't love him, but I suppose I need to decide whether that, when weighed against what he does have to offer, upsets the balance in his favor or not."

"You sound so logical."

"I'm attempting to be logical. To make a wiser decision, and a better thought-out one, this time. I seriously doubt I'll have a third opportunity to alter the course of my life."

"True enough. Just don't forget the details."

Camille looked over her shoulder at her friend. "Which details would those be?"

"Keating Blackwood." Sophia rolled over again, putting her back to Camille. "Now stop talking to me. All of your logic is going to give *me* nightmares."

"Very well. Good night, Sophia."

"Sweet dreams, Cammy."

Rather than remove her pretty mauve gown and climb into bed, Camille sat where she was for several long minutes. Once Sophia's breathing leveled out and a soft snoring began, she stood up again. Below them she could distantly hear the sounds of the club; after all, The Tantalus never closed its doors.

Slipping her feet back into her shoes, she pulled her gray wrap from the hook on the wall and left the room, shutting the door quietly behind her. A hard heartbeat shuddered through her. Swiftly she reminded herself that she wasn't up to anything. She felt restless, and it was chilly. If she decided to go out-of-doors, then she would do so.

Inside the common room Lily Banks lay curled up on the large, deep sofa beneath the window. Camille didn't know if that meant Lily's roommate Emily Portsman was entertaining a gentleman again, but it certainly wouldn't have been the first time. And she certainly didn't think any less of Emily for inviting a gentleman or two up to her bedchamber. Quite the opposite. Emily might never have left the club's grounds since she arrived, but at least she wasn't terrified of her own shadow.

She descended the back staircase and wandered into the kitchen. At this late—or rather, early—hour only one cook and two helpers were present, and with a nod she walked past them and out the rear entrance of the club. The predawn air had a heavy, damp chill to it, and she unfolded her wrap to cover her head and down past her shoulders.

An owl hooted, and she jumped a little. In the dark her sanctuary of the garden didn't seem quite so safe or comforting. The streets of Mayfair would be even less so—if she chose to stroll down one or other of them, that was. Skirting the carriage drive and stable yard, she stepped over the low stone wall that bordered the far edge of the garden and found herself alone on Vigo Street, around the corner from the club.

Well, not entirely alone. A smattering of carriages passed by, the coaches with their curtains tightly closed and a phaeton driven by a man who looked vaguely familiar and who stared at her until he was out of sight. She shivered again. This was a very poor idea for a large number of reasons, not the least of which was the fact that she'd been offered a second chance and this seemed to be the very best way to ruin it.

Another coach rattled by and she turned away, pretending to inspect a half-wilted rose dipping over someone's wall. Stupid, stupid, stupid. Under the best of circumstances she didn't want anyone—strangers or former friends—to see her where she couldn't swiftly vanish. And these were not the best of circumstances.

The coach that had passed her stopped, then made a wide turn to head back toward her again. *Oh, blast it.* Gathering her wrap more tightly around her, Camille stepped quickly back in the direction of Regent Street and The Tantalus Club drive.

When it drew even with her, the coach slowed to match her pace. She refused to look over, even at the sound of the door opening. Instead she sped her steps, sending up a prayer that she hadn't just made her worst and last mistake.

"Camille?"

The low drawl made her heart lurch in sudden relief, and she nearly stumbled. Stopping, she faced the large black vehicle. "Keating? What are you—"

He stepped out, grabbed her forearm, and half dragged her back inside with him. At some unseen signal the coach rumbled into motion again. "What the devil are you doing out on the streets at this hour?" he demanded. "It's dangerous."

She sank back onto the seat opposite him, far more relieved than she likely had a right to be. "What are *you* doing out here?"

"I asked first. Out with it."

"Very well." She swallowed. "I was contemplating paying you a visit." His light brown eyes, black in the dimness of the carriage, seemed to widen a touch. "Are you shocked?"

" 'Contemplating,' were you?" he repeated, leaning forward and lowering the wrap from around her ears. "You do that quite actively."

"I don't know quite how I ended up in that location. It . . . happened."

"And what would you have done next, in this contemplation of yours?"

"I think I might have hired a hack to take me to Baswich House. You said you were staying there, with the Duke of Greaves."

"I am, indeed." He tilted his head as if studying her, though she had no idea how much he thought he could see in the dark. "And once you reached Baswich House?"

Camille frowned. "I don't know. The butler would be asleep, I presume, and I certainly had no intention of sneaking in and peering into bedchambers until I found you. Heavens, what if I stumbled across the duke? That would have been—"

"Unacceptable," Keating interrupted, his voice unexpectedly harsh. "It would have been unacceptable."

"I was going to say that it would have been embarrassing, but as you will." She wrinkled her nose. "You smell of cigars."

"I was at the Society Club," he returned.

"That's nowhere near here."

"Isn't it? My driver must have become lost."

A smile touched her mouth. "You came by The Tantalus Club on purpose. Did you wish to see me?"

"Yes. But then I realized you would be to bed." He shifted a little. "I should return you there."

She heard the hesitation in his voice, and she knew immediately what it meant. He wanted her to stay. With him. It was an unexpectedly heady feeling, to be wanted. Desired. And considering how carnal her thoughts had been, it was also something of a relief. She doubted there could be anything worse than desiring someone who didn't want anything to do with you. "Now that I know your ruse, are you going to stop sending me birthday flowers every day?" she asked, even though that wasn't the question on her lips.

"I think I can manage five more bouquets, unless you wish me to stop."

Camille shook her head. "I don't. I like receiving flowers, even if you lied to me about sending them."

"I told you, I didn't lie. I skillfully evaded the question. And if Fenton hadn't been so shockingly obtuse, you never would have been the wiser."

"So you say. Don't you think it would have hurt matters if the flowers were what swayed me, and I found out at the very last moment that he never sent them?"

He scowled. "Stop being such a clever chit. It'll do you no good."

"Won't it?"

"No. It's far better to be mercenary than clever. Act for your own preservation rather than wasting your time deciphering everyone else's motivations."

She sighed, wishing she could simply sit and chat with him forever. Well, not just chat, but be there alone with him. The coach could go round and round London, stopping only for someone to fetch them some tea. "You sound so very cyni—"

He leaned forward, capturing her mouth with his. "I'm attempting to become a better man, you know," he muttered, yanking her forward across his thighs.

Heat spread through her like lightning. "That's very obvious to me," she said unsteadily, and tangled her fingers into his hair, drawing his face down to hers for another heady kiss.

"I swore I'd never step between a husband and his wife again. Ever." Warm fingers slid up from her hips, brushing the outside of her breasts and pulling her against his hard chest.

"You aren't."

"You're betrothed to my damned cousin, Cammy. And he still wishes to marry you. And marrying him would be better for you than anything else I can imagine."

"Better for me how?" she retorted, pulling and pushing at him, wanting to be even closer. Their stupid, stupid clothes were in the way, chafing and far too hot.

"For your life. You'll have back your family and your friends, pretty gowns and soirees."

"Then convince me tomorrow."

Keating pushed her back a few inches, his tawny gaze

full of secrets and wishes and other things that she badly wanted to discover. "Tomorrow," he whispered.

Camille nodded. "Now stop talking, before I lose my nerve." The coach bumped over something, and she dipped an eyebrow. "Where are we going, anyway?"

"Baswich House."

"You told the driver that before I ever climbed in here."

He claimed her mouth again, his fingers slipping beneath the shoulders of her gown. "Yes, I did. I said I'm trying to be a better man. I didn't say I was succeeding. And I want you. I have wanted you from the moment I set eyes on you and that buffoon who was insulting you."

So when he'd claimed he was only after friendship, he'd lied. Or very skillfully evaded, at the least. At the same time, he was certainly not some random gentleman who behaved himself in public and then insulted and belittled her whenever he could get away with it. His warm palm closed over her right breast, and she gasped, pushing into the embrace. "We're also friends, are we not?" she managed unsteadily.

"You need better friends than me."

"No I don't."

By the time the coach stopped, her lips felt swollen, her dress too tight and scratchy across her breasts, and her heart as though it would rattle straight out of her chest. Keating handed her down from the carriage, then stepped to the ground behind her and tugged her back against his front. "You will stay right here," he murmured in her ear, shifting his hips so she could feel the hard bulge of his trousers pressing against her backside.

Wordlessly she nodded. Keen arousal sped through her, and it took more willpower than she expected to not turn around and throw her arms around his neck for more kissing. As a nearly attached duo they climbed the trio of front steps. A stern, sleepy-looking fellow in trousers and a nightshirt opened the door for them as they reached it, then stepped silently out of the way.

Keating nudged her in the direction of the stairs, staying close behind her as they ascended to the first floor and then down the hallway to the west wing of the large, dark house. At the far end he reached around her to push open a door. "This way," he murmured, following her inside.

At the sound of the door locking, Camille turned around and kissed Keating again, sliding along his hard, lean body. In the back of her mind she knew she should be wary or worried—or one of those emotions she generally felt when she'd stepped away from her secure little haven—but mostly she felt intoxicated. Heady and excited and shivery.

"You are wearing too many clothes," Keating said softly, and her heart pounded at the edge of unsteadiness in his deep voice.

Good heavens, he intoxicated her. "So are you," she returned, pushing the coat off his shoulders. "Tell me again that you want me."

With a slight smile he bent, lifting her in his arms and carrying her over to his large bed. It had already been made down for the evening, and she sank into the soft pillows and sheets. Oh, she'd forgotten what it was like to have such a fine, soft bed.

"I want you," he said, taking one ankle to pull off her shoe, then doing the same with the other. "You've been driving me absolutely mad with desire for over a fortnight, and I don't know that I've ever wanted anyone as much as I want you at this moment." Keeping hold of her left ankle, he slowly brushed the palm of his free hand up her calf to her knee and up her thigh, drawing the heavy material of her skirt with him.

Oh, this was utter madness, and she was so thankful she'd had the courage to venture away from The Tantalus Club, at least for one night. To be wanted . . . for anything, felt significant, especially from someone she had come to value as a friend. Especially one who had been with enough women to know what he wanted. And to be desired by the man whom she lusted after in return . . . She'd heard enough talk at the club to know that that was a fairly uncommon occurrence.

Keating shifted to sit on the bed beside her. His gaze on her face, he brushed his fingers into her hair, pulling out pins and setting them carefully onto his bedstand. As her light-colored hair fell past her shoulders, he spent a long, breathless moment twining the strands around his fingers. "Lovely," he whispered, almost soundlessly.

"Thank you," she returned in the same tone. "So are you."

"And so polite." With a half grin he undid the buttons of his waistcoat and then dropped the thing to the floor. A moment later he pulled his shirt off over his head and tossed it aside, as well. "But you're being quiet," he observed, placing a hand on either side of her shoulders and leaning in to kiss her again. "Have you changed your mind after all?"

"No. Of course not. I'm absorbing and observing."

"Well, we'll have to take care of that then, won't we?"

"What do you—"

He shifted his attention to her jaw, nipping and kissing, the sensation so pleasurable it almost hurt. When she couldn't help moaning, Keating took a deep breath and made his way down her throat and over to her collarbone. Slowly he slipped his fingers beneath the shoulders of her gown and drew the material down her arms, kissing every bit of her skin that he exposed. When his mouth closed over a bare breast, she gasped again.

Oh, he was right about one thing: it was difficult to be an observer when every touch seemed to flood her with sensation. Her mind simply wanted to enjoy the moment, and her body already was. With an excited grin, Camille put her hands on his shoulders and ran her palms down his bare chest. His skin was like velvet just covering iron. Muscles flexed beneath her touch, and she couldn't hide her satisfaction. Being wicked definitely had its merits.

"What's so amusing?" he murmured, glancing up at her before moving his very capable mouth to her other breast and licking across her nipple.

"Good heavens," she rasped, arching her back. "It's not amusing; it's . . . splendid."

"That it is. And that you are."

She squirmed beneath his ministrations, almost wishing they'd remained in the coach so that at least he would have had to get on with it. Because as much as she was enjoying his hands and his mouth on her, she was very aware of the taut bulge in his trousers. And she was aware that kissing and his . . . oh, his mouth on her breasts was not all she wanted from him.

Keating, however, seemed to enjoy torturing her with his exquisite tongue, removing her gown as slowly as anyone could possibly manage and making her shiver in the most delicious way possible. Heat spread from everywhere he touched, until she thought she must burst into flames. "I have to be . . . back at . . . oh, at the club by seven o'clock," she said shakily.

"I don't think I'll be finished with you by then."

"Not at this rate."

His low laugh echoed through her breastbone. "Impatient, my dear?"

She couldn't help smiling breathlessly at his amusement. "I didn't come looking for you to have a chat."

Hauling her up by her hips, he stripped her gown and chemise down her thighs and off. "So anxious to be ruined, are you?"

"Everyone believes I already am ruined. I decided I might as well enjoy myself, then."

"With me." His palms slid up her thighs again, dipping inward as they climbed.

"Yes. With you."

Keating parted her legs, trailing his mouth down her belly, around the most impatient part of her, inside her thighs, and then . . . there. The sensation sent her floating skyward, shivery and gasping for breath.

"Oh, my word."

Never had she expected anything to feel so naughty and intimate and very, very good all at the same time. Arching her back, Camille dug her fingers into the bedsheets and moaned. Yes, he was still teasing at her, but she was closer to where she wanted to be now, closer to him. And the tightness running through her abdomen, stretching at her muscles, demanding a release—shifting her grip, she dug her fingers into his hair again and pulled his face up to hers.

"I want you," she whispered tightly. "Now."

From his expression he was still enjoying his ministrations. And that would kill her. She reached down between them and took gentle hold of the tented crotch of his trousers. He hissed in a breath through his teeth, jumping. "Stop that, or you'll finish me off," he growled.

"That is how *I* feel."

Tilting his head to gaze at her for a hard half-dozen heartbeats, he sank down along her body and kissed her again. "There is some pain involved. I want you to feel pleasure, first."

"I feel pleasure just being with you. And pain—I can manage a bit of pain. Be with me."

He lifted his hips, unfastening his trousers and shoving them down past his thighs. "You say some very nice things, Camille. Last chance to come to your senses."

"I *did* come to my senses. That's why I'm here." She lifted her head, angling her neck so she could get a look at the impressive erection jutting toward her. For the first time uneasiness touched her, but she banished it. Tonight she would not be afraid. Not with Keating.

"Look up at me," he ordered, and she complied, lifting her gaze again to meet his light brown eyes. "Hold your breath."

She took a breath and held it in, sweeping her arms around his shoulders to keep him from disappearing down her body again. He nudged her knees a little farther apart with his own, then angled his hips forward. All she could feel was the hard pounding of her heart and the warm, hard slide of him entering her.

Keating paused, something she couldn't quite interpret passing across his lean face, before he pushed deeply inside her. Sharp pain cut through her, and she clenched her jaw. A little pain in exchange for being with him. The question of whether it was worth it barely took time to form before it dissipated into a haze of sensation and heat.

"You can breathe now," he murmured, humor in his voice.

She gasped in a breath. "Oh, my."

He kissed her, slow and deep, at the same time pulling half out of her and then entering again. His weight across her hips, the fullness of him inside her, made her feel like lightning. The tension in her drew tighter and tighter until she thought she would break. When he slid deep inside her again, she did break, shuddering and shivering with a deep groan that shivered from her into him.

"God," he whispered, increasing his own pace, entering her again and again. Their moans and breaths and the slap of flesh against flesh filled the room. Finally he left her to surge against her stomach, holding himself hard and close as his seed spilled warm onto her skin.

That wasn't how it was supposed to happen. He wasn't supposed to leave her like that, just at that . . . moment. But then she knew enough about horses and dogs to realize that in the midst of thoroughly ruining her, he'd done something noble. But then he'd said he attempted to avoid repeating his mistakes.

Breathing hard, Keating grabbed a cloth to clean them both off, then sank down alongside her. Brushing a strand of hair out of her eyes, he kissed her again. "Now we're both in for it," he said with a smile that made her heart twist.

That, they were.

Chapter Fourteen

Six or eight years ago, Keating had pursued any female who caught his attention—which category encompassed nearly every chit under the age of forty in London. He hadn't cared whether they were married or not, as long as they were pretty and willing. He hadn't wanted a romance or a marriage, or even a connection beyond the bedchamber, and he hadn't offered any more than that, either.

He shifted a little, running his fingers along the slope of Camille Pryce's shoulder as she lay curled up against him. Her pale hair draped across his chest, delicate and ethereal strands as striking as the long-vanished moonlight.

The rosy tinge of sunrise looked for a way past his heavy curtains, with only a sliver or two finding their way into the bedchamber. And Camille's breath caressed warm across his skin. He drew in a slow breath of his own, wishing he'd found a way to hold back time. But he'd made that wish once before, and no one had listened to him then, either.

"Camille," he murmured regretfully, "it's past six o'clock."

She stirred, stretching like a cat. His cock twitched

again in reaction. "I fell asleep," she said, lifting her head to look at his face.

"Yes, you did. I wasn't certain whether to be insulted or flattered." He grinned to make certain she knew he was jesting.

Her sunrise blue eyes danced. "Flattered. Definitely." Camille sat up, arching her back and stretching her arms up over her head.

Well, he wasn't going to ignore that. Sitting up next to her, Keating ducked his head to take her right breast into his mouth. The nipple budded beneath his tongue, and he reached up to flick his thumbnail across the other one. Her responding groan made him immediately hard.

"Oh, you—stop, please, Keating."

With a last suck he released her. "Does that displease you?"

She scowled. "Of course it doesn't displease me. But I have to leave, and if you continue, I won't be able to walk."

He leaned in again. "I'll drive you."

A hand across his mouth stopped his advance. "I have to leave," she repeated, a laugh in her voice.

How odd, that he was the one cajoling his lover to stay. It was the first time he could remember being the one who wished to remain. "Very well." Reaching over the side of the bed, he grabbed her shift and handed it to her.

She pulled the cotton material over her head, then paused, glancing at him. "Do we need to talk now?"

Keating shrugged. "Not unless you wish to. I mean, I understand that you wanted to be the woman everyone seems to think you are. I don't expect this to have meant anything more than it was—a very, very pleasant evening spent together."

As he spoke he studied her expression carefully, though

he wasn't certain what he was looking for, or what he hoped to see. His best interest would be served by her marrying Fenton. And by her certainly never telling his cousin that the two of them had shared a bed. For the devil's sake, everyone knew he was a notorious rogue without feeling or sentiment. Even he knew that.

"And is this a pleasant evening you might care to repeat?" Camille asked, standing to go find her gown.

He couldn't see her face, which might or might not have been on purpose. At the mere thought of having her again his cock rose to half staff. "Definitely. As long as it doesn't interfere with anything."

"And by 'anything,' you mean me going back to marry Fenton, I presume?"

"You don't wish to be a ruined employee of a gentleman's club forever, do you?"

She glanced over her shoulder at him. "You know, there are moments when you are very unlikable."

"Yes, well, I've had a great deal of practice." Sliding to the edge of the bed, he grabbed his trousers and yanked them on. "Wait here until I return. I'll go order the coach brought 'round."

"I can hire a hack."

That made him scowl. "No. You can't."

"I don't want—"

Stalking around in front of her, Keating grabbed both her forearms. "All I'm attempting to say is that I am doing my damnedest not to be a villain. Your path to regain your life remains, and I won't set snares in the shrubbery."

"That's all I intend, as well," she shot back at him, yanking free. "For heaven's sake, you don't think I've done something as foolish as falling for you, do I? After all the stories I've heard? After all the stories you've told me yourself? You may very nearly turn my blood to steam, but I'm not a fool. I only wanted to explore the benefits of my tattered reputation. And I—"

"Cammy."

"And I know full well," she pressed, "that you have ten thousand pounds wagered on my marrying your cousin."

"It's not a wager."

"No? It's a matchmaking fee, then. Call it whatever you like." She stepped into her shoes, grabbed up her wrap, and headed for the door. "Now if you'll excuse me, I'm expected to be at my station by seven o'clock."

Before he could conjure a retort that wouldn't have her kicking him in his recently exercised loins, she stalked out the door and closed it hard behind her. He stared at the heavy oak. Now that had been unexpected.

The entire evening had been unexpected, ill-advised, and very pleasurable. And apparently meant to satisfy him—and her—with no encore performances planned. *Damnation.* Because while he had been sated, that had felt more like a beginning than an end.

A sharp knock sounded at the door. *Ha.* Of course she'd returned for a second go-round. Striding forward, he pulled the door open. "I hope you—"

"You hope I what?" the Duke of Greaves asked, folding his arms over his chest.

Keen disappointment edged through him. "Nothing. What do you want?"

"No, tell me. What do you hope? That the chit you sent away had the sense to walk a block or two before she hired a hack? That she put her wrap over her head so no one would think that Greaves is bedding other men's women?"

"Oh, shut up. I didn't think of you at all."

"Now that doesn't surprise me." Greaves regarded him. "That was Camille Pryce."

"What were you doing, lurking in the morning room to spy on visitors? I was under the impression that you weren't running a monastery here. Or was I mistaken?"

"I thought . . ." Adam scowled, closing his mouth again. "Never mind. Do what you will."

"I always do."

The duke turned down the hallway. "Yes, I know."

Keating cursed. Pulling on a fresh shirt, he picked up his boots and stalked, barefoot, down the hallway toward the stairs. "What the bloody hell is that supposed to mean?" he demanded, leaning over the railing to view the descending Greaves.

"Nothing. I was going to make some comment about learning lessons, but as you're not an idiot I will simply assume that you're proceeding in the way you are because it is your choice to do so."

"I *have* learned my lesson, Adam," Keating snapped, gripping his heavy boots and making a conscious decision not to throw them at Greaves's head. "She won't be returning. And I'm fairly assured that she'll be marrying Fenton—who will never know about tonight, and who already assumes she was ruined long before I returned to London. So bugger off and go lecture someone else."

Greaves reached the foyer and barely paused as Hooper pulled open the front door. "I happen to have a breakfast appointment at The Tantalus Club. Attempt to stay away from there at least until nine o'clock. After that you may cause as large a spectacle as you please."

For the second time that morning, Keating had a door close on his face before he could conjure an adequate reply. More than likely that was because there was no reply. He'd erred, his friend knew it, and he couldn't excuse his behavior.

Growling, he summoned Pidgeon and returned upstairs to dress. There were myriad places he could go for breakfast other than The Tantalus Club. And myriad women with whom he could spend the morning if Camille wished to be elsewhere. Half a dozen calling cards had appeared on his dressing table just since yesterday afternoon. For a moment he wished Camille had taken the time to notice them, to see that he was sought after and give him a chance to tell her that he'd abstained from chits since his return to London—with only one exception.

He picked one of the cards up. "'Lady Georgiana Hefferton,'" he read, and tossed it into the trash receptacle on the floor. "'Barbara Cossinglen.'" Into the trash it went, as well. "'Eleanor, Lady Bal . . .'"

He trailed off, staring at the embossed calling card he gripped far too tightly in his fingers. For a moment he considered whether he might be dreaming. The last letter he'd received from Eleanor had been posted from Madrid. "Pidgeon," he said in a low, tight voice, "fetch me Hooper."

The valet set down the spare cravat he held and backed toward the door. "Right away, sir."

His mind began spinning in a dozen different directions, following a dozen different scenarios that might end with Lady Balthrow's calling card in his hand. If she'd come to London, had she brought the boy? Would Michael look like him? Had Eleanor raised him to detest his murdering father?

"Mr. Blackwood, you wanted to see me?" the butler queried from the doorway.

Keating stood, holding out the card. "Who delivered this, Hooper?" he asked. "Did a message accompany it?"

"I believe it was a footman, sir, though I didn't recognize the livery. And no, there was no message. In fact, the fellow only said three words. 'For Keating Blackwood.' That was all."

Nodding, Keating waved at him dismissively. "Thank you."

"Sir." Inclining his head, the butler retreated once more.

No address, no sentiment, no time or place for a rendezvous. Evidently he was only to know that Eleanor was in London, and nothing more. Either that or someone simply wanted him to believe that Lady Balthrow was nearby, but he couldn't conjure anyone who would risk annoying him to that degree without a damned good reason.

So yes, she was somewhere in the vicinity. Which meant he might encounter her anywhere, at any time. He took a short breath. If she'd meant a genuine ambush, she wouldn't have sent a card over first—the warning shot across his bow, as it were.

Pidgeon finished brushing out the shoulders of his coat and stepped back. "Very nice, sir," the valet said. "It's been a pleasure to see you dressed in fashion again."

Keating glanced at himself in the dressing mirror. Dark blue superfine coat, light gray waistcoat, and dark gray trousers. He *did* look like a proper gentleman, however little he felt like one. "Yes, well, I couldn't very well wear this to shear the sheep," he said aloud.

"No, sir. Shall I have the sideboard set for your breakfast? His Grace went out to eat."

Yes, he knew that. "No. I'll be dining at The Tantalus Club." Whether Greaves wanted him there this morning or not.

"Very good, Mr. Blackwood." The valet hesitated. "If I'm not being too bold, I'm relieved to see that your megrims seem to have subsided."

They both knew quite well that his frequent morning headaches weren't megrims, but Keating supposed he appreciated both the intentional misnomer and that his valet had bothered to notice that he'd remained more or less sober for the past week. "So am I."

"Perhaps the London air agrees with you."

Perhaps something *in* London agreed with him—or so he'd nearly fooled himself into thinking. As of this morning he wasn't so certain of the Town's enticements. And not only because of Eleanor's arrival. He'd seduced his share—more than his share—of females, but this was the first time in his recollection that a chit had come to find him, gotten what she wanted, and left again. Hell, she might as well have patted him on the cock and given him a shilling.

In fact, the more he considered it, the more it felt like *she'd* seduced *him*. He'd been willing, of course, whatever his gentlemanly sensibilities should have said in protest. At any rate, if Fenton ever discovered what had occurred . . . Keating rolled his shoulders. Camille had stomped off, and Fenton would never know who'd deflowered his bride. As she'd said, the marquis already considered her to be ruined.

Even so, adding his confusion over Camille together with Eleanor's arrival made it very nearly seem the opportune time for him to leave London again. Except that he hadn't yet earned his ten thousand pounds, and that he didn't yet feel like he'd finished with Camille Pryce. Or Eleanor Howard, for that matter.

The most surprising part of the morning hadn't been the sex or the argument or even the reappearance of Eleanor. No, it had been the realization that the face he'd conjured in his mind, the person with whom he'd most wanted to speak about all this, had been Camille. It was nearly enough to drive a man back to drink.

Camille stopped just short of the door in the dining room to catch her breath, smooth her skirts, and fix the pins in her hair. Then she squared her shoulders, pulled open the door, and strolled into the Demeter Room.

She was late; by the time she'd returned to the club and changed into an appropriate morning dress, it was nearly half seven. For a moment she attempted to convince herself that no one had noticed her tardiness—until she caught sight of the figure standing in her usual place beside the podium.

"Lady Haybury. Diane," she said, inwardly cursing. "I apologize. I completely for—"

"Here you go." The marchioness handed her the book with the current seating notes jotted neatly inside. "I don't require lies or apologies or excuses, Cammy. I only ask that you be here when you're expected."

"Yes, my lady. It won't happen again."

Nodding, Lady Haybury put a hand on Camille's shoulder and then walked away to chat with some of her guests. Of course on the one morning she was late, it couldn't have been Lucille or Sophia or Rachel standing in her place. It had to be The Tantalus Club's owner and proprietor. And that after she'd been warned the night before to mind her duties.

Even with the additional trouble, though, she kept catching herself smiling at the oddest of moments. Not only had the early morning's . . . exertions been exceedingly pleasant, but she'd successfully set Mr. Keating Blackwood back on his heels. He was a practiced rogue, and of course he expected that he would be the one to guide the course of an encounter, to decide where it would occur, how intimate it would be, and when it would end. But not this morning. Not with her.

So perhaps she wasn't as skilled at seduction as he was. Whatever he'd been telling her about second chances, she'd been listening to some other things, as well. About the freedom of being scandalous. About for once taking action instead of sitting on her stone bench and watching something she wanted pass by. And she'd wanted Keating.

She still wanted him; the general trepidation and mild . . . annoyance she felt at the gentlemen visiting the club when they muttered and glanced sideways at her was gone this morning. Now she knew what lay beneath the immaculate clothing and intricately tied cravats—and some of them who looked her up and down must have been truly hideous naked.

"What are you smiling about?" Sophia whispered as she glided up behind Camille.

"Just thinking," Camille returned, mentally shaking herself.

"Well, the next time you mean to pretend not to slip out and spend the night elsewhere, you should at least rumple your bedsheets."

Oh, dear. Triumphant thoughts fleeing, Camille turned around to face her friend. "And how do you know I didn't merely rise before you this morning?"

"Because the gown you're wearing now was still in your wardrobe when I left the room earlier. And the one you wore last night was nowhere to be seen." Sophia kissed her on the cheek, her light green eyes dancing. "Was he wonderful?"

A heated blush creeping up from her neck, Camille sent her gaze across the room. "Yes," she murmured back, unable to keep from smiling again.

"I knew it. But be cautious; you look happy, and that will make everyone suspicious."

Swiftly stifling her smile again, she nodded at Sophia. "Excellent advice. Now go away and let me see to my duties."

Before she could do more than take a deep breath and seat Douglas Trevor and his party, she looked up to see the Duke of Greaves gazing at her. Immediately her skin heated again, and she turned away on the pretext of jotting something in the daily book. She'd been at the man's home last night. Did he know? He'd been polite, if a bit reserved, when he'd taken her and Sophia to see the Tower menagerie, but this was different.

When she turned around again, he'd begun chatting with the Duke of Melbourne, and she relaxed a little. "Your Graces," she said, walking up to them, "would you prefer to sit beneath the garden windows, or in a more central location?" She and the other ladies had swiftly discovered that some of the club's founding members wanted mainly to be seen by others, and "central location" had seemed the best term to avoid offending anyone. She used it at least a dozen times every morning.

"The garden windows," Greaves said. "And a large pot of that very good American coffee of yours, if you please. I had a very restless night's sleep."

Oh, heavens. She nodded, hoping her embarrassment didn't show on her face. Whatever rebellion she'd been enjoying didn't include people actually knowing what she'd been up to. Gossip, she'd discovered, she had the backbone to tolerate. But facts . . . "This way," she squeaked, and led them toward the far side of the room.

Evidently her newfound bravado still needed a bit of bravery and devil-may-care added to it. Camille took a deep breath. It was odd, treading the line between rumor and fact. And if she still wished to keep hold of a chance for a normal, proper life, she couldn't allow herself to fall too far toward fact. Because while Lord Fenton might believe that she'd strayed, providing him with proof would very likely cause him both to withdraw his offer and shoot Keating.

She blanched. Keating had already engaged in an armed brawl over another man's woman. No wonder he'd been so hesitant about last night. Of course she'd already known that, but somewhere between leaving the club last night and returning there this morning, she'd put it aside in favor of what she'd wanted. And that had been him.

But now . . . Oh, this was becoming far too complicated. Narrowing her eyes, she turned back to the podium—and smacked into Keating's chest. "Oh!"

He grabbed her elbow to keep her from falling on her arse. "Steady."

The warm soap-and-leather scent of him washed into her like summer. "My apologies, Mr. Blackwood. I didn't see you there."

"I was being sly."

"Well, my compliments, then."

At first she didn't see any indication in his light brown eyes of his mood, until she caught him glancing beyond her at the Duke of Greaves's table. *Ah.* He knew that the duke knew, then, of their rendezvous. When he returned his gaze to her, his mouth curved, but his eyes flashed. "I thought we might go for a stroll when you've a moment later."

Inwardly she squared her shoulders. "Have you spoken with Lord Fenton, then?" she asked in a lower voice. "He's agreed to walk in public with me?"

Something crossed his expression. "So you're all agreement and propriety-minded today, are you?" he murmured back, making her feel as though they were completely alone rather than surrounded by several dozen curious gentlemen. "Ready to don your wedding gown and return to finish the ceremony?"

"Isn't that what you wanted?" From the books she'd read, beginning an argument and leaving before the man in question had had his say—or his fill—was supposed to send him lusting even more strongly after a female. Perhaps she argued too well. He took a half step closer. "Don't test me, or I'll have Fenton set a date. Whatever game you've decided to play, Camille, keep me out of it."

He *was* the game. "Don't pretend you're more proper than I am," she retorted in the same hushed tone. "Why shouldn't I have what I want before I . . . settle for what's good for me?"

"It's not settling if it's an improvement to your life, ninny."

"Do not call me a ninny."

"Then do not take me for a fool."

She wasn't certain whether she wanted to slap him or kiss him. Both entailed touching him, which was likely the point. If he hadn't been so cynical and suspicious, flirting with him would have been much easier, and likely more productive. Of course he faced the very same dilemma that she did; if she happened to fall in love with Keating Blackwood or something equally ridiculous, the more likely she was to want him to have what he required—in this instance, the ten thousand pounds.

Across the room she caught Jenny looking at her. No, glaring at her. "Go away. I was already tardy this morning, and if I'm sacked, I'll have to live in Hyde Park and eat raw duck eggs."

His jaw twitched. "No, you wouldn't," he said very quietly. "Be on your bench at two o'clock." With that he went through the Demeter Room to one of the gaming rooms at the back of the club.

Well, that might possibly have been the nicest thing he'd ever said to her, both because it proved that he *was* still interested, and because she now knew for certain that there was one person in the world with whom she could have a disagreement and not be discarded. Returning to the podium, she closed her eyes for just a moment. As long as she refused to consider what the final outcome of all this might be, today had been a rather splendid day.

For the first time she'd discovered the merits of bad behavior. And it would be exceedingly difficult to begin behaving again.

Because she'd been late, she volunteered to stay at her post through most of the busiest luncheon hours, helping Rachel when the queue of men waiting to be seated ran almost out the foyer. Whether it made up for her earlier absence or not, it made her feel better about it.

Of all the rooms in The Tantalus Club only the library boasted a clock, and she had to ask one of the Helpful Men for the time at least thrice. She could of course have declined to meet with Keating in the garden, but since she had decided to seduce him again rather than merely make him angry, that didn't seem a wise thing to do. After all, as generally amusing and obliging as he'd been with her, he did have a proven darker side. And that part, she had no wish to encourage.

When she finally escaped through the kitchen door and into the garden it was nearly nine minutes past two, and she found herself trotting. For heaven's sake, if he saw that, he would realize that all—or rather, most of—her aloofness and arguing had only been to draw him closer to her, and that would never do.

Slowing to a walk, she rounded the mass of roses and

found him seated on her bench, a book in his hands. For a moment she stopped and simply looked at him. He was tall and lean, his dark brown hair a shade too long and his brown eyes a shade too dangerous, and the long line of his cheek and his hard jaw simply made him look . . . delicious. And he'd been hers, as much as she'd been his. Of course he'd been with other women before her, and likely would be with other women after she'd gone back to Lord Fenton, but this was now.

"What are you reading?" she asked.

He looked up. "*Pride and Prejudice*. Darcy's a stuffed shirt, isn't he?"

"He's shy. And cautious. Why are you reading that book?"

Keating shrugged. "Because you were. You have a fair sensibility, and generally better taste than any other chit I've encountered, so I decided to attempt it. I won't weep at the ending, will I?"

She grinned, both at his wit and at the idea that he seemed to be attempting to return to her good graces. "You may at that. Wait until you're somewhere private."

"Good advice." With a snap he shut the book and set it onto the ground at his feet. "I need to talk with you for a moment."

"You aren't going to lecture me about making poor choices, are you?" she returned, half seriously. "You did just compliment my sensibility."

"Come and sit." He rested his palm on the stone beside him.

Hm. He was sounding reasonable. Had he seen through her attempts at being coquettish? Hiding her hesitation, she complied. "Very well, I'm seated."

He looked down at his hand where her skirt half cov-

ered it. "You twist my head around," he said quietly, his
eyelashes still shuttering his brown eyes.

A thrill went up her spine. Whatever she wanted from
him, at the moment she was very aware that they were
Camille and Keating. Unlikely friends. And that he'd been
proving himself to quite possibly be the dearest friend
she'd ever had. "I feel a bit spun myself," she said aloud.

"Yes, but I'm jaded. No one is more cynical than I am."
Finally he looked up at her. "I received a calling card."

She forced a smile. "What? Someone's invited you
somewhere?"

"Evidently Lady Balthrow is in London."

Camille snapped her mouth shut again. Ice froze her
fingertips. But beyond the shock, and the dismay she felt
on his behalf, her keenest emotion was a dark squeezing
in her heart. Good heavens, was she jealous? She knew
that she had the immediate urge to hunt down Lady
Balthrow and slap her. "Goodness," she finally muttered.

"Not the first word that came to my mind, but yes.
Goodness." He squared his shoulders. "I don't know where
she's staying, but I will discover that."

"Is there anything I can do to assist you?"

Swiftly he leaned over and kissed her. "You just did.
Don't trouble yourself, Cammy. I just wanted you to be
aware, since I've told you more about my . . . connection
with her than I've ever told anyone else."

They sat there in silence for a moment. She knew
what he had to be thinking; this would be the opportune
time to present Eleanor Howard and their son with a
very large fortune. That he would like to be able to feel
for once that he'd done his duty as he should have, made
all the amends that he could. And there she sat, lusting
after him when they both had obligations elsewhere.

She took a breath. "As long as you're here, would you mind informing Lord Fenton that I had a very agreeable time, and that I would very much enjoy that stroll he mentioned? I will make myself available at his convenience."

Keating took her hand and kissed her palm. "We're a pair of sad sacks, aren't we?"

"Don't forget the 'ruined' bit."

Finally he smiled. "Extremely ruined."

Oh, yes. And despite the arrival of Lady Balthrow, and despite where her friendship and duty seemed to be leading her, she very much hoped she would have the chance to be ruined by him again.

Chapter Fifteen

"So first you barge into The Tantalus Club when I expressly asked you not to, and now you want me to bring you along to Lord and Lady Voss's soiree. Do I have the word 'halfwit' scrawled across my face somewhere?"

Keating kept his annoyance deeply buried, and smiled at the Duke of Greaves. "I did not make a scene at the club, you'll note."

"No, you merely stood and gazed longingly at your cousin's betrothed for ten minutes and then vanished. Very unnoticeable."

"But you forget that as I'm always scandalous, the only thing people would remark on is if I did something proper." Frowning, Keating followed his friend down the main staircase of Baswich House. Before, he'd never missed the invitations to various proper and semiproper parties, but tonight he did. Because Lady Voss was a dear old friend of Lady Balthrow's, and as far as he knew they'd stayed in touch with each other over the past six years.

"No, Keating."

"As if you're a saint. Good God, Adam, when did you lose your nerve?"

The duke turned to glare at him. "I have not lost my

nerve. I'm thirty years old, and I'm attempting to behave accordingly."

"Time for you to be gelded and sold to a cart driver, then."

"This is not how you convince me to change my mind."

"Fine." Blowing out his breath, Keating pulled the calling card he'd been carrying with him all day from his pocket and pushed it against Greaves's chest. "I need to attend."

Adam pulled the card free and looked at it. Unless Keating was mistaken, even his jaded friend's face paled just a little. "When did you receive this?"

"Sometime yesterday afternoon. If she'll be anywhere in public, it will be at the Voss soiree."

"No good can come of a confrontation, Keating. You said you've been paying her way, so she has no reason to make trouble for you—unless you throw a gauntlet in her direction."

For a long moment Keating looked at the duke. In six years he'd told one person what, precisely, lay between himself and Eleanor Howard. Camille had been shocked, but because she was a kind, fair-minded individual, she'd understood. Greaves's heart was a much stonier place, but lately Keating had been exploring the value of . . . trust.

"I want to know if she's brought my son with her to London," he finally said.

Greaves blinked. "Your . . . son? You're certain?"

"She was Balthrow's second wife, and he was married for a total of sixteen years without producing an heir. And she gave birth nine months after I last slept with her."

"So that's why—"

"Yes, that's why I need that damned blunt from Fenton. Eleanor may detest me for what I've done, and the boy may hate me as well, but by God he'll have a comfortable life and a proper education. And she will not have to worry about money for the remainder of her life." He took a breath. "Now. Will you take me with you to Voss's party?"

"Yes, damn it all."

"Thank you."

As they made their way outside and climbed into Greaves's coach, the duke eyed him. "Does Fenton know about the boy?"

"No. I think he's realized that I fund Eleanor's household, but I would never tell him about the parentage of her son. He barely tolerates me as it is."

"And . . . your new friend?"

"She's aware. I wanted her to know that Eleanor was in London on the off chance that the two of them set eyes on one another. Eleanor loathes me, and I don't know if she's above making a stir simply because she can. And that wouldn't be fair to Cammy."

There were several things that had already occurred that weren't fair to Cammy, at least one of which Greaves knew about. But thankfully the duke seemed to realize that his good looks would be at risk if he brought any of them up at the moment.

When she'd asked him to arrange a second meeting with Fenton, he'd had the distinct feeling that she'd done it only for him. And that had hurt. Whatever he'd intended when he'd first arrived in London, he liked Camille Pryce. He liked her a great deal. And if she'd convinced herself to return to Fenton only because it would gain him ten thousand pounds . . . *Damnation*.

Who the devil did he think he was, anyway, to even think of pursuing Camille Pryce, much less bedding her? And why was he still thinking about it? He'd wrecked himself, Eleanor, their son, and certainly Lord Balthrow.

He had no right to receive affection from anyone, or to think he could manage to give it.

"I have a thought."

Keating shook himself. "What might that be?"

Greaves scowled. "You wait in the coach, and I'll go inside and see whether Lady Balthrow is in attendance or means to attend this evening. Because if she sent you that card, she must know you'll attempt to track her down. If she's not at the soiree, there's no reason for you to show your hand already."

The man had a point. A good one. "Thank you, Adam."

"Yes, well, I may be attempting to reform, but once a schemer, always a schemer."

Adam gazed at his friend as Keating rolled his shoulders. Six years had made Keating Blackwood into a different man. He was more thoughtful, more reserved, and capable of emotions that Adam had once thought had never been present in his soul in the first place. Clearly Keating didn't know what to do with them, but at least he was making the attempt.

And Adam *had* been a schemer, had spent years watching and manipulating the people around him. To some extent he still did so, though he'd lost the appetite for most of it. One thing his cynicism had granted him, however, was the ability to recognize the same quality in others. And Eleanor Howard had been a schemer herself. He had to wonder, then, whether she'd continued on that course as a widow whose life was being funded by the former lover who'd killed her husband.

Keating wouldn't see it, because the idiot was racked with six years' worth of guilt. Of course the lummox also didn't see that he was halfway to falling in love with the very last woman he should ever be looking at. Or perhaps

Keating did see that, and he was only attempting to cause himself more of the pain he thought he deserved.

It was a damned conundrum. Luckily, Adam still enjoyed unraveling conundrums. Especially for those few people he called friend.

Three days. For three days he'd been hunting for Eleanor, and she'd failed to appear. Her old favorite haunts—the shops on Bond Street, teatime at the Green Apple Inn, late-afternoon barouche rides in Hyde Park—were full of every chit in London with the exception of Lady Balthrow, and Camille, of course.

Keating stepped down from Greaves's borrowed barouche and handed out Sophia White and Camille. Primrose Hill was part of St. James's Park, but most of the *haut ton* stayed at the other end, where the carriage paths meandered. It was a park within a park, essentially, and while they were likely to encounter a few faces who might recognize them, the odds were at least in their favor.

Sophia took a turn to look all around them. "This is pretty. I thought perhaps we would have to drive well outside of London to go for a stroll."

Camille made a face at her friend. "Hush, Sophia. We are behaving today."

"Oh, very well."

Light blue eyes glanced in his direction again, and then pointedly looked away. She'd been like that since he'd retrieved her from the club half an hour ago. He didn't like it, but he understood it. At least part of the unease between them was his fault; after all, he hadn't called on her for three days. Not since he'd informed her that Eleanor Howard was somewhere in London.

He understood why she might wish to distance herself

a little from him. In fact, he'd anticipated that she would, which was one of the reasons he'd made himself scarce—despite the restless nights and the way she colored his every thought. She'd made a mess of her own life, and she now had a chance to set her cart back on the road. He'd destroyed four lives including his own, and the carnage continued.

And then there was what she'd implied—that she would make amends with Fenton not because it was what she necessarily wanted, but because of the blunt that would fill Keating's pockets as a result. It was precisely what he wanted, but he didn't like it. At all. He didn't like the idea of her sacrificing herself, and he didn't like that she would be removed from his embrace.

"Shall we?" he said, offering an arm to each woman.

"What about Lord Fenton?" Sophia asked.

"I think he'd prefer it if our meeting looked coincidental," Camille put in, before Keating could do so. She wrapped her gloved fingers around his sleeve.

With a lovely lady on each arm, Keating left the carriage path and guided them in the direction of the low rise that comprised Primrose Hill. With the sun in the early afternoon the dew had fled the grass, and the breeze brought them the light scent of flowers and greenery. It was an oddly . . . content set of moments, despite the trouble that seemed to surround him. Both of them.

"I've been listening to the club gossip," Camille said into the relative silence. "Gentlemen can be terrible wags."

"You have no idea. They're far worse than any chit," Keating agreed with a smile.

"I haven't heard any mention of Lady Balthrow. You haven't tracked her down, have you?"

"No. Not yet. She's being surprisingly subtle. And I have to say, that worries me."

"Lady Balthrow?" Sophia squeaked from his right. "Is she in London? Oh, dear. You never said, Cammy."

"I asked her not to say anything until I was certain what Eleanor was about," Keating responded, before Camille could.

Sophia looked all around, as if she expected Eleanor might be lurking in the shrubbery. "Is she as pretty as everyone says?"

"Yes." Or she had been, six years ago. That was the entire reason he'd bothered with her.

He hadn't cared anything about wit or morality or character—unless either of the latter two happened to oppose his seductions. And he distinctly recalled that Eleanor had lifted her skirts for him on the first evening they'd met. In the silver closet of Lord and Lady Wincott's home. The salvers had received an excellent polish while her thick husband dined in the next room with three dozen other guests.

Beside him walked a woman who'd made a poor decision and suffered its consequences, just as Eleanor had. Never, however, would he compare the two otherwise. Camille was by turns shy and then brazenly bold, cautious and foolhardy, still naïve about some things and completely jaded in others. And eminently desirable, always.

She fascinated him. As a man who'd allowed his past to govern his present, she seemed a breath of fresh air. For God's sake, she'd carved out a new life for herself in a matter of weeks, and had managed to tolerate it for a year now. And while she might not be entirely happy with it, she hadn't sunk into the bottom of a bottle and vanished from the accusing glances of her peers as he had done.

"Why are you staring at me?" she muttered, keeping her gaze on the park.

"Am I?" he returned, inwardly shaking himself. She wasn't his. She couldn't be. Regardless of what he wanted. "Perhaps I'm merely attempting to look in that direction and you're blocking my view."

"I see." The soft curve of her mouth jumped upward.

"Oh, there he is," Sophia whispered.

Keating glanced over his shoulder to see Stephen Pollard dismount from Brownie, his imaginatively named brown Thoroughbred. His arrival was supposed to be good news, but it didn't feel that way. With a hard breath Keating stopped and waited. Kicking and scratching against the inevitable would only gain him bloody fingers, he supposed.

"Good afternoon, Lady Camille, Miss White, Keating." The marquis sketched a shallow bow and then offered his arm to Camille.

Well, that was promising, if a bit surprising. Camille relinquished her grip on Keating's sleeve and transferred her hold to the marquis. Unclenching his jaw, Keating nodded at his cousin. "I've made assurances that everyone will be behaving themselves this afternoon. Even me, odd as that is."

"Of course. I pride myself on being a gentleman."

He prides himself on nearly everything, Keating reflected, but kept that thought to himself. Reconciliation was the best thing for everyone concerned, and if Fenton had decided to make the effort of being charming, that could only bode well for Cammy.

Stephen pointed out a falcon and a wayward goose and then a brown-and-green-feathered chiffchaff. "Ornithologist Louis Viellot formally classified it just last year as *Sylvia collybita* in his *Nouvelle Dictionnaire d'Histoire Naturelle.*"

"I had no idea you were an ornithologist," Camille said with a slight smile.

"Oh, I've always been a bird-watcher, haven't I, Keating?"

Not that he recalled. "Yes. Since we were children," Keating said aloud.

It was more likely that Stephen had known they were going to be walking in the park and had therefore fished about for a topic of conversation that wouldn't have everyone hanging themselves from the tree branches. If he'd bothered to look up the Latin names of local birds, however, Keating had to give him some credit for making an effort.

As the marquis continued reciting the various classifications of birds found in the area of London, Keating attempted to distract himself from his unkind mental commentary, and from the way his gaze seemed to insist on lowering to Camille's swaying hips. "Were you friends with Cammy before you both went to the club for employment?" he asked the petite, scarlet-haired chit walking beside him.

She shook her head. "I was raised by my aunt and uncle in Warwickshire. At age eighteen they turned me out, and that's when I came to London."

"You seem well educated."

"Oh, I am. I think the duke must have sent a stipend of some sort to my uncle Harold, because I had a governess and went to boarding school. But then someone found out about my parentage and that I grew up on a farm all at the same time the income stopped and my aunt and uncle lost interest in me, so I had to look out for myself."

"You don't seem bitter about all that."

She shrugged, light green eyes glancing up at him and

then away again. "I was at the time, but I've been in London for nearly three years now and, believe me, I've seen girls who've lived much less pleasant lives than I have."

"I don't doubt it." Now Camille was actually chuckling at something, and he clenched his jaw. "So you've only known each other for a year or so."

"Yes. We've all talked about that. How we've become . . . comrades in arms, I suppose it is."

"A mutual fight against the idiocy of the *ton*. I understand. Except that you invite the enemy into your midst every night."

Sophia grinned. "And we take their money."

Keating laughed. "I feel utterly despoiled. And yet, I shall continue to come calling. I'm evidently a weak, weak man."

"Yes, well, I could regale you with my theories on men and weakness, but then you might leave me here to hire a hack."

"You're a friend, Sophia. I wouldn't abandon any friend, disagreement or not."

She looked up at him. "You know that's why Camille decided she liked you. Because you're one of us, and you understand."

Now this was abruptly becoming more interesting. "One of 'us'?" he repeated.

"Ruined. Scandalous. Minxes, blackguards, and rogues."

He grinned. "I have the feeling that we are much more fascinating in conversation than the proper, the closed-minded, and the meek."

With a snort, Sophia nodded. "Most definitely."

Camille glanced back at them over her shoulder. "What's so amusing?"

"We've decided we enjoy being rogues," Keating offered.

"That doesn't surprise me at all," Fenton commented, his shoulders lifting. "Propriety takes more effort. It's not for the weak-willed or weak-minded."

Silence.

"Evidently it *is* for the men who speak without thinking first, however." Keating wanted to smirk, and he pushed against the urge. Yes, Fenton had just shown his stiff-backed side, but that was who he was. And Camille knew that about him. Perhaps it was better if she became used to it in small doses. Like arsenic.

"Simply because you have an inability to follow the rules doesn't make misbehaving acceptable. I would imagine that Lady Camille would agree with that, whatever her reasons for turning away from her peers."

"I prefer not to discuss it at all, since I cannot help but relate every aspect of the conversation to myself."

The four of them stopped beneath a stand of elm trees. "True enough," Fenton agreed. "We have larger considerations than our differing opinions of your past actions."

Ah, and he still manages to sound like a complete nidget. "Shall we have a late luncheon?" Keating said, wondering once again whether it was God or the devil laughing at him for landing himself in the position of diplomat. He motioned to the tiger down at their carriage. The lad unstrapped the blanket and large picnic basket from the vehicle's rear and carried it forward. "Or at least some Madeira and biscuits."

"Biscuits, definitely," Sophia agreed, taking the other end of the blanket and, with the rather surprised tiger, spreading the plaid thing onto the grass.

Keating folded his legs and sat with Camille on his

left and Sophia on his right, and his cousin seated rather
more stiffly opposite him. Fleetingly he wondered when
Stephen had last partaken of a picnic. Well, Camille loved
the out-of-doors, so the marquis would simply have to become accustomed to it.

"This was thoughtful of you," Camille noted, sending
him a smile.

"With our mouths full I thought we'd have fewer insults flinging across the park," he returned, handing her
a pair of glasses.

"Very wise."

"I don't see the point of pretending to be polite and
eating sweets. If this is what you claim I neglected to do
earlier, it seems a poor reason to avoid a marriage."

"Stephen, shut up," Keating said, and handed him a
plate of biscuits. "Eat."

"In itself," Camille took up, her expression more
thoughtful and less apprehensive than he would have expected, "yes, a single picnic—or lack thereof—would be a
poor reason to avoid a marriage. I'd like to think I wasn't
quite that idiotic."

"I'm not romantic. We're still promised to each other.
Did you ever think that perhaps I would have preferred
to marry someone else?"

"I can't imagine who." Keating looked at his full glass
of Madeira and set it onto the blanket beside him, un-
tasted. "Statues don't generally marry. Not even with mar-
quises who might admire their stoicism."

Fenton looked at him for a moment before he returned
his attention to Camille. "You're deliberately mistaking
my meaning. I merely meant that you weren't the only
one promised in marriage to someone you'd never met."

"You know, my lord, I find myself more interested in

the future than in the past. If we are to reconcile, I would first like to know what I might expect."

She'd changed. Somewhere in the past weeks, Camille had become more assertive, less timid, and, as far as Keating was concerned, more intriguing. He bit into a biscuit and chewed, unable to take his eyes off her.

"Ah. Well, we'll be spending the Season here at Pollard House. It's been in my family for six generations, as has Fenton Hall. The hall burned down a hundred or so years ago, and was redesigned by Christopher Wren himself. In fact, the family has long claimed Wren as a distant relation. When he began the plans for St. Paul's Cathedral, in fact, he—"

"There's a pond," Keating interrupted. "Good for swimming, better for fishing."

"A pond," Camille repeated, smiling. "So you mentioned before. Is it at the front or the rear of the house?"

"The front. The carriage drive loops around it, and my uncle had a small dock built so Stephen and I could take out a boat. It's sunk somewhere out in the middle."

She snorted, then covered her mouth with one hand. "So you were adventurous boys, were you?"

"Yes, Keating was forever dragging me from one disaster to the next. *I* grew out of it. Keating still enjoys his mayhem."

"It wards away the dullness," Keating said lightly, reminding himself that he was behaving not for himself, but for Camille. And for young Michael. "Tell her about the views and the people and the local soirees, Fenton. Not about how the stones were laid."

"What? Oh, well, I suppose there's a soiree monthly at the Clackfield assembly. And the Duke of Sommerset lives only five miles away. I've been to Sommerset Park on three

different occasions, but unfortunately His Grace doesn't
entertain often, and he is frequently abroad. Th—"

"When I resided at Fenton," Keating interrupted, just
barely refraining from rolling his eyes, "there were frequent fairs and races at the village. I once saw a lamb
with two heads there. The fellow had two small leashes
made for it, one for each head."

Camille chuckled again, a merry, musical sound that
for some reason put him in mind of angels. Naked, wanton angels. "I remember attending a fair. No two-headed
lambs, but we used to see the May dance performed
nearly every spring."

A fleeting image of a young, nearly white-haired chit
spinning amid ribbons around a Maypole flitted into his
mind. She would have been laughing, smiling, completely
unaware that the man she'd already been promised to in
marriage would never bother to send her a letter or a single rose.

"Blackwood."

He blinked. "What?"

"I said, Clackfield hasn't hosted a fair in years, so
there's no need to chat about one. Keep your advice to
yourself."

"I see. Shall I leave, then?"

Camille reached out as if to grab his arm before she
clenched her fingers and shifted to reach for the plate of
biscuits. "That isn't necessary. Tell me more about Fenton Hall, why don't you?"

"We'll have time to see to that. But as you were speaking about the future, I have a surprise for you."

Keating caught Camille's sideways glance, but he
hadn't a clue what constituted a surprise in Fenton's eyes.
A puppy? Flowers? An accounting sheet or a book about
mud?

"What might it be, my lord?" she asked after a moment, clearly realizing that Fenton expected to be asked.

"On Tuesday you and I will be dining at Pryce House."

Her face paled alarmingly, and Keating had to steel himself against the abrupt need to comfort her. Damned ham-fisted Fenton. "Perhaps you should approach things a bit more slowly," he suggested.

"Nonsense. I've spoken with your parents, my lady, and they've agreed to dine with you, as long as I am accompanying you. So you see, marriage to me does have its benefits. Your parents will welcome your presence again."

However much she thought she'd learned since that moment standing in the church doorway, Camille's first instinct was to stand up and run. Sitting there and being civil and ignoring Stephen Pollard's self-important prattling with the much more compelling Keating close by had been difficult enough, but then the marquis had done this. He'd gone to her parents, spoken to them, without saying a word to her first. "I don't wish to go," she blurted, every instant of the fear and desperation she'd felt on that night flooding back through her.

"Fenton, stop being such an a—"

"Of course you'll go," the marquis said, interrupting his cousin. "This is about reconciliation and recovering your reputation. You can't do that if you're still disowned. And I remain a laughingstock whose bride fled to a gentlemen's club and only changed her mind about marriage out of hopelessness." His voice growled over that last part. "Meeting with your parents is vital."

Perhaps it was, but for heaven's sake, he might have been a bit more diplomatic in telling her about it. She could feel the warm dismay of Sophia sitting across from her, and nearer still, the solid warmth of the man who was swiftly becoming her greatest advocate and dearest friend. "I won't go alone with you. I will be outnumbered."

"But—"

"You can't expect Cammy to voluntarily subject herself to that," Keating put in, his own voice low and tight. "I suggest you invite one or more of her friends to accompany you."

"Ha. As if Lord and Lady Montshire would allow the likes of you through their front door. The rabble their daughter has attracted over the past months is not to be permitted to cross their threshold."

"You have a very odd method of courting," she managed.

"Let me make myself clear. I am not courting you. I am attempting to put right the mess you made a year ago. For both of us. As we will both benefit from the results, I don't think you have a right to complain."

That made sense, in a horrid, unsympathetic sort of way. A chasm opened up in front of her, filled with her nightmares and memories of the past year. Everything her parents had said to her. Sleeping in the servants' quarters of her aunt's house. The realization that she'd lost . . . everything because she'd wanted her future husband to be someone she could view as a friend and lover.

Dimly she was aware of Keating standing up and putting a hand beneath her shoulder to half lift her to her feet. She heard him cursing, and Fenton's defensive-sounding responses, and then Sophia taking her other arm and guiding her to the coach. Finally the blood pounding in her ears quieted a little, and she looked up.

The first thing that met her gaze was Keating's angry, concerned expression directly across from her. "Did I faint?" she asked, realizing they were in the coach and it was moving.

"Very nearly," he returned darkly. "Idiotic, ham-fisted, thick-skulled boob."

"I am not!" she protested.

He grabbed her hand. "Not you. Him."

His fingers were warm, his grip solid and more possessive than comforting. It helped to steady her more even than Sophia's arms across her shoulders. "Perhaps," she said, taking a welcome deep breath. "But he's correct. I need to go."

"Then I'll be joining you," Keating said immediately. "I dislike bullying."

And she liked him, very, very much.

Chapter Sixteen

"Oh, he was angry. For a moment I thought he meant to flatten Lord Fenton. His own cousin!" Sophia brought a glass of water into their shared bedchamber and poured it into the vase holding the latest bouquet of roses.

"If I'd been a man, *I* might have flattened Fenton," Camille conceded, giving up on reading the book on her lap. Nothing seemed to distract her from the thing that loomed before her like a gigantic cloud of doom—tonight she would be dining at Pryce House. A place she'd not set eyes on in over a year.

"But my point is," her friend continued, bending to sniff the yellow and white profusion of flowers, "he stood up and defended you. Without hesitation."

Yes, he had. And because she knew how much he had at stake in this, his support meant even more to her than anyone else could ever know. "I should have been prepared for something like that. Of course my parents need to . . . forgive me if any of my reputation is to be recovered."

"So you're going through with all this? With dinner and with . . . marrying Lord Fenton? He's not very kindly." Sophia sat in the deep windowsill next to her. "And if I'm not mistaken, you've become acquainted with a man who *is* very kindly." She grinned. "Despite his reputation to the contrary."

Camille nudged her shoulder against Sophia's. Sometimes it seemed so odd that friends she'd known since childhood, with whom she'd shared secrets and infatuations, had turned their backs on her rather than be touched by scandal. She'd known Sophia for just under a year, and there were times she felt closer to Miss White than she ever had even to her own sisters.

"I have to tell you something," she said, glancing up to make certain their door remained closed. "Fenton has offered Keating a . . . bounty for retrieving me. It's a tremendous amount of money, and Keating needs it badly."

Sophia furrowed her brow. "Just a moment. You're saying that Keating was paid to bring you back to Fenton? You know this? And you still sympathize with Keating?"

Oh, she more than sympathized with him. "He's the one who told me. During our second or third conversation, actually."

"But then why has he . . . why have you been . . ." Sophia stood up and paced to her bed and back again. "He likes you."

"We've found a kinship, yes," Camille agreed, though that seemed an utterly inadequate description for the deep satisfaction she found in his presence and the keen longing she felt when he was elsewhere.

"No. He *likes* you, Cammy. And you like him."

Her heart flip-flopped. "I admit that I am becoming very . . . fond of him."

"And you're going to marry his cousin. The man who couldn't be bothered to send you a flower in twenty-one years."

"He needs the money, Sophia."

"This is awful." Her friend turned around again. "But you . . . were with him," she whispered. "Weren't you?"

"You said I should have a bit more fun with my reputation."

Finally Sophia quirked a grin. "And did you?"

"Suffice it to say that Keating is extremely wicked."

And now that she considered it, she couldn't come up with a decent reason she should stop being with him. At least until the marriage. She couldn't very well be more ruined. If she was going to marry that stuffed shirt Fenton, she wanted something for herself first. She wanted someone for herself.

With a deep sigh, Sophia shook her head. "I do not understand you." Walking over to the wardrobe they shared, she pulled it open. "But if I'm to meet your parents, should I attempt to be proper, or more scandalous so that you look better in comparison?" She held up two gowns, one light blue and demure, and the other dark burgundy and very low-cut.

Camille laughed. "I do love you, you know."

"And I'm glad that you're finally happy. I hope Fenton doesn't ruin that for you."

Sobering, Sophia shifted to gaze out the window. This was a ladies' evening, and the regular employees of The Tantalus Club weren't required. Lady Haybury had discovered very early on that the thing that made the club so popular with the gentlemen also worked for the ladies. Every available man under the age of thirty who was employed at one of London's other gentlemen's clubs took this evening off—to work at the Tantalus.

If she married Fenton, she supposed she could attend the twice-monthly ladies' nights. As a guest. Perhaps she could even hire Sophia as a companion, and she could bring her friend to grand balls and soirees. She knew a great many ladies who had very little to do with their husbands, so she could do the same with Fenton. They could have separate bedchambers and separate lives. Of course she would be expected to bear an heir, which would mean the marquis would touch her and be inside her as Keating had. Her heart thudded again.

Previously her complaint about Fenton had been more about intangibles; did he care about her, was he romantic, did he even want to be married to her? Now she had answers to some of those questions, but thanks to Keating she had a completely new set of concerns.

Sophia was still looking at her, her expression shifting from amused to concerned. Camille mentally shook herself. "Please wear the demure gown," she said aloud. "I do have younger sisters, and I suppose I should worry about them being led astray."

"Very well. But if your parents or anyone else is mean to you, I think I'll have to speak up. And I *know* Keating will."

"Please don't make me even more nervous. I've only just found the courage to leave the club at all, if you'll remember."

"I remember. And I'll behave. But you'd best have a word with Bloody Blackwood."

She wanted more than a word with him. "I shall," she replied, knowing Sophia expected a response. With a glance at the side table and the small clock they'd purchased, she took an unsteady breath. "I suppose it's time to dress for dinner."

However much she'd wished for Tuesday never to come, it had. And now she could no longer put off the moment when she set eyes on her parents again. She donned a simple green-and-brown silk evening gown, but her hands were shaking so much that Sophia had to assist in putting up her hair. Thankfully Keating would be escorting them to the house, and she kept her attention on that moment while she did everything in her power to keep from thinking of anything past that point.

When she couldn't put off the time any longer, she and Sophia went down the back staircase and outside through the servants' entrance. The proper ladies in attendance tonight intensely disliked having the scandalous chits of The Tantalus Club anywhere in sight, much less in their midst, and Lady Haybury had actually gone as far as putting a gate into the back fence to allow her girls, as she called them, to enter and leave the premises without having to go down the front drive.

On the street just beyond the gate, the Duke of Greaves's grand black coach sat waiting for them. Keating Blackwood leaned against the door, smoking a cheroot and looking the very portrait of strong, dark masculinity. A delicious shiver went through her, much more welcome than the nerves that had been assaulting her for the past three days.

As he saw them, he dropped the cheroot, grinding it out with his boot heel as he straightened. "You both look far too lovely for a private dinner," he drawled, taking Camille's hand and brushing his lips against her knuckles. "What say we go to the theater, instead?"

"Don't tempt me," she returned, belatedly retrieving her hand.

"That's why I'm here. If you don't wish to go, say the word. If you wish to leave once we arrive, tell me. You may feel the need to be diplomatic because you are thoughtful and . . . nice, but I am not." He gave her a wicked grin. "And I've never been happier to be a rogue."

She wanted to kiss him. There, on the street, where anyone and everyone could see. The expression in his eyes changed, and he took a half step closer. The heat of him seemed almost palpable. When they'd first met, she'd never expected him to become a friend and a lover, someone whose company and opinion she valued more than she felt comfortable expressing.

"If we're going, we likely shouldn't be late," Sophia said from the depths of the coach.

His jaw muscle jumping, Keating straightened again. "Damned chaperone," he muttered under his breath, taking Camille's hand again to help her into the carriage.

"I heard that," Sophia commented. "Do as you will, but Cammy would be embarrassed if you mauled her in public."

The coach lurched into motion. "We're not in public now."

Before she could say anything, Keating leaned across the short distance dividing them in the coach. His warm mouth caught hers in a deep, swift kiss that left her breathless. Looking extremely self-satisfied, he sat back and crossed his arms over his chest.

"That should do me for a short while."

"The two of you confuse me," Sophia commented, her expression amused and troubled at the same time.

Camille knew precisely what she meant. Before long, she and Keating were going to have to have a serious chat. She had the feeling that she wouldn't like the outcome, however, and as nothing had been decided with Fenton, no wedding date set—or set again, rather—she preferred to be able to kiss the man presently gazing at her.

Considering how alone she'd felt after her parents had thrown her out of the house, it was genuinely surprising to arrive at their front door only fifteen minutes after leaving The Tantalus Club. She supposed there were longer distances than those bridged by roads. Rubbing her hands together, she attempted to warm her abruptly chilly fingers.

"Wait here," Keating said, rising. "I'll make certain Fenton's already arrived."

As soon as he left the coach and closed the door, Sophia grabbed her arm. "I want to be kissed like that," she whispered, giggling.

"Hush. Don't encourage him." She smiled, grateful for the momentary distraction. "Leave that to me."

"Oh, you're naughty! Good for you."

The door opened again, and Keating leaned inside. "He's here. Arrived ten minutes ago. I would imagine they're going over battle plans. Showing a united front and all that." He cocked his head at her as he helped her to the ground. "Do *we* have a battle plan?"

"I'm going in there, and I'm going to be polite. I think the remainder of my plan depends on their plan."

And for a moment she wondered what would happen if they refused to allow her back into the house, much less back into the family. Undoubtedly Fenton wouldn't want her then—he didn't seem the sort to marry an unredeemably ruined chit. She sent a sideways glance at the tall man walking beside her. He would lose the money he needed, but nothing would prevent them from doing as they chose.

The front door opened as they topped the granite steps. "Smythe," she said, nodding at the butler, and supremely thankful that her voice remained steady.

Holding the door wider, the butler stepped back. "Lady Camille. Do come in, my lady. Lord and Lady Montshire are upstairs in the drawing room."

"And my sisters?"

"Lady Marie and Lady Joanna are also in the drawing room."

"Thank you, Smythe."

She hesitated at the threshold. Had it only been thirteen months now since she'd last been inside this house? It felt like years. Inside Pryce House she'd lived a different life, been a different person. Clearly she could never be the old Camille Pryce again. Since meeting Sophia and Emily and Lady Haybury and most definitely Keating, she wasn't certain she wanted to be her old self again. But her parents were inside, waiting. They'd been furious when she'd run away from her own wedding. She could only imagine what they must think of her present employment and her new friends.

A hand touched her arm. "I imagine you've already anticipated anything they might say to you," Keating said quietly. "And if—or when—you leave here, you won't be alone this time."

"Not alone," Sophia affirmed.

"You're going to make me weep," Camille said, her voice quavering a little. "And I know how that disturbs you."

Keating grinned. "I'll manage."

"And don't punch anyone."

He sighed. "Anything else?"

"No." She wanted to lean into his shoulder, breathe deeply of the scent of him, and sternly stopped herself. For heaven's sake, her fiancé—or whatever it was she was supposed to call Lord Fenton now—was just inside. "Just thank you."

"You're welcome, my dear."

With a deep breath she put one foot forward. Then one more, and she was inside Pryce House. Screaming banshees didn't come shrieking out of the walls, and no small children began wailing, but from the way her heart was pounding ghouls and goblins might well have been parading all around her.

Up the stairs, she ordered herself. The stairway seemed twice as long and twice as steep as it had once been, and if not for Keating's warm presence at her back, she might have reconsidered her decision not to flee. It helped to remind herself over and over that she wasn't a coward any longer, that she was learning how to stand up for herself and not be so afraid of what other people thought of her, and she kept reciting the words as she climbed.

Stopping outside the closed drawing room doors would only make things more ominous, so she kept walking. She pushed open the doors and took two solid steps into the room. Then she looked up.

Stuart and Victoria Pryce, Lord and Lady Montshire, stood side by side in the center of the room, Lord Fenton directly to her father's right. Her sisters stood behind them, half hidden and clearly expected to remain silent.

Then her mother sighed. "Really, Camille. You return home after months and months, and you choose to bring . . . these people with you?"

Oh, thank goodness. Of all the things her parents might have said or done at this moment, her mother had chosen the one thing guaranteed to make her angry. To make her brave. "Lord Montshire, Lady Montshire," she said, her voice low and calm and steady, "may I present my dearest friends, Miss Sophia White and Mr. Keating Blackwood? Sophia, Keating, my parents."

To her left, Sophia curtsied neatly. On her right, Keating remained unmoving, a formidable, beautifully sculpted statue. Before a glaring contest could begin, Lord Fenton stepped between the two groups.

"I suggested she leave her companions behind, but they are part of the problem we need to address. Perhaps it's beneficial to have them here."

Part of the problem. "I believe the main part of the

problem was my actions," Camille said, shifting her hands behind her back so she could clench her fists. "If you wish to fault people for befriending me at the worst moments of my life, well, I think we may all be wasting our time here."

"I don't think debating anyone's presence will accomplish anything this evening," her father finally put in. "Let's sit, shall we? Smythe, please fetch the wine."

"Right away, my lord."

The door closed behind them. From his position at Camille's shoulder Keating saw her spine stiffen, and he stepped forward, offering his arm. "I never refuse a glass of wine," he drawled, taking her fingers and placing them over his sleeve when she didn't move.

"Yes. Of course," she blurted, then swallowed.

It was a damned shame she'd ordered him not to punch anyone. Both Fenton and Lord Montshire seemed prime candidates for a nose-bloodying. "I assume you've told the viscount and viscountess all about Lady Camille's friends and activities since her departure, Fenton?" Keating asked, taking a seat on the low couch between Sophia and Camille.

As little practice as he'd ever had at being a protector or a guardian or whatever might be necessary this evening, he'd meant what he'd told her. No one was allowed to hurt her. If they did wish a fight, he would be more than happy to stand as an opponent. At the same time, Camille had stood her ground so far. He felt . . . proud of her. Her bravery also made him want to rip off all her clothes and have his way with her, but that would cause her sisters to faint. Fenton likely wouldn't appreciate it, either.

"So." Her parents sat on the smaller, facing couch, while Fenton took the chair at one side. The silent sisters took seats on the opposite side of the room, apparently content to stay out of matters. "Stephen tells us you're amenable to marrying him, after all," Lord Montshire commented.

"I'm amenable to discussing it," she corrected.

Something tore loose in Keating's heart and began flopping weakly and painfully in his chest. He'd almost forgotten that this wasn't simply a reconciliation before Cammy and her parents. Apparently their reacceptance of their daughter truly did hinge on whether she would do as they insisted or not.

He didn't like that. Almost as much as he didn't like the idea that she was willing to discuss marriage to Lord Fenton. It wasn't as if he would make her a better husband than Stephen, however; God knew he had no right even thinking about . . . marriage. He'd destroyed too much, ruined too much to ever risk involving someone else so closely in his life. No matter how fond he might be becoming of her.

"Explain to me why this was unacceptable to you before, and now it isn't," the mother said, her own expression tight. Keating wasn't certain whether she was holding in her desire to embrace her daughter again, or if she was simply annoyed at having to discuss this mess in front of strangers.

"I've learned some things since then."

"Enlighten me."

Camille frowned. "Do you want me to regale you with how frightened I was when you threw me out of the house?" she asked, her voice unsteady for the first time since she'd entered the room. "How my supposed friends wouldn't open their doors for me? How I cleaned the floors and shared a bed with two other maids in Aunt Douglass's house? Or are you more interested in how I came to find employment, friends, and a place to live?"

"Your vitriol is unbecoming, Camille. Surely you know that I have friends who've visited that . . . club of yours. Do you have any idea of the embarrassment you continue to cause your mother and me? Your sisters?"

"Then perhaps you should have let me remain at home. Otherwise, I find that my interests lie in finding a way to stay alive. I am not about to apologize for that."

Good for you, Keating cheered silently. He'd been more than prepared to step in and have just this conversation on her behalf, but she was managing it exceedingly well all on her own. She might think herself timid and a coward, but tonight Camille was a lioness. He looked at his cousin's pinched, annoyed expression. Fenton didn't deserve her. Whether the marquis realized how difficult tonight was for her or not didn't signify, because he didn't care. He wanted to marry her so people would stop laughing behind his back. Period.

"And yet if you're so proud of how you've managed to claw your way to survival, why succumb to propriety now?"

"I believe, my lady, that the point of this meeting is Camille's willingness to return to propriety. Demanding to know the hows and whys seems . . . counterproductive." Fenton cleared his throat. "If I may, of course."

"Yes, yes, of course you're correct, Fenton," Lord Montshire said with a nod. "The match was beneficial to all parties concerned before; Camille's actions have made the same match now even more necessary."

That was enough of that. "And of course Lord Fenton is going to exert himself enough to become acquainted with Lady Camille so that she has a reasonable expectation of happiness—if a marriage is to occur." Keating allowed himself a slight scowl for effect; he knew most noblemen at best felt uncomfortable around him, and at

worst feared him outright. If he could use that reputation
to aid Camille, he had no hesitation in doing so. None.

"Interesting choice of sides," Stephen observed, gazing
at him coolly.

"I'm not choosing sides. I'm ensuring that—if anything is to go forward—no one is placed at a disadvantage.
I'm contrary, as you'll recall."

"Why so concerned with my daughter's well-being?"
Montshire asked stiffly.

"Because she is my friend." That was all she was allowed to be, as long as he could be assured that a union
between her and Fenton was to her benefit. That it would
allow her to regain the things she most missed, and that
it would give her happiness.

"After less than a month she is your dear friend. You.
Who never met a female whose skirts you wouldn't lift
and whose husband you wouldn't kill."

Clearly Fenton didn't realize that if not for Camille sitting straight-backed beside him, Keating would have been
across the room thrashing his cousin for what he'd just
said. Keating took a slow, steadying breath. "Perhaps you
should keep that in mind, if you're to be married."

"Keating," Camille said under her breath, the sound
disguised beneath the squeaking of the other females and
the offended rumbling of the males in the room. "Stop it."

"I won't see you attacked," he returned in the same tone.

"I embarrassed them. To Fenton and my parents, their
own discomfort is more significant than mine. Let them
scratch at me. I want to know what the end result will be."

And now she was more circumspect than he was. Was
her heart not becoming as tangled as his? The realization
was like a slap in the face. Had he fallen to the point that
he cared more for her than she did for him? How the devil
had that happened? He was the jaded one. The one whose

past continued to send him calling cards to remind him that he'd put nothing behind him, and that he had no right to do so. "Then perhaps I should go."

She sent him an abrupt glare. "Don't you dare."

Well, that made him feel better. "As you wish."

Of course she was most likely utilizing him to make herself look better in comparison. As he'd meant to do the same thing if required, he wasn't offended. If his damned reputation could do someone—her—some good, then so be it.

"Mr. Blackwood does make a good point about my wish for happiness," Camille said once the offended uproar had quieted. "I'm in a position where I'm able to support myself. I have a roof over my head, employment, and friends. What are the benefits I would receive if I decided to marry Lord Fenton after all?"

"Don't be so mercenary," her mother snapped.

Keating saw the flinch of her jaw, but only because he was directly beside her and looking for it. To anyone else, she likely looked utterly impassive. "I've learned a great deal in the past months. With no one else to look after my interests, I've had to do it myself."

"We would welcome you back into the family," Lord Montshire said. "You would once again be the beloved daughter of a viscount."

"You would be a marchioness," Fenton took up, sitting a little forward. But then he'd always been better with logic than with emotion. "With my declaration that you were only timid, and that we've reunited as a result of a love match, you'll be seen as romantic. And we will be welcomed back into Society. Soirees, luncheons, assemblies, outings will all be open to both of us once more."

"How in the world could you guarantee such a thing?" Camille queried, her voice skeptical.

"Because that is how it's done."

"It *is* how it's done, Camille." Her mother gestured across the room at the still silent sisters. "Think of Marie and Joanna, if nothing else. Marie has had such a time this Season. One prospective suitor actually asked her if she'd visited you at that club. And if she could procure him entrance! Joanna will be out next Season, and by then it may be too late to salvage anything. Heavens, what if no one proposes to her at all? It would be your fault. You've dragged us into the mud with you."

Quiet, girlish sobbing began, giving the entire evening the feeling of some torrid gothic horror. Next the batty grandmother would begin growling up in the attic. Before he could say any of that aloud, Camille's fingers brushed briefly against his. "Don't do it," she breathed.

"You're thinking it, too."

On her other side Sophia made a choking sound. "Might I have some water?" she squawked.

"Yes, of course."

By the time a footman arrived with a glass, Sophia's coughing fit had subsided, but it had served its purpose. The line of argument had been broken, whatever annoyances the family had been ready to utter, interrupted. A moment later they moved into the large dining room. Miss White was a cleverer chit than she let on. He'd already known that about her, but this confirmed it.

He handed her into a chair himself. "Well done."

Sophia nodded. "I don't know what you're talking about."

Dinner was stiff, silent, and awkward. Keating would have attempted to engage the silent sisters in conversation, but they'd been pointedly seated as far from him as the table allowed. Accustomed as he was to being seen as a pariah, tonight he was at least as annoyed as he was amused. And it gave him a new appreciation of just how unique Camille Pryce was. Wherever she'd learned her gentleness and compassion, it hadn't been from her family.

"So we'll meet here on Thursday afternoon to go for a drive," Fenton was saying, and Keating snapped back to attention again.

"Pick her up at the Tantalus. That's where she lives."

"Stay out of this, Keating. The idea is to return her to propriety, not to deepen the scandal around *me*."

"You'd be surprised how many of your fellows you'll find at The Tantalus Club. I think you're only embarrassed because you've been barred from entry."

The marquis glanced at Camille. "That was not my doing."

"Yes, I will meet you here on Thursday," Camille interrupted. "But I'll wait outside. I'm not going to stand about and be yelled at."

The evening ended fairly swiftly after that, and Keating had to concede that the speed was more likely due to his presence than to Camille's. Her parents simply didn't want him under their roof. Briefly he wondered what they would think if they knew he'd been under their daughter's skirts. That he'd become obsessed with her.

The coach stopped on the street backing up to the club, and he stepped down to hand the two ladies to the cobbled ground. "I apologize if I was less than helpful," he said, holding Camille's fingers a moment longer than he needed to. If everything continued as it was, he wouldn't have many more opportunities to touch her. "Obtuseness aggravates me."

She nodded. "Sophia, I'll meet you upstairs in a few moments. I need a breath of air."

"I'm going to find us a bottle of brandy," Sophia said,

heading around to the servants' entrance of The Tantalus Club.

"Would you like company?" Keating asked, still gripping her warm fingers.

"Certainly."

At least she didn't seem angry with him for his less than diplomatic outbursts earlier. He offered his arm, and she tucked herself up against his side. "Was it what you expected?" he asked, as they stopped beneath the garden's central oak tree. The light scent of roses hung low in the crisp air.

"I'm still attempting to figure out if it's them or me who's changed so much. I never felt unloved, you know. Not until the night they sent me away. Is love that easy to give and deny?"

"I don't think so." He shrugged. "Though I'm not an expert."

Shifting away, she faced him squarely. "I'm going upstairs to the back sitting room. I think you should join me."

"Weren't we just negotiating your future marriage?"

"I'm not married, yet. And I want to be with you. Unless you don't wish to—"

Keating closed his mouth over hers. Heat flooded down his spine all the way to his cock. Whether she cared for him or not, at least she still desired him. "I wish to," he murmured.

Chapter Seventeen

The two of them slipped down the hallway, the subdued sounds of women talking and the more distant sounds of the club with its weekly supply of aristocratic ladies laughing and chattering surrounding them. For a moment Keating felt like he was sneaking into a nunnery.

The Tantalus Club, however, was nothing close to being a cloistered sisterhood. He'd heard the rules; the employees were allowed "visitors" as long as their presence didn't interfere with the running of the club. Previously one or two of the ladies, Camille's fellow hostesses, had even asked him upstairs for the evening.

He'd refused, of course, at first because he'd come to London determined not to make trouble, to earn his ten thousand pounds and leave again. Later, he'd declined because another chit had lodged herself into his thoughts and refused to be dispelled.

"The door doesn't lock," she whispered, leading the way into the small sitting room. Luckily it was deserted; most of the female employees seemed either to have gone to bed or made themselves scarce on ladies' nights at the club.

Deftly he took a wooden chair and lodged it beneath the door's handle. "Now it does."

In a very short time Camille had become quite the seductress. She swept up to him, planting her hands on his chest and leaning up to kiss him again. This time she wasn't tentative. Camille knew what she wanted, and afraid or worried or not, she went after it. And that was only one of the things he loved about her.

Love. Blinking, Keating grabbed her shoulders and pushed her out to arm's length. Light blue eyes narrowed as she gazed at him, no doubt wondering whether he'd lost his mind. Her soft, cream-colored hair was drawn up in a simple, neat knot, a few straight strands escaping to brush against her cheek.

"What? Is something wrong?" she asked, plucking at his sleeves with her fingers.

"No. Nothing is wrong." He tried to steady his swirling thoughts, no easy task when most of his blood had already fled downward. He could never tell her what he'd just realized, hard as it had struck him. It didn't take much sense to know that she was near to striking a bargain that would benefit her much more than he ever could. "I like looking at you."

She smiled. "I like looking at you. I believe some ladies even consider you to be handsome."

Slowly he drew her in again, sliding his hands down her back to her waist. "Is that so?" He pulled her closer, knowing she could feel his growing arousal against her front. "I consider you to be exquisite."

"Oh, tell me more," she purred, slipping her hands beneath his jacket and pushing it to the floor.

Keating laughed, remembering at the last moment to keep his voice down. "You've become a tigress. A lioness."

"I've been learning some things from you about courage and speaking my mind." Twisting around, she took his hands and pulled him to the low couch at the back of the room. Letting her lead the encounter was very different for him, the man who knew what he wanted, took it, and left again in pursuit of other amusements. Watching her unbutton his waistcoat, her clumsy efforts at unknotting his complicated cravat, aroused him to an astounding degree.

"Doesn't what—who—I am bother you?" he asked, running his palms under her skirt and slowly up her thighs. Her skin was warm, soft, and utterly intoxicating.

She sat forward, placing feather-soft kisses on his mouth, his cheeks, his throat. For a moment he thought he would completely destroy his reputation as a jaded rogue and come right there in his trousers.

"I didn't know you then," she said, removing his waistcoat and the ruined cravat, then running her fingers and her lips down his chest. "I see who you are now. You've protected me, encouraged me, educated me," and her hands crept down to brush across the uncomfortably tight jut of his trousers, "and made me think I don't have to be so afraid."

Keating closed his eyes for a moment, concentrating on her curious, novice hands roving his half-clothed body. "And yet I'm still bedding another man's wife."

Rising up, she tangled her fingers into his hair. "I'm not yet married," she whispered, licking the curve of his ear.

His well-honed control snapped. Keating pushed her backward on the couch, rising up over her to plunder her mouth in a hard, deep kiss. Yanking down the front of her demure gown, he ran his fingers across her breasts to lightly pinch and tug at her nipples.

Camille whimpered beneath him, pushing at his hips so she could reach the fastening of his trousers. It reminded him that she'd instigated this, and he complied.

A low moan escaped from his chest as she undid the last button and shoved the material down over his hips. As he sprang free, new arousal coursed through him, and he lowered his head to take her soft left breast into his mouth.

She gasped, arching her back to bring him still closer. In response, Keating flicked his tongue across her captured nipple. The taste of her, the scent and feel of her . . . He hadn't been celibate over the six years he'd been away from London, but she made him feel as if he had been.

"Take off my dress," she said, pushing at him again and half twisting so he could reach the trio of buttons running down her spine.

He actually had to take a mental breath to keep from simply ripping the offending fastenings off the gown. Women didn't appreciate having their clothes ruined. And she wasn't in the position where she could simply purchase a new gown every other week.

Keating paused with his fingers on the last button. She would be in that position, very soon. And he wouldn't be the one stripping her out of them. He would have to stand back, watch her go home with her husband, spend his nights imagining her in another man's arms.

With a low growl he undid the button and lifted her half upright so he could pull the soft silk over her head. As she settled into the couch's deep cushions again he went to work on her hair, pulling out the dozen carefully placed pins so the butter-white cascade tumbled down her shoulders.

"Now you," she breathed, taking the tail of his superfine shirt and pulling it over his head.

Disliking being confined around the thighs, he sat to yank off his boots, and then kicked out of his trousers. "Much better."

"May I touch you . . . there?" Camille asked, her gaze lowering to his cock.

"Please do. No jabbing or yanking, though."

Shifting so they could both look at what she was doing, Keating ground his jaw shut when her fingers stroked the length of him and then curled around his girth. "I'm glad I'm not a man," she finally said, the edges of her voice shaking despite the matter-of-fact words. "I would be like this every time I set eyes on you. Everyone would know."

That was the problem, wasn't it? Not that he developed an erection every time he thought of her, but that people would know just from looking at the two of them that he'd fallen. And hard. "It takes some practice," he returned. "And I'm also glad you're not a man."

Camille grinned a bit breathlessly. "Show me why that is," she suggested, sliding her fingers across the sensitive head.

He jumped. "Good God," he muttered, tugging on one of her legs to turn her flat onto her back again and rising over her.

She bent her knees, opening to him, and with a slow, relentless thrust he entered her. Tight, warm flesh enclosed him, pulling him deeper, and he groaned. She was damp, hot, and panting, and he had no intention of disappointing her.

Keating stroked into her again and again, holding on to every sliver of control he owned to keep from spilling into her. He wanted to; he wanted to claim her as his, and have everyone know it. But that would only hurt both of them—and everyone else involved in this mess.

Beneath him, around him, she grew taut, and then he kissed her deep and openmouthed to stifle her cry as she came. He pumped harder and faster, then raised up to pull away from her.

"Stay," she gasped, wrapping her legs tighter around his thighs.

"But—"

"What does it matter? Stay."

Before his brain could compose a counter to that, his body took charge. Moaning, he thrust forward and spilled into her. Breathing hard, Keating lowered himself onto her, tucking his head against her neck.

Confounding, mesmerizing, unique—he was beginning to run out of known adjectives in his search to adequately describe the woman currently running her fingers languorously down his spine.

He lifted his head. "What do you mean, 'what does it matter?'" he rumbled, his heartbeat still fast and hard. "It's one thing to be gossiped about, and quite another to be unmarried and sport a babe on your arm."

"I won't be unmarried, will I?" she returned, stroking his arse with both palms. "And I daresay your cousin firstly would think a babe of his would look something like a babe of yours, and secondly wouldn't dare confront you with any suspicions."

It made sense. "That's rather mercenary of you."

"I've discovered that there's a difference between comfort and happiness. Between propriety and pleasure. Whatever you wish to call it. And before I surrender to one, I want the other."

He frowned into her serious blue eyes. "It's not surrendering. It's returning to a position that will leave you happier."

"Happier than what, precisely?" She took an unsteady breath. "But of course you're correct. I certainly know what it is to have nowhere else to go, and no one to care for me other than myself. I prefer a roof and security."

"As you should."

Her change of mind seemed rather sudden, but then perhaps her pleasures interfered with logical thinking as well. It happened that way with him. This time he kissed her slowly, savoring sensation, the body-to-body heat of the two of them.

He couldn't remember the last time he'd savored anything. The next pleasure, the next risk or reward, always waited just ahead, and by the end of one he was already looking to the next. "May I ask you a question?"

"Certainly."

"Do you like Fenton?"

Her brow furrowed, and he smoothed at the lines with his thumb. "I'm disposed not to," she said after a moment, "but I'm not entirely certain that's completely his fault. After all, how many times have I complained that I didn't wish to marry a stranger? No one listened. I didn't even listen, until I was forced to do so."

"You've walked and dined with him now, at least. Does he seem . . . pleasant?"

"Pleasant enough to marry, you mean? He claims excessive wealth, several properties, a title, and he's not old enough to be my parent. That's something, isn't it? When my requirement is security?"

Kissing her breasts as he rose, Keating sat up. "You are walking a very winding path to avoid answering me. I'm not an idiot. Generally."

Camille sat up in front of him, their legs still comfortably entangled. If eight or nine months ago someone had told her that she would be employed at a gentlemen's club, living under its roof, and bedding an impossible rogue, she would have scoffed. Or more likely fainted in horror.

But as she looked up at the lean, hard-muscled man

currently toying deliciously with her hair, it wasn't horror she felt. Not in the slightest. In fact, if not for the matter of ten thousand pounds, his cousin, her parents, and a son he'd never met, she would be the most content—and most alive—she'd ever felt.

"I'm not trying to be evasive," she said slowly, his touch still making her shiver in delight. "And I don't particularly want to discuss marriage at the moment."

"I insist," he returned in a low voice.

"Very well. He doesn't seem horrid, and even though I embarrassed him and continue to leave him feeling . . . harmed, as far as his reputation is concerned, he hasn't said anything truly terrible."

"I believe that's called 'damning with faint praise,'" he observed.

"What I mean is, I require some things, and you require some things. We'll both receive them as a result of this match. And he's not terrible." She scowled. "Actually, he's rather handsome, and if he at least remains polite I think I might eventually grow to like him. At this moment, I will tolerate him. And I think he will tolerate me."

"You think he's handsome?" Keating asked, something dark and predatory and chill entering his voice.

"You're the one who came here to send me after him, so don't complain that he isn't some warty toad."

He blinked his pretty brown eyes. "Point taken." Gently he tugged at a curl of her light hair. "Perhaps I'm being foolish, but I *do* want you to be happy. Not merely secure."

If all she required was happiness, if all *he* required was happiness, she didn't need to look any further than this little couch. For a moment she almost suggested that she would be happy if he continued to call on her like this, even after her marriage. That, however, would not happen. She knew enough about his past and his regrets to understand that.

"I imagine I'll be perfectly fine," she lied, keeping her voice light and disinterested.

"Then you will agree to marry him."

"Unless something untoward occurs between now and the date of the wedding, yes. I believe I will."

What he likely didn't realize was that she wasn't agreeing to this for her own security, and certainly not for her happiness. She was doing it for him.

From what she'd seen, Stephen Pollard was stiff, easily embarrassed, and without a romantic bone in his body. In a sense it was reassuring that her first, brief impression of him had been spot-on. But while she might be twenty-two years old, a mere one year older than she'd been when all this chaos had begun, she felt miles wiser.

Some of the gentlemen members of The Tantalus Club appalled her with their airs of superiority, the way they sized up every lady employed by the club as if they were sides of venison. These were supposedly the best of Mayfair, the most powerful, the gentlemen every gentleman wished to be. She wouldn't dare meet any of them in private—unless she was very much mistaken they were concerned only with their own enjoyment, their own reputations, and everyone else could go hang themselves.

Lord Fenton didn't appear to be one of those men. Yes, he was entirely self-absorbed, but he didn't seem . . . cruel. Merely uninterested in anything other than her hand with his ring on it. In light of what had transpired over the past year, and particularly over the past few weeks, she could tolerate that.

What she *wanted* for herself was another thing entirely. Perhaps being presented with Keating Blackwood,

being literally close enough to touch him and not be able
to keep him, was her punishment for straying from propriety in the first place. If that was so, it seemed utterly
cruel to show her joy and delight and happiness, let her
taste it, and then take it all away from her again.

For a moment or two she wished she could be one of
those self-absorbed aristocrats and demand either that
Keating continue to call on her after her marriage, or that
he keep her for himself. But she'd seen the regret in his
eyes when he talked about Lord and Lady Balthrow,
and the . . . need he had to make things right for young
Michael.

"You look very solemn," he commented, tilting his head
as he gazed at her. A strand of his dark, tousled hair fell
across one eye, making him look younger and far more
innocent than he truly was.

"I've a great deal to think about," she returned, stroking the stray lock back behind his ear.

He cleared his throat. "Are you and your sisters close?
Because I did notice that they barely spoke a single word
between them earlier."

"I thought we were. I can't imagine what my parents
must have said to them after I left, and they're both far
too young and . . . dependent to risk being put out of the
house. If I'm able to mend any more fences, perhaps I'll
be able to talk with them about all this."

Keating nodded. "And are you and I going to continue
with our . . . friendship until your marriage?" he asked
slowly.

The wisest thing would be to say no. She felt so tangled up in him, literally and physically, that prolonging
the pleasure would only increase the pain. But giving him
up when she didn't yet have to would be even worse. "I
am amenable to that."

"Good." Cupping her cheeks with both hands, Keating leaned into her for a deep, plundering kiss. "Then let's not waste time."

Keating didn't leave The Tantalus Club until just after sunrise. Enough people had tried the jammed door in the upstairs sitting room that likely every employee knew what Camille and he had been up to, but she didn't seem to mind. These women, after all, had all faced their own scandals. If nothing else, the club had at least gained her some true friends. Of course, whether they would be welcome at Pollard House after her marriage was another question entirely—and he had a good idea of the answer.

Greaves's coach driver had evidently decided Keating wouldn't be returning, because the vehicle was nowhere to be found on the street behind the club. With a sigh he hailed a hack and gave the address of Baswich House.

He had what he wanted, apparently. Camille had outright said she would marry Fenton. A few weeks ago he would have been ecstatic, already contacting his solicitor with arrangements to portion the blunt out to Eleanor and packing his trunks to return to his home in Shropshire. Havard's Glen and the sheep and the quiet had been his haven when he'd desperately needed one. Without them he would likely have put a ball through his head by now.

Looking back, he'd been restless and angry and drinking far too much. His brawls in the local taverns were to the point they'd almost become local events, scheduled for the nights he'd sent off most of his income to London for dispersal to Eleanor. He hadn't been angry that the money was going out; no, he'd been upset that there wasn't more of it.

Now, however, he'd have ten thousand quid for her and the boy. It still didn't excuse what he'd done—nothing could do that—but it would make things easier for Eleanor and Michael. And perhaps he would get to see the boy now.

But nothing would be the same after this. Yes, he'd return to Havard's Glen. He wouldn't brawl any longer, because the anger and frustration already filling him wasn't the sort he could excise with drink or pounding fists. He was giving Camille to his cousin, because it was the best thing he could do for her. But he didn't have to like it. Ever.

Hooper pulled open the Baswich House front door as he topped the steps. "Mr. Blackwood," he said in a low voice. "His Grace has expressly asked for you to go directly to his office. Without detour or delay."

Keating lifted an eyebrow. "Oh, he has, has he?"

"Yes, sir. And if you should balk, I am to say please."

Well, this was different. "Why are we being so quiet?" Keating asked, lowering his voice to match the butler's.

"It's imperative, sir. Please. His Grace's office."

"Very well, Hooper. I'm convinced, whatever the devil is afoot."

"Without detour or delay."

"I'm going, for Christ's sake."

Tired and frustrated as he felt at the moment, a good argument with Greaves might be just the thing. With the butler close on his heels as if to prevent him from veering into one of the side rooms or dashing back outside, he climbed the stairs and headed down the hallway to the duke's large office.

"What?" he demanded, shoving the door open.

"Shut up and close the door," Adam ordered in the same low, direct voice the butler had used. "Hooper, back to your previous duty."

"Yes, Your Grace."

Scowling, Keating closed the door. "You have my attention."

Greaves rose from his chair. While Keating had never seen him less than impeccably dressed, this morning he couldn't help noting that the duke's cravat was very simply tied, and that he had an air of distraction about him. In a way, it was a little . . . alarming.

"Sit down." The duke motioned at one of the chairs facing the desk.

Keeping an eye on his friend, Keating complied. "Why do I feel like I've been caught at university with a naked chit in my rooms?"

"Am I permitted to ask where you were? I sent Pidgeon in to wake you twenty minutes ago, and he said your bed wasn't slept in."

"You're not my nanny, Adam." Keating frowned. "And since when have I made a habit of sleeping in my own bed, anyway?"

"Since you've been back in London," the duke retorted. "Fine. Don't tell me. I have a good idea, and I can only hope you know what the devil you're doing."

"Instead of interrogating me, perhaps you could tell me why everyone in the house is creeping about on tiptoe," Keating suggested, his jaw clenching. He would have to give Camille up soon enough; no one was allowed to try to part them before it was absolutely necessary. No one was even allowed to discuss such a thing.

"Very well." Greaves took a breath. "Someone arrived here twenty minutes ago. She's waiting in the morning room for you to dress and come downstairs. I sent Pidgeon out to The Tantalus Club to look for you, so I wouldn't have to make your excuses."

Ice curled through Keating's fingers. "So you sit here and chitchat with me when Eleanor's in the house?" he hissed. "Is the b . . . is anyone with her?"

"I wanted to give you a moment to think before you walked directly in to her. And she's alone."

As angry as Keating was at being delayed now that Eleanor Howard had finally made an appearance, the new, more thoughtful man he'd evidently become had to note that the Duke of Greaves actually looked concerned. Over him.

He stood. "I'll behave," he said, lowering his voice as he pulled open the door again. "I've already done her enough harm to last several lifetimes."

Just outside the morning room door he stopped, flexing his fingers over the door handle. He hadn't set eyes on her in six years. In fact, the last time he'd seen her had been at the Old Bailey when the solicitor had listed the charges against him. She hadn't even stayed for the trial. No doubt she hadn't needed to hear that Keating shooting her husband had been to preserve his own life.

Abruptly the image of Camille stepping back into her parents' house after being thrown onto the streets came to his mind. If she could do that, he could damned well do this.

He pushed open the door. "Good morning, Eleanor," he said, keeping his voice cool and steady.

At first he didn't even see her; the servants hadn't yet opened the room for the morning, and with the curtains drawn and only a pair of candles by the door, it was dull and dim. Then she moved away from the fireplace in his direction.

She wore a dark gown, brown or gray in color, and her long, deep red hair was bound up in a very . . . matronly knot. Six years ago she'd been stunning, and she was still petite and shapely and very, very pretty.

"Keating. I'd begun to wonder whether you meant to leave me standing here or not."

"I couldn't find my boots," he improvised.

"Interesting, then, that you're wearing evening clothes."

"Is that what you wanted to discuss? My attire?" He stepped further into the room, walking to the windows to throw open the heavy curtains. Dramatic dimness or not, he preferred being able to see.

"No. Of course not."

He faced her again, taking a closer look at her own wardrobe. "You look very demure," he commented, leaning back against the strip of wall between the windows and folding his arms over his chest.

"My circumstances aren't what they were six years ago. What do you expect?"

She had a point. "Why did you leave your calling card here and then vanish for a week?"

"I had some matters to attend to just outside of London. I've been away for longer than you have, after all." She tilted her head at him. "I admit to some curiosity. Why are *you* in London after so long?"

"I also had some matters to see to."

"Matters that include a woman who works at The Tantalus Club. I'm not without eyes and ears, you know." She moved over and eased into the chair by the hearth.

If any other female in London—with one exception— had attempted to chastise him for his actions or his associations, he would have said something insulting and turned his back on her. He couldn't say it to Eleanor Howard, however, and instead he decided to try a different tack. "I want to see Michael."

"No."

"If he's mine as you say, then I insist."

"At the moment I can pass him off as Edward's son."

"Then why did Edward's cousin inherit Balthrow?"

She scowled. "Why? Because the courts refuse to acknowledge Michael as the heir." She waved her hands in the air. "Evidently a child born nine months after the supposed father's death and after an affair on the part of the wife is 'suspicious.'"

"You did try to have him named the new viscount of Balthrow?" He wasn't certain he liked that, though it certainly would have lessened Eleanor's money troubles. And thereby, his money troubles.

"I looked into it. Discreetly. Everyone seemed very happy—ecstatic even—to have Edward's cousin Roger inherit and me gone from London and from memory, so they had their way. If I'm cursed to live on a pittance with a son to raise and no friends or family, then so be it."

"I send you every cent I can," Keating returned, his jaw clenched tight. "More than I can afford."

"It isn't enough. I had everything, you know—a title, wealth, friends, parties, the latest fashion in gowns and hats. Now I have nothing."

He scowled. "You have a son. And I wasn't the only one rolling about in your husband's bed. You invited me, after all."

"Don't blame Edward's death on me! Everyone knew how much trouble you liked to cause. I should have known better. You have no right to be as handsome as you are when you're such a devil on the inside. And I certainly didn't ask you to murder my husband."

"I'm aware of that." Keating blew out his breath. "I'm doing a favor for someone. When I'm successful, I'll earn ten thousand pounds. I intend to sign it all over to you. For

Michael's education and so you'll be able to afford . . . nicer accommodations."

She blinked. "Ten thousand pounds? That's . . . That would be marvelous. Such a weight taken from my shoulders." Eleanor sat forward. "How much of a certainty is this? Because I don't wish to get my hopes up only to have them dashed again."

According to Camille, it was very certain. "I'm quite confident." *And not at all happy about it.*

"Then you aren't in London simply to go back to your old ways? I have to say, from the rumors I've heard I thought perhaps you'd forgotten about me and your son."

"I will never forget that."

Eleanor stood again. "Good. Because neither will I." Halfway to the morning room door she hesitated, facing him again. "If you are able to get me the money, perhaps I will begin to think you have indeed changed. And then, perhaps . . . Well, we'll see."

He pushed away from the wall to watch through the window as she left the house and hailed a hack. After six years this was the closest she'd come to saying she might allow him to see Michael. He should have felt hopeful. At the moment, however, mostly what he felt was despair. Apparently God had a sense of humor, putting a woman in his path who made him truly happy and then making him watch as she walked down the aisle with another man. Generally he enjoyed irony. Not, however, this morning.

Chapter Eighteen

"We can wait here for as long as you like," Sophia said, sinking back in the hard, lumpy seat of the hack.

Beside her, Sylvie Hartford nodded her agreement. "I'm happy to be out of doors. Pansy's become obsessed with lavender cologne; our room reeks of lavender."

That explained why Sylvie smelled rather strongly of lavender herself. Camille didn't say anything, though; she had enough turmoil in her mind and too few friends to risk hurting one of them.

"Just give me another moment," she commented, still gazing at Pryce House through the coach's cracked window.

Keating had volunteered to escort her to her rendezvous with Lord Fenton, but she'd declined. Having him present gave her courage, made everything a bit easier, but it had occurred to her sometime last night or early this morning that she was only making things more difficult for both of them.

Once she married Fenton, Keating would be gone. The heat and temptation of him would return with the rest of him to his small estate in Shropshire, and she would remain. Married. To the cousin of the man she . . . the man she adored.

Swiftly she pushed the door open and stepped down to the street. Moving, doing something, was much better than thinking about whether what she would gain was better than what she would lose. Because she was fairly certain she already knew the answer to that—at least from her point of view.

As for Keating, though, Camille knew quite well that the entire reason he'd come to London had been to earn ten thousand pounds. He'd chosen that as the method by which he would make amends to Eleanor Howard, and see to the son who more than likely had been raised to detest him.

So was she doing this for the wrong reasons? If so, what were the right reasons? Yes, her reputation would benefit from the match with Fenton. If she'd married him thirteen months ago as everyone had intended, her reasons for doing so would have been even less than she'd discovered since being ruined. A signed agreement made by his parents and hers when she was only three days old. And nothing more. At least now she could help Keating.

"Cammy?"

Starting, she released the coach's door and faced her friends inside. "Wait for a moment just to be certain I'm not to be left standing at the front door." She handed Sophia two shillings to pay the hack's driver. "And then, if all goes well, I shall see you this evening."

Sophia gripped her fingers as she took the coins. "If you aren't back at the club by six o'clock, I will come here to find you. And I shan't be polite about it."

Camille grinned. "That would almost be worth seeing. I'll be fine."

The door remained closed as she reached the short portico. Well, if they wanted her to knock, then so be it. Curling her fingers around the brass knocker, she tapped it against the door three times. Part of her hoped no one would bother to answer, so she would be free to leave again.

With a rattle the heavy oak pulled open. "Lady Camille," the butler said, with a formal nod.

"Smythe. Has Lord Fenton arrived?"

"He is speaking with Lord Montshire, my lady. If you would wait in the morning room, I shall inform him of your presence."

It annoyed her that her supposed fiancé was more welcome in her childhood home than she was, but it certainly didn't surprise her. Not after the way she'd left. "No. I shall wait outside."

"My lady?"

"That is what I agreed to. If anyone objects, they may argue with me in the garden."

She walked around the side of the house, intentionally keeping her gaze away from the windows as she meandered around the lilies and roses. It all felt so familiar; she couldn't even count the number of times she'd paused in that very spot. The person she'd been then, however, would scarcely recognize the one she'd become.

"Camille."

She looked up as her mother strolled around into view. Inwardly cringing, she kept her expression neutral and nodded. "Mama."

"You look like you're ready to bite my head off."

"I've learned that I need to do a better job of protecting myself."

"And that man, Bloody Blackwood? If you were looking for a way to injure us further, you certainly found it."

"Yes, a man who made a poor decision, found himself in an untenable situation, and was ostracized from Society and lost most of his friends as a result. I haven't a clue why we might have felt a kinship." Much more than a kinship, at least as far as she was concerned, but telling her mother that would likely make the woman drop dead of mortification.

"Your sharp tongue does you no credit."

"I would have preferred it if I'd never had to sharpen my tongue in the first place." She wanted to clench her fists and march about, but that would seem overly aggressive. However angry she might be at the woman presently glaring at her, Victoria Pryce was first and foremost her mother.

"Abuse me, then, if you wish," Lady Montshire returned sharply, "but mind yourself in Lord Fenton's company. I doubt there is an arrangement to be made that would convince him to give you a third chance."

"I'm aware of that."

"Ah, there you two are," her father said, entering the garden from the carriage drive. Lord Fenton walked at his heels. "Having a nice coze, I hope."

Hm. She doubted she would ever have a nice coze with her mother again. Not for a very long time, anyway. "Good afternoon, Papa, Lord Fenton," she said, reluctantly offering a curtsy.

"Lady Camille." Fenton cleared his throat. "Shall we be off?"

"You can't go without a chaperone," her mother stated.

Goodness. A chaperone. She'd nearly forgotten about that sort of annoyance. At the same time, she was quite happy not to have to be alone with the marquis. Not until she had no other recourse.

Lady Montshire turned toward the house. "Marie! Come out here at once!"

A muffled door-slam later and eighteen-year-old Marie hurried around the house. "What is it, Mama? I was in the morning room, reading."

Considering that the middle Pryce sister was already dressed for walking, Camille wasn't certain who the play was meant for—though it more than likely wasn't for her benefit.

"Your sister and Lord Fenton are going for a stroll. Be a good girl and accompany them."

"Of course, Mama."

When Camille returned her attention to the marquis, he was looking at her. She tried to assess the gaze, to determine whether he was annoyed or interested or curious or angry, but she couldn't narrow it down at all. On the surface she supposed that was something he had in common with his cousin, but that wasn't quite true, either. When Keating looked at her, even if she couldn't decipher his mood, she always knew that she was safe. That no harm would come to her in his company. That she was respected and cared for.

"Shall we?" he said, offering his arm.

Hiding her reluctance, she tucked her fingers around his sleeve and they headed down the drive to the street. A passing phaeton nearly crashed into an oak tree, the driver so occupied with staring at them that only the horse's abrupt balk saved him.

"You know people will talk again," she commented, determined not to cringe. "And we've already been seen together."

"I am taking a risk," he agreed, speeding their pace just a little in chorus with his words. "My reputation as a member of the aristocracy might not have been harmed, but I became a de facto cuckold, a fool, a weakling who couldn't convince a woman with whom I had a contract to marry me. I will not go through that again."

He was certain, then, that she would agree to go through with this. And so she would, but not for *his* reputation. Or even for hers. "What if your cousin had been unsuccessful? What if I'd decided never to speak to him?"

He gave a short smile. "Keating is very charming. When he wants to be. I'm actually somewhat surprised, though, at some of the things he's said. You do know I agreed to pay him for bringing you back to the table, as it were."

"Yes, I know."

"Truly?" He lifted an eyebrow, a nearly-as-handsome, if less warm-blooded, version of his cousin. "He told you that?"

"Yes, he did. It was our second conversation, I believe."

"And you still agreed to meet with me."

"Shall I speak honestly, or do you prefer that I simply nod and smile?"

For the first time faint surprise crossed his features. "My preferences never seemed to concern you before. I see no reason to begin dissembling now."

Camille preferred when he became cold and insulting; it made her own anger and determination easier to maintain. "Very well. You offered ten thousand pounds for me. It was the first time you ever went out of your way to gain my company."

"And now you'll say that flowers would have been much less expensive."

"It was too late for flowers." She glanced over her shoulder to see Marie behind them, close enough to overhear the entire conversation. No doubt she would repeat it verbatim to their mother once they returned.

"Why were you so angry at me?"

Camille blinked. "I wasn't angry. I was ... disappointed."

His arm beneath her hand stiffened. "Yes, well, I would have preferred a woman with more meat on her bones and less prone to flights of fancy. We all make do, I suppose. Most of us do, anyway."

"Yes, but if you'd bothered to become acquainted with me, you might have realized that we aren't compatible, or even that we are, which would have saved the embarrassment at the church."

"Yes, yes, I should have written you a letter and sent you posies. I didn't. I'm not going to apologize or tell you I intend to make amends. We've both been injured by your actions, Lady Camille. Time to make things right. For my sake, your family's sake, and your own sake."

And for Keating's sake. "Yes, I suppose it is," she said aloud, attempting to ignore the rebellious stammering of her heart.

He stopped, lowering his arm and moving to face her. "Then no more of this idiotic faux courtship is required, I assume?"

"No. I don't see the point in attempting to convince myself that you're someone you're not. All I ask, in fact, is that you have as little to do with me as possible after our marriage."

"I require an heir. And your fidelity. I won't be laughed at again."

Her heart jolted again. "Other than that, then."

"Agreed." He tilted his head a little. "Oddly enough, if you hadn't fled a year ago, we would have had the same arrangement."

"I was more naïve then. I suppose I wanted more."

Lord Fenton nodded. "I expect you to remove yourself

from The Tantalus Club immediately. You cannot work there and prepare for a wedding with me. I won't have it. And neither will your parents."

That statement hurt worse than she'd expected. "They have been very kind to me. I daresay if I hadn't been able to find employment there, my next choice would mean that neither you nor my family would be welcoming me back now." She took a breath, fighting abrupt panic at the thought of moving back into a hostile household and then into a cold, uncaring one. "I will give my notice, and work until they are able to replace me." Which wouldn't happen until the day she married him.

"No."

She lifted her chin. "Yes."

The marquis opened his mouth, then closed it again. "Have it your way. But there will be no announcement, and no money will be exchanging hands, until you leave that place. Tell that to your new friend and see how supportive he is." He took one step closer. "That's the difference between Bloody Blackwood and me. I am direct and honest. I don't pretend to be a friend when I'm not one."

"And yet no one knows he's your cousin," she commented, ignoring the remainder of his statement. Only someone who'd never had a friend would think he could sway her away from one with a few biting words. "How direct and honest is that?"

"That's a matter of him being unable to behave. If he could do so, I would happily tell everyone of our connection."

This was getting them nowhere, and the more they talked about Keating, the more likely she was to say something in his defense that his cousin couldn't overlook. And concerned with the appearance of propriety as he was, Lord Fenton likely would take serious issue with the knowledge that she'd had sex with his cousin. And that she fully intended to do so again.

After a moment spent looking about as though he were seeking for something to say and not succeeding, Fenton turned back toward the house and offered his arm again. With a sigh, she took it.

"Your parents and I will make the arrangements for the wedding," he said, his tone cool and unconcerned once again. "And you will not flee this time."

"No, I won't flee. As long as you honor all the things you've promised. To everyone concerned."

"I will."

They walked in silence for the remainder of their stroll, until he parted from her at the foot of the short drive. "Your father knows how to reach me," he said. "Good afternoon, Lady Camille."

"Lord Fenton."

When he'd vanished back up the street, Camille turned to look up at the house. She'd grown up there, and yet nowhere seemed more foreign and less welcoming. The idea of moving back there—well, she wouldn't do so. Not until the very last possible moment. She'd never seen more than the front of Pollard House, but evidently she would be its mistress very soon.

"How did you do that?" Marie whispered.

She'd forgotten her sister was there. "Do what?" she asked, turning around to face her.

Marie's hair was three or four shades darker than her own, and her eyes a much deeper, prettier blue. "You just said whatever you wanted to. I would have died of mortification."

"I've discovered there are things worse than mortification." Camille cleared her throat, less certain about how to proceed with her sister than she had been with her prospective spouse. But then she didn't know him. "Have you and Joanna been well?"

"Mama barely lets us leave the house. We almost didn't come to London for the Season, because she knew we would be laughed at. I hate it. The only thing that would be worse would be if she'd decided I was to miss my debut after all."

"Everything should be well resolved and forgotten very soon," Camille offered. "And as a marchioness, I'll be able to introduce you to a great many handsome young men."

"They all know you now, don't they? From The Tan . . . from that place."

"It's a gentlemen's club, Marie. Not a brothel."

Her sister's cheeks turned red. "Don't say such things. My goodness. We were never raised to act as you have. I don't understand it at all. I thought . . . I thought we were friends, as well as sisters."

"We were. We are. I can't explain why I did what I did, because in retrospect it seems very silly. But I've learned some very important lessons since then."

"Well, I should hope so." Marie started up the drive, then slowed when she realized Camille wasn't following her. "Are you coming inside?"

"No, I don't think so. I have some things to see to."

"But Joanna and I have missed you." Returning, she took Camille's arm in both of her hands. "We truly have. It's been terrible having to listen to the things Papa and especially Mama said after you left."

She didn't want to know what those things were. "What if I come by tomorrow and take you two to luncheon?" she asked instead. "Then we can chat without Mama frowning at everything we say."

"I would like that." Marie kissed her cheek. "And you

could tell us about meeting Bloody Blackwood. Did he truly shoot the Viscount of Balthrow?"

"He says he did."

"He's so handsome. I can see why Lady Balthrow fell in love with him." Squeezing her arm, Marie giggled. "Is he deadly dangerous?"

"Not to me." Not in the way Marie meant, at least. In other ways, he'd stabbed straight through her heart before she'd ever realized it.

Abruptly the need to see him again shoved through her. There might not have been a date set yet for the wedding, but it was inevitable. And then he would leave.

"I'm sorry, Marie, but I really must go," she said, her voice wobbling a little. "I'm still employed at that place, you know."

"Not for long." With a last kiss to the cheek, Marie climbed the front steps and vanished back into the house. Camille watched after her long enough to be certain she was safely inside, then went to hire a hack.

"Where to, miss?" the gap-toothed driver asked as Camille climbed inside.

"Baswich House. On South Audley Street."

Once Keating realized that Camille was actually heading for Baswich House, he cursed and spurred Amble down a street parallel to the hack.

The walk had been briefer than he'd expected, and even halfway down the street from the conversation he could tell that the meeting hadn't been cordial. At the same time he hadn't seen anything to make him race to the rescue, and the devil knew he'd been more than ready for any excuse to do that.

No, she'd kept her head up, her back straight, and what-

ever she'd said had kept Fenton from looming over her
and yelling. In fact, as well as he knew his cousin, he
could tell that Stephen didn't quite know what to do with
his bride-to-be.

Another thought struck him. Perhaps she was racing
over to the Duke of Greaves's house to tell him that
she'd changed her mind, and she was no one's bride-
to-be. Keen hope tumbled through him, immediately followed by worry. After all, whether she'd considered it or
not, The Tantalus Club employed young, lovely ladies. For
the moment she could continue there, but it was no way to
fund the remainder of her life.

And while he would have been happy, ecstatic even, to
offer her a home, it wouldn't solve anything. He was a pariah and always would be. Even worse, once he'd funded
Eleanor, he barely took in enough income to pay his servants and keep his land. With Fenton and his substantial
holdings, she could have everything.

As of this morning it had become even more complicated than that. While Eleanor hadn't outright agreed
to introduce him to Michael, she had intimated that she
would. That, however, depended on the ten thousand
pounds Stephen had promised him.

He cursed again. They all should have left him alone
at Havard's Glen. He would never have met Camille Pryce,
never had the hope that he would meet his son, never
think he could somehow make amends for what he'd done
six years ago.

Amble galloped up the Baswich House drive, and he
jumped from the saddle before the gray gelding had managed to come to a stop. "See to him," he ordered a groom,
and ran for the house.

A surprised-looking Hooper pulled open the door as he

strode through it. "I've been here all morning," he said, panting, and thundered up the stairs without waiting for an answer.

In his rooms he pulled off his riding boots and jacket and dug into his wardrobe for something a gentleman staying in for the day would wear. What that might be he had no real idea, but when Pidgeon appeared to assist him, at least the valet didn't faint.

The butler knocked at his door. "Enter," he called.

"Mr. Blackwood, Lady Camille Pryce is downstairs and wishes to speak to you. She is alone, sir."

"Did you tell her I'd been here all day?"

"She didn't ask, sir. I couldn't think of a way to mention it without arousing suspicion. I can go tell her if you wish."

"Don't be an ass, Hooper. And don't pretend to be scandalized. I know in whose household you serve."

"My apologies, Mr. Blackwood. I've put her in the morning room."

"Good. I'll be down directly. Offer her some tea."

"Yes, sir."

Keating lifted his chin as Pidgeon knotted his cravat. More than anything he wanted to charge down the stairs and discover what he'd missed in his observation of that little jaunt earlier, but he didn't want her knowing that he'd been spying on her.

"Are you finished yet?"

"If you would stop moving about, sir," Pidgeon said with a grimace.

"Just hurry it up."

Finally the valet stepped back. "I suppose that'll d—"

"Make yourself scarce," Keating ordered, pulling open the door and charging down the stairs.

The morning room door stood open, and he was halfway inside when he realized that Camille was seated very calmly beneath the front window and sipping a steaming cup of tea. Slowing his charge, he made for the chair opposite the side table from hers and sank down into it.

"Is this a good or a bad visit?" he asked, attempting to disguise the fact that he was breathing hard.

Without answering or even looking at him, Camille set down her tea, stood up, and walked over to shut and lock the morning room door. His insides clenched in response. Instead of returning to her chair, she put a hand on his shoulder and sat across his thighs. Then, to his surprise, she leaned her head against his shoulder.

If Fenton had hurt her, he would die. Old friends, cousins—it didn't matter. Slowly, reluctant to give her reason to move, he wrapped his arms around her shoulders. The quiet . . . joy at just sitting quietly with Camille in his arms stunned him down to his very cynical soul.

"You were right about Lord Fenton," she finally said, twining her fingers around the top button of his waistcoat.

"In what way? I said a great many things about him, as I recall."

"He isn't a monster."

Keating closed his eyes for a moment. "That's a good thing, isn't it?" he forced himself to say.

"I suppose so. Marie chaperoned us on our stroll, and she was quite impressed that I'd spoken my mind. Evidently I never used to do such a scandalous thing." She opened the button and slipped her hand inside his waistcoat, her palm warm over his heart.

Desire rumbled through him. "Tell me what you said. I'm all aflutter."

She chuckled. "I merely said that I wasn't impressed with his warmth then or now, and that with the exception of producing an heir I expected to be left to pursue my own interests and run my own household, and that he and I would have as little to do with each other as possible."

Every word she spoke was like a punch to his gut. But she couldn't be allowed to know that. This was for her benefit, and he would keep repeating that to himself until he believed it. "And he didn't suffer an apoplexy and drop dead?" he asked lightly.

"He wasn't amused, but he agreed." Lifting her head a little, she softly kissed his jaw. "I left it to him and my parents to set a date for the wedding; I simply didn't have the stomach for that."

"I don't blame you."

Another button opened. "Have you been able to find any further sign of Lady Balthrow?" she continued, her lips on his throat nearly making his eyes roll back in his head.

Keating could practically hear her thoughts. If he couldn't find Eleanor, if there remained no hope of his ever seeing Michael, would he still need the ten thousand pounds? Would he consider completely ruining her life as he'd already ruined his own? And to his shame, it was tempting. So damned tempting.

"She was waiting for me when I returned here this morning," he said, the words sticking in his throat.

Her head shot up, her blue eyes widening. "What? You met with her?"

He nodded.

"What did she say? Is Michael with her? Were you able to see your son? D—"

Keating put a hand over her mouth. "I can't answer if you won't shut up," he said, replacing his palm with his lips and touched that she would be so concerned over his son and his troubles when she had so many of her own.

She pulled away from him and stood, smoothing her skirts. "Tell me."

"Eleanor seemed concerned that I was in London to . . . return to my old ways—which I seem to be doing."

"No you aren't. This is different." She gestured between him and herself. "We are different."

"Because I I . . . Because I'm more fond of you than I ever was of her? Otherwise I see a very strong resemblance, my dear."

Christ, he'd almost said it. Almost admitted that he loved her. As if that would do anything but make an untenable situation even worse for both of them. He drew in a shuddering breath. Calm. He only needed to be calm.

"Anyway," he continued after a moment, "she said Michael wasn't with her, but she intimated that she might allow me to see him if I could prove that I would continue to support the two of them."

"I hope you told her about the money you'll be receiving."

"I did. That's when she said I might see my son."

A tear ran down her cheek, and at the sight of it Keating felt like someone had ripped a hole in his heart. If this was love, he wished he'd never discovered it. The damned thing hurt like the devil, and he couldn't see any merit in it at all.

"I'm so happy for you," she said, wiping at her eyes.

"Really."

"Yes! Of course I am. You deserve to see Michael."

"I don't know about that, but thank you for saying so."

Camille gazed at him for several hard beats of his damaged heart. Then she visibly shook herself. "I should go. I just wanted you to know that Fenton and I have reached an agreement."

Keating reached out for her hand and drew her down onto his lap again. However much self-control he'd been attempting, there were moments when it simply wasn't worth the effort. She consumed him, and if he didn't have her, he was quite certain he would expire well before her wedding to another man.

He placed her hand back on the buttons of his half-open waistcoat. "Are you finished with being wicked, then?" he murmured, lowering his head to nibble at her exposed throat.

She gave a shuddering sigh. "Not quite yet, I don't think." Her slender fingers opened a third button, then the fourth. "But I'm to work at luncheon, so don't ruin my hair."

Keating chuckled. "I shall endeavor." With an open-mouthed, tongue-tangling kiss, he shifted so that she straddled his lap, then pulled her skirts free. They settled around them, disguising the fact that the only thing keeping him from her was the stretching material of his trousers.

"Oh, my goodness," she said with a shiver, wriggling her hips experimentally.

She would be the death of him, he was certain. "Lift up a bit," he ordered, reaching between them first to unfasten his trousers and shove them down, and then to slip a finger inside her damp heat. "You look so demure above your skirts," Keating commented, taking her hips and drawing her down around his hard, straining cock.

Camille shut her eyes as he impaled her. "Mm," she murmured, her hands on his shoulders. Slowly she lifted up and then sank down again. "I don't feel at all demure," she said raggedly, opening her eyes again.

"Neither do I. Hold on."

With that he surged up into her, lifting and lowering her hips over him until she took up the hard, fast rhythm herself. Panting, she smiled wantonly at him as she bounced enthusiastically up and down on his cock while he lifted his hips to meet her. "I like this."

Keating cupped the back of her head, keeping in mind that he wasn't to destroy her hair, and drew her face forward to kiss her again. Tense need speared through him, his already ragged control splintering. As she came around him, he let and found his own release deep inside her.

Leaning forward, Camille rested her cheek against his shoulder. For a long moment they stayed that way, breathing hard, his cock still inside her. He could hear the faint pop of the fire in the hearth, the carriage wheels rattling by outside the window, the distant sound of voices chatting, hawking wares, and someone loudly proclaiming that he knew a Thoroughbred when he saw one. If time could be stopped, a moment savored, he would have chosen this one.

Finally Camille straightened again, looking down at him. "This is a very handy way to do this," she said, grinning.

"It is, though I prefer to see you naked. And to have a bit more time with you."

A shadow crossed her vision. He knew precisely what had caused it; more time was something they simply didn't have. Every moment was one less he could look forward to sharing with her.

"When is Fenton to pay you?" she asked abruptly, lifting up and then recovering her legs to stand up again and smooth down her skirts.

"The day after your wedding." He stood, as well, fastening his trousers and buttoning up his waistcoat again.

She frowned. "You should have it now, while Lady Balthrow is in London. She might have Michael with her, after all."

The thought had occurred to him as well, but he had no wish to end this . . . whatever it was between them before he had to. "After the wedding is what I agreed to. I imagine that will be soon enough."

He took her hands in his and leaned down to kiss her. Her soft, warm lips molded with his, stealing his breath and his thoughts and his soul. She was what he might have had, if he'd lived a better life. He hadn't, and the best he could do now was have a taste and then watch her walk away.

Finally he let her go, and she started for the door. With her hand on the latch, though, she faced him again. "Is this it?"

If he had any sense at all, it would be. If he'd learned anything six years ago, he would nod his head and tell her good-bye and stay inside this house until the day after her wedding. "That depends," he said, anyway, forcing a slight smile. "I thought I might attempt a picnic luncheon on Tuesday. Would you and Sophia care to join Greaves and me?"

Camille actually looked relieved, as if she hadn't realized that he was making things worse. "I think that would be splendid."

She was wrong about that, but if he would be spending the remainder of his life without her, he wanted more—just a little more—to remember her by.

Chapter Nineteen

For two days nothing untoward happened, though Camille had to admit that the lessening of insults and sideways glances might have simply been because she no longer cared enough even to notice them. But she knew something was amiss the moment she caught sight of Juliet Langtree slipping through the crowd of men and into the Demeter Room.

Juliet was the face of The Tantalus Club every evening. Someone had even written a song about the angel-faced butleress guarding the door to happiness, or some such thing. She did not leave her station at the front door. Not unless something extraordinary was afoot. And at the moment the butleress's gaze was on . . . her.

Camille disliked working evenings as it was. The club members had had time to drink, which made them all seem less . . . refined. Lately it bothered her much less, and considering the long memories in Mayfair, she assumed she would be tolerating those looks for the remainder of her life. Even as a marchioness, even as they dined at her home and complimented her for her fine jewelry.

But at the moment she watched Juliet. "What's wrong?" she asked in a low voice, the moment the butleress stopped in front of her.

"Lord Montshire and Lord Fenton are here," Juliet murmured.

All the blood left her face, and she grabbed onto the podium to keep from swaying. "But . . . they aren't members." And Fenton, at least, had been banned from the premises.

"They procured an invitation from Lord Cleaves. Lady Haybury said I'm to ask you before I admit them."

Oh, dear. A few weeks ago she would have fainted already. Or more likely, she would have gathered up her skirts and fled up to her room, locked the door, and hid under the bed. "Let them in."

"You're certain?" Juliet whispered, lifting an eyebrow. "I have several well-rehearsed excuses to hand."

"Evidently they are prepared to be stared at and gossiped about," Camille returned. "And I'm accustomed to it. Let them in to share some of my discomfort."

With a somewhat incredulous nod, Juliet turned on her heel and headed back to the foyer. Camille caught Sophia's quizzical, concerned glance from halfway across the room and sent back a half smile.

This was her chance, she supposed, to show both her father and her almost-betrothed that she had learned to stand on her own two feet. That she held her head high, and was returning to the proper side of Mayfair because she chose to do so. Not because she had no other choice.

And they'd best thank Lady Balthrow as well, because if not for her and Keating's need to support her, Camille would have been much less inclined these days to find propriety once more. That was the thing about courage, she was discovering. It opened so much more of the world to her than she'd expected.

A few moments later the two men, her father and her

almost-husband, strolled into the Demeter Room. Fenton, at least, looked like he wanted to tuck his head inside his coat like a turtle. At the same time, his gaze roved everywhere, taking in the opulence of The Tantalus Club for the first time.

"Good evening," she said, pleased that her voice was steady. "May I show you to a table?"

Her father's jaw clenched. He'd always been more tolerant of her high spirits than her mother had been, but he'd had as much of a hand in tossing her out of the house as anyone. "Yes, thank you," he finally said.

"Ordinarily I'm afraid we would have had you wait in one of the gaming rooms," she said, turning to lead them through the room and attempting to ignore the dozens of speculative male eyes gazing in their direction, "as we're always quite busy on Monday nights. But we keep a table reserved for special guests."

Stopping beside the neatly set table beneath the garden window, she gestured for them to be seated. "Your menus are here, or if there is something for which you have a particular fondness, our chefs are phenomenal. One of our waitresses will be by in a few moments. Have a grand evening."

"Camille," her father muttered, his gaze on the list of wines set on the table, "you do this every evening?"

"I have Sundays and every other Tuesday free, and usually I work in the mornings. I've been . . . working less, so when someone needs an evening off, I stand in for them."

"But who are these other women? You *live* with them?"

"We are all sisters here, my lord. For many of us, this was a last chance before complete desperation." Another trio of gentlemen walked into the room, and she took a step backward. "Now if you'll excuse me, I have my duties to see to."

Sophia caught her arm as they walked across the dining room. "Did you know they were coming here?" she whispered.

"I had no idea. And I'm not certain why they did so. If they meant to embarrass me into leaving, I won't—"

"You know you can't be a marchioness and work here. Not unless you're Lady Haybury and own the establishment."

"I know that. But I'm not walking away from a bed and an income until I have somewhere else to go."

"You could go home."

To her surprise, she felt tears in her eyes. Swiftly she rubbed at her forehead, pinching the bridge of her nose until the sensation went away. "This is home."

"Oh, stop it, Cammy. You'll make me cry." Sophia hugged her arm. "I'm happy for you. Not many of us get to come here and then be offered more."

Yes, she was supposed to be grateful for a second chance. When Keating had first delivered the news, the thought that those glances and mutterings would stop had seemed a delirious dream. In the midst of all her wishes that things could be the way they used to be, however, she'd discovered something in an entirely new and unexpected direction.

Keating, though, needed something more than she could give him. Yes, her parents were wealthy, but she'd been cut off the moment she'd left her own wedding. And the only way she could help him was to return to Fenton. It was a very small sacrifice, really. After all, she would have everything she wanted. With one notable, heartrending exception.

"What do you think they're doing?" Sophia asked.

Camille shook herself, and a daydream of the impossible splintered into nothing. "I think they're setting a date for the wedding. And they want me to know it—though I'm not certain why they think I would be surprised. I agreed to it, after all."

"And what about Keating?"

Reaching the podium, Camille flipped through the notes in the daily book. "I don't want to talk about him. Not out here."

"Of course. But I think I'm going to procure a bottle of whiskey for later."

Camille forced a smile. "A very good idea."

"Yes, I know."

For two hours she attempted to avoid the table by the garden window without appearing to do so. What a difference from the first time a date had been set for her wedding to Fenton. Back a year ago she'd been so excited she could barely sit still, drawing sketches of the flowers and the ribbons she wanted for the church, imagining how romantic it would be when Stephen Pollard finally arrived on her doorstep to introduce himself.

Now all she cared about was that Keating would have his money—in which case the sooner the event took place, the better. On the other hand, once she married she wouldn't see him again. He might be Fenton's cousin, but she had the feeling that he didn't attend family holidays. Or he wouldn't after this, at any rate.

"A word with you," her father said from behind her.

She turned around to see him and Fenton. *Oh, dear.* A shiver went through her. With a nod she led the way through the crowded foyer and out to the front drive. "I only have a moment."

"Very well. Your wedding will take place in a week, on Saturday the eighteenth. That should shorten both the anticipation and give you too little time to change your mind again."

"I won't change my mind."

"Even so. I've applied for a special license from Canterbury. We're making arrangements to let a small church in Knightsbridge, and we will decide the guest list. Only afterward will all financial considerations be settled." Her father glanced at Fenton. "Is there anything you wish to add?"

"No, my lord. Only that I'm pleased we could come to this agreement. For all our sakes."

And what little hope she'd had for a bit of romance crumbled into dust. "Very well," she said aloud. "I'll give my notice to Lady Haybury for the seventeenth."

"You should leave now. There's no need." The marquis frowned. "Everyone sees you here."

"You've made your arrangements, and these are mine. Now I need to return to my station. Excuse me."

She turned away swiftly, so they wouldn't see the tears overflowing her eyes. This would be the second time her wedding would be the saddest day of her life. Only this time she had so much more to lose.

"Explain something to me," the Duke of Greaves commented as he took a seat in his large, lush barouche.

"This again? What?" Keating wasn't much in the mood for questions, but considering that Greaves was missing a session at the House of Lords to eat sandwiches on the grass, he supposed he owed his friend a conversation.

"Camille Pryce."

"No."

Greaves lifted an eyebrow. "I haven't asked my question yet."

"I'm not talking about her. Choose another topic."

"We're going to retrieve her and her friend what's-her-name from the Tantalus. Are you going to ignore her, or just not talk about her?"

"Sophia," Keating supplied. *Damnation.* He supposed the questions would come sooner or later. Best work out his replies now, so he'd have them memorized the first time he became too drunk to summon an original thought. "What do you want explained, then?"

"You've given her to Fenton, yes?"

"I've returned her to Fenton."

"In exchange for money."

"A great deal of money."

Adam eyed him. "And she's willing to go."

"Wouldn't you be, if you'd spent the past year or so ruined? She's a lady. And while she might have made friends at her club, I very much doubt she would choose to live the remainder of her life surrounded by rogues and roués."

"Meaning you."

With a scowl, Keating turned to view the street as they passed by. "I suggest you stop attempting to decipher me before I attempt to thrash you for it." He folded his arms across his chest. "And I notice you aren't disagreeing with my assessment of her situation."

"I'm still doing my own assessing."

"Keep it to yourself, then."

"The eighteenth. That's four days from now."

"Yes. I have a calendar."

Greaves sighed audibly. "This should be pleasant," he muttered, just loud enough for Keating to hear him.

Keating supposed he might have made an attempt to be more pleasant and to explain that of course he *wanted* to keep Camille in his life, craved her presence and her touch, but that logically she would simply be better off elsewhere. Early on she'd made it quite clear what made her happy—and that was friends and luncheons and dances and strolls where no one looked askance at her.

He had his own reason for seeing her married to Fenton, of course, and the question of what he was willing to give up in exchange for a faceless boy and a mistake he'd made six years ago had kept him from sleep for the past week. For him it was a miasma without a positive outcome—so all he could do was arrange for her to be happy.

"One more question."

Shaking himself, he looked back at his friend. "Good God."

"Do I know that she's agreed to marry Fenton, or am I ignorant?"

"It was in the newspaper this morning, if you'll recall. And you might as well know, anyway. Sophia more than likely does, and it'll give the two of you a chance to gossip."

This time Greaves looked affronted. "I don't gossip. And certainly not with a gentlemen's club hostess."

"Then sit there and look pretty. If I can, I want a word or two with Camille." Because while he couldn't do it the other day, today he needed to say good-bye. Seeing her again after this, knowing what had to come next, or worse, what had happened—it was more than his ill-used restraint and self-control could manage.

For several moments they drove on in silence.

"A last question, then."

"Damnation, Greaves, what do you want from me?" Keating exploded, facing into the barouche to glare at his companion.

The duke gazed at him coolly. "Never mind. You just answered it." He rapped on the back of the driver's seat with his cane. "Here will do, Saunders."

The barouche rolled to a stop. Greaves stood and

unlatched the door, then stepped down to the ground. "What are you doing?" Keating demanded. "I need you to chaper—"

"The other chit can chaperone for you," Adam interrupted. "I have something to see to."

"So you're simply going to walk from . . . here," Keating returned, looking at the busy Mayfair street around them.

Greaves swung his cane in his hand. "I've a good idea I'll be fine. Drive on, Saunders."

The fine-grained mahogany cane concealed a razor-sharp rapier, and Adam Baswich knew precisely how to use it. He stood at the side of the street for a moment as the barouche and the annoyed, frustrated-looking Keating Blackwood drove off in the direction of The Tantalus Club.

Once the carriage turned the corner, Adam headed up a side street to hire a hack. Generally he would rather have chewed off his own foot than ride in one of the ill-sprung, smelly contraptions, but evidently haste was of the essence.

He'd expected Lady Camille to balk a bit longer before her second attempt at marrying Fenton, just as he'd thought Keating would put another tree or two in his cousin's path. Evidently, however, two martyrs aimed in the same direction could easily conquer and destroy any possible means to happiness before them.

In front of a small line of shops and offices in Knightsbridge he stepped down from the coach. "Wait here for me," he said to the driver.

"I ain't g—"

"Right here," Adam repeated, and flipped the man a gold sovereign.

The fellow snapped his mouth shut around his complaint and instead tugged on the brim of his hat. "Aye, m'lord. Right here."

"That's 'Your Grace,'" Adam muttered, but kept his voice low enough that the driver couldn't hear him. Anonymity was damned annoying. It was also necessary, however.

Stopping in front of one of the narrow doors, he pushed it open and stepped inside the dim office. "Harrow?" he called, removing his blue beaver hat and dropping his gloves into it.

"Your Grace? Back here." A tall, thin man with spectacles and a slightly hunched back appeared in the rear doorway and then vanished again. "I didn't expect you today."

Adam followed him into the even smaller room behind the first. Stacks of books and papers filled the ceiling-high shelves and the two worktables wedged into the space, barely leaving room for a single chair and a trio of sputtering lamps. "Time is more of a factor than I'd realized," he said, dropping his hat onto one of the shorter stacks of books. "Have you found anything?"

"You nobles are a tight-lipped lot, Your Grace," Harrow returned, digging through a stack of papers and pulling one of them free.

"Yes, I know. Am I paying you for your insightful commentary, or for results?"

"Both, I hope." Harrow held the paper closer to one of the lamps, squinting even with the spectacles. "I've an appointment on Thursday. First time that Evans bloke has agreed to see me. But it will cost you."

"Pay it. Add it to my tab." He reached out and took the paper to look at it for himself. The information there stirred in him an emotion he generally sought to avoid these days. Anger. "You're certain this is accurate?"

"My people don't stay in my employment by imagining facts."

"Then I'll see to this." Folding the paper, Adam stuffed it into his pocket. "I need an answer by Friday. Any later will do me no good."

"You'll have it then, Your Grace."

"I'd better."

Four days to avert a disaster. A difficult task in itself, but when he factored in a rogue who thought he deserved all the pain he'd incurred, he wanted to begin using the word "miracle." It would take one to resolve this, and another measure of luck on top of that.

Adam sighed. Best get to it, then. And hope he didn't find himself bloodied and battered for his trouble.

"I can't imagine why they won't allow you to invite any of your own wedding guests," Sophia said ruefully as she handed a platter of biscuits to Keating.

He took four of the ones with cinnamon in them. "For people attempting to step back into Society's favor, they're rushing this rather alarmingly."

"I'm inviting the two of you, anyway," Camille stated, taking one of Keating's biscuits from him and biting into it. "And Lord and Lady Haybury and whomever else I wish to see there."

Keating glanced sideways at her. "Invite Greaves, will you? Your family's not likely to turn a duke away from the church doors."

"Certainly."

He took a breath. "I meant to tell you, I'm leaving for Shropshire on Saturday. I've been away for too long, and I wore out my welcome here years ago."

She wanted to argue with him, tell him that she wanted to catch sight of him at the wedding to remind herself that what she'd agreed to was worth it. That what they would both gain might balance what she felt she was losing. Of course neither of them had ever said anything about forevers, so perhaps she was daydreaming and deluding herself again. But she didn't think so.

Leaving it unsaid, however, might be infinitely less painful. It was only that she had nothing with which to compare it. "What about the money?" she asked aloud.

"I've left instructions for my solicitor to deposit everything in Eleanor's name." His gaze lowered to her mouth as she devoured his biscuit. "So if you don't mind, I'd prefer to wish you well today."

Sophia abruptly stood up. "Oh, look! A duck," she commented, and sped off in the direction of the quaint wooden bridge.

"Did I frighten her away?" Keating asked, handing over a second biscuit.

"I think that was her way of subtly giving us a moment of privacy." Camille forced a smile. "Relatively speaking."

"If I'd realized she was so willing to leave us be, I'd have attempted rendering you naked and having at you weeks ago. Subtlety be damned."

As if in response to that statement a quartet of young ladies strolled by on the path, all of them gawking. Camille just refrained from sticking out her tongue at them. They'd likely faint, and in addition she might well be entertaining them or their families at dinner in the next month.

He tapped the back of her forefinger with his. "I have a proposal for you."

Her face must have looked as startled as she felt, because he sat up straight and scowled. For that second, before she'd realized that he meant something else entirely, she'd felt . . . joy. "A proposal," she repeated dubiously.

"Don't faint, Cammy."

"Oh, very amusing. I'm not the one bandying about words like 'proposal,' sir."

A faint, warm smile cracked his face. "I apologize. All I wanted to do was suggest that for the next five minutes we say whatever we wish, whatever comes to mind. And then, after the five minutes is done with, we never mention them again."

Light brown eyes met hers, daring her to agree. "You know nothing good will come of it."

"I know. But this is our last chance."

Oh, it was the worst idea ever in the history of ideas. And at the same time the desire to tell him precisely how she felt about him pulled at her, much like the man himself. She'd been saying it to herself for days and days. To say it to him, to hear him perhaps return the sentiment, to know that in the world someone—he—loved her . . .

She closed her eyes for a moment. "No."

When she opened them again he was still gazing at her, his expression unreadable. "Why not?" he asked in a low, flat voice.

"Because it will hurt. And because you'll use those five minutes to torture yourself, just as I will. And because I have noticed that you've nearly stopped drinking, and I won't be responsible for you taking it up again and hitting people who look askance at you. Because I'm happy—very happy—to have met you, and I don't want to regret it."

After a long moment his mouth curved up at the corners. "And you didn't even need five minutes for all that."

Camille snorted. "I hate you."

His smile softened. "I hate you, too." Clearing his throat, he handed her a glass of Madeira. "I do want to say one thing to you. If Fenton makes you unhappy, if he gives you a moment's pause or concern, promise that you'll write me."

"And what would you do? Keating, he's your cousin, and I . . . you have a history. I wouldn't do that to you."

"I wouldn't shoot him, if that's what you're worried over," he said, his voice tightening. "But I could damned well make my concerns very, very clear."

She stroked her finger down his wrist, unable to resist touching him. "You are a very peculiar sort of knight in shining armor, you know."

And on a different day, in a different life, he might have been *her* knight in shining armor. If she'd required any more proof that wishes were for little girls and simply didn't come true, all she needed to do was look into the eyes of the man she loved—four days before she walked down the aisle to marry someone else.

Chapter Twenty

Once Keating saw Camille and Sophia safely back to The Tantalus Club, he sent the barouche away. While in the past he'd preferred smoky midnight clubs and darkened boudoirs, fresh air and a walk seemed much more conducive to clear thinking.

For some reason his mind refused to let go of the idea that he'd missed something, that he could do . . . something to send his personal nightmare onto a better path. He wanted Camille for himself.

He also wanted to have been a better man than he was, he wanted never to have spent time in beds that legally belonged to other men, and he wanted never to have met Eleanor Howard. If he'd known—but that didn't suffice, either, because Camille had been promised to Fenton practically since her birth.

His own troubles merely made the impossible *more* impossible. And yelling at the heavens and shouting that it wasn't fair—well, coming from him, all the angels must already be laughing at him.

When he looked up he found himself on Bolton Street, and in fact directly in front of Pollard House. Hm. That was interesting. He'd meant what he'd said to Camille, that if she found herself less than happy in Stephen's company the marquis should expect a visit from his cousin.

Best make that clear in advance, as well. Squaring his shoulders, Keating walked up the front drive and swung the brass knocker against the door. The stout, ancient man who opened the door had been at his position for as long as Keating could remember, and he nodded. "Anders. Is my cousin at home?"

The butler stepped back from the doorway. "Master Blackwood. If you'll wait in the morning room, I shall inquire."

He took in the view of the morning room much as he had several weeks ago. The tall windows with slightly faded brown and gold curtains that matched the gold-threaded fabric of the furniture, the tasteful selection of Staffordshire pottery dogs and cats on the mantel and shelves, the cast-iron swan on the hearth. For a moment he felt twelve years old again, and he scowled at his hesitation before sitting on a chair.

Perhaps Pollard House wasn't as opulent as the home in which Camille had grown up, but she would have a maid and new gowns and a place where men wouldn't pinch her arse simply because they thought they could get away with it. And he had no doubt she would make the place feel comfortable, alive. Of course he would never set foot in the foyer again, but he supposed that wasn't the point. He wouldn't let it be the point.

The door opened. "What is it, Keating?" Fenton asked, still pulling on a light blue jacket. "I'm rather occupied at the moment."

"Yes, you've a wedding in four days. I just thought we might chat for a moment."

Stephen looked at him, then leaned back into the hallway. "Anders, a pot of tea, if you please."

"My lord."

Keating kept his seat, watching as his cousin closed the morning room door and walked over to gaze out the window. What did Camille see when she looked at the Marquis of Fenton? Stephen was fairly tall, and he rode almost daily, which kept him fit. A trio of lines bisected his forehead, a result of too much frowning, and Keating doubted such a thing as laugh lines would ever trouble the marquis's face.

"I'm waiting," Fenton said into the silence. "If this is about your money, I told you when you'd receive it."

"I know. The day after your wedding." Keating attempted not to growl over the word. "I'm attempting to decipher the quality of luck."

His cousin turned around. "What? You interrupted my day to discuss luck? You're the gambler. Decipher it yourself."

"That's the thing. I can't. I mean, here you are, a cold-hearted, stiff-spined bastard who never cared about anything but your own comfort, and you—"

"Excuse me, but you're calling *me* self-involved? After the way you tore through London six years ago? You embarrassed me, you embarrassed your family name, and you embarrassed everyone who called themselves nobility. Not to mention the fact that you killed a man."

Keating stood up. "Yes, let's not mention that. I don't deserve luck; I'm perfectly aware of that. My question is about you. How is it that you deserve someone like Camille Pryce?"

" 'Deserve'? That's an interesting word. I suppose you mean that she's some sort of reward of which I'm unworthy. I see it differently myself."

"How so?"

"Suffice it to say that I've only met one other person

with a worse reputation and a greater tendency toward self-destruction. So, no, I don't deserve her. I deserve a wife who has a grasp of duty and propriety and who hasn't attempted to drag my name through the mud for the past year."

"Then why marry her now?"

"Because she ran. And because when she walks back into that church and marries me, I win. And she loses. And because everyone who said my wife would rather work in a bawdy house than be the Marchioness of Fenton loses. A deal was agreed to. And I insist"—and Fenton slammed his hand against the top of the side table—"that it be honored."

Hm. This was the most passion Keating had seen from his cousin. Ever. But once again it wasn't about Camille. Rather, it was about himself. His victory, the agreement he wanted honored.

"You know," he said, attempting to keep his voice level, "if you would consider just for one damned minute *why* she didn't want to marry you, you might understand why you shouldn't be marrying her now."

"I *am* marrying her now, and I'm certainly not going to take advice from you." Fenton took a step closer. "And if you've developed some sort of infatuation with my fiancée, stop it."

" 'Stop it'?" Keating repeated, using every ounce of willpower he possessed to keep from launching himself at his cousin.

"You heard me. She belongs to me, and I won't have you shooting me because you think she'd be happier elsewhere."

It was a damned shame he'd already promised Cammy that he wouldn't do violence to Fenton. "I suggest you consider that the happier Camille is, the more pleasant your own life will be. Treat her well, cousin, or I *will* come looking for you." He turned on his heel, sidestepping the footman carrying a tea tray.

"Don't tell me you imagine yourself in love with her," Fenton said incredulously. "You? She's hardly your usual sort, Keating. Unless the rumors of her activities at that club are true."

Keating faced the marquis. "Camille Pryce is a magnificent young lady who deserves far better than you. And far, far better than me. Do right by her, Stephen."

"And you stay away from both of us."

He'd expected that. And considering that he couldn't stand the thought of her marrying someone else, hanging about the newly married couple would be worse than a stay in Purgatory. "I'm leaving on Saturday morning."

"Good. Good-bye, Keating."

With a stiff nod, Keating turned away again and left the house. For the last time ever. And then he went to get drunk.

"Camille, a moment, if you please."

Sophia patted her arm as they both turned to see the club's owner and proprietess approaching. "See you in a bit."

Lady Haybury looked stunning as she always did in her daring black attire. The rest of the ladies heading for their stations at the beginning of the morning shift moved around them, but Camille waited.

"Diane. I wanted to thank you for allowing me to stay for another few days."

The marchioness waved her hand, dismissing the notion. "You're an asset to the club; don't thank me for helping myself." She stopped in front of Camille. "I wanted you to know that you will always be welcome here."

"Even as a runaway marchioness?" Camille asked, forcing a smile.

"Oh, definitely then. The scandal alone would see us full to the rafters." Deep green eyes regarded her for a moment. "I'm not your sister, and heaven knows I'm not old enough to be your mama. But I am nearby, and generally people are afraid to cross me. And my husband is exceptionally devious." She sighed. "What I suppose I'm attempting to say is, if you need anything, you have only to ask."

"I don't suppose you could conjure a different husband for me, then?"

"Beg pardon?"

Camille shook herself. "I'm just rambling. It's only that an arranged marriage is nothing like a love match. I wish I'd realized that years ago." Then she wouldn't have run, and by the time she'd ever met Keating, she would have long ago given up such childish dreams.

"I told you that my first marriage was arranged," Diane said unexpectedly. "My husband wasn't a cruel man, but he certainly cared more for his own comforts than he cared for mine. It's the most miserable feeling in the world, the morning you awaken and realize that . . . this is all you'll have."

Camille swallowed. "If you'll excuse me, I don't wish to be late."

"Certainly."

Oh, she hadn't wanted to hear that. It was difficult enough to convince herself to go through with the wedding. If not for Keating . . . She shook herself. There were no more *if only* or *perhaps* moments left to her. Only two days of enjoying the company of friends and attempting to forget that Saturday loomed closer and closer over her head.

As she walked into the Demeter Room, even more gazes than usual were turned in her direction. The announcement of the wedding had appeared in the newspaper two days ago, so the interest didn't surprise her. She'd spent twenty minutes reading and rereading the short, concise notice. Even in stark black print it hadn't felt real. Not yet. She doubted it would until the moment she said "I do."

When she looked forward again, she slowed. Sophia stood at the podium in her place, but it was the tall, lean figure speaking with Miss White that caught her attention. The Duke of Greaves wore his usual cool, unflappable expression, but there was something in his light gray eyes that made her heart shiver.

"Good morning, Your Grace," she said, stopping beside her friend and unable to prevent herself from looking past the duke just to see if a particular friend of his might be present.

"Camille," he returned, inclining his head. "I've misplaced Keating, I'm afraid. You wouldn't happen to know where I might find him, would you?"

The chill in her deepened to ice. "No, I don't. When . . . when did you last see him?"

"Tuesday afternoon. Shortly before your picnic."

"When Keating said you abandoned us."

A brief frown crossed his face. "I did not abandon you. I had something to see to. Something quite important, as it turns out. But I need to find him before I can . . ." He trailed off. "Did he say anything to you?"

"He returned us here and then left," she answered. "He said he would be returning to Shropshire on Saturday." Scowling, Camille glanced sideways at Sophia's concerned expression before returning her attention to the imposing duke. "You truly haven't seen him for two days? Might he have simply gone home to Havard's Glen already?"

"Not likely. His valet's still at my home, for one thing. For another . . . No, he wouldn't have left yet." The duke swore under his breath.

"Have you tried the various other clubs?" Sophia suggested quietly. "I mean, Keating does have a certain reputation for drinking and wagering and . . . other things."

Camille didn't like hearing that at all. Had he simply found another chit to keep him company and forgotten about her already? Even as the thought occurred to her, though, she put it aside. The Keating of six years ago might have gone through several ladies since she'd last seen him, but he wasn't that man any longer—whether he felt comfortable acknowledging that or not.

Greaves was shaking his head. "I've been to a dozen clubs. No one's seen him. And he's not the type of fellow that people don't notice." He hesitated. "There are several places he used to frequent, but I can't imagine that he would go back to any of them." He looked at Camille. "Or perhaps he would," he said after a moment. "Excuse me, ladies."

Camille put her arm on his sleeve, and he stopped. "If you hear anything, Your Grace, please inform me," she whispered, her voice wobbling.

"Don't fear, Camille," he returned, patting her hand in a rather un-Greaves-like manner. "If he's learned one thing, it's how to live badly."

"But he has enemies."

The duke nodded. "That he does. I'll send word when I've tracked him down."

"Thank you."

With a last glance at Sophia, the duke excused himself and left the club again. Unsettled, Camille pasted on a smile and began seating the morning's guests.

What she wanted to do was run out the front door, hire a hack, and go searching for Keating. She had no doubt that he could defend himself if attacked, but that only worked with outside, tangible enemies.

She had resolved to wed Fenton. It was the action she chose to take because it would help Keating. In a sense, she had the easier side of things; she would be the one moving forward with a purpose, while Keating was forced to stand by and simply watch.

"Cammy, stop staring into nothing," Sophia whispered. "You're frightening the men."

Camille shook herself. "Sorry. I'm worried."

"I know."

"I want to go looking, but I have no idea where to begin." She edged closer to her friend. "Two days, Sophia. He's been missing for two days."

"Perhaps he did go home to Shropshire. I doubt he would miss his valet for a few days."

That made sense. She didn't like it, because it meant that that one last look she'd hoped to have, that one last kiss, had already happened. She hadn't been ready for it to be over.

"Well, if I haven't heard from His Grace by this afternoon, I'm going to call on him. I need to know." Because without knowing where Keating was, much less knowing if he was well or not, she could barely breathe. If something had happened to him . . . Well, there would be no reason to marry Fenton, would there? There would be no reason for anything.

Adam Baswich was beginning to feel distinctly soiled. Beginning with the loftiest of clubs—White's, the Tantalus, Boodles, the Society—he'd been searching for hours. By now he'd reached the dregs, and was quickly running out of places to look. For the devil's sake, he'd visited Jezebel's an hour ago. The places he had been reduced to visiting now barely seemed to exist in daylight.

Picking his way through an alleyway of trash and unconscious drunks and some other things he didn't care to examine too closely, he reached the half-rotted door at the end. Someone had carved the words "The Deval's Club" into the wood, leaving him unimpressed with both the penmanship and the spelling.

Once he pushed open the door, the scent of piss and sour ale hit him like a blow, and he had to stifle the urge to gag. The candlelight inside sputtered and smoked, the cheap tallow adding to the indescribable smell.

As his eyes grew more accustomed to the dimness, he made out a long, rough-wood bar in the far corner of the room, a skeleton standing behind it. "Christ," he muttered under his breath as the skeleton leaned its elbows on the bartop and gazed at him.

"What's yer poison?" the skeleton asked through a mouth half devoid of teeth.

"I'm looking for someone," Adam replied, beginning to realize the difference between someone who drank to maintain a reputation and one who drank . . . here.

"The girl's occupied upstairs. Wait ten minutes and ye can have her. Two shillings."

Oh, good God. "Not a chit. A man."

The skeleton squinted one eye. "Three shillings. Louis! Get yer cock over here. Someone wants it."

A chair squeaked along the floorboards behind Adam. "No," he blurted, reflecting that this was one of the few times he felt truly uncomfortable somewhere. "Someone who might have come here to drink. Tall, dark brown hair, nice teeth, likes to punch things?"

A hand pressed down on his shoulder. Whipping

around, Adam straight-armed the fellow hard in the chest—and Keating stumbled backward, falling onto his arse.

"Damnation," he said aloud, squatting down to eye his friend. "What the devil are you doing here?"

Keating fumbled up to a seated position on the floor. "I don't know," he mumbled. "Where am I?"

"I'll tell you later. Come on." Grabbing an arm, Adam hauled Blackwood to his feet.

"No." Keating pulled away. "I'm staying here. I'm going to live here."

"Oh. Very well, then."

Adam clenched his fist, pulled back his arm, and hit Keating in the jaw. Hard. His friend grunted, then collapsed.

Catching Keating as he fell, Adam hauled him over his shoulder, grabbing an arm and a leg to balance the considerable weight. "My thanks," he said to the skeleton, and left the club. Outside he carried Keating over to his waiting coach and dumped him inside onto the floor. "Home, Millet," he instructed his impassive driver, climbing in and taking a seat.

"Right away, Your Grace."

Keating peeled open one eye. Or at least he thought he did; the outside of his eyelid was as dark as the inside. Then the knife blade shot through his skull and lodged there, vibrating. Ah. Definitely awake, then.

With a groan he levered himself onto one elbow. As his one open eye focused, he realized he was in the bedchamber he'd been using at Baswich House. When had that happened?

At least someone had not only drawn the curtains, but had thrown blankets over the already heavy coverings.

Pidgeon, most likely. The valet had learned over the years
how best to limit his own exposure to his master while
Keating was . . . recovering from an evening—or several
of them—of overindulgence.

A glass of water sat on the bedstand. It would likely
make him ill, but his mouth and throat felt like they'd
been stuffed with sour cotton. Frowning, he took a single
swallow and slowly sat up, waiting to see what the effect
might be.

His door rattled and opened. At the flood of light coming from beyond, he closed both eyes again. "Shut it," he
rasped.

The door closed again. "I have tea with an absurd
amount of sugar," Greaves's voice came. "Pidgeon continues to insist that it helps, but I have my doubts."

"It does help. Sometimes." A hazy memory swam
through his brain. "You hit me."

"Yes, well, you said you intended to live at The Deval's
Club with an *a*. I couldn't allow you to reside at a place
where such poor spelling is tolerated."

"How did you find me?"

"A great deal of searching at some places I used to
know, and some I never wished to see again. Are you
coherent enough to answer a question?"

Keating squinted an eye open enough to grasp the hot
cup of tea and shovel several lumps of sugar into it. "Depends on the question."

"What, precisely, were you hoping to accomplish? You
send a chit off to the chapel, earn your eight pieces of silver, and then crawl off into the sewer? What's the point?"

"That's three questions." The pieces of silver refer-
ence, at least, seemed very fitting. Whatever Camille had
agreed to, he *felt* like a traitor. Because he knew deep

down that she would manage, but she wouldn't be happy. Not that he could make her happy, but damned Fenton certainly couldn't, either.

"Take the first one, then."

For a moment he couldn't remember what the first question had been. "I thought to make myself unavailable until after the church appointment on Saturday."

"Ah. You nearly made it, then."

Nearly? "What day is it?"

"Friday. Late afternoon."

"Damnation, Adam. You should have left me there."

"Hm." Moving silently even in the near total darkness, the duke reached the side of the bed and handed over a piece of paper. "I would have, except for this."

"What is it?"

"Since we can't light a lamp, I'll tell you. I had someone look into a few things. More specifically, I tracked Lady Balthrow's movements over the past six years."

Keating scowled. "What? She's been in Madrid. I told you that."

"So she and your solicitor have told you. I'd sack him, by the way. I decided to be suspicious and look into matters myself. Your dear anchor did spend a year in Madrid. Previous to that, she's rented homes in Vienna, Paris, Rome, Florence, and Venice." The duke glanced down at the paper. "She seems to enjoy Italy."

"What does this have to do with anything?" It didn't make sense, but even if she had traveled more than she'd told him about, he didn't see why Greaves would care. Or think it significant.

"I can also give you the names of the men with whom she's kept company. Six years ago it was a Prussian count, followed immediately by some fellow known

only as Jean-Pierre, which brought her to Lord Eme-
reaux, then a Spanish troubadour, as unlikely as I found
that. My source then couldn't determine whether the
Conte d'Adinolfi was before, during, or after the Marchese
de Migliore. Th—"

"You're making my head ache," Keating grunted.
"And I still don't see the point of reciting her residences
or lovers."

"I'll leave you the list. Finish your tea. And think about
it." Halfway to the door, the duke paused. "There is no
one so blind as he who thinks he doesn't deserve to see."

After Greaves left the room, Keating sat on the side
of the bed and finished his cup of tea. The tea tray also
had several pieces of toast, he discovered, and he slowly
downed those along with a second cup.

Previous to his return to London he'd had more than a
few mornings—or afternoons, rather—like this one, but
even so he couldn't remember when his skull had hurt
quite this much. But then he'd evidently been drinking
for better than two days. Generally he only had a single
evening from which to recover.

Finally he stood up and went to find a cravat. Knotting it tightly around his forehead, he picked up Greaves's
list and cautiously inched one of the curtains aside until
he could make out the writing.

Evidently Eleanor had been living better off his money
than she—or his solicitor—had wanted him to know. Because not only had she resided in the cities Greaves had
mentioned, she'd lived on well-appointed streets and in
houses with names.

In addition, she seemed to have a new lover every few
months, beginning with the moment she'd fled London.
But then Eleanor had always disliked being left to her own
devices.

While he didn't much care that she'd lived well, he'd sent that money so she could see to nannies and tutors and clothes for the boy. Not so she could attend every soiree on the Continent over the past six years.

Keating frowned. Then he shoved the curtain open the rest of the way and read the carefully compiled list again, more carefully.

And then, swearing, he yanked on his boots and charged downstairs to order Amble saddled. Eleanor Howard had some bloody questions to answer. Before it was too late.

Chapter Twenty-one

Camille stirred the potatoes on her plate, wondering if food would be this tasteless from now on, or if it was only her nerves unsettling her appetite.

"You'll be happy to know that Lord and Lady Clarkson will be attending the ceremony tomorrow," her mother said. Lady Montshire's appetite didn't appear to be affected at all by her daughter's impending nuptials. "As will your dear friend Amelia."

"My dear friend who's flung insults at me on every occasion for the past year?" Camille countered. "How delightful."

"That's enough of that," Lord Montshire put in. "You should be grateful. At the least, you will refrain from being insolent and insulting."

And to think, she'd agreed to have dinner with the family. Whatever she'd been thinking or imagining about a return to her old relationship with her parents and sisters, it would evidently have to wait until after the wedding. Which meant it wouldn't be the same as it had once been at all.

"I'm only happy you're going to marry Lord Fenton after all," Joanna chirped. "I can't imagine that anyone would wish to marry me knowing that the Pryce girls run away from their responsibilities."

"I can only hope you find a man who adores you, and whom you adore in turn," Camille said to her youngest sister. "Then you shan't have any cause to wish to run away."

Joanna cleared her throat. "I heard a rumor about your friend," she said, grinning.

"Which friend?" If Joanna intended to gossip about Sophia or Lady Haybury, or anyone employed at The Tantalus Club, Camille meant to stop her. Immediately.

"Bloody Blackwood. I heard that Lady Balthrow arrived in London just after he did, and that they've taken up just where they left off when he killed her husband."

"That's a lie!"

"Camille," her mother chastised. "Calm yourself. And Joanna, we do not speak about unacceptable persons at this table. You know that."

Clearly Keating wouldn't be welcome in Pryce House again. It didn't matter, of course, since she wouldn't be living here herself. He would always be welcome at her new home, whether his cousin wished to see him again or not, but she doubted Keating would ever come calling.

At least he was alive; Greaves's note earlier in the day hadn't said much other than that he'd found Keating, and that he was attempting to sober him up. It bothered her that he'd returned to drinking, but considering that she wished she had a bottle of whiskey herself, she supposed she could understand why he'd been tempted. She only hoped that he wouldn't return to his old ways; he deserved to be happy and to forgive himself for a mistake he'd made six years ago.

In fact, she would write and tell him so. Surely

corresponding would be acceptable to him. And even if she couldn't see him or hear his voice, to read his thoughts and sentiments—it would be something, anyway.

"At least your wedding dress still fits you," her mother went on, as if she'd banished everything unpleasant just by saying it would be so. "You're costing us enough as it is."

Camille frowned. "Why, are you bribing people to attend the ceremony?"

"Nonsense. Everyone wants to come."

"I heard there's a wager in the book at White's over whether you run again or not," Marie whispered. "One man wagered a hundred pounds that you won't be in the church by the end of the wedding."

"I can hear you, Marie," their father snapped. "That's enough."

"Who is it?" Camille breathed.

"Lord Bram Johns, from what I heard. They say he never loses a wager."

Camille didn't know how much of that was fact and how much was embellishment on Marie's part, but in an odd way it gave her some hope. At least someone thought she might escape the absolute dullness of the remainder of her life. If only Lord Bram Johns had mentioned what she would do after she fled.

"I only meant that you've cost us in friendships and reputation," her mother said in a high voice, her cheeks reddening.

That seemed odd. Her mother was much better at self-righteous indignation. Fumbling and embarrassment over . . . over what? Money? A dowry, perhaps? "Have the terms changed for my dowry?" she asked aloud. "As I recall, last year it was two thousand pounds."

"Which we paid to Lord Fenton, anyway. It was a Pryce who fled the wedding, after all."

"And this time?"

"None of your affair, Camille. Just don't embarrass us again."

Something began tickling at the back of her mind. Clearly, though, she couldn't ask or answer the questions she had here at the dinner table. She sent a sideways glance at Joanna. If anyone could be tricked or cajoled into discussing something the rest of the family seemed to want kept quiet, it would be her youngest sister.

What she might discover, she didn't even want to think about. It would lead to too many other thoughts and easily dashed hopes. But she insisted on knowing precisely what arrangements had been made with Lord Fenton. She was done with being a naïve, oblivious bargaining chip.

She managed to down enough dinner to avoid more criticisms, and then made her way with the rest of the female family members to the upstairs sitting room. No one seemed to wish to talk about anything, which she understood, but which made learning the information she wanted even more difficult.

Finally she stood up. "Joanna, I had a necklace hidden in my bedchamber which I particularly wanted to give you."

"Why was it hidden?" Joanna asked, while their mother frowned.

"Because it was precious to me. I thought to take it with me . . . after the wedding. The first time, that is. But now I'd like to give it to you."

Once she'd left the room to find her old bedchamber, she only had to count to five before Joanna hurried into the hallway after her. "What does it look like?" the seventeen-year-old asked, grabbing her arm. "Is it pearls? I particularly want a pearl necklace."

"It's a surprise."

Her bedchamber door was locked, but the key rested in the lock just below the handle. She hesitated before she opened it; she hadn't been inside in what felt like forever, and evidently no one else spent any time in there, either. In fact, other than her wedding gown she hadn't seen anything of hers emerge into the rest of the house.

The room was dark except for the pale moonlight squares on the wooden floor. Taking a breath, Camille retrieved a candle from the hallway before she ventured inside the room that had been her place for daydreams and reading mad adventures and sketching portraits of a Lord Fenton she'd never met. One who didn't even exist.

"It's dusty in here," Joanna noted, stifling a sneeze.

"Someone needs to open it up and dust. And for heaven's sake, someone could make use of the reading chairs and the writing desk."

Joanna wrinkled her nose. "I don't like reading. It's dull."

While her sister snooped through the bedchamber, Camille removed the key, quietly closed the door, and locked it again—this time from the inside. Then she pocketed the small brass key.

"What did Mama and Papa promise Fenton as a dowry?" she asked.

"You know I'm not supposed to tell you that. Where's the necklace?"

"Technically it's *my* dowry, Joanna. I want to know what I'm worth." Or rather, what her hand with a ring on it was worth. The rest of her didn't seem to matter all that much to anyone. Well, to anyone except Keating, the only one who was to be removed from her life.

Joanna faced her. Wrinkling her nose, she looked past Camille to the closed door. "There isn't a necklace, is there?"

"You'll only find out if you answer my question."

"You're mean."

"I'm learning to be so." She preferred to think of it as taking more of a hand in her own destiny, but she didn't much care what anyone else might call it. Not any longer. "Dowry, Joanna."

"Oh, very well. Two bay coach horses and twelve thousand pounds. It had to be twelve, because Lord Fenton already promised ten of it to Bloody Blackwood. You know Blackwood tricked you into getting married to Fenton."

"He didn't trick me," Camille returned, only half listening now. "I know all about it."

The money for Keating wasn't coming from Fenton. It was coming from her parents. For a bare moment she locked her knees against the urge to flee from the house and go find Keating. She would throw herself into his arms and never let him go. Fenton didn't have the money. She didn't need to marry him.

In the next instant, though, she realized that the information didn't change anything. Her parents would give Fenton the money once she'd married him. Fenton would give Keating the money once she'd married him. In fact, the only thing it actually changed was the idea that Fenton had spontaneously decided he still wanted to marry her. It was far more likely that he'd approached her parents to ask how much money they would be willing to part with to have this scandal go away.

"You aren't going to say anything to Mama or Papa, are you?" Joanna asked into the silence. "Because they'll know I told you."

"No, I won't say anything. There's no point to it."

"Good." Joanna took another turn about the room. "Is there a necklace?"

With a sigh, Camille went to her writing desk and

pulled open one of the trio of drawers. She lifted out the box of pencils inside, and opened it. "Here."

"Oh!" Joanna took it, her excited expression slowly folding in on itself. "It's . . ."

"It's clam shells. From the stream at Montshire. I used to pretend they were ivory and pearl. I made it when I was seven."

"And why do you want me to have it?"

"It reminds me of dreams."

"Oh," Joanna said again. "If it's so precious, I think you should keep it." She handed it back.

Quite possibly it would be the only thing she had left of her childhood dreams. "Thank you. I will." Camille carefully set it back into the pencil box and tucked the wooden container under her arm.

Once they'd returned downstairs, she could practically hear the seconds ticking away on the long case clock out in the foyer. When she couldn't stand it any longer, she stood up. "I should be going. I'll have a busy day tomorrow, after all."

Her father stood up. "We're not going through that again."

"Going through what?"

"You changing your mind the moment you're out of earshot. Everything you need for tomorrow is here. You'll spend the night with us, in Marie's bedchamber. With Marie."

Abruptly the house seemed to close in around her. "No. I'm expected back at The Tantalus Club. I haven't said my good-byes yet."

"Send them a note. Better yet, *I'll* send a note to Lord Haybury. You embarrassed us once, Camille. I'm not so stupid that I'd allow it to happen again."

But if she stayed, she couldn't go find Keating. She

couldn't see him one last time or feel his warm hands on her skin. "No!"

"The more you argue, the more I'm convinced that you mean to do something to avoid getting married. Again. If you persist, I will lock you in the cellar. Now go up to bed. You'll find nightclothes waiting for you."

"And your wedding dress for tomorrow," her mother put in, her expression tight and very, very determined.

Camille narrowed her eyes, wishing for once that she had the same temperament as Keating. Then she could punch her father in the nose and make her escape. But he'd warned her; if she argued further, she would be locked away with no chance even to send word about her discovery. "Very well," she snapped. "But I will not forget this."

She stomped back upstairs, Marie on her heels. "It's not so bad, you know," her sister said once she'd closed the bedchamber door. "We used to sleep in each other's beds all the time."

"You do realize you've been tasked with being my guard dog."

"Which is why you must promise not to do anything foolish."

While her sister changed into her night rail, Camille pulled a book off a shelf and sat down in front of the small fire. Hm. *Pride and Prejudice* again. It didn't quite suit her mood any longer; all of Miss Austen's heroines seemed to find husbands to love, and who loved them in return. Her own story wasn't going to end nearly as happily.

"You need to go to sleep," Marie said as she hopped into bed and pulled the covers up to her neck. "Brides aren't supposed to have ugly circles under their eyes."

"I don't think it much matters," Camille noted. "You get some sleep. I'm not tired yet."

"Will your . . . friends worry over you?"

"Sophia will. And Emily. If Papa doesn't send over a note he may find half a dozen disreputable chits on his doorstep."

Marie giggled. "Mama would have an apoplexy."

"I only hope some of them come to the wedding tomorrow."

"You didn't ask them!"

"I did." Camille shrugged. "They'll know how little wanted they are, however. I doubt they'll make an appearance. It would be grand, though, since I don't . . . I don't know when I might see them again." A tear threatened to spill over, and she willed it away. Tears wouldn't help anything. And she didn't want Marie staying awake to do something as absurd as attempting to comfort her.

"I heard that your club has ladies' nights. Perhaps eventually Fenton might allow you to attend one."

Camille refrained from pointing out that the ladies didn't want to be attended by other women, and that only men worked on those two nights each month. It didn't matter. "Perhaps," she said aloud.

Not bothering to read, she sat slowly turning pages while she listened for her sister's breathing to quiet. Finally she carefully set the book aside and stood. The entire house had fallen silent, early as it was. If she wanted to see Keating, now was the moment.

Silently she walked to the door of her sister's bedchamber. She'd given her word, so she would return. But as far as she was concerned, what she did with the remainder of the night was her own affair.

"I knew it!" Marie sat straight up.

Camille jumped. "For heaven's sake," she gasped, putting a hand over her heart. "You frightened me half to death."

"You're going to run away again. And it will be my fault, because I'm in here with you."

"Hush," Camille ordered, stepping over to the bed. "I'm not running away. I need to give Mr. Blackwood a message."

"Then write him a note. Smythe will see it delivered first thing in the morning."

Panic touched her for the second time that evening. "That will be too late. He's leaving for Shropshire before the wedding."

"Then send it to Shropshire. I'm certain Papa would frank it for you."

"Marie, just go to bed. I'll be back before anyone wakes up. I promise."

Scowling, Marie stood up and stalked over to her wardrobe. "I can't do that. If you're sneaking out to go see Bloody Blackwood for God knows what reason, I have to go with you."

"What? No you don't. I give you my word that I'll come b—"

Marie pulled a dark blue dress on over her night rail. She scooped her long, blond hair into a knot and pinned it up, then faced Camille again. "Well? Let's go. And hurry. I don't want dark circles, even if you don't care."

So not only had she become some wanton, ruined woman, but now she was dragging her sister into trouble as well. Unless she decided to stay where she was. Camille frowned. Even if she couldn't . . . be with Keating again, at least she could see him one last time. And that seemed more important than anything else she could ever conjure.

"Put on a wrap," she whispered. "It's cold outside."

"You, as well."

Taking the dark shawl from her sister, she pulled it over her shoulders. Then putting her finger to her lips, she opened the bedchamber door and crept down the stairs. The front door was locked, but if they hurried she could be back and have the house shut up again before any of the servants could rise and lock them out.

Outside she took Marie's hand and hurried them down the street to the nearest main intersection. It was still early enough that people and carriages roamed the avenues, and it only took a moment to encourage a hack to stop for them.

"I've never been in a hack before," Marie said in a hushed voice as Camille finished giving the address to Baswich House and shut the door. "It's very . . . dirty."

"You didn't have to come."

"Yes I did. Just remember that if you do anything foolish, you'll ruin me, too." Her sister's brow furrowed. "You won't do that, will you?"

"Of course not. I never wanted to hurt anyone in the first place. I only wanted to be in love."

"But you're marrying Fenton now. Do you love him? It didn't look like it."

"No, I don't love Fenton."

For a long moment Marie gazed at her. Then her blue eyes widened. "Bloody Blackwood? Oh, my heavens!" She put her hand over her mouth, as though trying to hold the words—and the thought—in. "But he's . . . he's a killer. And he's dangerous."

"No he isn't. I mean he is, but not any longer. And don't call him that. His name is Keating."

"You *are* running away, then. You can't! I have to stop you."

"I'm not running away. I just need to tell him about the money. About the dowry."

"Why? What difference does it make?"

"None. It's . . . His cousin lied to him. He needs to

know. It's important." He'd been used, by both Fenton and her parents. And while it didn't change the outcome, she'd promised to always be honest with him. Even if there were some things—one thing—she could never say to him, she would never lie. Or allow anyone else to lie to him.

The door of Baswich House opened the moment she touched the brass lion-head knocker. Evidently the duke, at least, kept less civilized hours than her own family. Except that the Pryces didn't feel like her family any longer. Her family resided at The Tantalus Club.

"Good evening, Lady Camille," the butler intoned.

"Good evening. Is Mr. Blackwood in?"

"He is not, my lady. Would you care to leave him a message?"

Damnation. The hope that had lightened her heart died away into ashes. She wouldn't see him again, after all. Already she had only her memory of his light brown eyes, his dark, tousled hair, his mouth on her mouth. "I—"

Abruptly the door opened wider, and the tall, black-haired Duke of Greaves stepped forward. "Come in," he said, taking her hand and drawing her across the threshold.

"I don't—that is, I just wanted—"

"You must be a sister," he interrupted, eyeing Marie.

"This is Lady Marie Pryce, Your Grace," Camille put in, as her sister gave a wide-eyed curtsy. "She's making certain I don't run away."

"Ah. Keating had something to see to. I don't know when he'll return." The duke cocked his head at her. "You do know he's leaving tomorrow."

"Yes. And thank you for sending word that you'd located him. I was quite worried."

He released her hand to lean back against the foyer wall. At some unseen signal the butler vanished, leaving just the three of them there. "You're marrying tomorrow, then. Given that you've a bodyguard, I at least assume that's the decision you've made."

"I am. I have. You're attending, I believe."

"I am. I'm certain I won't be welcome, but . . . he asked me to witness it."

He. So Keating wanted someone he trusted to report that she had actually done the deed. Fighting the latest in a hundred bouts with tears, Camille shrugged. "I suppose my odds of completing the ceremony are poor. There are even wagers, I believe."

"Camille," her sister hissed, her cheeks turning bright red.

"I believe His Grace has heard of wagering before, Marie."

"I have indeed." Brief amusement touched his steely gaze. "But your odds are not poor. They are even. Unless you decline again tomorrow." Gray eyes studied hers. "Why are you here?"

Because she wanted to see Keating one last time. "I discovered something at dinner this evening, and I wanted to tell him," she said aloud.

"Is it something I might pass on to him?"

That was more than likely a poor idea, since a rumor could begin that the Marquis of Fenton had no income of his own, and that he was forced to rely on advances from his almost in-laws to pay his debts. But then, she really didn't care about rumors.

"The ten thousand pounds Fenton promised Keating upon my wedding. My parents are paying it as part of my dowry."

"Oh, heavens," her sister said faintly.

His eyes narrowed. "Well, isn't that interesting?"

"It doesn't make much of a difference, but it seemed

like something he would want to know. He should know about it, I mean."

Slowly and to her surprise, the Duke of Greaves smiled. "Yes, he should. I'll tell him."

This time she scowled. "Is there something afoot?"

"At this moment? I'm not certain. But you should go, before we begin a whole new set of rumors."

"Yes. Of course. I'll see you tomorrow, then."

"I wouldn't miss it."

Keating had never been thankful for an aching head—until tonight. It settled his mood nicely into angry, frustrated, and determined, which was just what he required after spending three hours tracking down a woman who had good reason not to want to be found.

"I told you already, I don't know where she's staying," Lady Graslin said, backing from her morning room. "And you need to leave."

Stepping forward to match her retreat, Keating drew himself up to his full height. He knew he looked intimidating, and he meant to use that. He was not in the mood for evasion. "I am one minute away from searching every room in this house, Vivienne. She didn't take a house in London, and she isn't residing with Lady Voss. That means either that she's here, or you know where to find her."

"Keep your voice down," the viscountess hissed at him. "I have a dinner party upstairs. I allowed you into the house as a courtesy. But I will call for the butler to remove you if you don't leave now."

"Forty seconds," Keating said, unmoving.

"I don't know why you would think I would have anything to do with Eleanor after such a scandal, anyway. As far as I know, she's in Europe somewhere."

"Thirty seconds."

Her face paling, Vivienne backed away another step. "Your silly numbers won't do any good, Blackwood. I don't know where she is. If I did, I would tell you."

"Then you have twenty seconds to do so."

"Be reasonable, Blackwood. You can't behave like an animal any longer. No one will tolerate it."

Keating blew out his breath. "I can smell her perfume, Vivienne."

"I have no idea wh—"

"No sense in waiting any longer, then," he grunted, and pushed past her into the hallway.

"No! You can't!" She trailed after him, grabbing onto his sleeve. "Miller!"

The butler appeared from the foyer. "My lady?"

"Get this man out of my home immediately!"

Miller put a hand on the back of Keating's neck. So many people had attempted to push him over the years that he reacted almost without conscious thought. Whipping around, Keating leveled a punch directly into the butler's nose. With a *whumph* the fellow collapsed.

"Let go of me, or you're next," he said, sending a glare at Lady Graslin.

With a shriek she backpedaled, then, skirts flying, she hurried up the stairs. "Graslin! Robert! Husband! We're to be murdered!"

Every instinct he possessed shouted that Eleanor Howard was here, somewhere very close by. And he would have a damned answer from her tonight. Anything else was simply unacceptable.

Generally the rear of the first floor housed the guest rooms; they were slightly less convenient to the main stairs and the dining rooms than the rooms of the residents. He charged after Lady Graslin, shoved past her stupid, weak-chinned husband, Robert, and headed down the corridor.

As he passed each door he shoved it open, looking inside. A sitting room, the library, the billiards room, then one, two, three empty bedchambers. Clearly no one resided in them, because the sheets had been stripped from the beds and the fireplaces banked. The fourth door, however, was locked.

"Eleanor," he bellowed, shoving against the heavy oak.

A slight whimper sounded from inside. It was all he needed.

Backing up a step, he kicked open the door. The frame splintered, a now useless key on the interior side clattering to the floor. As he charged in, he caught sight of a green gown vanishing into an attached dressing room.

Keating strode forward, reaching the door as Eleanor came charging out of it, a pistol in her hand. Not slowing, he grabbed the weapon from her and flung it back into the dressing room behind her.

"What do you want?" she shrieked, the very image of a distraught and helpless female.

"Shut up. I have a question for you."

"You would injure the mother of your son? What sort of monster are you?"

"Who is Arnulf Herrmann?" he asked. "Reichgraf Eberstark?"

She blinked. "What?"

"Who is he?"

"He's . . . Eberstark? He's someone I met after I fled London. A friend."

"A friend who consoled you after the demise of your husband."

"Yes. After you killed my husband, you mean."

"I find it interesting that not only did you reside in his

castle for eleven months, but you attended a grand ball eight months after you fled London. You danced with King Friedrich."

"They were very kind to me in Prussia."

"I'm more impressed with your considerable charms, seeing that you were able to convince a king to dance with you while you were nearly ready to give birth—and carrying the bastard of the man who murdered your husband."

"No one knew whose child he was," she snapped back, glancing toward the room beyond him.

He heard a stifled gasp, then surprised murmurings. "Evidently your host and hostess didn't know about your child at all," he commented.

"I—" She snapped her mouth shut again, her face growing gray. "I don't know what you're talking about, Mr. Blackwood. Leave at once."

"I want to hear one of two things from you, Eleanor. And you will answer me. I have a list of every house where you've resided over the past six years, and every man with whom you were ever seen in public, so consider your answer carefully."

"Not here, Keating," she hissed, backing toward the dressing room again.

Oh, so now she was embarrassed. He turned his back on her to glare at the dozen aristocrats now crowded into the room behind him. "Leave."

"This is my home, Blackwood," Lord Graslin stated. "I will not have you in—"

Keating hit him. The viscount fell onto his arse with a thud. "I'm not warning you again. Get out."

"Out of . . . of the house, or the room?" a long-necked chit whimpered.

Good God. "The room."

"I'm sending for Bow Street, I'll have you know!" Graslin grunted, stumbling for the door ahead of his wife.

That still gave him a few minutes. More than enough time. Stalking forward again, Keating found Eleanor on her hands and knees, digging through a stack of hat boxes. "If you're looking for the pistol, you've missed your chance to use it."

"How could you?" she wailed, standing to face him again. "You've ruined everything!"

"*I've* ruined everything?" he repeated, his jaw clenched. "For six years you made me think I had a son. For six years I've paid for you to decorate half the beds in Europe. For six years I thought . . ." He trailed off.

For six years he'd thought that God had selected a punishment for him that would last the rest of his life. Something he could never escape, never turn away from, never, ever forget. And it had all been a lie.

"You deserved to pay," she snapped back at him. "You killed Edward."

"Yes, I did. I've been thinking about that, you know. How was it that he returned home so early that night?" he asked carefully. She'd built a tale, and he'd believed every word of it. He'd been a fool. But now that he could see the holes, the entire building felt ready to crumble. "After you practically tied me to the bed to make me stay?"

The apprehensive expression on her face relaxed a little, as though she'd let out a breath she'd been holding. "What are you going to do now, then?" she asked in a much more even tone. "Murder me? With all those witnesses? You'll never be able to claim this was self-defense."

For a moment he stared at her, stunned. In all the incarnations of his dreams and nightmares, in all the sleepless nights he'd spent in the past six years, he'd been a monster. A man who'd erred so gravely that he deserved nothing but pain, and earned nothing but the illusion of a good life he could never touch. A Tantalus, ever looking for a son and a future just out of sight over the horizon.

"You didn't need to invent Michael," he finally said, his tone rough-edged over the breaking bits of his soul. "I would have paid to support you for the remainder of my life."

"Not as well as I wanted. And I wanted an assurance that you wouldn't simply change your mind." She actually looked angry at him. "What now?"

" 'What now?' " he repeated. "If I were the man you took to your bed six years ago, I would likely do something very violent, very nasty, and very final."

The apprehensiveness touched her gaze again. "And if you weren't still that man?"

For several hard beats of his heart he held her gaze. And then he turned on his heel and left.

He wondered if Eleanor realized she was still whole and standing thanks to one person. One woman who'd decided to be his friend despite having every reason to avoid him. One woman who'd come so close now to being his that he could barely breathe for thinking about her.

And he wondered what would happen when Camille heard that he didn't have a son, that if not for his awful reputation and the much better one she would gain by marrying Fenton, her wedding would have been a very different event than the one they had planned.

Chapter Twenty-two

"Where the devil have you been?"

Keating glanced over his shoulder at Adam and then went back to brushing down Amble. "I wanted a ride," he said, keeping his voice low in deference to the grooms sleeping in the back room. "It's been a long evening."

"It's not evening any longer. I was about to send a query to Bow Street, on the chance that you'd been arrested."

"If I wanted a wife to nag after me, I would have found someone prettier than you," Keating commented, appreciating the worry even if he wasn't in the mood for more conversation.

"There is no one prettier than me. You found Eleanor, I presume?"

"I did." Keating closed his eyes for a moment. "My head weighs at least five stone, and I'm . . . I'm tired, Adam. I'll talk to you later, before I leave."

"I understand. It's just that I have a bit of information, but I'm not certain how important it might be. So I'd like to know—if you'll tell me—do you have a son?"

"No. I don't. It was all a ruse to gain her more money and my continued cooperation." He took a breath. For a moment he'd felt free of everything. Free to begin anew.

But the more he considered events, the more weight returned to his shoulders. The death of Lord Balthrow, whether Eleanor had thrown her husband to the wolf or not, was still his fault. The drinking and wagering and whoring in which he'd buried himself from his seventeenth to his twenty-first year were still his fault, as was the brawling in which he'd engaged regularly since then.

"She's clever; I'll give her that. Is she dead?"

The fact that Adam had to ask that question spoke volumes about the man that Keating still was. Or everyone thought he was. The two seemed virtually the same. "No. Murder seemed counter to my best interests."

"Thank Lucifer for that."

Keating dropped the brush into a box and went to fetch a bucket of oats for Amble. "What the bloody hell does it matter, Adam? It's changed nothing other than the fact that I'll have ten thousand pounds for my own use. Perhaps I'll be able to patch the holes in the roof at Havard's Glen."

" 'Instead they bade him live in shame, / With a bloody murder to his name. / So mind your manners, mend your ways, / Or you'll join Blackwood in hellfire's blaze,' " Greaves quoted. "Isn't that how the poem ends? And the way you end as well, I suppose."

"Tired as I am," Keating said, his jaw clenching as he faced the duke full on, "I very much want to hit something. So thank you."

For a heartbeat Greaves actually looked surprised. "I don't want a fight, Keating," he said, taking a step backward.

"You hit me earlier; it's only fair. Aside from the fact that you're a self-righteous bastard who pretends he's never done anything nefarious in his life—which we both know is a lie."

"Dammit, Keating, stop."

"No."

Greaves raised his hands, palms open. "Your ten thousand pounds isn't coming from Fenton. It was part of the new wedding bargain he made with Montshire."

Keating stopped his advance. "What?"

"Evidently your dear cousin barely has two coins to rub together. He made an agreement with Montshire that if he could return Camille to the altar and to her family's good graces, they would pay him something over ten thousand pounds prize money. And a team of coach horses." Greaves slowly lowered his hands again.

"Bays?"

"Yes."

"And how the devil did you discover this?"

"She came by a few hours ago, looking for you. With her sister; evidently her family won't take their eyes off her until the wedding." He pulled out his pocket watch and flipped it open. "Which is in five hours."

She. Camille. She'd been here, and he'd been away, hunting Eleanor. He might have seen her once more, but Eleanor had ruined that as well. He took a breath. "It doesn't change anything. She needs Fenton for his reputation; not for his blunt."

Greaves looked at him for a moment. "Oh, well, now *I* want to hit *you*." Shaking his head, he turned his back and walked toward the stable door. "I wash my hands of both of you," he said over his shoulder. "I've never seen a pair so concerned with the other's happiness that you just won't see what's directly in front of you. Good night."

The duke didn't understand. He didn't see that Camille would be far better off with a proper life. Even if Fenton was a liar and a buffoon and a cold, cold fish, she'd manage. Certainly she'd have to learn to rein in her good humor, and she'd make good use of that caution she had about everyone and their opinions, but she would have a roof over her head, and her own household.

It was a rather shabby-looking household with decades-old curtains and furnishings, and those new gowns he'd imagined seeing her in would be cotton rather than rich silk, but on the positive side Fenton would never dance with her and would send her off with a maid for her daily walks through the park.

She would never see her friends—her odd new family—from The Tantalus Club again, because that would offend the sensibilities and thin layer of hide her husband possessed, but she would be able to have tea and biscuits with the chits who'd insulted her at every turn over the past year, the ones who'd turned her away from their homes when she'd been desperate and frightened.

He, on the other hand, would have a new roof, a solemn promise to himself and to her never to drink to excess or get into meaningless fights with people, and ten thousand pounds. And no need any longer to send every penny he earned off his land to someone else.

Keating sat down hard on one of the stable's wooden benches. Perhaps it was the ache in his skull fooling him, but optimism nevertheless began to seep into his soul. Into his heart. Could he do this to his cousin? Would she do it to Fenton for the second time? Would she choose . . . him? A brawler and a drinker and a killer?

The thought made him giddy and light-headed. Could he have her? Worthy of her or not, he supposed it boiled down to one vital thing: Did he have the courage to ask her, and to face whatever her answer might be?

He pulled out his battered old pocket watch. Twenty after four o'clock in the morning. Standing again, he gave Amble a last pat and strode out of the stable for Baswich

House. Hopefully Adam hadn't yet gone to bed, because they had a few things to discuss.

And he needed to see whether he could rewrite the end of that damned poem, once and for all.

Lady Montshire pinched Camille's cheeks. Hard.

"Ouch! Stop that," Camille protested, leaning away and putting her cool palms over her face.

"You need some color."

"Then use paint. There's no need to maim me."

Her mother frowned. "You aren't maimed. And considering that this is the liveliest you've been all morning, I'm not going to apologize."

"No, why would you apologize? Your daughter is marrying a man she dislikes, and who dislikes her, for a very large sum of money. And in return you get to tell your prissy friends that I've come back to my senses."

"I only hope Lord Fenton realizes how poorly you govern your tongue," Lady Montshire snapped back at her. "If you'd gone through this the first time as you promised, you and he might have learned by now to be friends. Now you have to begin with suspicion, which is your own fault. But you will be married today."

"I gave my word." What her mother didn't realize was that the promise she was keeping wasn't to her family or even to her almost-husband. It was to a man she would likely never set eyes on again. A man she loved and would never forget and whose happiness mattered more to her than her own. And for that the Pryce family should be very, very thankful.

Finally her mother stopped poking and pinching and stepped back. "You do look lovely," she said.

"I look better in darker colors," Camille countered, eyeing herself in the dressing mirror. With her fair skin and yellow hair, she felt far too pale and exposed in her white wedding gown.

And aside from the fact that this time she was not a wide-eyed virginal bride, seeing herself in that dress again brought back that flood of uncomfortable memories, her hopelessness and panic at being trapped into a marriage with a complete stranger, a man who'd remained aloof from her completely by choice. Nothing had changed since then. Well, nothing except for her.

"We need to leave for the church," Lady Montshire said, turning to face her two younger daughters. "Stay here. I'll be back in a moment."

No one seemed to believe that she wasn't going to flee. At least the company of her sisters kept her from dwelling too much on all the might-have-beens and should-have-beens that had kept her from sleep for the past week.

"What do you think?" Joanna asked, spinning a slow circle that made her light blue gown swirl around her legs. "I wore that green one last time, but everyone saw me in that."

"You look pretty," Marie supplied, sending Camille another sideways glance. She'd been doing that since their secret outing last night, but Camille wasn't certain what she thought to see.

"Come downstairs, girls!" their mother's voice came. "The coach is waiting!"

Camille took a breath. This was for Keating, she reminded herself for the thousandth time. She was the only way he would receive the money he needed. And that was the only path to him hopefully getting to see his son.

The trip to the church thankfully only took twenty minutes, because no one seemed to want to do anything but sit and stare at her as if they expected her to turn into a bird and fly out the coach's window. At least Marie realized that if she'd wanted to run, she could have managed it last night. That was something, she supposed.

Once at the church, she and her sisters were bundled into the small dressing room at the rear. The door opened once to allow her mother in, and she wasn't surprised to see her father standing directly on the far side, his arms crossed over his chest. Guarding her—or guarding against her, rather.

By now Keating had said he would be gone. She could imagine him on his pretty brown gelding, Amble, riding beside the hired coach that would carry his things and his valet. She wondered if he'd ridden by the church, or if he'd made an effort to avoid it.

Abruptly she heard a low-voiced argument just on the far side of the door. She couldn't make out any words, but someone wasn't happy. With a scowl her mother slipped out of the room again.

Marie came over and sat down beside Camille. "If you love Mr. Blackwood, how can you marry Lord Fenton?" she whispered. "I would die of heartache."

"People don't die of heartache. And I suppose marrying Fenton because of the money Keating gets is a better reason than marrying him because twenty-two years ago someone said I should."

The door opened again. "Your 'friends' are here," her mother snapped, her brows thunderously low. "Those light-skirts and tavern wenches, all sitting as nice as can be in the back pew. They told your father they would strip naked if he made a fuss, and promised to mind themselves only if we let them be."

Camille grinned. "Good for them. I'm glad they're here."

"They're ruining this ceremony. This is supposed to be about your return to propriety. Now the dregs of Society have dragged themselves in to make trouble."

"The dregs of Society put a roof over my head and allowed me to avoid some very unsavory things," Camille noted. "They stay."

Her mother glared at her. "I am very glad that you will cease to be my responsibility in ten minutes. Because I know I didn't raise you to be so defiant. I only wish Lord Fenton good luck."

That seemed to signal the end of the discussion, and for the next ten minutes they sat in silence except for the sharp tick of the small clock in the corner. It seemed to echo her heart; steady, unaffected by events, merely concentrating on beating and not breaking.

Her father stuck his head into the room. "It's time."

Finally her heart shivered nervously. Time for a marriage. Time for her daydreams finally to die. Time to square her shoulders and do what needed to be done.

Lady Montshire and Joanna left, presumably to take their seats at the front of the church. Then Marie left, sending her a last glance that held more sympathy than she would previously have expected. Then her father offered his arm.

Taking a shallow breath, she wrapped her fingers around his sleeve and stepped into the church.

This was the moment, thirteen months earlier, that she'd fled. She looked up to see Fenton staring at her as though he was worried that if he blinked, she would vanish. Not this time. This time she at least had a reason for being there.

While what must have been a hundred pairs of eyes watched, she advanced until her father handed her off to Fenton and the priest began droning on about the sanctity of marriage. She wished he would finish with it already.

Finally the priest asked Fenton if he agreed to take her as his bride. He didn't even glance at her, but kept his attention on the fellow officiating the ceremony. "I do," he said.

Then it was her turn. Evidently she was supposed to love, honor, and obey the marquis. She wondered whether he would settle for one out of the three as she opened her mouth to marry him.

The rear doors of the church slammed open. Jumping, she whipped around—and froze.

Keating Blackwood strode up the aisle, his gaze on her. Only on her. Her heart broke free of its leash and began hammering crazily. What was he doing?

Amid the mutterings of "Bloody Blackwood" and loud speculation over his presence, she caught sight of her friends in the back pew. Sophia, Pansy, Sylvie, Lord and Lady Haybury, the Duke of Greaves—and to a one they were smiling.

He stopped directly in front of her. "Camille," he said in a low voice that shook ever so slightly.

"Keating," she returned. "What are you d—"

"I need to ask you a question," he interrupted. "I'm a rogue, you know. A blackguard. The worst sort of man there is."

She shook her head. "No, you aren't—"

"People have lied to me, and used me, and I've lied to myself. You, however, have never lied to me." Abruptly he sank down onto one knee.

For a moment, her heart simply stopped. Time stopped. She was twelve years old, imagining her charming hero storming castle walls and sweeping her off her feet into a world of kisses and chocolate sweets. That man finally had a face, and he was presently looking intently up at her.

"Camille, I love you with every ounce of my rotted soul. I worship you. I draw strength and courage from watching you. I never, ever, want to be without you." He hesitated, the shaking of his deep voice touching her somewhere deep inside her soul. "Camille, will you marry me?"

"Just a damned minute, Blackwood!" Lord Fenton growled, stepping forward. "You can't propose to her! I'm in the middle of marrying her. We have an agreement!"

"Shut up, Stephen," Keating returned, not even sparing his cousin a glance.

Oh, she wanted to marry him. So badly. Hardly trusting herself to keep her balance, much less her wits, she put a hand on his shoulder and leaned down. "But what about the money? What about Michael?"

Light brown eyes held hers. "There is no Michael," he murmured back. "She lied. And as for the money, it's hardly a difficult choice, under the circumstances." Reaching out, he took her free hand in his. "But it is your decision. Do you wish to spend the remainder of your life with a man like me?"

Camille shook her head. "No. I do not wish to spend the remainder of my life with a man like you."

"You see?" Fenton broke in. "Leave, Keating. Now."

Keating blinked. "I—"

"Hush. I don't want a man *like* you. I want you. I want to marry you. I love you."

He stood up, tangling his hand into the careful knot at the back of her head and tilting her head up for a hot, crushing kiss. Somewhere beyond the range of her caring she thought she heard her mother scream, but she barely noted it. Keating wrapped his arms around her, pulling her hard against him.

"I love you," he whispered again, brushing her lips more gently with his.

"I love you," she whispered back, knotting her fingers into his lapels so he couldn't get away from her.

"Then come with me. I have a coach waiting to take us to Gretna Green."

She grinned. "Oh, yes."

He took her hand tightly in his, and together they ran out the back of the church as chaos erupted around them. The coach he had waiting bore the Duke of Greaves's coat of arms, which explained why her friends hadn't been at all concerned over her.

As he handed her up and climbed in after her, the last glimpse she had through the open church doors was Fenton standing beside the priest, his mouth hanging open. She laughed.

Keating kept hold of her hand as the coach rolled swiftly toward the north. "I took the liberty of removing most of your clothes and things from The Tantalus Club this morning," he said, his gaze never wavering from hers. "Sophia says to give you this." He leaned forward and slowly, gently kissed her again. "Perhaps not quite in that way, but I interpreted."

"I still can't believe this is real," she returned. "I'm dreaming."

"You're not dreaming." His expression sobered. "You will be utterly ruined now. No parties, no dances, no unnoticed walks through the London parks."

"I imagine Havard's Glen has paths."

"It has some lovely paths. And a pond. And deer." He ran his fingers down the side of her face as though memorizing her.

"And it has assemblies?"

"It does." He smiled. "In fact, I swear to you that if

there isn't an assembly in the next three weeks, I will hire musicians and dance you through the house. Just the two of us."

That almost sounded better than a party. "Thank you for saving me," she said. Her childhood self had been correct; dreams did come true. She'd just begun living one. A single warm tear ran down her cheek.

He brushed it away and kissed the spot where it had been. "Thank you for saving *me*," he returned. "My friend. My wife. My love."

Keep reading for a sneak peek at the next sensual
romance in the Scandalous Brides series:

RULES TO CATCH A DEVILISH DUKE
by Suzanne Enoch

Coming Fall 2012
from St. Martin's Paperbacks

Adam Baswich, the Duke of Greaves, stood looking down
at the naked young lady in the cast-iron bathtub. Steam
rose from the water to straighten the damp strands of
unusual scarlet hair that tangled deep red and lush at the
top of her head. If she hadn't been wearing the remains
of a bonnet earlier, he would have recognized her even in
the middle of the River Aire; he'd never encountered anyone with hair of quite that color.

Realizing that Mrs. Brooks wasn't present, he hesitated
for a brief moment, then moved forward anyway, stopping
halfway into the guest bedchamber. Saving a chit's life
should grant him some license to speak with her. "Miss
White. You're unhurt, I hope?"

She nodded, sinking still lower in the tub so that her
lips were only a fraction above the rippling line of water.
If they hadn't been chattering, he might have considered
them kissable, but that was neither here nor there.

"Bumped and bruised I think, now that I can feel my arms and legs again. But yes. This is much better than being drowned." She offered a smile. "And as you're the reason I didn't drown, I think you should call me Sophia."

"Considering that the coachman was saving the mail and the turkeys, aiding you seemed the least I could do," he returned. "I hate when my guests expire while answering my invitations. It puts people off."

"I can see where that might happen."

This seemed an odd and rather amusing conversation to have with someone—a chit in particular—who'd nearly drowned, but on the other hand she would have need of her good humor. "I'm afraid that this was all we were able to recover of your luggage." Putting a sympathetic expression on his face, Adam lifted up the wet, misshapen hat box that dangled by its fraying handle. "I'm sorry. We did look, Sophia."

Sophia White looked at him, then at the box. Then she laughed, her mouth upturning and eyes squinting at the corners in genuine amusement. The sound, her entire reaction, in fact, was completely unexpected, and he frowned, even more intrigued now. Although he didn't have much experience with half-drowned women, he doubted most of them would laugh at additional misfortune.

"I enjoy a good joke," he said. "Is this one?"

Choking a little, Miss White lifted one hand out of the water and pointed at the hat box. "I detest that hat. I only purchased it on a dare and meant to wear it to shock Cammy and your other guests." She chuckled again. "Oh, it's dreadful. I daresay it only survived because Poseidon refused to have it in his river and cast it back upon the shore."

If there was one thing Adam insisted on, it was having his curiosity satisfied. For the moment he put aside the information that she meant to shock his guests. Some of them could stand to be upended. That had been one of the reasons he'd invited her to his party in the first place, actually. He hadn't thought she'd known that, though. Or did she? She likely didn't receive many invitations to noble houses, after all.

Keeping half his attention on Miss White, he set the box down on a chair and with his boot knife cut the string holding it closed when the wet knot wouldn't budge. Once he'd removed the lid, he reached in and pulled the sopping wet thing out into view. It was blue, with what looked like the remains of two bright blue ostrich feathers arching over the top of it and shading two concentric rings of red and yellow flowers. A faux bird—either a sparrow or a bull finch—nested in the center of the yellow inner ring. "Good God." She was absolutely correct. The hat was hideous.

Even considering the ugly hat, her reaction wasn't anything he'd anticipated. After all, he'd just informed her that everything she'd brought with her to Yorkshire was gone. Perhaps she hadn't understood that. Or perhaps that had been hysterical laughter, though he abruptly doubted that. Previously acquainted to her or not, he was beginning to suspect that Sophia White had rather more facets to her than he'd expected.

"I'm certain we'll be able to find something for you to wear," he began again, setting aside the hat and noting that if he took a step or two closer, he would be able to see her bare legs beneath the water. He had no objection to seeing them again, actually, but it seemed a bit like taking advantage.

"Camille is nearly my size," she commented, sending a glance at the towel across the foot of the bath tub. "I know she would lend me a gown."

"Mrs. Blackwood isn't here."

Her pretty green eyes blinked. "That complicates things
a bit, doesn't it?" She sighed, her mostly submerged shoulders rising and falling beneath the thinning curtain of
steam. "Perhaps one of your other guests could be per-
suaded to lend me a cast-off, then, until Cammy arrives.
Or I'd be happy to purchase something from one of the
maids."

So in the space of a very few minutes she'd lost her
clothes and the presence of her dearest friend, but Sophia White didn't seem overly concerned by any of it.
Adam almost hesitated to tell her the rest, out of character as it was for him to sympathize with any but a very
select circle of friends. But he found himself more curious as to what her reaction would be than concerned that
she would be overset. Miss White didn't seem to overset
easily.

"You are my first guest, Sophia. And as long as the
bridge and the river and the weather continue in their
present state, you shall be my only guest."

This time uncertainty crossed her face. Practiced as
he was at deciphering people who made their way by
deception, he could practically hear her thoughts. Was
she trapped at Greaves Park for the winter? Was there
anywhere she could go to escape her situation? He could
answer all those questions, of course, but he wanted to
hear her ask them aloud first. Miss Sophia White might
be a child of unacknowledged parentage, and one who
worked in a profession many of his peers considered highly
unacceptable, but there were times a few months ago when
he'd actually found her amusing. And interesting. Had it
been a facade, or was she actually as good-humored and
practical as she pretended?

She wrinkled her nose in a thoughtful scowl. "Well. Unless I'm to remain submerged here until spring thaw, I shall have to hope that Mrs. Brooks liked me well enough to allow me to alter one of her old dresses. Unless you have a supply of onion or potato sacks to hand, of course."

Considering how rarely anyone accomplished the perturbing feat of surprising him, Adam couldn't quite believe that she'd done so unintentionally—though under the circumstances, unless she'd taken a powder keg to the bridge, he had to believe that she'd had no idea what awaited her on the road to Greaves Park. "You mean to tell me that as long as someone has enough charity to lend you a gown, you have no other concerns over your situation?" he asked, unable to keep the well-honed skepticism from creeping into his voice.

"I *am* somewhat concerned that you've barged into my bath without so much as knocking," she returned promptly. "But I'm also aware of precisely what sort of female everyone thinks me." She tilted her head, a straying strand of her autumn-colored hair dipping into the water as she assessed him. "Is that why you came in here? I'm still dreadfully cold, you know."

Hm. Perhaps it had crossed his mind, but he wasn't about to admit to it. "You are the friend of my friend's wife, Sophia. I wasn't aware that you would be naked."

"Fair enough. And considering that you pulled me out of a river, even if I were prone to be otherwise offended, I certainly wouldn't be now."

Now that he *did* know she was naked, he likely should have left the room. Instead he hooked his ankle around a chair, dragged it closer, and sat. "You're well educated."

"I am quite well educated."

"And yet I recall one evening at The Tantalus Club

when you complained to Lord Effington that if that Cleopatra chit ever showed her face in London, she would regret attempting to steal the Nile from us."

Her mouth lifted at the corners. "And Lord Effington laughed so hard at me that he didn't even notice he'd lost seven hundred pounds at faro to the club." She lowered her gaze briefly before her green eyes met his squarely again. "Should I dissemble, then? It gives me an aching head after a while, but I can pretend stupidity if it benefits me."

In the company of Keating Blackwood and Camille, Adam had once escorted Sophia to the Tower of London and had even untangled a lion cub's claws from her hem. He couldn't recall that she'd said anything ridiculous, or if he'd been lured into saying anything haughty or condescending in return. The fact that he was attempting to recall several brief conversations with her, however, spoke volumes. She'd just elevated herself from mildly interesting to intriguing. "I prefer that my guests be themselves," he said aloud. "So I suppose I shall converse with whichever face you choose to show me."

"I just showed you my actual face, so that will have to do, I'm afraid."

All of the ladies of The Tantalus Club were beauties; the owner, Lady Haybury, only hired the most tempting of chits. The fact that they were untouchable except by their own choice made them even more attractive to most of the lordlings of Mayfair. Some of the young ladies came from good homes and bad circumstances, and all of them were well-spoken and charming.

He'd noted months ago that Sophia White was an attractive young lady, just as he'd noted that she had a very unattractive parentage. In the same way, he noted now that she didn't blush and hide when a man disrupted her

bath, and that she'd looked him over from head to toe at
the same time she'd stated that she wasn't offended by his
presence, but was simply too chilled to leave the bathtub.
A living, breathing conundrum, when he'd expected a tire-
some, fluttery, complaining headache.

"So I am your only guest."

"You are." He drew a breath, wondering if she realized just how . . . vital that made her to him at the moment. "But you are not the only female in residence. My
sister arrived a week ago. As I am unmarried, Lady Wal-
lace hosts my Christmas gatherings. I don't invite guests
in order to deliberately ruin their reputations."

Color had begun to touch her cheeks again. "If that's
so, then I wager I'm your only pre-ruined guest."

He smiled. "Several of my guests—would-be guests—
walk close to your side of the dividing line, though none
of them currently work at The Tantalus Club."

Her brow furrowed, the amusement in her eyes fading a little. "Should I volunteer to leave, then?" she asked
abruptly. "Your large holiday party has become a small
family gathering. As Hanlith is only a mile away, I could
t—"

"No."

"No?"

"It's too complicated to explain with you sitting there
in cooling water, but you will stay." He stood. "And I will
see that you have a suitable wardrobe."

"I will see to my own wardrobe. If you begin dressing
me, I'll feel . . . obligated to you. Even more than I already do."

People rarely turned down his offers of generosity. He
didn't make them very often. And while it somewhat annoyed him, he had to respect her wishes. And her. "As
you will, then. I'll send Mrs. Brooks back in to tend to

you. Work your wiles on her if you wish a gown. I'll have Mrs. Beasel the cook save a potato sack, just in case."

Sophia snorted. "Thank you."

In the doorway, he stopped again. "You are my guest, Sophia, whatever the oddities that led us to this moment. You may have as many potato sacks as you wish." He hesitated. "You may ask anything of me that you wish." And hopefully she would never realize how rarely he made such a statement. Evidently half-drowned chits with stunning red hair were a weakness he'd never realized he had.

"At this moment, all I ask is that you please knock the next time you wish to enter a room you've provided for me."

So now he was to be chastised, and by a female employed at a gentlemen's club. But he supposed this once that he deserved it. He pulled open the door and exited. "I shall do so."